13th May 2014

For Tricia,

With best wish

Hope you en[illegible]

£2

CALL ME CATHERINE

Helen D. Newman

Helen D Newman

Reuben Books
2012

First published by Reuben Books, Faringdon
September, 2012

British Library Cataloguing in Publication Data.
A catalogue record for this book is available from the British Library.

Typeset in 9/14 Bookman Old Style
Typesetting by Jean Saunders
Printed by Copy tech (UK) Limited, Peterborough

ISBN: 978-0-9562828-6-6

In memory of

my dear parents

Nora Edith & Alfred Edwin Newman

£1 –

CALL ME CATHERINE

Helen D Newman

CHAPTER ONE
1324

He would not come now. She had waited too long. The sun was beginning to dip beyond the horizon in a last flood of light. Its glow singled her out, burnishing the copper tints in her hair and staining her tears. She thought of his promise. Was it not solemn and binding? Had he not reassured her that he would find a place for her in his lady's household, that their child would be raised as his own, entitled to all the perquisites of a lord's bastard. She had felt so certain that his word was his bond, that he was indeed a man of honour, a man who would not leave her to face the world alone, their child without a father. And so she went on waiting, inventing all manner of reasons to explain the delay, though with each passing moment she sensed the betrayal. Maybe Lord Elliston had detained him at Runnarth Castle for the purpose of discussing ways and means of preventing further Scottish incursions into these vulnerable lands of Northumbria. He had told her that Elliston was a hard task master, disillusioned with the ineffectual help he received from a faraway capital that showed little concern for him or his people except when it happened to coincide with its own precious interests.

She looked up at the sky now darkening to night. The wind took up a low dreary moan, the ache in her heart resembling its note of seeming despair.

"A man of honour!" she sobbed half defiantly, her voice flung out on the breeze.

Awareness brought hurt, the dreadful pain of realising that, despite his reassurances, she had meant little more to him than a pleasurable interlude which had now run its course. She had felt so certain in his regard, and yet he had deceived her like any common light of love. She began to shiver, not from the cold but the knowledge. And yet she continued to wait, still deluding herself that what she had so freely given could not be so lightly cast off. She had entrusted her whole life to him, not to mention that of the life she was now carrying as a result of that unreserved trust.

"Not now, not ever," she said at last.

A steel coloured moon kept her chill company as she descended to the valley below. Autumn leaves clung to her hem, their brittleness crushed beneath her feet. She showed no inclination to hurry. Matthew and Miriam would be wondering at her absence. If she could turn to anyone in her trouble it would be Miriam, but Miriam was married to Matthew and Matthew was not of her ilk. But they must be told, told of her shame. What a boon it would be to the gossips. She could see it all before her, the years that were left, and the vision was cheerless.

The latch creaked on its hinges as it always did. She lifted it gingerly, hoping against hope that they might have retired early. Once the light faded it was customary to do so, for work on the land began at dawn. She should have known better than to think it, for as soon as she entered the room the feeble flame of the fire threw their huddled outlines into relief. They were waiting as she had waited, worrying for her as she had so recently worried over another.

"And what do ye think ye hae been about lass?" Matthew sourly enquired. "Decent folks hae beds to go to."

"Gently Matt," Miriam pleaded, already aware of her sister's distress. "Give her time."

"Time!" he retorted, sliding his legs nearer the fire. "She may be your sister, but she lives in my home and by my leave she'll answer to me or feel the strength o' my fist."

Miriam put her hand on his arm. She was alarmed, but not unduly so. Despite his raging talk, she had never known him to raise his hand to her, or indeed to any other woman. Isobel knew it too. It was a stern rebuke, but even with the sting of the recent betrayal still uppermost in her mind she was not easily cowed.

"Well, we're waitin'," he said, his voice calmer under Miriam's restraining influence.

"I thought to meet someone," she explained.

"Someone," he echoed impatiently.

"The father of the child I am carrying," she promptly replied. They would know soon enough anyway, she thought.

A lengthy silence ensued, the kind that none of them would quickly forget. Miriam put her hands to her face. Matthew slumped heavily in his chair. Isobel clutched her belly. The mice could be heard in the wainscot, even the breathing of the children beyond the thin partition.

Matthew was the first to break into the quiet.

"A child," was his only remark.

"Yes, a child," she answered, leaning against the wall to steady herself.

"Why did you not tell us before?" Miriam mildly reproached.

"Am I not telling you now," she replied, her voice breaking under the strain of the confession.

"The child of the man ye were waitin' for?" Matthew queried in a voice lacking spittle.

She shook her head wearily. What courage she had displayed suddenly left her and the sobbing commenced. Miriam hugged her close, her eyes pleading with Matthew not to be harsh.

"So, we're to hae a bastard in the family. Do ye mark that wife. Ye sister, who has so many airs and graces, ye'd think she had not come o' the same stock as we, is to make of us a byword. A byword." He spat dispassionately into the fire. "A byword. Well, twould seem we hae somethin' to be proud on at last."

"Matt, for the love o' Holy Mary, the children will hear," Miriam pleaded.

"They'll hear soon enough, hae no fear."

Isobel knew it would be like this. She had played out the very scene in her mind. In a few words, he had reduced everything she held sacred to the level of a dung infested runnel.

"You speak in ignorance of the facts," she said, her voice shaking with emotion. "He was a noble man, a man of standing in his own domain." But she knew how hollow the words sounded, and that her reactions were those of a woman desperate to hold on to her self respect despite the indignity and hurt of a misplaced affection.

"We hae nae ordinary man to thank for your deflowerin' then?" he laughed cruelly.

"Dunna Matt" Miriam begged. "Let her speak."

"He was Lord Elliston's adviser from London," she continued, the memory of their first meeting softening her expression and easing the tears.

"London," he groaned, the word rolling round his tongue as if he were spewing it forth. The idea of the capital always turned his stomach thus. Such innate distrust owed nothing to experience, he had heard things though and that was enough. London was his idea of Sodom, a place where squalid men made squalid laws with which to cheat and trick their fellow countrymen, particularly the hard working men of the north. He wanted none of them. They were on a par with the Scots, common vermin both, and the sooner wiped out the better.

Ignoring him, Isobel proceeded to tell them of how, on hearing that she was to have his child, her lover had promised to take her into his lady's household on that very day.

"An adulteress as well!" Matthew interrupted. "Better and better!"

"I loved him," she sobbed, "and I am not ashamed to own to the feeling, do what you will."

"Love!" he retorted. "Didna seem he felt the same o'er you, now did it? I might hae seen it comin'. Ye visits to the Father to try and learn letters, wantin' to do better than God hae placed ye. Well mark me well. Ye'll hae nae bastard in this house."

"You need not worry on that count. I shall leave on the morrow," she replied with some spirit.

"Will ye now," Miriam said, looking at Matthew with ill disguised anger. "Ye'll do nae such thing on my account. Ye'll stay here and hae the bairn, and if ye say anythin' against it Matt I'll leave with her, for I'll no see my own flesh and blood treated sae uncommon cruel."

Stretching himself, Matthew got up from his chair, giving vent to a nervous sort of yawn. "I'm away to my bed" he said, reserving a last look of contempt for the disturber of his peace and the bane of his household.

"We all be too tired and fretted by far," said Miriam. "The morrow we'll see things in a better kind o' light."

Putting her arms round Isobel, she gave her a reassuring hug.

"Twill be all right. Matt 'ull see sense."

As she turned to go into her own partitioned space, Isobel heard him mutter, "I suppose she could get rid on it. Mother Jomfrey 'ud to it for a free supply o' mutton."

Her space was but tiny, but it allowed her a measure of privacy, and she felt lucky to have it.

Sitting on the edge of the bed, she let her thoughts wander. There was truth it what Matthew said. She did want something better than the circumscribed life of the village and the three large fields which helped to sustain it, each of them divided into scattered strips of land on which men like Matthew eked out their back-breaking existence, where the yield was a matter of chance and the vagaries of the weather the main topic of talk. There had to be more to existence than that. Had *he* not told her of his splendid London house, of the gilded palaces and the fine garden walks leading down to the river, of its gaiety, above all, its life. She had never doubted the promises he had made to her; it was as if her whole existence had depended on them, but then she had never doubted his love, which made his desertion all the more bitter. The dreaming was over, the reality all too apparent, but she had to look to the future if only for the sake of the new life inside her.

"*My* child," she wept, for she now revoked any share he had in it.

And as the shadows began to thin into light, she vowed that *her* child would do better.

ɞ ɞ

The dawn brought small comfort, only revealing the narrowness of the world outside and its aspect of sameness. It was bitterly cold and her feet felt imprisoned in ice as they touched the earthen floor. Already the cock was crowing and Daisy's heavy tramping could be heard in the outside shed. That meant Matthew would be milking his precious cow. "A good milker," was his oft repeated phrase, and so she was, though sometimes it seemed to Isobel that she took precedence over everything, Miriam, the children, in a word the whole lot of them. The thought brought a smile to her face, the first for some time. Matthew and her sister made the best of what they had. If only she could be similarly content. Miriam certainly made the best of Matthew, actually loved him in a soft maternal way, yet for Isobel he epitomised a hundred others of his class, thin featured and drawn, living for the land with a dirt encrusted determination to succeed in the face of whatever difficulties fortune threw in his path. His dream was to eventually become a free man so that he could devote every hour of the day to tending his own strips instead of being obliged to give up part of it to work on Lord Elliston's lands. This was the sum of his ambition, as it was of most like minded men in his position. And it was not for her to fault it. If anyone was at fault it was herself, for not accepting the pattern of things as they were.

She brushed vigorously at her dark hair, reflecting on the kindness of Miriam. As sisters they owned little in common, neither in looks nor temperament. It gave rise to idle gossip, and though there was nothing of truth in it, the differences between them were there to be pointed out and remarked on. Isobel was tall and slender, Miriam short and plump. Isobel's hair was long and dark and without any curl. Miriam's was fair and given to curl. Isobel's eyes were brown with a touch of the sloe in them, witches eyes said some. Miriam's were blue and placid. Being so different only seemed to draw them closer together.

Miriam had made up the fire which helped to alleviate the grey veil of weather outside. The still damp twigs spat sparks on the floor, occasionally setting the rushes alight. Rob trampled on them with glee. He was nine, bright and hardy, the very image of his father. Annie, his sister, sat demurely at the table winding her hair round her finger; a born seductress, thought Isobel, visualising the transition from child to young woman. She was Matthew's only weakness. He doted on her, indulging her every whim and making it impossible for Miriam to exercise any influence over her whatsoever. Everyone else was aware of her guile, but Matthew seemed blind to it. She was his little girl and he idolised her. Rob took it well considering he was much the better child, but he felt it nonetheless. Quiet and dependable, he rarely lost his temper, but Annie, secure in her favouritism, knew how to goad him, and did so with fiendish delight.

The milking over, Matthew's coarse hands gripped the bread platter; he never lifted his head until he had finished both the bread and its contents. In the bright blaze of flame he looked old.

Flecks of grey showed in his hair and his shoulders were prematurely rounded. Already he was taking on the appearance of his father before him, weighed down and overburdened for those in his care. Rob waited for him to rise from the table and then followed him out.

"I'll be away," he cursorily nodded to his wife.

"I'll come as soon as I can," Miriam replied.

It was the time of harvest, the season when the women were expected to take on a thousand extra chores in addition to those they already performed.

"Aunt Isobel, tell the story about St. George, the one with the white knight and maiden," Annie simpered in that irritating way she used when addressing her father.

Isobel was a wonderful storyteller. She had an inexhaustible fund of tales and both children delighted in listening to her rich expressive voice, but it was Annie who delighted in them most.

"Let your Aunt be," Miriam said. "She is not feeling well."

"Why?" enquired Annie, assuming an air of knowingness beyond her years.

"Because she's not. Now off with ye. Ye father 'ull be glad of a pair of extra hands."

Annie scowled. Work was a thing of which she was not over fond, and she would much rather have stayed behind to learn why her aunt was not feeling well and why it was she was unable to tell her a story. When she was gone, they sat and talked. For sisters of dissimilar temperament, they were well in accord. Knowing her as she did, Miriam was not surprised when Isobel chose to draw a veil over what had gone before, and though she was curious to learn the name of the man involved she knew better than to press her. What she was willing to talk of were her plans for the future, or rather the child's future, for it was noticeable how all her thoughts revolved round the child and not round herself. To Miriam it was touching yet sad.

"I want my child to have learning Miriam, to have the chance of doing better than I have."

"I see," said Miriam guardedly.

"You do not approve, because of Matthew?"

"No, but ..."

"But you'd never go against him?"

Miriam remained silent. Isobel knew what her thoughts were. As far as Matthew was concerned any kind of learning, apart from husbandry and the uses of the land, was a complete waste of time.

"This is my child Miriam, and I will do as I think fit."

"In truth," replied Miriam. "Twould never do if we were all to think alike."

"Like Matthew you mean?" she laughed.

"Mayhap," agreed Miriam, turning a pleasing shade of red.

There was nothing more to be said, Miriam going out to assist Matthew as promised. With the house to herself and the sun growing stronger, she began to look to the future with much more certainty and hope.

It was noon in the fields and the men were busily employed in gathering the harvest. The sun had lost its summer heat and the crop looked a good one, the sickles creating their own special music, a steady swish, swish as they cut through the corn. It was the men that lacked music, their faces wearing the same haggard look, their hands red and calloused. Annie was leaping and shouting and generally getting in the way, but Rob was already assuming the duties of a man, for he knew that one day the land would be his and it behoved him to learn his responsibilities early. As quickly as the corn was laid low, Miriam and the other women bound it up into stooks. Miriam noticed that the woman next to her was very near her time; it made her think of Isobel and the plans she had in mind for her own child and what Matthew would have to say when she told him. Life was exacting and cruel; it was also full of beauty and wonder. She stretched her back and looked at Matthew's bent one. Best leave it to God she decided.

In their absence Isobel began to prepare the herbs that she had spread on the table. She had learned such skills at an early age, mainly from an elderly man called Peter the Hermit whom she had befriended as a child. She made few friends, and such as she had were usually learned and willing to impart their superior knowledge in response to her longing to better herself. Father Craven was another such friend, but Craven was narrow and exacting whereas Peter was warm and expansive. The villagers thought her a bit above herself, just as Matthew did, but they came to her because they relied on her skills to alleviate their sickness. Minor ills she was able to cure, but there were others which made her only too well aware of her own limitations and for which she could only prescribe pain-relieving palliatives. In attending the mortally sick and the dying, she was often obliged to witness the most pitiable suffering. Even so, she was proud of her gift, seeing it as a valuable asset to pass on to her child. The grinding of the leaves had a soothing effect and she began to hum to herself, strangely enough the delightful French air *he* had taught her. She recalled the foreign sounding words of unrequited love which now seemed so cruelly appropriate. The lettering she used to mark up each pot of cure was awkward, but considering the little tuition she had received in letters from Father Craven it showed remarkable promise. Her mind drifted back to her childhood, of which she had few happy memories, she and Miriam being the only surviving children of their mother's long sequence of pregnancies, the last having resulted in her early death. Unable to account for her strangeness as he termed it, their father was more than relieved when Miriam, naturally the favourite of his daughters, married Matthew, thereby ensuring that his own strips of land would devolve upon his son-in-law when he himself died which was not long afterwards the birth of Rob. Isobel had not been so obliging when it came to the taking of a husband, her learning and her aloofness disinclining the local men of the village to seek for her hand. Smiling to herself, she patted her belly.

"You will do better," she said.

CHAPTER TWO

The days grew shorter. Strong winds whipped the land into dust followed by rain that turned it to mud. Miriam was forever laying a fresh covering of rushes as Matthew and Rob squelched back and forth in a desperate attempt to finish winter ploughing. Dusk saw them return heavy eyed and muddied and Matthew developed a cough that kept him awake when sleep was essential. Isobel prepared some physic for him. He took it grudgingly and the symptoms soon eased.

Only in the dry intervals between the driving rain were they able to finish ploughing. Then it grew colder. Heavy snow in the night brought an unnatural glare with it, causing them to wake even earlier than usual and giving Rob the unenviable task of breaking the ice in the pail. Morning ablutions were more akin to cat licks and only Isobel kept to her customary habits despite the raw weather. Miriam was convinced she would kill both herself and the baby, but Isobel paid no heed. Annie was fretful and had to be amused. Isobel made her a straw doll, but in a fit of pique she tore it to pieces and then had the effrontery to ask for another. But with the onset of winter, Isobel's time was taken up in tending the sick and decrying the quackery of Mother Jomfrey. An old woman, old that is beyond the normal span, Mother Jomfrey preyed on the minds of the weak and the timid by offering false hope to those often beyond it. Trading on fear and superstition she made up worthless concoctions or mumbled pathetic incantations as a means of effecting her cures. Unlike Isobel, she demanded a fee, either in pence or in kind, but those who sought her advice genuinely believed she had special powers and were willing to pay what she asked. It was easy enough to simply regard her as a meddlesome old woman, but Isobel saw she was dangerous.

And all the time the child was growing inside her. With the approach of spring it occasionally gave a kick. She liked that kick. It showed tenacity. Now that her belly bulged and she was no longer able to conceal her condition, the gossips had their day and naturally Mother Jomfrey headed the throng; it gave a few of the women similar in age to Isobel and long since married the chance of gathering together to pride themselves on their own sense of virtue, their haughty contemporary having turned whore. For the most part, however, they were kind, for although such an independent nature as hers was strange to them she was their mainstay in sickness and they had no wish to offend her.

With her time drawing nearer, she would have to see Father Craven regarding the baptism. She had delayed the interview for as long as she could, but now she could delay it no longer. Miriam offered to accompany her, but she preferred to go alone. It was a fine day in April and there was a vitality in the air that belied the ravages of winter. Putting their hardships behind them, the villagers were busy scattering seed across their meagre strips of land, praying that the earth would sustain it and bring it to fruition, just as the life inside her was being brought to fruition. Beyond was the common land where she found many of the plants and flowers endowed with the healing properties she prized, the brightly coloured ones not necessarily being better than the dull and plain variety which often turned out to be the most efficacious. It occurred to her that in this respect people and plants were not all that different and that it was always advisable to look beyond the exterior of things to find those of true worth. As the day was fine, she was not disposed to hurry. It also served as an excuse to delay her interview with Father Craven, the workings of whose mind she found it difficult to fathom.

She soon spotted the plants she was seeking, placing them in the front pannier of her gown which she had made solely for that purpose. Cows were drinking at the river, their moon–eyed reflections rippling in the water, their tails warding off flies. She almost felt envious of such a trouble-free existence. It was the human condition that was worst, invariably obligated, invariably fraught.

Grey stoned and lichened in places, the church stood at the heart of the village, the meaner dwellings cleaving to it at a respectful distance. For the villagers it represented the very centre of their being, the sanctuary to which they turned in times of trouble and hardship. In a world where life was easily expendable, they clung to its promise of paradise to come tenaciously. Their faith was strong and rarely wavered, and combined with their faith was a belief in their priest, to whom they attributed a divine link with Christ. And Father Craven did epitomise the spiritual refinement they felt themselves so in want of, yet at times Isobel was repelled by his seeming refinement; to her it was as if his emotions were stunted. The Latin mass was a mystical joy to them, utterly removed from the humdrum round, the monotony of their day to day toil. It gave them spiritual strength, gave meaning to their appointed place in the pattern, a pattern from which, according to Father Craven, they were never to deviate. Only she herself had dared, which was why she was dreading the forthcoming interview. In refusing to be bound by the constraints of the pattern, she could hardly expect Craven to be sympathetic. As a child she had been in his favour when, prompted by nothing but her own initiative, she had begged him to teach her the meaning of the squiggles from which he read. Surprisingly, he had agreed, in the hope that the learning she acquired would fit her for the quiet of a cloister, but once she had left her childhood behind he found her increasingly independent of mind, expressing a desire to debate as well as to learn, dangerous traits in a woman. Gifted with belief in herself, it was this that set her apart, as it set her priest apart, but there the similarity ended, she finding expression through an excess of feeling, he through the exercise of a dispassionate intellect, and years of acquaintance only added to her long held belief that he was not a man to confide in. She knew that the villagers regarded him as he wished to be regarded, with a mixture of reverence and awe. But she felt neither of these things, seeing him simply as a man and a flawed man at that. The door of his dwelling was open, allowing beams of light to play on the walls or tremble their way across the low structured ceiling. He sat at his desk, studying some volume, but the moment she obstructed the light he looked up with a kind of awareness that made her go cold. It was this quality of icy remoteness that put her on her guard. Above the common height, he was gaunt and pale, his close cropped hair as fair as a young child's, his eyes blue and disconcertingly penetrative.

"I have been expecting you," he said. "Pray be seated." Even his speech had the slow deliberation of the extremely articulate.

"You will know why Father," she replied, resenting the manner in which her own voice lacked its usual tone of confidence.

"Your absence has not gone unnoticed Isobel. It has been many months since your last confession. You should have come to me sooner. Did you think I would deny the comforts of Christ to the child, for the sin is not of its making."

She felt her knees begin to tremble. It suddenly seemed exceedingly chill and his proximity made her shiver. The words of comfort were to her a pretence, but it was the knowledge that they were an unconscious pretence that disturbed her. It was as if his emotions were untried, dried up in a kind of self-imposed repression that he saw as strength. She recollected his arrival in Runnarth; then he must have been a comparatively young man, but he gave no evidence of it, always behaving from the outset as their elder, father to them all, a stern exacting father whose example was one of restraint. There was no better illustration of it than in his response to a particularly virulent form of sickness that had swept through the village; throughout it his conduct had been exemplary, his dedication to his flock total, yet never once could it be said that he had suffered with them, for them.

"This child, though conceived out of wedlock, is the one joy left to me," she said, her voice becoming stronger, her eyes pleading with him for the understanding he lacked.

"Let me hear your confession in church," he replied.

The church was a comforting place, more comforting still when its priest was absent. Wall paintings depicting stories from the bible, crudely executed and all in bright primary colours, served as a means of instructing an illiterate flock, few of whom had ever handled a book, let alone read one. Her personal favourite was that of the Virgin and Child; the Crucifixion in all its excruciating detail was too disturbing to look at for long, as were the sores on the leper. She often wondered what Craven made of them. Things so unabashed and uninhibited must have jarred on his own repressive nature but, wary of his possible response, she had never seen fit to draw him out on the subject. She made her confession much as she had made it to Miriam, without revealing the name of the father of her child, despite Craven's subtle attempts to wheedle it out of her. They then knelt to pray in front of the altar, her long dark hair draping her shoulders and lending her features a Magdalene aspect. His prayers were just as she envisaged, calling on Holy Mother Mary to intercede with God to forgive her grievous transgression, and asking that the sins of the father be not visited on the child. "My child not yet born," she longed to cry out. Instead she kept her eyes fixed on the beatific gaze of the statue of the Virgin, silently framing prayers of her own. "Holy Mother, make my child, conceived in love though not in wedlock, the instrument of my salvation. Let the child atone for the wrong I have committed."

So fervent were these prayers that their silent pleading drowned out those of his spoken ones until she scarcely heard what he was saying. The sun beamed on the face of the Virgin, giving an illusion of life to the sweet calm of her expression, and

Isobel felt at peace. The serenity of her features filled him with unease. She did not seem humbled at all.

"Think on the words I have spoken," he said, as they parted.

"Yes, Father."

What a blessed relief it was to escape. The sunlight seemed to flood her whole being. The singing of birds was enchanting.

"I best not hear ye usin' such language again, do ye hear Rob!" Miriam scolded.

"Ay, but I heard Mother Jomfrey say, and others too."

"Speak to him Matthew," she urged.

Annie sat looking at them with a knowing look on her face, outwardly absorbed in her doll, inwardly digesting every word that was said.

"Rob, ye know your Aunt's havin' a bairn?" Matthew tentatively began, wondering why he had to be burdened with such matters,.

"Ay, everyone knows it."

And that's the problem, mused Matthew to himself, before going on to give a more thorough explanation of the way of things to his son. Men were impossible when it came to plain speaking, thought Miriam. All this wavering was only having the effect of making everything seem that much worse than it actually was, though as far as Matthew was concerned nothing could be much worse, but then he was a man and prejudiced.

"Rob, your Aunt canna marry, so the bairn will hae no father," she spoke out.

"Is he dead then?" asked Rob, thinking that he had at last solved the riddle.

"No, he isna dead, but he canna marry your Aunt!" she explained, beginning to feel exasperated.

"Why?" interrupted Annie, feigning innocence, her sphinx eyed look fixed on her mother.

"Annie, ye are not supposed to be listenin'," chided Matthew, but only in a tolerant way because she was his pet.

"He canna ..." Miriam hesitated, her face hot and flushed. The whole issue was becoming a headache.

"He must be wed then," simpered Annie, much more a child of precocity.

Matthew was visibly shaken. Not so Miriam. She was well aware that Annie was far more advanced in the ways of the world than ever Rob was.

"Tis so?" enquired Annie.

"Tis so," replied Miriam.

"Rob wouldna believe me," said Annie, adding insult to injury and enjoying every minute of it.

"That's enough," Miriam reprimanded. "Ye'll never use such language again, that's all we ask."

"I never did in the first place," she retorted. "Twas me who told Rob to say nothing because I knew what it meant anyway, but Rob is still such a baby." Thereupon she grabbed up the doll, glowered at Rob and calmly left them to it.

Rob felt humiliated, and by his baby sister at that, and took the first opportunity he could of escaping.

"To think my little lass should know such things," Matthew sighed when he was gone.

"Not such a child as ye think," said Miriam, placing her hands on his shoulders. "She's too pert by far, but Rob, now he's another mould, and all the better for it if ye ask me. Ye spoil Annie Matt. A little slap now and again wouldn't be amiss."

"I couldna do it, Miriam. Ye know how it is."

"Ay, I know, but ye dote on her too much, and Rob's a good lad."

"Twas ever thus, sons to their mothers, lasses to their fathers," he remarked.

He even smiled which was not very often, but then there was a bond between these two that had increased rather than diminished with the passing of the years.

CHAPTER THREE

Without wishing to dwell on the past, it found a way of creeping into Isobel's thoughts, like so many scenes from a pageant, some gloomy, some gay, her first and only love, its resultant pregnancy and the religious bigotry of her priest. She longed for someone to whom she could really open her heart. Miriam was warm and practical, but there was a limit to her sympathy, and that limit was Matthew who had only agreed to let her go on living in his house because she was Miriam's sister and Miriam insisted upon it. And aside from Miriam, there was no other woman to whom she was close. In wanting to better herself she had become an outcast, her contemporaries thinking her haughty and full of pretension, and if she was honest she had to admit that there was more than an element of truth in the charge.

The only person she felt she could trust was her friend the hermit Peter who lived a good two miles beyond the confines of the village. Winter had made it impossible for her to visit him previously and anyway she was aware that the first three months of pregnancy were the most prone to miscarry. Now, having gone beyond six months, and with the weather more settled, she was set on seeing him before the child was born.

Peter, a Benedictine friar who had found his own way to God, lived a life of austerity and prayer. His dwelling was a cave hewn out of rock, covered in by an abundance of fern to hide it from sight, and only accessible by boat; from its proximity to the river it was often flooded, the water flowing over the stone steps leading to the entrance and thence into the interior. His bed was a rough stone slab, the altar consisting of another block of stone on which stood a simple wooden cross that he had formed out of twigs bound together with rushes. Whatever the season, the altar was always adorned with flowers or plants picked from the wilderness around him, or God's wider garden as he preferred to call it. They had met by chance. Liking to escape from the village whenever she could, even at a young age, she had been wandering along the edge of the river when she saw him slip down a rough stony slope. He had fallen in trying to grasp at a plant just out of reach. There was no way of getting to him except by the boat which was moored on her side of the river, so she took up the oars and rowed across. She was only a ten year old girl and he was amazed at the quick thinking she exhibited. He had not broken any limbs, but he was cut and bruised and badly shaken, though she noticed that the plant he had been pulling at was firmly clenched in his hand. After tending his wounds she enquired about the plant and why it was so important to him. From that first meeting they became firm friends, and it was from Peter that she acquired her knowledge of healing and herbs. No one knew much of his history and none knew him by any name other than that of Peter. He had then been a relatively fit man, but time and the conditions in which he lived had prematurely aged him.

Her belly now swelling ever more under the weight of the child she was carrying, she took her time to unmoor the boat and row across to the cave.

"Peter!" she called, as she neared the other side of the river.

It was not long before he ambled forth from the cavern, his former strong frame bent a little from the harshness of his existence. His sandals were well worn as was the frayed corded cassock, but none of this seemed to matter for his face was one of serenity and the lines of age showed kindly upon it. Deeply tanned, more by the vagaries of the weather than the sun, an unruly tangle of wiry white hair gave him the appearance of a prophet.

"Isobel, Isobel," he said, helping her step from the boat, enfolding her hands in his own, now so heavily veined. "This is a visit most welcome, most welcome." It was clear that he spoke as he felt; there was nothing contrived in the man, and his smile was genuinely full of welcome and concern.

"Come now, we must go inside and talk."

The cave was dry if slightly dank, but the scent of the yellow primroses lying on the altar and the pungent smell of herbs hanging in clusters to dry gave forth a pleasant odour.

"You will have heard, no doubt?" she said, running her hand over her belly.

"How could I not," he replied, his smile one of understanding and forgiveness.

"You know then what people say of me? I loved unwisely, but..."

She could not continue. The strain of the past months culminating in the interview with Craven had been too much to bear and the tears, though long in coming, were a necessary relief.

"Isobel," he soothed, gently putting his arm round her shoulder. The gesture was more reassuring than all of Craven's words. "Whatever is done is done. It cannot be altered, and who knows, maybe, God himself has a purpose in it."

"I am so tired," she wept. "Tired of being stared at, ridiculed, despised. I am not the woman they would have me to be. My love was not given lightly. Surely you, of all people, know better than to think it."

"I do know," he answered, as the girl wept beside him. For a moment he was lost in quiet reflection as if he himself had experienced what it was to give in to desire unadvisedly, the gentle lapping of the river outside and the girl's obvious distress only serving to quicken his remembrance. "The love you speak of is a sin, yes, but a sin mitigated by the feelings it engenders. Such love as you speak of is not governed by reason, nor ever will be. We are flesh, we are blood, and thereby we suffer. As for the consuming mystery of the love between a man and a woman, why in this we are found at our weakest. To love where love is not permitted, that is bitter. There is too much pain involved in it, and deeper pain still to the one who is by right entitled to that love." He felt his eyes blur in the memory of things long ago.

"You understand," she said, looking up at him. "I knew that you would."

Her faith in him was so strong that she was able to tell him everything, including the name of the man who had fathered her child, although she made him promise that he would never divulge it to anyone else. Contrasting his understanding with Craven's lack of it, she began a fierce indictment of the priest and would have continued had Peter not interrupted her somewhat abruptly.

"For all his faults, Isobel, Father Craven is a good man, who has striven tirelessly on behalf of his flock. That he has no ruth on others is because of his want of it in regard to himself. To understand our fellow men, we must first understand ourselves."

His dealings with the priest were few, but they were sufficient to know what Isobel meant when she referred to his coldness, his lack of compassion. He had met men like Craven before, so convinced of God's special favour that they could not distinguish the infallibility of God from their own, thereby causing everyone to suffer, but most of all themselves.

"But what of the bairn to come, Isobel," he said, tactfully

changing the subject. “Have you thought of the education that befits such a child, albeit born out of wedlock.”

“Indeed, I have thought of little else, and Peter, there is no one but you to whom I could entrust such a sensitive task. Please say you will do it in token of our past and present friendship.”

“And what of Father Craven, surely he has a right to be involved.”

She was about to contradict him, a spark of disdain in her eyes, but he too could command with a look and she let him continue.

“He taught you your letters, and I recall the time when you thought very well of him by virtue of the knowledge he imparted.”

“A time long ago Peter,” she corrected. “I was very young and malleable then, but as I grew older I saw him for what he was, eaten up by the sense of his own worth, narrow and shrinking of soul, and quite unfitted to have any child of mine under his guidance. I fear the influence he might wield, which is why I beseech you to do what I wish.”

Peter raised an eyebrow and then chuckled quietly to himself.

“Why do you laugh!” she retorted.

“Not because of anything you say, Isobel, but the vehemence with which you say it, which makes me think that the possibility of his retaining any influence over a child of yours is extremely unlikely. Let him instruct her in letters at least, and I will do the rest. Tis fairer that way. And, who knows, she may grow to love and understand him far better than we do.”

A slip of the tongue perhaps, but he had said “she”. Ought she to tell him, or let it be. She decided to let it be, for it might break the spell if spell there was, for during the long winter months she had dreamed of a girl like herself, but with flame coloured hair, the colour of *his,* thick, dark and red.

“I take it we are agreed then?”

“So be it,” she replied.

He rowed her back across the river and bade her take care. She left him standing at the water’s edge, a man noble in spirit because he was humble where humility counted.

Her labour was drawn out and protracted and there were moments when Miriam feared she might die, but once she held the baby in her arms the pain was forgotten; the child was beautiful, the child of her forbidden love, the girl with the flame coloured hair that Peter had unwittingly foretold.

CHAPTER FOUR

She called the child Catherine after her favourite saint, Catherine of Alexandria, whose faith had been put to the test on the wheel. Such courage appealed to her and as far as she could recollect there had been no other Catherines in the family; she herself had been named after some distant aunt and for as long as she could remember she had been constantly reminded of this lady's virtues and how far she fell short in living up to them and this, she felt, was sufficient reason for breaking with tradition. Insistent that the name she had given her daughter must never be shortened, Kates, Kats and Kathys were not to be used, but even Miriam would lapse into the habit occasionally and Annie took a delight in doing so on purpose, though never in Isobel's presence. Catherine herself did not mind, but tried to warn the others when they were in danger of lapsing. She was now ten and had grown into a lively and affectionate child. Like any child she was sometimes unruly, but not to the extent that Isobel felt the need to give her a beating; to guard against her being spoilt in the way that Annie was spoilt was her primary thought. She also managed to avoid any tendency to become over possessive or over protective by maintaining as loose a rein as possible for the purpose of encouraging the development of a nature akin though distinct from her own. It was a method that seemed to work.

Her arrival into the family had caused various reactions. Matthew had hoped for a boy who would be able to help out on the land, but as Catherine grew up he saw she could be useful. For one thing she did not baulk as Annie baulked at doing common tasks such as bird scaring. In fact, she rather delighted in it, her wild leaps and yells attracting the notice of the villagers who wondered what manner of man could have sired such a high spirited creature. She also had an affinity with the land and that pleased him. Miriam found her much more willing to assist in the home than her own daughter, but then Isobel had taught her the value of work for its own sake. Rob was devoted to her, far more than he was to his own sister who infuriated him by the way she was able to twist their father round her fingers. It followed, therefore, that Annie detested her. From the minute of her arrival she was fiercely resentful, exhibiting all the jealousy of which her nature was capable, and it did not diminish as Catherine grew older. Though she remained her father's favourite, she saw Catherine not only as a threat but as an inescapable bugbear, but then for Annie life was a perpetual competition where to be first was the only lesson worth learning. For her part, Catherine tried to be tolerant and there were occasions when they actually got on together, particularly when Catherine complimented her on her prettiness, for there was no denying that Annie was pretty.

Catherine quickly took to lessons and learning. She was soon a firm favourite of Peter and he had no difficulty in teaching a pupil so willing to learn. She loved him too, probably seeing in him the father figure that was missing in her life. Isobel had told her very little about her father, except that important business kept him away; she had been tempted to tell her that he was dead but that seemed such a patent lie that she was unable to do it. Occasionally Catherine would ask her aunt or uncle, but they never gave her satisfactory answers, always implying as her mother did, that his duties kept him absent. Rob hated the questions and would skirt round them awkwardly, all of which gave a more sinister edge than ever to the mystery. Annie was far more obliging, sniggering and trilling in sing-song fashion, "I know something you don't," which was guaranteed to make Catherine lose her temper and be blamed for any scrap that might follow. The only person who enlarged on the subject was Peter, but it was more in the way of assurance than any real facts. In her innocence, she had even asked Father Craven, who like Peter found her a very willing and able pupil, a pleasure to teach, in fact, just as her mother had been when she was of similar age. "You are a good child," he had said, "a good child. Always be good," but he had looked more stern and unbending than usual and she concluded that she was not to speak of it again.

Peter had finished the lesson. The hot and humid day was not conducive to learning and Catherine lolled against the trunk of a great beech tree, drowsily scooping up stones and tossing them into the river. She watched the tiny whirlpools form and then vanish. Only the midges were active, hovering in feverish dance above the surface of the water.

"Surely the unbeliever will be convinced of a Heavenly Creator on a day such as this," Peter remarked. "What say you?"

She was dreaming and not really paying attention.

"Catherine, where is that mind of yours wandering to now?"

The sun blazed down, but it was sheltered where they sat. They were at peace with the world and content in the ease of one another's company.

"I was thinking of my father," she dreamily replied, running her fingers through her hair. Her mother was justly proud of that thick red hair, reaching well beyond her waist, and shining like the colour of autumn in sunlight. Once Catherine had asked her if *his* hair was of a similar shade, but Isobel was evasive and she never asked again.

"I know very little about him, Catherine," Peter answered. It was all but true, even though Isobel had told him more than anyone else. Catherine looked very hard at him, her soft brown eyes seeking for veracity in his rapidly failing blue.

"But you know more than you are willing to tell?" she questioned, rather too emphatically for the old man's comfort.

"You must not press me Catherine," he replied a little sharply.

She could see she had unsettled him and she was sorry for it. There was no one on earth dearer to her excepting her mother. She loved the others naturally, even Annie, but Peter was special, he was gentle and patient, and apart from Father Craven there was no one more knowledgeable, but she would never be able to warm to Father Craven as she did to Peter.

"I wish you were my father!" she suddenly said, flinging her arms round him.

"Catherine," he soothed. "If only your real father knew you as I do, what a proud man he would be. You must be patient and always trust in God."

She then told him about the jibes that Annie frequently made and the odd looks she sometimes received from her neighbours. In response he told her that he thought her more than capable of dealing with taunts from Annie and she assured him that she could with a seriousness well belying her years.

A kingfisher suddenly flew across the water, causing the other birds to panic, as it soared high above them, making pale the blue of the sky with its plumage.

"Look Peter!" she cried, rejoicing in the moment.

"Ay, I see him," said Peter.

"Is he not beautiful?"

"Indeed, child, indeed, surely a mark of God's love for the earth he created."

He patted her head as her own father might have done,

pleased because she was pleased, ridiculously happy that one so young should delight in his company.

Runnarth Castle shimmered in ghostly heat at the head of the river, and the scents and sounds of that summer day, the sighting of the kingfisher, and above all, Peter himself, would live on in her memory for many summers to come.

"Tis time you were home," he said.

"Must I go already," she pleaded. "I wish I could stay here forever. I wish ..." She paused.

"What is it you wish, Catherine?"

"That mother was as happy as I am."

"You think she is not happy, then?" he asked, not at all surprised by her perceptiveness.

"There are times when she appears to be sad. I think it is because my father does not return. Sometimes, Peter, I fear he will never return!"

"You leave it in God's hands, now," he consoled. "In God's hands."

He rowed her back across the river. A glorious sunset rounded their happiness, spilling its brilliance to drown in the water and swallow the earth in illusory flame. Only the after glow remained as he carried her home, its last glimmers tracing the ramparts of the castle in a tremulous outline of red, the sky putting out feelers of darkness to gather in the light.

It was a harsh winter that year and Isobel spent much of her time in treating the sick, particularly the young and the elderly who were always the most vulnerable. Catherine often went with her. She already had a basic knowledge of what was required, from the preparation of ointments and infusions to the lancing of boils, and Isobel was now of the opinion that she acquired some practical experience. The elderly were prone to loneliness as well as infirmity, craving company as much as physic, and with her childish warmth and vivacity she helped to lift their spirits at a time when they most needed it.

On a bitingly cold day in early January, Geoffrey Frincham came to the house begging Isobel to look at his wife. Catherine went with them. When they arrived they found Mistress Frincham clutching her stomach and writhing on her pallet, her face contorted with agony as she tried not to cry out and frighten the children who were huddled in a corner.

"What is this?" demanded Isobel picking up a phial that lay on the table.

"It was summat Mother Jomfrey made up for her," he admitted, looking slightly abashed.

She sniffed at it and then thrust it under his nose.

"Well, what is it?" she railed.

"I truly dunna know," he replied.

"Well, I will tell you. Coloured water! Do you hear! Coloured water!"

"She asked me to fetch her," he said by way of apology, pointing to the writhing woman.

She turned away from him and immediately went to the bedside. Mistress Frincham's stomach was hugely bloated like a cow's could become after eating something alien to its digestion. Catherine had never seen anyone so ill before and felt as frightened as the children; but then she had never seen her mother so angry before.

"Catherine!" she peremptorily ordered. "Fetch a bowl. The woman needs to vomit. Otherwise it will be the worse for her."

"No!" cried Frincham, whereupon the youngest child began to blubber.

She told him to take the children outside to spare them the distress of watching their mother retch into the bowl; taking a phial of emetic she forced it down the woman's throat and then waited. Catherine she ordered to stay by her side and watch closely. It was not long before the potion began to work and the woman retched as required. Catherine's legs wobbled, but she stopped herself from fainting as she guessed that Isobel regarded this as a test of her character. When the worst was over and the woman was given cold water to sip, Isobel told Catherine to call Frincham and the children back inside.

"Is she going to be well," he tentatively enquired, his look one of utter shamefacedness.

"Yes," Isobel replied. "Come and see for yourself."

He kind of tiptoed to his wife's side and grasped at her hand.

"I am feeling better Geoffrey," she whispered. "Tis all down to Isobel."

"What can I give you?" he said, looking at Isobel. "I hae a few pence saved, I hae a shoulder of mutton. We need pay our debts."

"I want nothing, only your promise that you will never ask Mother Jomfrey to assist you again."

"I promise, and God bless ye."

The children withdrew from the bedside as Isobel went to check on the patient's progress. Proud of her skill and confident that the woman would live, she informed them that she would call again on the morrow to see how they fared. She smiled encouragingly at her daughter. Catherine smiled too. The smile told her that she had not let her down. And the more she saw of her mother the more she grew to appreciate her inner strength and kindness; as to her father, whoever he was and whatever his faults, she was firmly convinced that he was no mean minded man if her mother had loved him.

For days afterwards she told the same tale of her mother's courage and strength until it grew tiresome and presented Annie with the perfect excuse for giving vent to one of her acid edged innuendoes.

"Anyone would think ye mother were a saint, but we know better dunna we Rob?" she hinted, darting a malicious glance in the direction of her brother.

"Shut ye mouth Annie!" came the response.

"What do you mean Annie?" Catherine demanded. "I hate your half told tales. Tell me."

"Ask Rob?" she scowled.

"I'm saying naught," he replied, unwilling to be drawn into Annie's sordid little games.

"Annie!" Catherine pleaded.

"Shan't tell ye anythin'," she taunted, provocatively tossing her curls and grinning slyly to herself.

"Oh yes you will!" Catherine cried, gripping hold of the curls and wrenching them with ruthless ferocity. Though she was seven years her junior, when Catherine was angry she seemed to have double her strength. Annie started screaming.

"Let her be," Rob said. "You know ye'll only get the worst of it."

But Catherine was in no mood to let be, and Annie went on screaming. Miriam and Isobel were washing in the lean-to when the rumpus began and it took them all their time to bring it to a halt.

"Holy Mother of God," exclaimed Miriam, crossing herself.

"She started it," said Annie. "I never touched her."

"Liar!" screamed Catherine. "You were saying things about mother again, you know you were."

"That is quite enough," Isobel cautioned. She was well aware of Annie's penchant for making trouble, but she preferred to keep Catherine in ignorance for as long as she could, though she knew the time would come when she would have to tell her the truth.

"Why take her side?" Catherine railed.

"I said that is enough," Isobel warned, but Catherine's temper was as inflamed as her hair and as little disposed to change its hue. For months she had been aware of a secret from which she was being deliberately excluded, and that this was in some way connected with her father only added to the torment, particularly since Isobel appeared to connive at their silence.

"Where is my father?" she demanded.

"I have told you."

"I do not believe you."

"I have warned you, Catherine. I'll not warn you again."

"Do your worst!"

It was then that the inevitable happened, Isobel's growing disquiet making her lash out at Catherine in a way that she had never done before. Catherine felt herself reel from the blow, holding her hand up to her face in amazement. It was so unexpected that they both stood staring at one other, utterly stunned. Annie clung to her mother, pretending to dab her eyes but secretly gloating.

"I hate you!" Catherine sobbed, brushing past them.

She had not gone far before she was stopped in her tracks by Mother Jomfrey, her scraggy arms locking round Catherine, who fretted like a bird to be free of them.

"In a hurry, are we?"

"Leave me alone," she cried.

"Now you tell ye mother that somethin' very unpleasant will happen to her love child if she meddles in my business again."

"What do you mean?" sniffed Catherine, at last fighting free of her skeletal impress.

"Just what I say. Now my pretty, where be ye father? There be a question, eh."

"I hate you all," Catherine wept, her small body shaking in a torrent of rage she neither could quell nor entirely understand. "I love no one, no one at all."

The very words betrayed her, for the denial was in essence the affirmation of a deeply sensitive nature inclined to feel rather too deeply. Her first and only thought had been to escape, above all to blot out the livid face of her mother.

Now she was alone and faced with the prospect of what to do next. Her first thought was to go to Peter, but she had never walked the distance unaccompanied before, her mother usually taking her on the two mile journey, and Peter bringing her back. She looked across the meadow to where the path began. Naturally, it looked familiar to her, but she overlooked all the twists and turns it entailed. At first she was reasonably confident, but when the second turn came she was not so sure. To make matters worse the sky had taken on an ominous look and before very long it started to rain, steady at first, but then like a deluge that mercilessly soaked her through until her hair stuck to her face and her feet to the mud. So heavy was the downpour that she could hardly see the track in front of her and her misery was only compounded by what had initiated it; even now she could feel the sting of the slap on her face. Apart from Mother Jomfrey she had seen no one of whom to enquire, and now that night was beginning to fall a feeling of panic possessed her. Under their shrouding of mist, all manner of dread seemed to spill from the hills, terrifying because it was invisible like the evil that ate up the souls of the wicked. Had not Father Craven spoken on such matters, warned of a nether world reserved for the damned. What if Mother Jomfrey had contrived her predicament for the purpose of sending her down into hell. The spectres were out there in the mist waiting to claim her for their own and there was no escape. She was trapped, flung out in a hostile world through her own wilfulness. Covering her head, she crouched down in the mud and awaited her doom.

She could not have been there many minutes when she became aware of a figure looming above her; was this then the end, had the devil come to claim her for his own. She was too afraid to stare her fate in the face.

"Can I help?"

The voice was soft and caring, hardly that of a phantom of terror. She peeped between her tightly clenched hands. It was neither a ghost nor the devil incarnate, but a slim willowy girl who looked in as sorry a plight as she was; she raised Catherine to her feet and together they huddled inside her cloak. Catherine said not a word. At last she felt safe. She had no idea where they were going, but there was something in the girl's attitude and voice that was so reassuring that she trusted her implicitly. Soon they were in sight of the village, approaching a dwelling which to Catherine looked vaguely familiar. The girl gave the door a decided rap with her knuckles.

"I knew this would happen," came the sound of a woman's voice as she scurried to open it.

Catherine seemed to have some recollection of the woman, but she was too wet and sorry for herself to give it any deep thought.

"Goodness!" was her exclamation on beholding the two sodden figures. "I told ye what would happen, but ye would be goin' off alone again. Tis not healthy, tis not indeed. And who is this ye've brought with ye?"

Hardly a pause between one sentence and the next, she ripped off the cloak and hurried them in by the fire. Without more ado they were divested of their garments, draped in warm covers and given mugs of warm ale.

"Why bless my soul, tis Kate Venners, Isobel's child," she said, once Catherine was looking more herself. "Ye mother's been lookin' for ye hours past. I canna think why ye be wantin' to worry a wonderful woman like that, ye must be a bad wee baggage that's for sure."

Then without further ceremony she took hold of Catherine and began to rub at her vigorously, urging the girl to follow her example and rub herself down.

"Walter!" she called. A skinny boy, slow of intellect, appeared from behind a piece of sheeting that divided the room into two; two small girls and another lad joined him. "Go immediately to Mistress Venners and tell her I hae her daughter safe and well. No dawdling now!" The boy fled, the others herding back behind the makeshift curtain.

"Where's Geoffrey?" the elder girl asked, as Catherine felt herself getting warmer and warmer.

"Went over Bardwick way, somethin about buyin' a cow. He reckons we can afford it, but what a day to choose."

Recollection was now coming to Catherine as her scalp was rubbed to soreness. It was the woman who her mother had saved from dying a few months previously, but now looking so well that she hardly recognised her.

"Mistress Frincham?" she said, looking up from the rubbing.

"Ay, so tis, and all thanks to ye mother, and ye worritin' her and I dunna know ..."

"There must a good enough reason," the elder girl intervened.

"Mary 'ull always find some excuse for wrong doers," said Mistress Frincham knowingly.

Mary smiled as if she were accustomed to this kind of badinage. It was a beautiful smile, Catherine thought, as warm and comforting as the way in which she spoke. She was not pretty but her eyes were tender and full of compassion.

"Alice is my sister," she explained.

"Ay," affirmed Alice Frincham. "Younger by some years, but o'er to visit us until I be fully fit like."

She would have gone on talking, but Mary prevailed on her to leave them alone together in order to give Catherine an opportunity of explaining her reason for running away on a day so inclement. Alice reluctantly concurred. She knew that if anyone could draw Catherine out, it would be her sister who had all the patience that she herself lacked. It did not take Catherine long to unburden herself, particularly as Mary was so forbearing and kind.

"Please say something," Catherine said when she had finished.

"What should I say," Mary replied softly.

"Why, that I am wicked, that Annie is wicked, anything that comes into your mind."

"As you wish. I do not think anyone is wholly to blame. I think you all let your tempers be your masters and now you are reaping the gall."

"What is gall?" Catherine enquired, furrowing her eyebrows in childish curiosity.

"Bitterness. However, I think that all will be forgiven when your mother knows you to be safe."

"Do you really think so, Mary? Do you?"

"Yes I do," her new friend maintained.

They then began to find out more about one another. Catherine discovered that Mary had received a little learning from her own priest, nothing like as extensive as that Catherine had received from Craven, but enough to make her valued by her own family who could neither read nor write.

Aged 18, she was ten years younger than Alice, and as yet unmarried. It was easy to talk to Mary, she was so undemanding, so undemonstrative, so unassuming, the kind of girl that would make a perfect match for her cousin Rob; it was only a thought but a pleasing one nonetheless. An ominous clatter of the latch brought her back to reality. It was Walter with her mother. Alice grabbed him by the scruff of the neck and hauled him behind the partition. Mary tactfully followed them.

"Catherine," said Isobel holding out her arms.

Catherine did not hesitate. The rift was healed, and all that remained was for Isobel to tell her the truth. The only reason she had withheld it so long was in the mistaken belief that she was not only protecting herself but protecting her child; she was also afraid of losing Catherine's respect. Censure from anyone else she could bear; should it come from Catherine, however, she knew that her heart would break. But Catherine was growing up, and instead of lessening the bond between them which Isobel had feared she clung to her closer than ever in her need to compensate for a hurt that could never be mended.

CHAPTER FIVE

Catherine had her wish. Mary did not return home. Furthermore, when she was introduced to Rob it seemed as if Catherine's wishes in that respect might bear fruit. Rob was undeniably choosy when it came to girls. He was in possession of reasonably good looks, albeit in a heavy, brooding kind of way, and they for their part found him of more than passing interest, but for all the notice he took of them they might as well not have bothered. The pretty ones put him in mind of Annie, shallow and too taken up with themselves; as for the practical ones, they tended to be plain and lacking in spirit. Catherine came close to his requirements, but he could never regard her with anything more than brotherly affection. Short of the frail rib of an Adam as she was before the Fall, it looked as if he would never find his so called ideal. Matthew was anxious to see him settled. He had recently bought his freedom which meant that the land was now his own to pass on to Rob unencumbered. It was therefore up to Rob to see that it was passed on to a son of his own, in a word to stop dilly dallying and take any reasonable woman that offered, but Rob kept on biding his time.

From the first moment of meeting Mary, however, he knew she was different. She had a soulful kind of beauty, a modest manner and a quiet way of doing things that appealed to him at once.

Though not quite Eve before the Fall, she was the nearest he had come to that model of perfection and having made up his mind he was not going to change it. Mary had not thought to marry. She was well aware that she had neither the looks nor the character that would appeal to the generality of men, but she also knew that men like Rob once having pledged their affection would not lightly rescind it. What is more their love was of a kind, outwardly undemonstrative, inwardly warm and enduring. Within a year of meeting they were making plans for their wedding. Catherine's wishes appeared to have been granted without her having to do anything at all, other than effect that first meeting, and if God had played his part then she had cause to thank Him for it; the suggestion that it was God's doing coming not so much from her as from Father Craven, and aside from her mother and Peter she could not deny the wisdom of her priest's judgement even if at times she found it hard to accept.

ꟲ ꟳ

That winter Peter died. They had found him one morning early in December; he was stretched on his bed of rock as if asleep, a look of sublime contentment upon his face. Catherine gave vent to hot tears, but her mother, though sad, was more accepting. In between her tears, Catherine asked if the dead always looked so happy. Isobel replied that she wished it was so, and though it was right to grieve over his passing they must remember that Peter had long had the mark of God upon him and that they should also rejoice that he had at last gone to his rightful place in heaven, for no one was more deserving of it than he was. It had been his wish to be buried close to his cave by the river, and Isobel and Catherine had persuaded Father Craven to agree to the request on the basis that Peter was a man of remarkable saintliness. Craven had agreed, albeit reluctantly, and Peter's aged bones were laid to rest by the river. After Craven had gone Catherine and her mother found Peter's crucifix and rosary, untidily folded in two pieces of cloth, which had been secreted behind the stone altar, the first marked for Isobel, the second for Catherine. On foreseeing his death, he must have hastily performed this last act, his crippled fingers falteringly trying to form the faintly scrawled letters.

"We should have been with him," Catherine sobbed.

"Maybe," replied Isobel, "but remember how happy you said he looked in death. Peter was comforted by his Saviour. We had more need of Peter than ever he had of us, believe me."

Catherine was not so certain, but when spring came and the riverside had cast off the coldness of winter and she was gathering wild flowers to put on his grave, she began to see the wisdom of her mother's words. A feeling of calm settled on her. Peter might have left them in body, but somehow his spirit seemed very near still, and without really comprehending it, she believed that she had been granted a glimpse of that peace everlasting.

ꟲ ꟳ

The plans for Mary's wedding were well in hand. Matters of dress never interested her and she was happy to leave things to

Miriam and Isobel. The two heads got together and with Isobel's flare for invention and Miriam's for sewing, the length of chosen material was soon taking shape. Expensive, it required careful handling and the adjustings and fittings were endless. Rob, necessarily excluded from the proceedings, grew impatient. Whenever he felt like talking to Mary she was invariably missing, his mother and aunt clucking over their bright new creation like two broody hens when all he desired was the being inside it. Annie enjoyed every moment, her mind filled with thoughts of the gown she would wear on her own wedding day. Of a surety it was bound to be finer than Mary's. As for the prospective bride herself, to give pleasure was an essential part of her nature and she readily agreed to whatever minor or major alteration was suggested. Catherine, like Rob, was bored with the whole procedure and spent her time idling by the river or scanning the hedgerows for herbs, an occupation her mother had temporarily abandoned.

The day prior to the wedding had turned exceptionally cold, an early morning frost having covered the land in a crisp silver sheen. Everyone huddled over the fire, its fitful glow sending forth showers of sparks which Catherine trampled out on the rushes. Breakfast was eaten hastily and for the most part in silence. It was Matthew's aim to squeeze two days' work into one in order to be free to enjoy the day of the wedding without feelings of guilt, which he would have felt otherwise, simply because he was that kind of man. The frost, coming so unexpectedly, had put him in a sour frame of mind.

"Tis a frost we could hae well done without," he complained.

"Ah, dunna take on so," Rob replied, for once forgetting the struggles of the labourer in anticipation of the morrow to come.

"Tis all very well," he retorted, "but dunna forget, I hae fought for this land, made it what it is for you and my future grandchilder."

With this, he glanced narrowly under his eyes at Mary, who scarce seemed strong enough to bring bairns into the world.

"I know tis so," Rob replied, "but surely we can be a little more cheerful. Why, tomorrow, I'll hae the best lass in all o' Northumbria."

He winked at Mary, who modestly lowered her eyes, while Annie grinned slyly into her half finished basin of porridge.

"Ye'll learn lad," Matthew muttered, scraping back his stool from the table. "Ay, ye'll learn as I've had to do," and with this final if somewhat obscure warning he hunched up his shoulders and trudged out into the frost laden air.

"See, how you've upset father," sneered Annie.

"I've done nowt of sort," he gave out in defence.

Mary, who in keeping with the others, found Annie very trying at times, but did her best to pacify her, intervened by offering to wash her hair, a chore which Annie particularly disliked doing herself.

"Now?" queried Annie.

"Yes, if you want me to."

Rob glowered at her.

"One day Annie all your hair 'ull drop out through being washed overmuch, and on that day I'll raise a cheer."

"Ye are just spiteful and jealous. I canna think why Mary should wish to marry such a dolt," she replied, flicking back her wealth of golden curls in defiance.

"Come along Annie," Mary cajoled, smiling faintly at Rob, who was in no way amused.

The others were busy in the outhouse baking when Annie was bustled in to have her hair done.

"Mary is going to wash my hair," she announced with an air of triumph.

"You are a baby Annie," Catherine remarked. "I much prefer to wash my own hair."

"Horrid red stuff!" Annie retorted. "Who would want to wash it anyway."

"It is not red," Catherine charged, looking to her mother for confirmation of the fact.

Isobel ignored her, much as Miriam ignored Annie. They were too busy for these petty squabbles. Seeing that she would get no satisfaction, Catherine went in search of Rob.

Rob was slumped over the table, for once reluctant to follow his father into another day's hard toil.

"She has been upsetting you too. I can see it," Catherine remarked.

"No more than usual. I just feel ... I cannot explain ..."

She knelt beside him, her hand on his arm.

"It will be all right Rob. Mary is the finest girl in the whole world."

"I know," he smiled, "and ye are the best o' cousins."

"Only because you have no other," she teasingly replied, always as quick to brush away compliments as Annie was eager to seek them. "What is that?" she said, as Rob fumbled to hide something under the table, the something in question being a straw like object which immediately aroused her curiosity.

"Come on, Rob," she persisted, poking her head beneath the

table and snatching it from him.

"Give it back!" he angrily demanded.

"I shall do no such thing until you answer me civilly," she replied, a word which she had often heard her mother use and one which she had quickly learned to imitate.

Furious, he grabbed at it, but she was altogether too quick for him, holding the prize at a taunting angle above her head.

"You have made it well, Rob," she remarked with a demon-eyed look, as he edged a little nearer, "and I know what it is!" The knowledge made her reckless and his fury only added to it.

"Tis a strand of your own hair and Mary's plaited into a knot, a lover's knot in truth. Why Rob, I never thought you so noble in love." She laughed, tossing the token from one hand to the other.

"Now give it back," he cried, only more imperatively this time.

"A surprise for Mary on her wedding night. Oh Rob, what a devotee you are," she approved in a real teasing humour.

There were occasions when Catherine seemed possessed by the devil, and this was just such an instance, and nothing, but nothing, was going to make her relinquish the prize, least of all Rob's growing frustration. The more angry he became the more she provoked him, but the token remained firmly in her possession, despite his attempts to retrieve it.

"Kate!" he raged, "give it back or else."

It was this shortening of her name that made her strike on a new and subtle way of tormenting him.

"Or else what?" she asked, all mock innocence. "My name is not Kate. It is Catherine. Call me Catherine and you can have your toy."

"You promise?"

"Of course," she lightly assured. "But say it civilly, as mother would say it."

"Catherine then, may I please have what is mine."

For a moment she looked so demure that he genuinely believed her, but the game was only begun and she was in no mood to curtail it.

"Call me Catherine, call me Catherine" she reiterated, dancing away from him. "I pray you, call me Catherine."

The fire blazed brightly, filling the room with an orange like glow, such as the sun gilds the earth with in autumn. She swished round the flames, Rob striving ineffectually to take his toy.

"Call me Cath ..."

The laughter was quenched, swallowed up in the fierce

ascending flame that had caught at the hem of her gown. Its blaze all but engulfed her.

"Kate!" he screamed. "Kate, oh Jesu, no, Kate."

Careless of the heat on his hands, he pushed her to the ground, rolling her writhing figure back and forth in an attempt to extinguish the flames. The two women ran in from their work. Miriam stood riveted to the floor, her look one of speechless horror. But Isobel, her face ghastly white in the glow, set to aiding Rob in the task of saving her child. Annie had let out a scream, but otherwise it was strangely silent.

"Tis bad?" Rob asked, when the flames were at last extinguished.

"Tis bad," Isobel affirmed in an outwardly detached manner.

"What must we do?" he said.

"Nothing Rob. I will do all that is to be done. The responsibility can be mine alone. No one can share in it."

They did not gainsay her, but she saw in their eyes what their lips dared not utter, the feeling that the child was beyond all earthly hope and it might be kinder were she to die. And instead of preparing for a wedding, they found themselves contemplating a possible burial. Refusing all offers of help, Isobel remained resolute that the care of the child must be solely her own. Wisely, they let her be, realising that if anyone was capable of such a task, she was.

Father Craven came to visit. He was deeply affected by the tragedy, Catherine being held in some special favour with him, perhaps more so than anyone since her mother, though he came principally for the purpose of shriving the child in the event of her dying, but Isobel refused to let him go near her. The very notion filled her with dread. To her the mere intoning of the words might undo the miracle she sought and reluctantly he agreed to confine his concern to prayers for the sick. Oblivious of everyone's concern, Catherine's only sensation was that of pain, a dreadful searing agony that refused to relinquish its hold despite her mother's tireless efforts to alleviate the worst of its torment. Over the years Isobel knew that the best way of soothing burned flesh was to douse it in water, and this did bring some minor relief. She also had a good quantity of herbal preparations in readiness for the winter; for minor burns the use of oak and elder was known to be beneficial, and this she used liberally, but the tissue affected covered a considerable area, and though all these treatments would ease Catherine's pain for a while, when it returned it was with a renewed kind of ferocity, wresting agonised screams from the poor tortured body, whose sole means of expression was reduced to the groans of an animal. It was at such times that Isobel underwent an agony of mind as telling as that of the physical hurt endured by her daughter. A lesser woman would not have coped, but Isobel was no ordinary woman and the love she bore for her child made her equal to the task.

Within a week there was a change, Isobel's unfailing devotion being rewarded by a poignant smile of recognition. No words passed between them, for none were needed. Aware that she had reached some critical point in her young life, Catherine had unhesitating faith in her mother to make everything well again. The weeks lengthened into months, but at last the flesh, scorched and blasted though it was, began to heal. She could now recollect the love knot, the mad caper round the fire, then the sudden blinding flare, but beyond that flare her mind refused to travel. Mercifully, her sight was unaffected, her first instinct having been to cover her eyes, but as a result her hands were badly burned and the right side of her face was extensively scarred. Catherine, however, was happily unaware of the extent of this scarring or the lasting legacy it would leave, since much of her body was wrapped in voluminous bandages which prevented her from seeing even the tiniest blemish. When it was necessary for Isobel to periodically remove the bands, she was told to look at the rafters and not at her body, Isobel insisting that it was better that she saw herself when she was thoroughly healed and not partially so, though in her heart of hearts she was resigning herself to the fact that despite her best efforts the scars would be visible for all to see. Catherine was also made to lie very still and not to move her limbs unnecessarily, so much so, that she began to think of herself, if somewhat irreverently, as a corpse about to be buried. It was an image that would come to haunt her.

One evening late in November when the first winter gales were raging outside and her mother had once again performed the same laborious unwinding process and she lay dutifully gazing at the rafters, of which she now knew the exact number, down to the knots in the third and seventh beam, it suddenly struck her as odd that she was asked to go through the same ritual time after time unless there was something to fear. Even now she was not allowed visitors. Admittedly, Isobel had brought her frequent messages of goodwill from friends and neighbours. Conversations with her aunt and uncle and Rob and Annie had been conducted from behind the partition, but she had not seen any of them for weeks. But of far more relevance was the fact that they had not seen her, or rather had not been permitted to see her which was a different thing altogether. Was she as hideous to look at as she was beginning to imagine. There was a time when she thought she might have exaggerated her fears, that they were nothing more than the result of spending too much time idly lying in bed and filling her head with morbid imaginings. Once she had been faintly apprehensive; now she was doubly so. But her mind was made up; whatever it was she had to confront, she would do it that day, and do it with courage.

"I want to see what I look like," she said.

"Tis not time Catherine," her mother replied, carefully winding the bandage, as Catherine lay staring at the knot in the seventh beam. "Believe me, the scars are healing well, but a while is yet needed."

"No, mother, I want to see now. I have only been obedient through a sense of fear, not only for my own sake, but also for yours. I know you are afraid as I too am afraid, but I cannot be kept in ignorance for ever. Best get it over with sooner than later."

Isobel went on rolling the bandages without saying a word. She had been resisting this moment for weeks, wondering how she was going to deal with it when it actually happened. Her natural instinct as a mother was to ensure that her daughter be protected from the gaze of what she knew to be an often vicious and uncomprehending world, but the depth of her own compassion would not permit it, and since it was impossible to spare Catherine hurt she saw it as her duty to make her strong to face the world as she was.

"Are you truly ready, Catherine. Despite my care of you, some scarring yet remains which you may think unsightly," she explained, desperately trying to keep her emotion under control.

"We will do it together," Catherine replied with a gentle squeeze of her hand which was slowly been unbandaged. "Now lift me up, and give me the mirror."

As requested, Isobel brought her the mirror which had until then been safely locked away. For the first time since the accident Catherine was allowed to look at herself. And what she gazed on seemed as a stranger. Although the left side of her face was much as she recollected it, smooth and free from blemish, the right was grotesque, the tissue cauterised and blackened into unnatural fissures; her hair had begun to grow again, but that on the right-hand side of her scalp was tufted and weak. Lesser scarring showed at the corners of her mouth and on her neck; her hands were scarred all over, the tips of her fingers especially so. Her eyes remained whole and well defined. Gazing at the distorted image, it was like seeing someone she once remembered well, but now scarcely recollected, so pronounced was the change. Letting the mirror slide on to the bed clothes, she involuntarily covered her face as if to shut out the image forever.

"Would you rather I left you for a while, Catherine," Isobel asked, her voice noticeably shaking.

Catherine nodded. After she had left, Catherine picked up the mirror, as if to convince herself that the image she had seen there was, in fact, her own. She had never felt so utterly alone. Suddenly alive to the realisation that she would have to bear this ghastly caricature of herself to the end of her days, she buried her head in the bedclothes and sobbed.

From wishing for company, she now shunned it altogether. The thought of being seen by anyone only filled her with dread. Refusing to eat, refusing to be comforted, it seemed to Isobel as if she was literally giving up the ghost, seeking for death as a form of release from the pain of having to live as she was. Sympathy only made matters worse. Catherine was fast sinking into a state of morbid self pity out of which it seemed impossible to lift her. Isobel had tried everything from coaxing to chiding, but unless Catherine was disposed to help herself there was nothing any of them could do but pray and ask for the spiritual guidance of their priest.

Isobel might regard Craven as emotionally stunted, but she had to own that he was possessed of great strength of character, similar to that which she herself possessed, and which had served them well during the present crisis. Neither was Catherine afraid to be seen by him; he was the same after the accident as he had been before it, but then Craven was not like other men. When Catherine's condition had worsened and Isobel had been obliged to let him shrive her, he told them without evincing a shred of emotion that they must be resigned to God's will. What he actually felt, he kept to himself. But even to them it would have come as something of a revelation. Were Catherine's life to be spared it would be a life irrevocably altered, and in that alteration he acknowledged the will of God working through himself as effecting its rebirth. Life would never be the same for her again. She would be shunned, isolated, apart, as in many ways he was apart, but to be apart was to be chosen of God, or so be believed. Thus, there was a purpose in it personally for him as a priest. From now on it would be his duty to see that she followed in the way that God wished her to take. Catherine Venners must become a bride of Christ. Of this he had no doubt, for was it not sanctioned of the Almighty, Creator of Heaven and Earth, and, incidentally, Creator of Father Craven who was to act as His supreme mediator in all things that mattered.

Everyone but Isobel was in awe of him, never attributing their obedience to anything other than his own superior worth and their lack of God's grace; his will over theirs, his demand of their unquestioning submission, his belief that God and himself were in some divine way one and the same.

When he was gone and Isobel had left the bedside for a moment's respite, Mary tried to comfort her by saying that at least she had the consolation of knowing that Catherine's soul would now be at ease, but Isobel was beyond being comforted.

"And of what use is that to me," she railed, crying out against the God who had seemingly forsaken her. "I want my child, body and soul. I want her to live, Mary. I want her to live."

"I know," Mary commiserated, feeling at a loss for the right words to say, "and I think that she will live Isobel, but you must have faith, you who have borne everything with such courage and resolve. You must not weaken now."

"And what has faith done for me!" she threw back at her. "I who have lost my man and am now in danger of losing my child. You are still young Mary. You know so little of passion and desire, love for a man, love for a child of that man. Catherine is all I have left."

Mary's eyes filled with tears. The harangue had not so much upset her as made her feel inadequate when she so longed to be of help, and though she was of a quiet disposition and not given to extremes of emotion, she had willingly delayed her wedding in the hope of supporting Isobel in whatever way she was able, and if she was at fault for urging faith on a woman who had already endured more than the normal measure of suffering then she was genuinely sorry.

"Forgive me," she said.

"Oh Mary," Isobel replied, putting her arms around her. "Tis I who should be seeking forgiveness of you. How would I have coped without your unfailing kindness. Tis anxiety that makes me thus. Please bear with me."

The solemnity of the atmosphere was suddenly broken into by the sound of laughter outside amidst much "hushing and "shushing" which mostly came from Rob. The laughter belonged to Annie who was clearly in a mood of determined high spirits.

Not consciously callous, she had simply been indulged to such an extent that to her Catherine's accident was only a ripple in her own stream of existence. She was sorry for her, but not greatly so. The fact that the accident would appear to have robbed her of her looks was of little importance. Hers were still intact, and that was what counted.

"What is going on?" said Mary. "I better go and see. You stay here."

It was Rob, Annie, Matthew and Miriam, not to mention her sister Alice who, looking flustered and hot, was trying to restrain a puppy she held in her arms. On seeing Mary she went redder still.

"Tis all my fault Mary. Only when I heard o' Isobel's misfortunes, let alone the poor bairn's and remembered her goodness to me I thought I might cheer the little un up by bringing round one of Meg's latest litter o' pups. But I hadna realised how badly things were," and with this she broke into tears.

"What's to do now?" sighed Isobel as they gathered inside. Mary thought how haggard she looked and suddenly everyone was quiet, even Annie. Only the puppy gave out little yelps as it tried to struggle free.

"Alice brought one of Meg's latest litter, thinking to cheer Catherine," Mary explained.

"I hadna thought her so poorly," Alice sobbed. "Only I know how the bairn loved animals, and ...

"Give it here," Isobel interrupted. Alice put the struggling puppy into her arms.

"Tis true what you say. Catherine has always loved animals. I taught her that. Perhaps, providence has sent you after all, Alice."

"Isobel, do you think this wise?" warned Mary.

"Yes I do. You said to have faith, and I have it!"

Leaving them, she went to where Catherine lay on her bed. She was very weak now and hardly spoke, but Isobel placed the puppy beside her, and the child's fingers felt at its coat. The puppy was pliant. Catherine looked at it. It hardly made a whimper, but snuggled into her arms.

"It likes you," Isobel smiled.

Catherine nodded. The dog accepted her for what she was, and it was this sense of acceptance that filled her with the kind of innocent pleasure she had not experienced since the accident.

The dog licked at her face, the best of it, and more importantly, the worst of it.

"You are going to get well, Catherine."

Catherine smiled, a beautifully plaintive smile, but a smile all the same.

Within a few weeks, she was able to leave her bed. She had now been seen by all her family, whose responses were different and varied. Uncle Matthew was awkward, never looking at her directly, not because he could not bear to look at her, but because he thought if he affected not to notice it would put her at her ease. Worse still, his manner was uncharacteristically polite which was not in the least bit like him. But once he got accustomed to the change, the old familiarity reasserted itself and he became the crusty and obstinate uncle of old. Miriam was weepy every time she looked at her, and would have treated her as an invalid had she not insisted that she was perfectly well and capable of resuming all her usual tasks. As with Matthew, it took time to convince her of the fact. Rob was overtly the same, although she guessed that in some way he blamed himself for the accident, but then Rob carried his responsibilities more heavily than most. At least there was no pretence with Annie. She looked her disgust and took no pains to disguise it, but since she rarely saw life beyond a superficial level it was hardly surprising. Cunning she might be, but in this she was glaringly honest. Mary was, in fact, the only one of them who treated her from the outset as a normal human being. For the others it was a time of adjustment, just as it was for Catherine herself.

It was Mary's wedding that would be the real test. Up until then she had felt relatively secure within her own family, but now she was to be faced with the harder task of learning to cope with the reactions of her neighbours and, incidentally, the reactions of strangers.

An unusually large crowd had gathered, ostensibly to congratulate the new bride, but also to see the change in Catherine Venners. They were neither vicious nor unfeeling, simply human.

The same reactions that she had observed in her family were also true of them, the revulsion, the pity, the awkwardness, when all she longed for was to be treated as a normal human being. "I am still Catherine Venners" she wanted to say. "Accept me as I am."

And in time they did accept her, simply because like her family they grew so used to the disfigurement that they no longer took account of it. But it was not so easy for Catherine. The overcoming of one hurdle would quickly lead to another, and so it would be to the end of her days. Wherever she went outside the village, she would be confronted with the stares, the whispered asides, the undisguised disgust, worse still, the inescapable pity. While she yet remained a child, she was not so acutely conscious of it. She continued to assist her mother in treating the sick, illness being a great leveller which took no account of its means of relief, besides which she was in possession of a good bedside manner, far less abrasive than her mother's, the kind that instilled confidence in those that she cared for, which in turn encouraged her own and occasionally made her forgetful of her difference altogether.

Since giving her the puppy, she regularly visited Alice and the Frinchams. She had named the puppy Peter in remembrance of her friend. Doubtless it would have amused him. It also served to remind her of someone who would have understood in a way that no one else could excepting her mother. Father Craven was mindful, if not understanding. He tried to convince her that God in His infinite wisdom had given her this special cross to bear and that it behoved her to bear it well for His sake. It would not have done to tell him that she wished God had chosen someone more deserving on which to place His burden. He spoke a great deal now about the religious houses, and how with her knowledge of physic and letters, she could be of service to them. He also asked her if she was willing to learn Latin and she did not refuse because learning was a thing she enjoyed. She was not so sure about entering a religious order and in the innocence of her twelve years' experience informed him of the fact.

"You are young yet," he would say, "but later it will be different."

Having her obvious difference to cope with, she wondered what he meant, but chose not to ask him. What she could not do was glory in her so called burden as Craven enjoined her, and it was the futility of confessing these thoughts to him that made her long for a different sort of confidant, such as Peter. As it was, many of the things that she ought to have confessed went unsaid, simply because Craven was lacking in humility to accept them as the natural outpourings of a very human heart.

As she grew older she became increasingly self-conscious; she was no longer the carefree child who used to tease Rob. The accident had changed her mentally as well as physically. She became reserved and withdrawn, tending to find solace in solitary pastimes and pleasures, and reluctant to go beyond the environs of the village for fear of meeting strangers. She also took refuge in imagination, where she could be herself and nobody noticed her difference. There the fear of rejection never arose. There she was safe and protected.

A year after the accident she pleaded with her mother to devise some means of covering the worst of the disfigurement in the misguided belief that it would not only help in promoting her own confidence but promote it in those who were made timid by her appearance. Isobel had always fiercely resisted the idea, and for all the right reasons. She saw it for what it was, a desire to conceal the scarring for fear of what people thought, and though she cared not a whit for the susceptibilities of a few faint hearts she cared very much for her daughter and the effect it would ultimately have upon her. It was her belief that once Catherine began to hide behind some kind of mask, she would in effect not only be concealing a facial flaw, but concealing her true nature under a new and disturbing reserve, signs of which were increasingly evident. Catherine vehemently denied it in a futile attempt to justify herself, but she never was able to lie convincingly, which was why her mother's bald appraisal hurt so much. She would not abandon the idea, however, and at last Isobel grudgingly gave her consent. Catherine chose a neutral shade of material and Isobel cut out the pattern which could be made use of again. Cut obliquely to the left hand-side of her face with a hole made for the eye, it was secured by two narrow strips of cord, one round her head and the other round her neck. Isobel thought it gave her a somewhat ghostly appearance, but Catherine was pleased. It puzzled the villagers. What they actually thought might have surprised her. Having grown used to seeing her as she was, by wearing the mask she simply appeared to be concealing one form of disfigurement under the guise of another, and in becoming familiar with the new image they soon forgot the true one. Father Craven disliked it as much as Isobel, but for different reasons. In his eyes Catherine was resorting to a form of vanity instead of proudly carrying her cross for everyone to witness.

Catherine might not have been so intent on concealment in the first place, had it not been for Mother Jomfrey who, not having forgiven Isobel for exposing her as a fraud, had taken to tormenting Catherine by allusions to her disfigurement. Only a week or so earlier, the old woman had been particularly vindictive.

"Ay, well, there's a pretty sight if I'm not mistaken," she began, barring Catherine's way by waving her stick. "He's been a long time about it, but he's placed his mark on ye now."

"What do you mean?" Catherine had hotly demanded.

"Why ye father, who else," she replied.

"Let me pass," Catherine said, having a good idea of whither the converse was tending.

"Ye are no denyin' it then?" said the crone.

"Denying what?"

"That the de'il hae put 'is fiery mark upon ye, for twere no ordinary man that bedded ye mother."

"Leave me be," she replied, covering her ears to shut out this new and hurtful accusation.

Mother Jomfrey could always draw a crowd; it was something she took great delight in and they were never slow in taking the bait.

"She dunna care for the truth," she railed at them.

"What truth?" came the challenge she looked for.

"Why, that Isobel Venners lay wi the de'il and now he's come from hell to claim his own. You only have to look at the child here to know it."

The words momentarily cowed them. In an uncertain world where death and disease were ever present, they were prone to superstition. What is more the name and nature of Isobel Venners lover still remained a mystery. The old woman knew she could prey on their fears; it was how she maintained her hold over them. In some ways it was similar to the power their priest exercised over them, only his mandate came from God, Mother Jomfrey's from they scarce knew what. Catherine felt their eyes upon her; she faced them with remarkable composure, but inside she was trembling. Thankfully, Alice Frincham came to her rescue. Knowing Mother Jomfrey for what she was from bitter experience, she was not easily cowed.

"And where's the mark on ye?" she charged. "Tis to be sure ye've got some wart or other well covered, ye besom o' trouble".

Spurred on, the others followed her example. They saw no harm in Catherine; as to her mother, she might be a little untoward, but compared to Mother Jomfrey she was a saint. The old woman accepted defeat, if only for the time being.

"Ye'll see," she forewarned, spitting into the mud.

Putting her arms round Catherine, Alice begged her to forget the incident, but she could not forget, and neither, she suspected, did they.

CHAPTER SIX
1338

The annual fair at Bardwick was in progress and Annie was set on going. A fair day was like no other, a bit like Christmas or a Holy Day all rolled into one, full of novelty and excitement, and there was nothing that Annie craved more. She was 21, extremely pretty, and full of tantalising airs which she knew how to use to excellent effect. A flirt, she had every man in the village practically eating out of her hand, and that was how she liked it. Marriage was another matter. If she married at all, and she very much wanted to, it was certainly not going to be to any common tiller of the soil; glorying in her good looks, she was going to flaunt them to the best of her ability in pursuit of a man who was not only handsome and rich, but would consider it a privilege to marry her. The idea of meeting such a man at the fair brought a flush to her face which made her seem even prettier. She was wearing a blue dress which flattered her figure and brought out the blue in her eyes.

The early morning sun shone brightly upon her, leaving the rest of the company cast in shadow as she wheedled her way into her father's affections with the minimum of effort. He was fully intending to go to the fair, but not until noon when he had done a full morning's work, whereas Annie was all for going earlier in order not to miss any of the excitement on offer.

"Ay, after noon, lass," he persisted. I hae work to do first."

"But that will be far too late," she importuned, a note of irritation in her voice. "I'm sure Rob can manage without ye for once, canna ye Rob?

Rob glowered at her. Fairs were not particularly to his liking and he did not envisage going anyway, but there was work to do and he would have preferred to have his father alongside him for part of the day.

"Do ye think ye can manage wi'out me, lad?"

"It looks as if I'll hae to," he remarked looking glum.

"You see," she said, looking immensely pleased with herself.

They knew that she would wear him down in the end. She

always did. No one else could have done it, but Annie had such winning ways when it came to her father. Whether it was her blonde curly hair, her corn blue eyes or the full cupid mouth, she only had to combine them into a smile and he melted like butter. And the more it infuriated her mother and Rob, the more she seemed to delight in it. Catherine and Mary smiled at one another across the table. For all Annie's whiles, it was fascinating to watch her assert her ascendancy.

But if Annie was longing for novelty and excitement, Catherine was determined to avoid it at all costs; the thought of being paraded amongst strangers and being endlessly stared at was little short of a nightmare. Before her accident she had enjoyed going to the fair as much as Annie, but since it she had deliberately kept away. Now 14 and on the verge of becoming a woman, she remained shy and withdrawn.

Miriam sighed and got up to prepare the victuals that would be needed. Catherine, mindful of the task, offered to help her, but Miriam told her to go and cheer her mother. And Isobel was in need of cheering. Up until the last week or so she had refused to acknowledge herself as ill; the lack of well-being had only crept upon her gradually and she had been able to disguise it from the others by keeping as busy as usual. The symptoms were known to her and also what they portended. She had seen them before in treating the sick, the growing air of listlessness, the want of appetite, the terrible thirst, finally the slipping away into everlasting sleep. For the time being, however, she was trying to ignore them in the hope that it was just a temporary malaise, but deep down she knew differently.

The flowers that Catherine had picked were wilting in the heat by her bedside. Isobel smiled weakly, attempting to raise herself up. Catherine went to help her. Her mother was still a beautiful woman, not a hint of grey in her hair, her eyes dark with a gleam in their depths, her figure even slimmer than before she bore Catherine, but this was now the third occasion on which she had kept to her bed and Catherine had good cause to be worried. There was no change in her spirit; if anything, it was more resilient than ever, but the dark shadows round her eyes and the thinness of her wrists were only too apparent.

"Come here, where I can see you," she said. "Now tell me, what is afoot?"

"Annie!" said Catherine, that one word encompassing everything.

"Ah, Annie," smiled her mother. "I take it she has got her own way again?"

"Why Uncle Matt cannot see her for what she is."

"He does not want to Catherine. You see he loves her. I suppose they are going to Bardwick this morning after all."

"Yes," Catherine said, gripping Isobel's fingers and squinting at the sun that suddenly revealed the strained look upon her mother's features.

"God help the man who weds her," said Isobel, squeezing Catherine's hand in reassurance.

"Now will you do something for me."

"Anything," replied Catherine, thinking she was being asked to undertake her mother's duties in the village, as she had done while Isobel was ill. "I have the physic prepared for Mistress Hardy and the infusion for the Proctors' child. Tis all ready."

"I know you have, Catherine. No, it isn't that. I want you to do something that you will find much more difficult, something that I know you will rebel against."

"What is it?"

"I would like you to go to the fair with Annie."

"No. I cannot! You know I never go. We have never gone, either of us since ..."

"Precisely," her mother interrupted.

"Listen to me Catherine. You are nearly fifteen, on the verge of womanhood and tis time that you learned to cope in the world without me. We have done well together, but I shall not always be here to help you."

"What are you saying?" cried Catherine in alarm. "You will soon be well again. You know that you will."

"We are all mortal Catherine."

"I will look after you until you are well," Catherine said, a note of panic in her voice.

"But in the meantime, you will go with Annie to the fair. That would do me no end of good."

"How can I? What of the stares and the whispers. I prefer to stay here and look after you. I am happy here. I love Runnarth. There is no need to go anywhere else."

"And we all know why you like Runnarth so much, do we not? You cannot bury yourself in the village for the rest of your life. You need to meet other people, Catherine. There is a life for you outside of Runnarth, believe me."

"I will not go to Bardwick, and certainly not with Annie. I would rather enter a nunnery."

"Ah, yes," replied Isobel, "that would suit you very nicely. There you could hide away forever."

"You are cruel to make me go."

"Sometimes we have to be cruel to be kind."

Catherine would not stay to listen. In the outer room Mary was quietly engaged in sweeping the floor of its rushes in preparation for new ones. By this time Catherine was very close to tears.

"What is amiss?" Mary enquired.

One look at Mary and her anger melted away. In relation to Mary's troubles, her own looked petty by comparison. She was just getting over another miscarriage, yet despite the pain and disappointment she never complained. She trusted in God to sustain her. Catherine often wished she had the same kind of faith and envied her for it.

"Come, tell me all about it," she coaxed. "It is not often we get the opportunity of speaking quietly together."

She looked so tired and drawn that Catherine almost wished that there would be no further pregnancies, although she knew that Mary would not thank her for such prayers. As ever, Mary was easy to confide in, but her reaction was not as Catherine had hoped. Rather did she tend to agree with Isobel.

"I never thought you would be against me too, Mary," she sobbed.

"Of course I am not against you," she consoled, "but would you be crying like this if your mother was wrong. She is naturally worried for you."

"And don't you think that I have suffered enough. I cannot bear to meet strangers. My happiest hours are spent here with you and mother."

"Catherine, that is because you forget what you look like when you are with us, but there is no reason why you should not feel that way with someone else if you persevere, and I do believe yours to be a persevering nature Catherine. Please your mother. She loves you so much. Tis not such a big thing to ask of you, really, now is it?"

"Mother is quite ill, isn't she Mary? She will get well though, won't she?"

"I am confident of it," Mary replied. "We must pray, continually pray." Catherine flung her arms round her neck. "Am I to take it that your mind is made up, then?"

"I will go," said Catherine.

And with that she ran in to tell her mother, who gave her a kiss and a hug and urged her to get herself ready. When she had gone, the tears she had held back began to trickle down her face. The thought of being separated from Catherine was the worst part of dying.

ଓ ଛ

There were only four of them going, her Uncle and Aunt and Annie. Catherine had wanted to take her dog, but Annie was adamant that she wasn't having it. The thought of a mangy old cur as she called it dirtying her finery was just too insufferable. Catherine had only wanted to take it as a prop to boost her confidence, but when Mary pointed out that Peter might get lost in the crowds she had to own that it was more sensible to leave him at home.

It was a beautiful day, but exceedingly warm. The three open fields of irregular strips were bathed in the sun in one great expanse of yellow, green and brown. Beyond lay the common, its rights of grazing as sacrosanct as Father Craven's confessional. A few ducks quacked ferociously across the pond, their noise set in motion by a dog intent on sharing their pleasure. The forest lay dark and quiet, hardly a beam of sunlight penetrating the tightly grouped trees. Anyone who entered it unauthorised did so at their peril, Lord Elliston's forest laws being swift and severe. Rob paused to wave them goodbye, his swart figure showing to advantage against its setting of wide earth and sky.

Annie linked her father's arm, as sweet and winsome as the weather now she was getting her way. Catherine walked alongside Miriam who had a basket of eggs to sell. She almost felt happy, not so much at the thought of going to the fair, but simply because it was such a heaven sent day in spite of the heat.

Mercifully, it was cooler by the river and they all felt glad of the shading of trees. Trees of England, Peter used to call them, the giant oaks, the sorrowing willows, the cool green beeches, the tall poplars, the brooding rowan with its blood red berries. What recollections the riverside brought of Peter and long summer days, days forever gone but not beyond recall.

It was not long before Runnarth Castle came fully into view, its massive keep towering high above them against a sky peculiarly drained of all colour. Originally a simple motte and bailey, over the years the descendants of the first Ellistons had successively added to it, so that now it boasted a complexity of buildings ranged round a wide and partially turfed courtyard where the famous Runnarth jousting contests were held. Matthew was the only one of their number ever to have entered that courtyard, but he never forgot the Great Hall nor the mark he had been required to put upon a lengthy legal document giving him right of tenure over his own strips of land.

"Kate, hae ye ever seen anything so splendid," Annie enthused, looking up with a raptured expression at the ramparts, her imagination lifting her from commoner to lady in a trice. "Just imagine the riches, the music, the dancing."

Catherine could well imagine, but to her it was an idea more forbidding than inviting. There were a few boats plying aimlessly up and down the river, no doubt retainers from the castle enjoying their off duty hours. Looking up from the river to the castle, the scene seemed to strike a chord in Catherine's memory.

"Annie, I have just recollected something. Years ago when I visited Peter I saw the castle bathed in the most wonderful sunset. It was at a distance, of course, but it seemed to ring the castle with fire. I shall always remember it."

Annie became more excited than ever, clutching at her father's arm, urging him to stay after nightfall, but even he was not open to persuasion on this point. Disappointed, Annie now turned her attentions to Catherine.

"I have heard stories about the castle," she began, looking up at the mighty keep towering above them.

"Have you?" said Catherine in rather a dull graceless tone, Annie's stories being noted for their accent on colour more scarlet than plain.

"Well, for one thing tis said the old Lord is close to death and that his son canna wait to step into his shoes."

"That is cruel."

"And for another, that he's a terrible lecher," she gleefully continued, waiting on Catherine's reaction to this new revelation.

As Annie rightly surmised, Catherine was ignorant of the word, but then Annie's vocabulary, limited as it was, consisted of a quantity of words never appearing in Father Craven's curriculum. But nonetheless it made Catherine curious and it was plain that Annie was itching to add to her knowledge.

"He has mistresses aplenty and canna stand his wife and childer."

"I find it strange, hating one's children. Are you sure these stories are true?"

"Yes, Kate, tis perfectly true," she confidently maintained.

"I think you want it to be."

"Well, it does make everything a lot more interesting. Anyway who wants a dull lord."

Catherine wondered if her father had been such a man, not that it troubled her greatly if only for the briefest of whiles he had genuinely cared for her mother. Another mile or so and Bardwick came into view and Catherine felt a churn in her stomach.

"Nearly there," Matthew announced, as the din of distant crowds became ever louder.

In no time at all they were edging their way into the main square where trestle tables displaying a diverse assortment of goods were set out to tempt them. Even Catherine had to acknowledge that the life and colour was intoxicating. The privileged and the common brushed side by side, all turned out in the best they could muster. Parti-coloured hose of green and yellow clashed with tunics of vivid red and blue. Beautiful women with carefully painted faces and tightly coiled hair whispered provocatively into the ears of their grandly attired male companions. Jugglers performed in the adjacent meadow and a mystery play being performed by one of the guild of craftsmen was well in progress. Quacks peddled miracle cures to a credulous crowd while a ring of men and women linked hands and made up their own kind of dance to the beat of a tambourine. But alongside this seeming gaiety and colour was the dirt it engendered, grotesquely painted whores peddling their disease laden favours, surreptitious pickpockets, many of them children, weaving in and out of the crowds, and fetid alleyways of brothels and taverns where Matthew forbade them to go. In contrast to the smells of the country, the town was abysmal. As they turned a corner they were confronted by a blood spattered bear being baited by an equally blood spattered pack of dogs. Catherine covered her face with her hands. Such cruelty appalled her.

Miriam eventually found a vacant spot to sell her wares and Matthew went off to look at some livestock. Having been told to be careful, the two girls were left to their own devices.

"I feel so dowdy," Annie said desultorily.

"You are being silly," Catherine replied. "No amount of frippery can make a plain girl pretty and you are one of the prettiest girls here. Surely you know that."

Annie was not unaware of the fact, but it made her feel immeasurably self-satisfied to be told so. Both girls were attracting a good deal of attention, one for her obvious good looks and the other for her want of a face to be looked at.

"Let us go over there," remarked Annie, pointing to the end of the street.

Before Catherine had time to resist, Annie took hold of her hand and forced a passage to the front of the onlookers. A trio of musicians was the cause of her interest. Two were ordinary looking men but the third was noticeably different, both in looks and demeanour, a swarthy, dark eyed man who was adept in attracting the gaze of the women. He had a foreign air about him. His hair was dark with plenty of wave in it, his white shirt slightly open to reveal the bronze of his skin. The ballad he was singing complemented the romantic aspect of the man himself, and from the moment she set eyes upon him Annie's heart began to beat in wild heady leaps. Whereas the other two men confined themselves to making the music upon peculiar looking stringed instruments, he was the singer, his voice full of vibrant emotion. Catherine was also enthralled. Music such as this was a rarity and she noted with interest the instruments which were being played. Until then she had only heard a few men from the village play upon a recorder, a pastime which Father Craven tended to discourage. She felt her feet begin to tap in time to the beat. A small party of men and women were already dancing. For a moment she forgot how she looked, but the stare of one of the dancers made her remember only too quickly and she put her hands up to her face. Between her fingers she could see that Annie was mesmerised by the singer, and even after the music was ended and his fellow musicians had drifted away Annie remained.

"Annie," she whispered, "tis time we were going."

The singer was taking note.

"But not yet Mademoiselle. Your friend, she like to stay."

His English was deliciously quaint, his accent irresistible.

"Many pretty girls I see," he continued, "but none as 'andsome as you."

Annie soon found her tongue.

"Girls canna be handsome," she promptly replied, "only men. Girls can be pretty though."

"Then I am 'andsome and you are pretty, yes?"

Catherine, though looking down at the ground, smiled faintly. It would seem that Annie had at last met her match.

"Who says you are handsome," Annie responded, somewhat put out of countenance.

"Why, you do."

"I dunna know what ye mean."

"I find that very strange. You look at me in admiration, no?"

"Ye are vain I warrant," she replied, eyeing him narrowly.

"But truthful. I see you have a little temper."

Catherine smiled hugely at this, quite content to watch the sparring unnoticed. In terms of enjoyment, it all but rivalled the music.

"Tell me, what is your name?" he resumed.

"Philippa," said Annie, assuming the Queen's name.

"And mine is Edward," he immediately answered, taking on that of the King, sensing her guile and matching it with a little of his own. "I guess your trick. My home is Gascony, and your king is my king, for the moment that is."

"Tell him the truth," Catherine shyly interrupted.

"This is your friend, yes?" he enquired.

"My cousin."

"Please, step closer, mademoiselle, I cannot see you to advantage."

Catherine suddenly felt awkward and abashed, but Annie pushed her forward. She felt herself flushing horribly, not only because he could now see her properly, but because of Annie who had a way of inflaming her temper.

"Ye are bad mannered," Annie accused him. "She canna help the way she is."

In response to this, Catherine looked up at the stranger. She could see he was clearly embarrassed and her one wish at that moment was to simply disappear.

"Please forgive," he said, looking at her contritely. "I meant no 'arm."

"Tis rude to stare so," Annie persisted, regarding him with a new kind of boldness. "Twas a pity she swept too close to the fire, but tis done and there is no mending it."

Tears welled up in Catherine's eyes. There were times when Annie was pointedly cruel, and had it not been for the fact of him being a stranger she might have let the matter go, but as it was she felt duty bound to defend herself, if only out of respect for her mother.

"Please do not worry on my account," she quietly asserted. "I am accustomed to being stared at, and if you want to know her real name, tis Annie."

"But that is charming," he smiled, approving her spirit. "Mine is Gerard, and yourself."

"Catherine."

"Ah, the blessed St. Catherine," he sighed, crossing himself.

"Kate will do," said Annie, peevishly.

"No it will not," Catherine maintained. "My mother prefers me to be called by my full name."

She no longer felt shy, in fact quite the reverse.

"You are right mon petite. Catherine is finer, I think," he loyally defended, but not without a hint of irony. "You girls are alone?"

"No," replied Annie, more chastened. "Mother and father are here. We live at Runnarth."

"Ah, Runnarth. I have entertained the Lord Elliston."

"Ye have," said Annie, wide eyed with envy.

"But only the once."

"Was it very grand? Were the women very beautiful?"

"Mm, it is how you say, magnifique, but I see no woman as beautiful as you."

Annie actually blushed, though Catherine noticed that for all his flattery his liking for her cousin was genuine.

"Where did ye say ye lived?" asked Annie.

"My 'ome is Gascony, in the warm lands of France, but I come to England where I learn you 'ave a liking for French ballads and make the music of my country, yes?"

"The warm lands of France," Annie repeated to herself in a haze of enchantment. "Tis so romantic."

"But lonely," he added, looking at her meaningfully.

Yet again, Catherine intimated that they ought to be going.

"Please, no," he pleaded, "not when we just get to be friends."

"Tis a pity, but I think we must," Annie said apologetically, a lovely note of sorrow in her voice.

"But we meet again, Annie. Yes?" he eagerly enquired, his dark eyes begging her consent.

"I canna say. I dunna come to town that often."

"Then I come to see you, eh?"

"I canna say," she replied, her eyes hugging his.

"I am well behaved, yes. I would do you no 'arm."

At this Annie broke into laughter.

"Can I be sure on it?" she said by way of teasing him.

He momentarily turned away.

"I think you have offended him," said Catherine.

Annie's face crumpled into one of utter anxiety. But of far more moment to Catherine was the fact that for once in her life Annie was thinking of someone other than herself. Seemingly, the Frenchman was having a good effect upon her.

"You laugh at me, I think," he said at last, his back disdainfully turned away from them.

"Annie," whispered Catherine. "You will have to apologise."

"I didna mean it," she tearfully implored.

He immediately faced them, his good humour fully restored, his dignity still intact.

"We meet again Annie, yes?"

"Oh yes," she meekly replied.

He then told them where he could be found, but impressed upon her that she must first seek her father's permission.

"You will ask your papa?" he said, looking not only at Annie, but also at Catherine who he was obviously relying on to see that she did so.

"Now give me your hand."

She readily gave it, whereupon he brushed it with his lips.

"And Catherine."

She complied with her left hand which was far less unsightly than her right.

"Au revoir," he said. "Now you say au revoir Gerard, eh?"

They said it without demur, Annie gazing into his eyes as if she were utterly besotted, which of course she was.

Miriam and Matthew did all the talking as they walked back to Runnarth. By contrast, Annie was uncommonly quiet, neither Catherine nor herself having said a word concerning their meeting with the Frenchman. They both knew Matthew's dislike of foreigners, but Catherine was reasonably confident that if Annie wanted to see the Frenchman again she would have little difficulty in persuading her father. Catherine liked him too, but not at all in the way that Annie did though there was something about him that was undeniably appealing.

"Catherine," said Annie, as Runnarth Castle once again came into view.

"Yes," Catherine yawned.

"He is so delightful, and to think he has entertained at the castle. Do you think he really finds me pleasing?"

It was noticeable to Catherine how the harsh demanding tone of her voice softened whenever she spoke of him.

"You know that he does."

"I believe I adore him already," she avowed, whirling round in a haze of contentment.

Catherine smiled to herself. It would seem that Annie was in that strange state of feeling called love, and the realisation brought to her mind what Father Craven had said in regard to herself. "You are young now, but later it will be different." Now she was aware what his "different" had meant. She was a woman not destined to marry.

CHAPTER SEVEN

Swishing the flails to and fro in repetitive motion, the two girls stopped at intervals to wipe their brows before wearily resuming. A tedious but necessary task, this separating the grain from the chaff, and everyone was required to take their turn at it. The tallest girl invented a slow steady hum to keep pace with her work, but the other looked tearful and dejected.

"Shall we rest awhile," Mary said.

Catherine did not answer, her thoughts drifting away with the chaff.

"Catherine, you are daydreaming again. Shall we stop now?"

"No, no, do not stop," she replied, under the impression that it was the song to which Mary alluded.

Mary put down her flail and repeated the question yet again.

"Look, there is chaff everywhere," she remarked, flicking it out of Catherine's hair.

Catherine stood quietly submissive as the offending particles were removed. At twenty she was slender and graceful in her movements, her hair having deepened to a rich and dark auburn.

"I am sorry, Mary, I was not heeding. I feel low in spirits, right here," she said, pointing to her heart.

Mary knew only too well the cause of the trouble, but it was beyond her capacity to help. Time alone could relieve her of that particular ache. It was four years since Isobel had died, but to Catherine it may as well have been yesterday. Despite Mary's assurances that time would heal the hurt, she still felt it keenly. Lying against two heavy sacks of corn, she was content to let Mary cradle her in her lap.

"I do try Mary, but tis so hard at times. She was everything to me. She gave me courage to face the world as I am. If only she was here with us now. Tis all so unfair."

"Life is very rarely fair," said Mary, "but I feel sure tis all to some purpose. It is not ours to question."

"But I do question all the time. I do not have your strength of faith."

"Catherine, your faith is stronger than mine, did you but know it."

Wiping the tears from her face, Catherine suddenly leapt to her feet and, grabbing hold of her flail, recommenced the work as if her very life depended upon it. Mary understood, but understanding wasn't of any real help. For Catherine work was a form of release, but it was also in danger of becoming her sole means of existence. She pretended to be content, but apart from the family she had little companionship and little enjoyment, and only Mary seemed to sense how unsettled she was. The others took her for granted, Rob and her uncle thinking her a boon when it came to tackling those niggling tasks for which they had no time themselves. Now that Annie was settled, Miriam relied on her more than ever where the running of the household was concerned. Mary did what she could to fill the gap left by Isobel, but she had Rob and the baby to think of, or rather the baby she still hoped to have.

Annie and Gerard were settled in Bardwick with two boisterous sons, Matthew having given his consent to the marriage despite reservations. Had it been anyone other than his favourite child, he might not have been so willing, but as ever Annie got what she wanted. Matthew tried to make the best of it, but Gerard always had the feeling that he was tolerated rather than accepted. Miriam did what she could to make up for Matthew's aloofness, but Gerard had hoped for a warmer welcome into the family.

Marriage was far from the bliss Annie had imagined, Gerard's trade making for enforced separations which she bitterly resented, but which were unavoidable if they were to live in the kind of comfort she wanted. She hated being left alone or, in her words, neglected. Neither was she maternal, having little interest in the doings of her children who, left to their own devices, were growing up to be as wayward as their mother. When he returned it was inevitable that they would argue. She would accuse him of having other women and become hysterical, but when he showed her the rewards of his profession, particularly the pretty trinkets to which she was so partial, her chagrin would soon be forgotten in the passionate reunions that followed. Both highly strung, it seemed that these extremes of emotion were necessary to keep them together. "Ebb" and "Flow" Mary amusingly termed them.

Catherine lay awake. Unable to sleep, she gazed into the blackness, reflecting on her life as it was; the endless procession of days that revolved around sameness. It was the first time in her life that she actually understood what her mother had meant by life being meagre, but no sooner had she given in to such thoughts than she felt guilty for craving more than she had. Then she would pray very fervently, thanking God for His blessings and begging His strength in her weakness, but her spirit was not lifted and her prayers went unanswered. And then there were dreams in which her mother would plead with her not to give in to Father Craven's persuasions and enter a nunnery. The most recent had been so real that she awoke with a start to find Peter licking her face. He was an old dog now but still very much loved. In the dream her mother had been telling her that even were she to dedicate her life to the service of God, He would know that she was not doing it for the right reasons, but merely as a means of hiding herself away, when in truth He had planned a different path for her. But in asking what this path was, her mother merely smiled, and then she awoke.

Harvest was nearly over, and to the satisfaction of them all it boded good. Catherine walked out to the fields, on her arm the basket containing the mid-day repast for Matthew and Rob who had healthy outdoor appetites. It was a fine autumn day, the sky a deep blue, the sun casting its equable warmth on the strips of golden corn which were rapidly being cut down. She paused to put down the basket and take in the scene. In spite of the dream, for some reason she felt unaccountably content, a pleasing contrast to her recent low spirits. Like the earth, she basked in the ambience of brighter hued weather and the feeling was good. On days like this she could not visualise another village as lovely as Runnarth, another part of the country as fine as the wilds of her own native home. No, Runnarth was not circumscribed, it was not mean, it was home and she had no desire to go anywhere else. Picking up the basket, she had not proceeded very far when two horsemen riding at a furious pace overtook her; they splashed her with mud and laughed as they did so. She drew to the edge of the path, vaguely wondering what had brought them to Runnarth. One of them she recognised as Sir Guy Talbot, bailiff to Lord Elliston and collector of taxes and dues. Without conjecturing further, she continued on her way, but at a much faster pace. The horsemen had somehow disquieted her.

"What are you going to say to them Sir Guy?" asked his companion.

"Tell 'em the facts," roared Talbot, his huge body making the horse foam and sweat from the weight it had to carry.

"What about the wench we just past?"

"I could not see her properly. Anyhow we can choose 'em like. No shilly-shallying though. We get the best we can. Young and strong."

"Strong for what?" the other laughed coarsely.

They had been careful in picking a day when they knew that most of the able bodied would be engaged in collecting the harvest, which would make for less trouble and a smoother outcome to the issue. Talbot knew how it would be otherwise. His reputation in the village was well known and they avoided him like the onset of a plague. Thus, it was strangely silent when they arrived, but Talbot was in no mood to be ignored.

"Hear ye," he bellowed at the top of his voice. "By command of Lord Elliston I am authorised to find one female, preferably young, but more importantly hale, to assist in the management of his lordship's kitchen."

Once it had been Bardwick that provided suitable skivvies for the castle, but now it would seem that Runnarth had been chosen for the doubtful privilege of serving the Ellistons.

"They are not going to play," he remarked to his companion after a lengthy period of quiet.

"Then we'll have to take the game to them."

It was then that Mother Jomfrey stepped out of her hovel, summoning them to her with a bony twist of her finger. They followed her inside where a gaunt, thin man was lying on his bed, being tended by an angular looking woman, her face as pale and drawn as that of the man she was tending. "Dunna worry yesell o'er them," Mother Jomfrey said. "Look at her, barren as the day she were born. As for him, he's my son for my pains and no the strength o' a fly. Longing for the day I die, both of 'em, like crows over entrails."

Sir Guy curled his lip in disgust at the image. Neither were his nostrils too taken with the peculiar stench the old woman emitted. Seeing no reason to stay, he was about to leave when Mother Jomfrey grasped his arm.

"Kind sir, stay awhile. I can tell ye where y'ell be sure to get what ye be lookin for."

"Speak, and have done with it."

"I'm a poor woman sir," she continued, holding out the palms of her hands in hope of some recompense.

"Rest easy old hag. Now say your say."

"Matthew Thompson's place, top o' row from here," she replied, grovelling in the rushes as he threw down a coin. "She has a niece, twenty, strong, unwed, nor ever like to be."

"What mean you by that?" he questioned.

"Ye'll see," she tittered. "Ye'll see."

When he had gone, she spat on the coin and rubbed it between her finger and thumb.

"That for Kate Venners" she cursed. "I've bided my time and I've served the bitch out."

ꕥ

"You have a girl here unwed," enquired Sir Guy, attempting to be as civil as he was able.

"Ay," Miriam had to admit, looking in alarm at Mary.

"This her," he said pointing.

"No, no, this is my son's wife."

"Then where is the other?"

Miriam's features blanched.

"You own your land?" asked Sir Guy pointedly.

"It is ours by right!" Mary bravely spoke out.

"You are quite a spirited lass for a slip of a thing," he remarked, eyeing her lasciviously. "Look here, Mistress Thompson, facts are facts. You have the girl. We want her. She'll be well taken care of, have no fear."

"She's my niece," Miriam stammered. "She's terribly marked. I promised my sister to care for her." He was interested.

"What do you mean, marked?"

Miriam tried to explain.

"Then you have no need to worry. No fear of her being tampered with, is there?"

"Your speech is too free, sir," Mary accused.

"I but speak to reassure you," he countered.

"You must not let them take her," Mary implored.

"Be sensible now Mistress Thompson. No girl. No land. Tis as simple as that," he intimated, the smile becoming a grimace.

In her dilemma Miriam started to cry. It was all too much for her. A few years ago she might have put up some kind of resistance, but now she was older and more inclined to worry than act. Mary had only words to fight with, and a touching faith that God would come to their aid. Completely ignorant of matters, Catherine arrived at the very moment when Sir Guy was beginning to lose what little patience he had.

"That her?" he said, alluding to the mask.

"Ay," sobbed Miriam.

"You will not take her," said Mary, standing between Catherine and the bailiff.

For Catherine the world began spinning. She was utterly

bewildered and totally unaware of what was about to happen. Guy pushed Mary aside and grabbed her by the arm.

"You are to come with me," he said.

"Why? What have I done."

Sir Guy was not inclined to be unnecessarily hard despite his unenviable commission and the sight of the obviously disfigured girl moved him much more than an ordinarily pretty one would have done.

"You have nothing to fear," he assured her, "but the castle needs a kitchen hand and you are my choice." She looked at him in amazement, not quite realising what it all meant.

"Look," he said, "I'll go outside and wait while you say your farewells."

Mary tried to explain everything to her, and Catherine was strangely calm, possibly because it was so sudden and unexpected. By this time Miriam's sobbing was loud and unrestrained and it was Catherine, more in need of commiseration, who found herself comforting her aunt.

"You must not worry Aunt," she urged. "I will come back whenever I can."

The three of them kissed and hugged and Peter started to growl. "Poor Peter," she soothed, "You will look after him Mary?" Mary merely nodded. She was very close to tears herself.

Sir Guy helped her into the saddle as the villagers, now convinced of their own safety, one by one emerged to witness her departure. It was oddly silent. Seated in front of Sir Guy, it was difficult to look back. Only once did she manage to crane her head round his massive girth to catch a last glimpse of Miriam and Mary, but the horse suddenly veered and they were gone.

As they made their way along the edge of the great fields, she looked for Rob and her uncle, but they were nowhere to be seen and soon they were proceeding along the river and the cave once inhabited by Peter. The knot of autumn daisies she had placed on his grave swayed gently in the breeze. "Peter" she silently prayed, "Be with me. Protect me."

Dusk was approaching when they arrived and a sinking sun glowed red across the ramparts just as it had done on similar occasions. The drawbridge was lowered and the two horsemen rode across, the mighty keep towering above them like some malevolent ogre eager to swallow its prey. Sir Guy assisted her to dismount and as they entered through the gates the sun disappeared to leave them in gloom. Calling for a torch, he led her to a tower, its steps spiralling down to the depths beneath.

The further they descended the hotter it became. Strange

odours began to waft up to them, mingled with cries and hideous laughter. It was the human element that disturbed her. She could feel her body actually tighten and her head begin to throb. With the reality of the day gaining momentum upon her, so her fear increased. Sir Guy steadied her once or twice as she stumbled against the walls. The courage she displayed drew his admiration and he came to the conclusion that notwithstanding her disfigurement this was no commonplace woman. As the heat grew ever fiercer, she was mindful of hell and the fiery descent.

"Wait here," he said, as they reached the level of a dingy passageway lit by one paltry brazier. The heat and laughter were far more pronounced now as she pressed herself against the wall in a futile attempt to stop her body from shaking. Suddenly a door was thrown open and the passageway was bathed in a fierce blaze of light. Without further ceremony, Sir Guy motioned her to enter the source from which it emanated. The glare and the heat were intense as she strained to see where she was.

"Tom Watkins," she heard Sir Guy call. "Your new girl."

It was the heat and the fire that terrified her, not to mention the unfamiliar surroundings and the dread of finding herself encircled by a hostile sea of staring faces.

"Let's hope she proves better than the last," Watkins retorted above the din and noise that somehow seemed in keeping with this hellish place.

"She'll be good enough," replied Sir Guy. "Tis no common slut I've brought you," and with this terse comment he left her to their mercies.

"Take ye hands away from ye face girl, and let's be havin' a good look at ye," said the man named Watkins.

She did as she was told and met the vulgar stare of a thick heavy set man with mean looking eyes set in a bald shiny pate. His teeth were rotten and the hair that should have covered his head hung from the nostrils of his nose; he also boasted a healthy growth of stubble. Strange men and women closed in on her, all begrimed with grease, their eyes bright and keen in the heat, their sweat mingling with the smell of rancid fat.

"What's up with ye?" he demanded, pointing at the mask.

She was unable to speak. The words would not come. And as her fear mounted, they began to taunt and prod her, their arms waving threateningly.

"Lost ye tongue," laughed one of the older women with warts and derisory wisps of hair sticking out from under a frayed and crooked coif.

"Leave 'er alone," said a girl of comely if dishevelled

appearance.

"Leave 'er to me you mean," sparred a thin spindly youth with close cropped hair and a fiendish kind of snigger.

This set in motion a variety of crude interchanges which were threatening to get out of hand had not Watkins silenced them with a thunderous "Enough!". Silence of a sort ensued as Watkins moved closer towards her.

"Now, let's be 'avin' ye," he recommenced, thumbing the mask.

"Canna ye see the lass is afeared," appealed the girl of comely appearance, but she was quickly shouted down by the others and withdrew to the outer edge of the circle.

"Well!" he roared, "we be waitin'."

Trembling and shuddering to think of the consequences was she not to comply, she tried to explain, hoping to appeal to any compassion they had.

"Speak up!" bellowed an old man hard of hearing.

"Ay, ay," joined in some of the others.

They grew quiet while she told them, but they were rough and unpredictable and she knew her position to be precarious at best.

"What did she say?" said the man hard of hearing.

"Got burnt in a fire you silly old fool," screamed one of the women.

This was followed by comments and murmurs, and then a general demand that she take the mask off.

"Ay, we mun look," was the cry.

"No, I beg you," she pleaded. "You mustn't, not for my sake, but for yours."

"Mustna," drawled Watkins, slowly parading round her. "Did ye hear that? She said "mustna" the forrard baggage. No one orders Tom Watkins, do ye understand!"

She bowed her head, her eyes pricking with the tears she was trying so hard not to spill.

"Remove it!" he roared.

"Remove it! Remove it!" they took up the chant, stamping and clapping in one horrific chorus.

She attempted to evade them, but their hands were upon her. A solitary shriek echoed through the flame lit labyrinth, and then as quickly died away in a babble of muffled incredulity. Their curiosity satisfied, the mask was held aloft. What they felt was exactly as others had felt; it showed in their faces, the horror, the revulsion, worst of all the pity. She ought to have become accustomed to it by now, but each time it happened the rejection still hurt.

"Here," said Watkins, handing her the mask. "Put it back on for sweet Jesu's sake."

Coming from Father Craven there would have been a note of profundity in the words; coming from Watkins they meant what they implied. He told them to get back to work and they did so immediately. Through her tears she tried to take in her surroundings. Vast was too inadequate a word to describe the cavernous kitchen, each end of which was flanked by a massive open hearth. In front of one of them an ox was being turned to roast on a spit, the boy in charge of it no more than nine years of age, half naked and covered in scabs from burning bits of fat. From menacing hooks high above hung game and carcasses of every description, some of them riddled with vermin. Running the length of the walls were trestles containing a quantity of utensils, skillets, pots, pans, dishes, plates; the two huge tables in the middle were where the bulk of the preparation was done, and the beings who had just abused her were now furiously intent on their work, the men hacking at pieces of raw flesh, the women busily kneading loaves, cutting fruits and rolling out pastry. One smell cancelled out another, but one of the better ones was that of newly baked bread. For all the apparent slovenliness and disorder the place was run with amazing efficiency, Tom Watkins' role appearing to be that of chief surveyor and guard against slackers.

"Get to that table and stop ye shriking," he said, directing her to one of the smaller tables strewn with herbs in various stages of preparation There were only two women at work, one of them being the girl who had recently tried to defend her. "Joan, show 'er what to do."

"Come on. Take no notice of 'im," she said encouragingly. "I'm sorry they treated ye as they did. They didna hae cause, but we dunna get much excitement hereabouts. Still, tis a pity. I bet ye would hae been a fine looking wench with that red hair o' yourn. Anyways, the one side o' ye face is hardly marked at all; we mun look on that and not the other, eh Maud." The other girl grinned and nodded her head in approval. "This is Maud," she said by way of introduction. "She's dumb, canna talk, but she knows what goes on, eh Maud?" The girl grinned again.

"I am Catherine."

"And I be Joan as ye've probably guessed. Pleased to meet ye. Tom," she called, eyeing him boldly, "just like ye not to ask what 'er name be, well tis Catherine."

"Enough of your sauce," he retorted. "Catherine what?"

"Venners," replied Catherine.

He slunk away to the trestles at the opposite end of the room. Joan made a face as he went. She was blessed with good looks in a buxom kind of way, her eyes sparkling and full of mischief, her hair abundant though unkempt which gave it an added attraction, her mouth full and firm, her complexion clear and unblemished with a healthy glow in it.

"Thank you for your kindness Joan," she said shyly.

Maud gripped her arm, the gesture intimating that she too wished to be included. Catherine squeezed her hand in acknowledgement. Small, waif like and extremely plain, it seemed as if she too looked to Joan for protection.

"Ye know ye dunna need lessons from me," Joan remarked after a while. "I daresay ye could teach me a few things." Maud agreed with an excited kind of look. "She be a clever one Maud I warrant."

"My mother and Peter taught me," Catherine explained.

"Who be Peter, ye young man?"

"No. Peter was a man of God who lived near to Runnarth."

"Ay, I believe I heard somethin' on 'im, but I come fro' Bardwick. Dunna know your village. You ever been to Bardwick?"

"Only on fair days."

Maud's eyes lit up at the word "fair".

"Ay, fairs be grand," Joan agreed, giving Maud a playful cuff.

"Is it always so warm?" Catherine asked, wiping her face.

"Ye'll get used to it. Ye'll get used to a lot o' things 'ere."

Catherine did not pursue the matter. She had seen enough for one day.

"Time!" bellowed Watkins.

"What is happening?" whispered Catherine.

"Ye'll see."

Some time honoured ritual was evidently in progress. It commenced with the emptying of pots and pans, the bringing out of copper salvers, the arranging of plates and dishes, all of them set in gleaming rows upon the central table. She gazed in amazement at the pride these coarse men and women displayed in arranging each dish, the hot and sticky discomfort involved in preparing it forgotten in the magnificence of the feast now taking shape.

"Never seen aught like it hae ye?" said Joan giving her a nudge.

And it was true. Catherine had never seen anything quite like it. To think that one household consumed so much in a single sitting was beyond her comprehension. The diversity, quantity and quality quite took her breath. It had been transformed into something wonderfully mouth watering. Even the juices that dripped from the meat smelt delicious. As for the succulent concoctions of marzipan sweetmeat, they were wondrous in themselves. If only Miriam could have seen it, she thought.

"Tis the same every day, whether they want it or no," said Joan pointedly, "but more so for banquets."

"I thought that this was a banquet!" said Catherine incredulously.

"Mercy, no," replied her friend. She signalled to Maud. "We got an innocent 'ere if ever there was one."

When at last everything was laid out, the men and women stood aside, allowing Watkins to examine their handiwork. Inspecting each dish, he prodded it here and there, testing the tenderness of a joint of meat, the thickness of a crust on a pastry, at intervals sampling bits of it with relish. Judging by the look on his face, he was obviously satisfied and orders were given for the wine to be brought from the buttery.

"To it!" was his signal for the final stage of the work.

The men carried the heaviest of the salvers head high, the women coming up behind with lighter dishes, all carried through the door which she had entered just a short while ago. Seven youths in fashionable attire were there to receive it, and this was the last the purveyors of the feast actually saw of it.

"Them's pages," explained Joan. "Knights' sons most of 'em, hopin' to take a step up in the world. Never speak to low folk like we be."

Catherine noticed. Their heads were disdainfully held high, none of them deigning to look at the menials from the kitchen.

"Ah well, that's that then. Now for ourselves."

"Ourselves?" Catherine queried.

"Ay, ye got to eat yesell, haven't ye. God bless us!" she exclaimed, perfunctorily making the sign of the cross. The trestles were now being piled high with what was left of the feast just departed. Wooden platters were haphazardly thrown down on them by Jack the unfortunate spit boy, that is for everyone apart from Watkins, who as head of the kitchen, was provided with a pewter one. Manners were crude. Knives, but mostly hands, were stuck into salvers to grab what they could. Miriam would have been appalled at such behaviour. In thinking of her home, she pictured them sat round the table, Miriam dispensing equal portions to all. How she longed to be with them now, even dear old Peter with his begging for titbits.

"Come on Kate, dig in else ye'll get naught," chivvied Joan, breaking into her thoughts, "and tis good food, better than ye are used to I'll be bound."

It was good, but her appetite was lacking. A dreadful weariness of body and spirit made her long for the day to be done. After an hour or so, the dishes that had looked so tempting on being conveyed to the household above, were now returned, and the mammoth task of scouring begun. It seemed never ending, but when it was done every sign of activity suddenly ceased.

"I'll wish ye goodnight," said Watkins, leaving them in the semi-darkness of the lowly glowing hearths.

"Where do you sleep?" Catherine asked.

"Where ye can," replied Joan.

Many of them had already claimed spaces along the walls, others retiring into the dingy recesses of the passageways outside. She blushed as she saw several men and women quite unashamedly lie down together.

"I know a good place for ye," said Joan, seeing the worried expression on her face.

She led her through the passageway until they reached a small alcove just out of sight of the main flight of stairs.

"How about that," she said. "No one 'ull bother ye here. Only thing, tis so draughty. Have ye got naught to cover ye?"

"No. Sir Guy left me little time in which to gather anything together."

"Dunna vex yesell. I'll get ye a sheet."

While she was away, Catherine sat shivering, gloomily reflecting on the past hours and the torment to which she had been subjected. Her hands involuntarily went to the mask, just to make sure it still fitted securely. This must be a judgement by God for her want of contentment. There could be no other reason. She buried her head in her hands and wept.

"Here ye are," said Joan, "just what ye need."

"Thank you," Catherine sobbed.

"Ye dunna want to take on so. Tis not so bad. Ye'll get used to it, we all do."

"I do not want to!" she tearfully countered. "How could they act as they did? I cannot bear to be looked at like that."

"Kate," she said, wrapping the blanket round her, "I have known ye but a short time, but to my mind ye let those scars bother ye over much. Anyways, they be not such a bad lot as ye would have 'em. There's good in all on us. It just takes ye longer to find it in some than in others."

She was right of course and Catherine felt a little ashamed of herself.

"Joan, I am feeling sorry for myself, am I not?"

"Well ..."

"Tis so, I know it. I shall try to guard against it in future, but the day has been so fraught."

"I know," Joan agreed. "I'd feel sorry for myself too put in your shoon. You are such a little innocent too."

"Joan, I am so glad I have you," she said, gripping her hand.

"Ye wouldna think so well on me, did you know me better."

"What do you mean?"

"Naught to mither on. Ye are different to us, somethin' about ye."

"Of course I am different," she replied, touching her face.

"No I didna mean that."

"What then?" enquired Catherine, looking somewhat perplexed.

"Well, the way ye talk for one thing. Y'eve had learnin' and such, and as I said to Maud there's naught ye dunna know about herbs that's worth knowin'."

"You flatter me Joan. I have had lessons in letters from my priest, tis true, but my Latin is poorer than I would wish."

"Lord o' mercy, Latin!" she exclaimed. "Ye see what I mean. What do ye be needin' Latin for anyways?"

Catherine became silent and Joan, taking this as a signal to leave, was just about to go when Catherine had a change of heart and told her to stay.

"Can you keep a secret?" she said.

"Bless me, I kep' more secrets 'ere than ye'll ever know, saving Christ Jesu."

It was strange, thought Catherine, how her sentences were punctuated with appeals to God, and yet there was nothing blasphemous in the habit. Perhaps it gave her security in such a place.

"Go on," she nudged, her eyes wide in the expectation of some hitherto unforeseen seamy side to this girl who appeared to have no vices.

"You will not tell anyone? Promise?"

"Promise," she said, spitting on her hand.

"My priest wishes me to enter a nunnery."

Joan fell back in astonishment.

"A nun!" she said contemptuously.

"Many women become such," Catherine replied with a hint of nervous irritation, as if in defence of the notion. "There is nothing wrong in a life of prayer, and what is more Father Craven sees it as God's chosen way for me."

"Catch me doin' that, not as they'd look at me," Joan laughed. "No, Kate, dunna ye get doin' that. Think o' all the fastin' and penance and such like. It wouldna suit ye. For all ye are quiet like, ye've got spirit. I admired ye for the way ye put up with them lot. Anyways if ye have any sense ye'll get wed."

It was a little disquieting that her mother and now Joan, who could not have been more dissimilar, both frowned on the notion while she as yet remained uncertain. Her appeals to God on the matter remained unanswered, unless, of course, her present situation was going to provide some sort of answer, the possibility of which seemed very unlikely.

"Shall I go now?" asked Joan, seeing that she had given her cause for thought.

"No Joan, stay a while longer if you can. I feel so tired, and yet I fear I will not sleep, my mind is reeling overmuch for that."

"I canna stay much longer. I'm wanted ye see."

"I am sorry, I was not thinking. You must have other friends."

"Ay, I suppose ye could call 'em that."

Catherine looked so puzzled that Joan thought it time she was a little more enlightened.

"Look Kate, ye best learn to be on your guard. Ye might know ye letters and ye Latin, but ye dunna know anythin' o' the ways o' the world do ye? I got someone waitin' for me, see. I reckon once ye know me better ye'll not want much to do with me."

"I do not understand."

"Ay, that's the whole trouble with ye. Do ye know how old I am?"

"Eighteen?" Catherine hazarded, trusting she had erred on the right side.

"Ye mun know I'm older," she smiled. "Twenty-three come January."

"Joan," she affirmed, "I only know that you are my friend, the first person here who has shown me a measure of kindness and, incidentally, the prettiest. I am surprised you are not wed."

"Surprised are ye," she laughed. "No one 'ud wed me."

"But why?"

"Jed Atkins, Sam Upton, and now Tom Watkins, the worst of 'em yet. Ye see I take my comfort where I can."

Catherine coloured. Vaguely she had suspected something of the nature, but had preferred to push it to the back of her mind, not wishing to give credence to such a thought.

"Ay well, ye know now. Ye could blame it on my upbringin'.

Sunlight Alley dunna give out much sunlight. In a place like that ye hae to grow up quickly."

The day of Bardwick Fair sprang to Catherine's mind, and those closely packed alleyways where Matthew had forbidden them to go.

"Leastways when I got sent here," she continued, "I set on makin' the best on it. How else do ye think I get away with cheekin' Watkins the way I do. Simply because I please 'im, and not many wenches 'ud be willin' to please 'im."

"But surely you cannot love him," Catherine replied.

"And what do ye know of love. I suppose ye are right learned in that art too!" she rounded somewhat harshly.

"Why so bitter Joan. I am not here to judge."

"No!" she threatened, raising her hand, "and ye better not, because I could make it hell here for ye."

Instinctively recoiling from the sudden harshness in the girl, she flattened herself against the wall. All she had wanted was comfort and reassurance.

"Ye didna think I was goin to hit ye, did ye," she replied, all the bitterness evaporating as quickly as it had arisen. "Come here."

She snuggled up to her beneath the blanket.

"Ye be a strange one, that's for sure. What lovely hair ye 'ave."

"The same colour as my father's."

"Ay, and what were he like?"

"I wish I knew," she replied. "I am baseborn Joan. I never knew my father."

"Sweet Jesu, and what o' ye mother?"

At the mention of her mother, her eyes blurred in the recollection of the finest love she had so far known.

"I am sorry, I didna mean to upset ye."

Lonely and insecure, she needed to confide in someone, pour out the depth of her feelings to a sympathetic listener. Patient and as honest as she could be, Joan listened. The castle had provided her with many an entertaining tale, but Catherine's was as good as any, from the beautiful and gifted mother to the enigma of the father who crept into the story like some mysterious knight of old.

Catherine had inherited her mother's gift for telling a tale, and as this was a true one and also her own she was able to imbue it with all the interest and poignancy it merited.

"I have not spoken so freely for some time," she admitted when she had finished. "You have been so tolerant and kind, Joan."

"I wouldna have missed that for anythin', I can tell ye. Look Kate, ye stick with me and I'll see ye are all right. Ye are a strange body, but I've taken to ye. Now I best be goin'. If I didna know ye better, I'd be thinkin' you be keepin' me o' purpose to deprive Tom o' my company."

"I wouldna do that," Catherine maintained, with a touch of unconscious guile.

"Ye know what, I think I'm corruptin' ye already. Ye are even talkin' like me now. Afore I go though, I'll tell ye somethin' for ye own good. Ye mother was right. Dunna ye go shuttin' yesell away in some nunnery just to please ye priest. Think on it now."

Before Catherine had time to thank her again, she was left alone in the darkness. Water trickled down the walls to form tiny pools on the uneven floor, but at least she felt more secure here than she would have done in the kitchen. She knew Joan to be intrinsically good and it was not for her to judge. By Craven's rigid code she would have stood unredeemed, but in Catherine's eyes she was as worthy as anyone. Curling up beneath the sheet, she slept better than she had expected.

During the following weeks her life settled into another routine, albeit very different to that she had known in the village. Joan kept her word and she was rarely troubled by the others. Progressively trained in the day to day running of the kitchen, she was found to be an excellent worker, Watkins inwardly commending his woman's cleverness in choosing to champion the girl. There were workers and workers, but the Venners' girl was out on her own and he made it his especial interest to see that she came to no harm. In time she came to realise that some of these men and women were potentially as good as Joan, but there were always the few who, given the opportunity, would have made her an outlet for their pent up frustrations and she dreaded to think what would happen if Joan were to leave.

At the end of the month she was given a whole day of freedom. After being immured in an unnatural world where the eye of pure light rarely intruded it came as a blessed release. Small wonder some of them became as animals when they were caged as such. Anticipating escape made her feel slightly skittish, particularly when the drawbridge was lowered and the certainty of putting the castle with all its fetid associations behind her became a reality. Mild and sunny, the morning heralded the promise of a fine day to come. Only the faintest whisper of a breeze ruffled the calm of the river where the reflection of Runnarth castle wavered and trembled on its surface. "Begone!" she said, tossing a pebble into the water, only to watch it emerge again to mock her with its illusory impermanence.

Turning her back on it, she fixed her eyes on the path ahead, away from the castle, away from the vulgarity of it, away from every last stone of it, away, away. It was disappointing to see how the season continued without her, the way in which autumn was revelling in fullness of colour for its own sake and not for her own, being but a sober reminder on the transitory nature of man as against his surroundings.

If the season had forgotten her, the same could not be said of her family. So much did they fuss over her that she felt like a prodigal daughter returned to the fold. Underlying it, however, she detected that all was not well. It was more noticeable at the mid-day repast when they were sat round the table, Miriam making nervous chatter to fill up the long awkward silences, Matthew and Rob hardly speaking at all, and certainly not to each other. After the men had gone back to the fields and Miriam was dealing with the dishes, Catherine took the opportunity of speaking to Mary.

"Whatever is amiss Mary? Come now, you cannot hide anything from me."

"Things are difficult enough for you already, and I do not wish to add to your problems, but ..."

"Mary, you are making excuses. The truth now."

She was putting Mary in a difficult situation. Torn between loyalty to Rob and sympathy for his father, she was wondering how to proceed without seeming partial either to the one or the other.

"Since you left," she began, "or rather since you were taken from us, Rob has been hard on Uncle Matt for not doing more to prevent it, or even to put up a case for getting you back. He blames him for ..." She hesitated, clearly perturbed.

"Tell me."

"In a word, Catherine, he accuses Uncle Matt of bartering you for his rotten piece of land.

There, I have said it, and Jesu knows, I wish that I hadn't," she said, beginning to cry.

"Oh, Mary, I had no notion that he would take it so hard, but tis not so anyway, you know that. There was nothing anyone could do."

"Yes, but Rob will not let be. He keeps telling us that it is only the basest kind of men and women who are taken on in the kitchen and that you will be exposed to all manner of degradation imaginable. He is so bitter Catherine."

"I will speak to him, make him understand. There is no need for any of you to worry on my account. It is not as bad as he would have you believe; indeed, I have already made a firm friend who I know will do her best to protect me."

Mary furrowed her brow and looked at her doubtfully. After all that Rob had told them, she was convinced that the castle kitchens were managed by a league of the damned.

"Her name is Joan," Catherine continued, "and she has done her utmost to help me. The men and women are not deliberately vile, tis circumstances that have made them so."

"But is she a nice girl, Catherine?"

"I know so," Catherine maintained, quick to defend, "but her life has been hard, and hence her view of right and wrong is not what yours or mine would be."

Mary felt less reassured than before, but nor was she entirely ignorant of how a certain section of the people lived. It was simply that she had never envisaged Catherine being drawn into it.

"Tis not fair Catherine."

"I seem to recollect you telling me that life was not fair anyway."

"Yes, but."

"No buts now."

"Mayhap Father Craven could help in obtaining your release. Naturally he is deeply concerned for you, and would do anything in his power to assist you."

At the mention of Craven she felt a coldness comparable in its way to the heat of the kitchen. Having made up her mind not to pursue a religious vocation, she did not know how she was going to inform him of the fact. It was true that to some extent Joan had influenced her in the matter, but there were other factors too, like the impassioned plea of her mother. That she could not ignore.

"If you think it would help," she eventually replied.

"Surely you would want him to intercede on your behalf?"

Catherine hesitated. She knew she ought to have done because the very thought of returning to the castle appalled her, but for some reason she could not give a ready response. Mary did not press her. For some time it had been clear to her just how unsettled she was, but only now did she realise just how much. Her silence was an open avowal of the futility of her existence and there was nothing she could do or say to make it better.

"Have faith, Catherine, have faith. Trust in God and I am sure He will give you an answer."

Catherine took her hand and pressed it affectionately. She wished she could believe as Mary believed and accept all with good grace. Because of their closeness, Catherine then told her of her decision not to go into a nunnery, curious to see how she would react to such news.

"I do not have the necessary vocation," she ended, waiting on Mary's response.

"Father Craven will be greatly disappointed," came her reply, "but I believe that God has guided you in this Catherine, and you must stand firm in your resolve. I think you fear Father Craven a little."

"Yes, I do," she said at last, her hesitation only confirming the fact. "I feel the mark of ingratitude upon me. I owe him much, but is my life not my own to do with as I deem fit?"

"What you say is true Catherine. Things may not have worked out as he had hoped, but he still has a great fondness for you, and given time I think he will come to accept your decision."

Wishing to put off the matter no longer, she immediately went to see Craven.

"My dear child," he said in greeting, adopting a benign sort of attitude which did not sit on him easily at all. "Since I learned what had happened you have been ever in my thoughts as, of course, my prayers. Now tell me. How is it with you?"

The same gloom as always pervaded his dwelling; even the late autumn sunshine was finding no niche in which to settle.

"I am well, Father," she assured him.

"You mean you are brave in adversity. I have prayed that you would come to no harm. You see, I know the manner of people with whom you will have been obliged to come into contact, mainly from Bardwick as I recall."

"Tis so Father, but I do not fear them so much as I once did."

She caught the sigh under his breath before he resumed.

"I know these people, Catherine. Their minds and hearts are closed to the word of God. Speak of repentance and they spit in your face."

"You have tried to assist them?"

"I did in the past and, the Lord forgive me, I failed. They have no notion of right. I pointed the way, but they still went their own, arrogant in their grievous falling away."

His words brought the flicker of a smile to her face. It was hardly surprising that they had refused the salvation he offered them in exchange for a decent show of repentance, when the prime cause of their indifference stared out at him from every rat infested alley. Condemnation would not save them, only compassion, and Craven never let his feelings get in the way of his calling.

"It is the conditions in which they live that make them so uncaring, Father. Therein lies the remedy."

"Catherine," he sighed. "You know not what you say. I have heard the like before, but had not thought to hear it from your lips."

"I only say what I think."

"Tis dangerous talk Catherine," he replied severely. "I have listened to itinerant preachers expounding such, those who have fallen away from Holy Mother Church and incite the mob to take up arms and free themselves from their so called oppression. They speak of equality for all men, causing them to be discontented with their God approved lot. Every man has his part in the pattern, Catherine. Tis a pre-ordained good."

Catherine felt her hair tingle at its roots. Everything he was saying was fallacious to her understanding, and why, if he genuinely believed it, had he sought to raise her up from the position in which God had supposedly chosen to place her.

"I am at variance in this with you Father. Have you not instructed me over the years in the hope that I might prove worthy of something better."

"I have," he acknowledged, impatiently tapping the table with his fingers, "but in your case tis different."

"I know not what you mean," she replied, her face reddening in the heat of the argument.

"Because you are Catherine Venners!" he said, raising his voice.

"But I see no answer in that."

"My child, you were chosen of God to overcome your humble beginnings, but this does not imply that every man, or indeed woman, has the right to abandon their origins and go in search of something they can never hope to attain."

She was not persuaded. There was no reason at all, as far as she could tell, why she should be singled out in preference to anyone else. Like his explanation of her disfigurement, it did not wholly serve.

"Surely Father men should be treated as equals. As an instance, I have a friend called Joan who works in the kitchen. She could have been as well versed as I am had she been tutored as I have. You are speaking of privilege Father, not of

God. God is for all men."

"Catherine," he angrily retorted. "You speak without knowing."

"But I do," she maintained, only now realising just how much in conflict her own belief was with the one he professed. "God desires the betterment of all men. He wants them to use their talents to the best of their ability, to take up the challenge and mystery of life, not to fit them into neat little niches from whence they are never to venture. Man is accountable to no one but his Saviour. Let him breathe and he will soar. Stifle him and he will fester."

"Stop!" he railed, bringing his fist down on the table. "Cease, I beg you. It would seem that the taint of the kitchen is already upon you. I must do all I can to obtain your release."

His hands were trembling as he reached for the book of homilies he was intending to lend her. Catherine remained seated, silently unrepentant if somewhat shaken by her own vehemence. Firmly convinced of the truth of what she had said, she was yet aware that her denunciation of what he so genuinely believed may have seemed to carry with it a taint of mockery that in no way was meant. That aside, she had witnessed those chained souls in the kitchen, seen for herself the atrophying of the common decencies and, being charitable, had adjudged them more sinned against than sinning.

"Catherine," he resumed, his manner more calm. "Have you yet come to a decision?"

The question took her unawares, the recent confrontation having made her forget the very purpose for which she had come. She faced him resolutely. Having found strength in her opposition to his false concepts of life, she was determined not to falter in this, her major decision.

He stood looking at her, the tallness of his figure emphasised by the cassock which draped its ample folds round his gaunt frame. So white were his robes, so translucent the pallor of his skin, that he seemed less a man than a wraith. Only the blue of his eyes, their pupils dilated, betokened the life force within him. For a moment the old fear returned. He had given her so much, taught her so well, how could she make easier the bitterness of the disappointment she was about to inflict.

"Yes, Father. I cannot enter a house of religion. I lack the necessary vocation."

She spoke the words quietly, but emphatically. He showed no emotion, his eyes alone betraying a mournful displeasure.

"I see," he said at last. "They have done their work well. What

I have striven to achieve over a lifetime they have achieved in barely a month."

"Father, you must understand that in many ways my decision was formed before I was taken to the castle. Going there just made it easier."

Seating himself before the open book, his hand cupping his chin, he reflected on the passing of a dream that had occupied his thoughts for year upon year only to be destroyed in a moment.

"I understand very well," he mused, a shadowy smile curling his lips. "I have failed. They have succeeded."

"Please Father, I am ever in your debt. I always will be, but you were asking of me what I could not undertake. Our way of looking at things is dissimilar in so many respects; for instance, the disagreement we had earlier can only have added to your hurt."

"Hurt!" he interposed. "I do not hurt easily, Catherine. My prime feeling is one of disappointment, but for you Catherine, not for myself."

He stretched out his fingers on the volume and then suddenly gripped them together; the rest of his body was still and the quick clenching action seemed to adequately express the manacled feeling at heart.

"I trust to retain your friendship?" she asked.

"I am your priest, am I not," he replied, wearily rising from his chair.

So utterly dejected did he look that she was tempted to throw herself at his feet and beg his forgiveness, but the feeling did not last, her pride and his obduracy of will preventing such abasement. Also he appeared beyond comforting, but then he always had.

Rob remained broodingly silent at supper and Matthew only spoke when he had to, so that it was left to the women to do what talking there was. Catherine, finding the situation completely unacceptable, especially as it all revolved round herself, and anxious to smooth things over before she had to return to the castle, drew Rob on one side so that they could talk in private.

"Dear Rob," she began, "this has to stop. It is all very noble, you wanting to champion me and that, but you are wrong. Uncle Matt had no real choice in the matter. Had he spoken out as you wished, he would have lost the land he has worked so hard to acquire and pass on to you."

"I never asked for aught," he sullenly replied. "And I dunna forget the promise I made to your mother to hae a care of you."

"I know that, but I also believe that my mother would have taken Uncle Matt's part in this matter. I am certain she would. Uncle Matt has done everything with you in mind. You vex him with this misplaced anger. What is more you are not only making yourself miserable but everyone else, me included. I am learning new skills in the kitchen, and I have already made friends."

"Ay, but you shouldn't have to. Had I been there, it would not hae happened. I blame myself as much as father. Tis a bitter price you hae paid."

"Let it be Rob. Let it be. No good can come of it. What is done is done and who knows it might turn out better than we think. Promise me now."

At last he mumbled a grudging assent, but sufficient to convince her that she had won him round. By way of thanking him, she put her arms round his neck and gave him a cousinly peck on the cheek. It pleased her to see that Rob made the first overtures of reconciliation, and after some initial if characteristic resistance on her uncle's part, the remainder of the time was spent very pleasantly. She could clearly see the relief in her aunt's face, as well as in Mary's. Having two estranged men of the calibre of Rob and her uncle must have been trying.

"Did you speak to Father Craven?" asked Mary.

"I did, and as you surmised, he took it ill."

"I feared as much, but you did right in telling him."

"Is something else amiss Kate?" Miriam anxiously enquired.

"No Aunt," she smiled. "Tis just that I have told Father Craven that I do not have the necessary vocation a woman should have who enters a cloister."

Rob and Matthew were a bit taken aback. Both of them, particularly Matthew, had thought it all but settled.

"Good for ye," said Miriam, unaccustomedly firm in her opinion.

"I dunna know sae much," put in Matthew.

"Well I hae no such quibblings on the subject," put in Miriam. "What sort of a life is that for a lass, a young lass at that."

Nothing more was said on the subject, their talk turning to Annie and Gerard and the difficulties they seemed to make for themselves. In the course of conversation, it also became apparent that the villagers were missing Catherine's cures for their ills, and she promised to do what she could to remedy the situation, although her duties in the kitchen allowed for little spare time.

Overall she was pleased with the way the day had gone. It was gratifying to know that she had left them in a far happier frame of mind than when she had arrived, and though she did not relish the prospect of returning to the castle, she was not dismayed by it either.

Within the quiet of his church Father Craven called on his God to sustain him in this his hour of most need.

"Oh my God, my God," he cried, "why hast Thou forsaken me. In what manner have I failed Thee. Show me the way Lord and I will follow."

Had he been shown that way, he would not have known how to follow it.

CHAPTER EIGHT

Approaching the castle, the sun discreetly withdrew from the sky leaving a watery trail of gold in its wake. Her arrival coincided with the return of the dirtied dishes and her friend full of questions.

"Ye look well pleased with yesell," Joan said. "Did ye hae a good day?"

"Yes Joan, very good."

"Come over yonder. I want to ask ye something. Did ye tell that scurvy priest of yourn what to do with his nunnery?"

"I told him of my lack of vocation," she replied, overlooking the graceless remark, though smiling nonetheless.

In reply Joan shrugged her shoulders.

"Ye are gettin sense at last," she said. "I'm right glad."

The dishes washed and put away for the next day, they were just about to settle down for the night, each scrambling for their respective plot of ground, when there was a deafening knock at the outer door which threw them all into panic.

"Tis somethin' amiss," whispered Joan. "God forbid there was aught wrong with the supper."

Already suffering from an excess of ale, Watkins lurched awkwardly to the door, the blaze from the fires throwing out sufficient light to guide him and distorting his heavy figure to ghastly proportions on the wall.

Fumbling to open it, a tall angular man stood on the threshold, his long belted tunic and cap of black velvet denoting his rank.

"You have a girl here by the name of Catherine Venners?" he clearly announced.

"In truth sir," slurred Watkins, wiping the sweat from his face.

"She is commanded to come with me."

Catherine trembled in the darkness, her heart beating so quick and fast that she was certain it echoed like footsteps in a void.

"Ye best go," said Joan, plucking at her arm.

She moved cautiously towards the figure who beckoned,

trying to smooth the creases from her gown and tidy the knots in her hair.

"You are Catherine Venners?" he asked, speaking more gently on seeing the look of alarm in her features.

"Yes, sir," she replied, not sure of the manner in which she should address him. His features weren't all that distinct in the shadows, but both his bearing and voice gave the impression of competence, of knowing his role and performing it to the best of his ability. She reckoned him to be about Matthew's age, his hair and beard threaded with grey, his eyes having a resigned quality in their lack lustre blue. Like Matthew, he was sparing of speech, yet he smiled on her kindly as if to relieve her of anxiety. Watkins slammed the door upon them with scant ceremony. A lackey stood by with a torch to lead them up the spiralling steps, every tread she took resounding to the thump of her heart. She tried to think what wrong she had committed, for wrong she felt sure it must be. At the top of the steps the lackey was dismissed, the man leading her through a series of dimly lit passages which eventually opened into a corridor where an occasional flambeau dipped its flame in the wake of a breeze which blew up from the courtyard below. The corridor ended in a small kind of lobby wherein an open door led into a well illumined room; at this point she was told to wait outside until she was sent for. She could hear muted speech coming from within, and then the man returned to conduct her inside. The sudden light hurt her eyes. Lit by a plenitude of candles in decorative sconces, three walls of the room were draped in richly woven tapestries, the fourth bare and containing a narrow casement. But she paid little attention to any of it, her eyes immediately being drawn to the centre of the room in which stood a massive oak bed framed by purple curtains. Two oaken chairs stood at either side of it, and at its foot an intricately carved chest. A woman not much older than herself was in attendance.

"Please to come here," she curtly instructed, turning to face Catherine who stared at the floor.

The man who had conducted her thither still hovered in the background as if reluctant to leave without some formal note of dismissal. The woman gave him a cursory toss of her head. For a moment his eyes fiercely kindled, but whatever rancour he felt he kept to himself and his departure was swift.

"I am Joanna Fitzsimons, personal attendant to Lady Elliston," she explained, her voice like velvet with an unashamed trimming of hauteur.

Catherine simply gazed at her. She was lovely beyond her imagining. Even the most beautiful women she had seen at Bardwick Fair were nothing in comparison, she being in possession of a unique kind of beauty that haunts and fascinates by turns, and revels in a glamour distinctly its own. To enhance her perfection of feature, she was clothed in white satin, tiny clusters of stars embellishing the skirts of her gown and encrusting her coif, from beneath which cascaded a stream of golden hair. She was fragrant with perfume that was sweet without being heady.

"Do you always stare so?" she asked, fingering her bottom lip in displeasure.

"I was not aware of it," Catherine replied, blushing to the roots of her own lovely hair, which with a good brushing could have rivalled Joanna's.

"Come closer," she commanded, the satin of her gown rustling faintly as she approached the heavily draped bed. "I see what they mean," she said, pointing at the mask. Do you know why you are here?"

"No," was all Catherine could say, quite forgetting her manners in the contemplation of her singular situation.

"Joanna!" came the strained and peevish tone of a voice behind the curtains. "What is happening? Is the girl here, the girl I sent for."

"Yes, my lady, she is here," she replied in soft polite tones, venting her growing impatience on Catherine who she eyed with manifest contempt. "Straighten your hair," she whispered, picking on Catherine's one asset as a cat might pick on a sliver of chicken. In vain Catherine attempted to smooth the flyaway tendrils which nature had endowed with a will of their own.

"The girl is not fit to see you," Joanna continued, flinging back her beautiful hair to add piquancy to the remark. "She is naught but a slattern, and as badly disfigured as we were given to believe."

Catherine was not going to be bested, nor was she going to give way to tears, so in keeping with the man who had recently left she maintained a dignified silence.

"Bring her to me!" demanded the voice behind the curtains. This time the voice was more acrid and in no humour to be disobeyed. "Now leave us."

"As you wish, my lady," replied Joanna, looking at Catherine with utter contempt as she drew back the curtains and led her to the bedside. Without so much as another word, she then left, the sweet smell of her perfume lingering in the shadows.

An elderly woman lay propped up on pillows. Catherine guessed that this must be Lady Elliston, the woman who was apparently despised by her son, or so Annie had informed her.

"Draw nearer, come, come now, do not hesitate! My eyes are so weak now."

Her voice was dry and brittle, and yet in the subtle play of light and shadow there were still vestiges of a once favoured face. "I knew of your disfigurement. Tis a pity. You have fine eyes and your hair is better than average, though of the wrong colour. But enough of preliminaries. You have knowledge of physic, or so I am told."

"Yes, my Lady."

"You speak well for a village girl. You have learning?"

"I am versed in letters, my lady, and speak a little Latin."

"Very commendable," she smiled, revealing a mouth of blackened teeth. "I am suffering Mistress Venners, and have been for many days past. The symptoms are persistent. Pains in the head, vomiting, and sleeplessness. My physician is a fool and my son cares not whether I live or die, and since all else has failed I am putting what little faith I have in yourself. In a word, you are to cure me."

Catherine had attended many sick beds in her time, but none as strange as this. She dreaded to think what would happen were she to fail or, worse still, if the patient were to deteriorate even further. The task in hand called for the utmost discretion, but strangely enough she did not feel intimidated by the old woman who seemed willing to try any remedy whatever it might entail.

"If I may examine you, my lady?" she tentatively enquired.

"Do as you will," Lady Elliston muttered impatiently, "but do something quickly. My head is fit to split."

Deep in her observations of Lady Elliston, she failed to notice the man who stealthily crept up behind her.

"What have we here Mama?" he bellowed.

Catherine's reflexes were well adjusted. She started from the bedside, her pulse racing, her heart pounding within her.

"That is typical of my son," the old lady grumbled. "He has a grotesque sense of what is fitting. Pray, ignore him, and by some miracle he may leave us in peace."

So this was the son of the mother, the man who, according to Annie, despised his wife, hated his children and whose loose living was common knowledge. She could sense him standing deliberately close to her, breathing down her neck and deriving a sense of pleasure from her obvious discomfiture. Afraid to look at him, she summoned up courage from she knew not where to complete the examination.

"So far I find her diligent but insolent," he casually remarked. "It is usual to acknowledge one's lord and master."

"Leave her be Roger," the old woman said wearily. "Your visit is inopportune. The girl has been brought to help me, which is more than you have ever done."

"Now Mama you are being unjust," he teased.

Catherine found his voice persuasive, deep and resonant with a quality that was warm and expressive, full of hidden meanings and delicate nuances of tone which gave richness to each utterance.

"My son, Mistress Venners," she said at last.

"Ah, an introduction, Mama, how very touching."

She felt the colour rise to her face as she turned to acknowledge him. He held out his hand in a kind of playful gesture.

"A small hand Mistress Venners and scarcely to be viewed properly under those bindings."

"My son is also tactless as you can see," said Lady Elliston.

He laughingly withdrew his firm grasp and scrutinised her hard and long, his ringed fingers tapping the arms of the chair on which he had seen fit to perch his foot. She could only do one of two things, either look at the ground, or return his gaze. Normally she would have looked at the ground, but there was something within her that was determined not to be cowed by this man who seemed intent on amusing himself at her expense. So they returned gaze for gaze. He was not a handsome man, but his eyes were blue and compelling and, as she rightly suspected, prone to subtly changing shades in accord with his humour; his jaw set and square, his thin underlip, whether rightly or wrongly, giving the impression of a refractory nature. Unruly brown hair, flecked with gold, just touched his shoulders, and although he was only of average height there was an underlying strength in his frame. Repelled by Joanna's calculating assessment, his did not unduly perturb her, for he seemed to pass over the mask as something of limited interest.

"What are you doing? Mistress Venners has work to do," his mother complained.

"We are taking stock of one another, or at least I think we are," he replied, roguishly winking in his mother's direction. Catherine smiled involuntarily, but she smiled nonetheless. "Ah, I have also found out she is human after all. She actually smiles," he resumed looking at his mother. "Contrary to what you think, I am rather well versed where my tenants are concerned. For instance, I can tell you all you need to know about this one. Her name is Catherine Venners, bastard born out of noble stock on her father's side." He paused here for effect. "Whoever he might be! Is skilled in herbal arts and purports to read Latin. Rather can!" he corrected, noticing the obvious challenge in Catherine's eyes. "All this, as well as the wretched business to which you allude. Are you not impressed Kate?"

She puckered her brow in response.

"You frown. I have omitted something?"

"If I could be called Catherine, my lord," she replied hesitantly, her unaccustomed audacity making her colour.

"You interest me Kate," he said markedly. "But if I might be so presumptuous, why the insistence?"

"I meant no offence, my Lord."

"None taken," he affirmed with a wave of his hand. "Proceed."

"My mother preferred me to be called by my full name, my lord."

"That was your mother. Here you will be called as I choose, Kate," he replied more emphatically.

"Roger," commanded his mother. "Enough! Mistress Venners tell Sir Edward what you require. Sir Edward Burgoyne is the man who brought you here and, incidentally, the backbone of the castle." She looked hard at her son, who did not gainsay her for once. Instead he held the door open for Catherine, making her a show of mock obeisance as she left. Outside Sir Edward was pacing the passageway.

"What are your orders?" he yawned.

When she told him, they returned to the kitchen where Watkins was trying to reassure Joan that the household above could have nothing of which to complain.

"Mistress Venners, quickly now," Sir Edward enjoined, trying to instill a note of urgency into the proceedings. He was tired, it had been a trying day, and he longed to get to his bed. As for Watkins and his woman, they simply annoyed him.

"What's amiss Kate?" Joan whispered.

"Silence!" Sir Edward demanded, putting an end to all further enquiry.

Catherine was frankly bemused by it all. The situation in which she found herself was both new and bewildering, the opulence of Lady Elliston's bedchamber being as far removed from the squalor of the kitchen as heaven is from hell.

Lord Elliston was still present when she returned. He sat at a small desk by the casement, idly thumbing through a slim volume and gazing intermittently into the darkness. A sad resigned look clouded his features which only a moment before had been full of good humour.

"My lord," she said softly by way of announcing her presence. He flinched and looked startled. She had obviously caught him off his guard.

"You come upon a man like a traitorous knife carrier. Where is Sir Edward?"

"He begs leave to retire."

"He has it. He is, as my mother puts it, a good and able man. Mama!" he loudly called, his previous mood returning so swiftly that she wondered if her eyes had deceived her and that the man she had just seen was another altogether. Resuming his bantering tone like an actor assuming a role, he graciously conducted her to the bedside.

"You may leave us Roger," his mother said somewhat imperiously. "There is no point in hovering about me."

"Have you a glass, my lady?" Catherine enquired.

Elliston immediately placed one in her hand and then took it off her again as, visibly shaking, she undid the leather bottle containing the physic.

"You make her nervous," his mother snapped.

"Believe me, I have no such intention, but I shall stay all the same. For all we know she may be about to administer some deadly draught that will sever us completely."

Lady Elliston winced, refusing to respond to his unwanted wit. Catherine coloured and wished him anywhere but there, where he eyed her keenly and once put out his hand to steady her trembling one. The gesture concentrated her thoughts and she did not tremble again.

"Come mama," he pretended to coax, raising her up on the mountain of pillows.

Catherine could not help but notice how she callously dashed away his hand.

"I want no assistance from you," she retorted, her voice breaking in her effort to retain control as she cowered from his touch. She took the glass and drained it in one gulp. "Nasty, bitter stuff. Tis to be hoped it has the desired effect."

"A sobering one, mama?" he queried, his eyes piercing her own which stared at him like venomous pinpricks.

"You are a blight on the world," she sneered, drawing in her lips to reveal her shrivelled gums and rotten teeth. "A thankless son I have Mistress Venners. Better he had been strangled in my womb. One who scorns and derides me, who longs for my death and curses each hour I live. I swear I will outlive you, Roger, not because I find any pleasure in life, but just for the satisfaction of avenging myself at your expense."

"My mama, as you see, is not in one of her maternal moods," he noted sardonically, looking at Catherine who was trying her best to remain quietly detached from the vicious altercation.

"You may jibe," his mother continued. "That is all you are good for. Ask him where his wife and children are?"

A frown appearing on his hitherto composed features, he withdrew from the bedside.

"You hit hard, mama."

"And why not," she maintained. "A man who cannot hold on to his wife is no man at all."

"It was not my intention to hold her by force. You seem to forget that I was mated to a vixen, which admittedly adds a certain piquancy to the marriage contract, but soon wears off when the novelty begins to pall."

"Bah, you did not even try!"

"No, my dearest mama. I was glad to see her go. As for the children, they were more hers than mine, but she saw to that. And lest we forget, I had little choice in the matter. Blame it on circumstance or what you will, it was an ill advised union. Come, admit it. I am no saint and she was scarcely chaste, but what need have you to worry. My duty is done. Runnarth has an heir. Three sons have I fathered, yet God knows I would one of them had been a daughter. Tis said daughters are a comfort."

A bitter laugh issued from the old woman, her face contorted in a mixture of dire mirth and pain.

"Oh yes, my son, you had your own games to pay. The Lady Joanna would appear to be in rude health, or am I wanting in tact."

"You forget we are not alone," he reminded. "Mistress Venners comes from the peace and tranquillity of the village. She is not accustomed to the subtleties of the court."

An interval of quiet ensued, Catherine not knowing whether to leave quietly even though she had not been formally dismissed. Lady Elliston's breathing had eased, now that the draught was beginning to take effect.

"Come here child," she entreated, her passion quite spent. "You have done well. The pain is less than it was and I feel I can rest. Forget what you have witnessed this night."

"I am sure," he interposed, "that Kate is a woman of discretion. Consider her conduct throughout our convivial talk.

Such restraint is deserving of praise."

"You may leave Mistress Venners," said Lady Elliston, grimacing.

"Not with my permission," he countermanded as Catherine was half turning to go.

"My mama is forgetful Mistress Venners, especially when it comes to her own flesh and blood."

Lady Elliston drowsily muttered an oath and then fell asleep.

"Your calm veneer is to your credit Kate," he resumed. "Just the merest trace of dismay which I assume was involuntary. Of course you have the advantage of me in that contrivance you wear on your face."

She touched it by habit. Never before had she heard it described as an asset.

"Tis a blessing that the left side is not so obscured. It is there I shall look for my guidance."

"My lord," she said, looking bemused.

"Why so curious Mistress Venners. You should know by now that I have a penchant for divining the nature of things as they are and not as they seem."

Lady Elliston was gently snoring, the silken sheets softly swaying to the rhythm of her breathing.

"Go on, Kate, you may leave, or should I say Catherine," he quipped resuming his seat by the window. This time his smile was genuine and she responded accordingly.

Sir Edward, having gone to his bed, she was left to make the tortuous descent to the kitchen unaided. As she curled up in the alcove, hugging the sheet close to her chin, she felt envious of no one, certainly not of Lady Elliston and her son, though their features were ever before her.

CHAPTER NINE

Confined to their vault like existence, it did not do to brood for the world outside or to lament for the passing of the seasons, but could she have seen the dawn unfolding subsequent to her interview with the Ellistons, she would have remarked on a sky of intense luminosity, its brilliance seeming to seal the day ahead with special portents.

The only portents in the kitchen were of the direst. Through some mischance the fires had been allowed to go out. Reduced to groping around in near gloom, Watkins was swearing and hurling abuse at everyone and everything against which he happened to stumble.

Wearied by a lethargy of the spirit rather than the body, Catherine joined the others in a dismal attempt to put this great wrong to rights. One of the men had been to fetch rushlight to aid in the task. Joan was counting the notches scored in a lintel of wood which Watkins had devised for keeping a tally of tasks; it was for each one of them to notch up his definitive mark upon completion of a particular chore. Haphazard at best, it was often ignored, and out of the few who did deign to use it the notches were less than definitive.

"Tis the wood Tom," she smiled archly in an attempt to soften his temper. "Tis no one to blame."

He spat his acceptance, his language remaining in keeping with his countenance, rich, red and florid. Having no one in particular on whom to vent his displeasure and being aware of Catherine's fear of fire, he picked on her to light one of the hearths. Struggling to clear out the ashes, she wondered what was worse, the bone cutting chill they were suffering now, or the blistering heat to which they were normally exposed. Naturally, her choice was determined by her experience, and the task imposed on her made her uncommonly fretful.

"Kate, let me help ye," said Joan. "Ye look in need o' some."

"I can manage," she replied irritably.

"Well, have ye got naught to tell me?" Joan persisted.

"About what?"

"Ye know, last night. Tom were right vexed wi' me, keep harpin' on ye as I did and not on his wonderful self, and this mornin' that about finished matters."

Catherine, vouchsafing no answer, continued to poke at the embers which were proving as obdurate as she was.

"Kate, ye are right mean. Blessed Mary, we hae little enough excitement as tis. Ye could tell me. Here, let me do that, ye got no idea."

She went to take the poker, but Catherine wrenched it away, her usually patient reserve snapping in frustration at not being able to do the job efficiently.

"I can do it for myself. Tis my duty, not yours," she retorted, "and as for last night, I cannot see that it is of any moment to you."

Joan leapt to her feet. She was not the kind of woman to take insults lightly.

"Dunna think I'll stand up for ye any more Kate Venners, ye mealy mouthed bitch."

"Do what you please," Catherine cried, hot indignant tears smudging her face, not to mention the mask which would have to be washed.

She knelt back from the chore, aggrieved at her own unreasoning behaviour, especially when it was directed towards someone who in no wise deserved it. But it was not only that. The interview with Lady Elliston and her son had unsettled her more than she thought. The fire crackled and hissed, emitting a brief tongue of flame which flickered and died. So much for her stubborn independence.

"Fine mess ye've made o' that Mistress Venners," smirked Joan, sidling up to her.

"Joan, forgive me. I do not know why I spoke so. Mayhap I am tired," she sobbed.

"I dunna know what I'll do with ye," she replied in mock despair, crouching down beside her in an attempt to create something out of the havoc before them. "Ye couldna roast a flea on that."

"I really am sorry Joan," she reaffirmed, the imagery of the flea making her smile.

The hearth was soon blazing fit for hell, as indeed was its sister hearth at the opposite end of the room.

"Now Kate, remember favour for favour. Ye got time to tell me afore Tom gets any more nowty than he already is."

Feeling bound to oblige, Catherine gave her a detailed account of her meeting with Lady Elliston in the presence of her son, carefully omitting all reference to the unseemly behaviour of both.

"What are ye blatherin' on about," Watkins bellowed. "We be late enough already by God!"

"Come now Tom, ye wouldna deny me a little talk with my friend, now would ye?"

Scowling, he moved away. Whatever was being related, he hoped to hear for himself in good time. The Venners girl was seemingly meeting with favour, a favour that he trusted would ultimately reflect well on him as head of the kitchen.

With the flames growing stronger, the blurred forms of listless men and woman began to take on the semblance of reanimated vigour, jerking like puppets pulled up on string. Owing to the unforeseen setbacks there was more bustle and hurry than usual, Catherine having to remain dirty and dishevelled as they rushed to prepare the late breakfast. When they finally sat down to their own, she had still not found time to tidy herself, and barely were they finished when a knock, similar to that of the night before, was heard at the outer door.

"Why dunna the bloody beggars just walk in like lesser beings," Watkins swore, his face a study in fermenting ire as he went to open it.

Once again it was Sir Edward Burgoyne impeccably dressed with a further order for Catherine. Watkins boomed out her name, but Catherine did not move. It was not only the summons that made her apprehensive, but the lamentable state of her appearance which, poor enough ordinarily, was now a disgrace.

"Joan, what am I to do," she whispered.

Before Joan could answer, Watkins roughly sought her out. "Ye be wanted again. Ye mun be deaf as well as look-less," he growled, bundling her unceremoniously to the door, the rest of them looking at her doubtfully and seething to know what was going on and what it was about the Veneers girl that caused her to be so much in demand.

"What have you been at, Mistress Venners?" Sir Edward enquired, noting her sorry condition.

"She's been workin', that's what she's been doin'," Watkins broke in, "like we always do 'ere."

Choosing to overlook his insolence, Burgoyne retraced their journey of the previous evening; daylight now squeezed its way through occasional apertures on each landing, bringing with it a welcome waft of fresh air.

"If I might tidy myself," Catherine implored.

"I have my orders," said Burgoyne "and they were to proceed

with the business at once. I fear you must come as you are."

The precarious security of the kitchen suddenly seemed infinitely preferable, even if it necessitated lighting a hundred extra fires.

"May I know who it is I am to see," she ventured to ask, thereby hoping to learn the extent of her forthcoming humiliation.

"By rights I should not say, but it is Lord Elliston."

A sigh of resignation escaped her. Somehow she had feared as much, and the thought of looking like a device to scare away birds only served to drain away what little confidence she had.

She was so accustomed to the unnatural light of the kitchen that the sudden burst of sunlight blinded her for a moment and she had to pause to gain her bearings. They were standing in a corridor which formed part of a quadrangle overlooking the courtyard where a group of men were saddling up horses and generally enjoying the well disposed weather.

"Mistress Venners, this is no time to stand and stare," he reprimanded, anxious to discharge a duty which was becoming not only irksome but far too frequent for his liking. After all, he was supposed to be Lord Elliston's adviser, not his lackey. Negotiating further corridors which took them into the interior, they eventually reached a remote part of the outer bailey from which the prospect was one of low lying hills stretching hazily into the distance. Halting in front of another closed room, she was told to wait while he entered. In his brief absence, her heart pounding, she attempted to rescue her appearance by flicking her fingers through her hair and wiping her face on the edge of her gown. Better she had not attempted at all, as her face was now covered in streaks of sweaty soot.

"Mistress Venners, you can now enter," he said, making her start as she swung round from her concentrated effort and let go of the hem.

"Now?" she said, looking reluctant.

"Now."

He looked her up and down and mumbled something inaudible. Worse than this he was leaving her alone to deal with whatever transpired. Lord Elliston was seated in the embrasure of the window, his back turned away from her, but there was no doubt in her mind that he was fully aware of her presence. The gold flecks in his hair caught the light as he looked out on the distant line of hills and the river winding below them. It was thin sunlight and fleeting, creating substance and shadow in equal measure. She stood for a while, but he did not acknowledge her presence in any way. It was disconcerting, but it did give her an opportunity of trying to compose herself as well as studying her immediate surroundings. Simply furnished, it was a small room and a fire was lit in the grate to offset the chill, but it was the scattering of books on the desk that took her eye; she had never seen such a large collection before, there must have been a dozen or more, all beautifully bound in pigskin or calf. One was open to display an illuminated page, the colours so brilliant that she had to restrain herself from touching it. They almost made her forgetful of his presence until he began to whistle to himself, thereby intensifying the silence. It placed her in a quandary. Should she go or should she stay, or was he intent on trying her reserves of patience. Deciding to withdraw, she moved tentatively to the door. "I do not remember having given you permission to leave Mistress Venners, but maybe I am mistaken. You will enlighten me, no doubt."

"No, my lord, but I chose to leave of my own volition as I thought you were engaged in other matters and had forgotten my being here."

"Well answered," he laughed, swinging round to face her. "I could not have done better myself. Such tact. Such discretion." Revelling in the game he was playing, his eyes roamed over her with that glint of amusement she had feared though expected. "I fear you are hiding from me again, Kate, or should I say Catherine. Pray forgive me. I have a penchant for not remembering names."

"I apologise for my appearance, my lord," she began "but ..."

"Never apologise Kate," he interrupted, "Never!"

"My lord," she acknowledged.

"Well," he resumed, now dismissing her tousled appearance. "Doubtless you are wondering why you are summoned so soon after our last interview."

"I admit I am curious, my lord," she replied, now able to meet his steady gaze with surprisingly little discomfiture, much of her anxiety being overcome by his attitude of disinterest, whether feigned or otherwise she could not determine.

"My mama," he commenced, adopting a solemn tone, "my mama is well pleased with you, so much so that she desires you to be in regular attendance upon her. I take it you follow me thus far?"

"I trust to my lord," she answered, her wide eyes unconsciously responding to the look of irony in his own.

"I think you mock me."

"No, my lord, no."

"Mm. I am not so certain. Still, let it pass. To spare you the preliminaries, my mama has taken to you. Why is beyond me." He paused to gauge her reaction, then smiled when none was forthcoming. "I put it down to that miracle draught you administered last night."

"I am pleased that her ladyship is feeling better," she said.

"I do believe you to be sincere in that at least," he replied, eyeing her closely, "and where my mama is concerned sincerity is often found wanting. For instance, her very contrariness is proved by her preference for your companionship rather than mine, is it not?"

She felt herself colour.

"Come Kate, such modesty is unbecoming," he teased, directing her to take his seat by the window. "All that remains is your answer. Yea or nae, tis as simple as that. I can assure you that it is a signal honour to find favour with her ladyship. She and I are not of like minds, but you may have gleaned that fact already. Come now, your answer."

"I should deem it an honour to serve Lady Elliston."

"Spoken like a true servant!"

She immediately rose, but he bade her stay seated.

"Sir Edward," he called into the corridor. "Ah, Sir Edward, inform my mother that Mistress Venners has agreed to be her lackey or words to that effect."

"Yes, my lord," Sir Edward bowed, his skill in diplomacy called on once more.

"You can also inform her that I shall not suffer the flouting of my authority again in the hiring of servants. My mama," he resumed, turning to Catherine, "requested that I fetch you, nae demanded. She seems to forget that she is now answerable to me for her wants." With a sweeping gesture he put out his hand, causing her to start. "You are nervous Kate. Be assured, you will get used to the vagaries of my nature ere long."

"Yes, my lord," she replied, thinking on the complexities of that nature.

He stared thoughtfully at her.

"I am thinking that my mama is more impressed by outer show than I am," he said, alluding to her dishevelled appearance.

"If I could tidy myself, my lord," she ventured to say.

"Come with me," he said, taking hold of her hand, his grip firm and warm and extremely retentive

He led her into a smaller room adjoining the main apartment. Compared with the airiness of the former, it was rather stuffy, being illumined by one tiny window that admitted a harsh line of light across the breadth of a bed that swallowed up all the available space.

"You will find water in the ewer on that table, plus a varied assortment of brushes and looking glasses, in fact anything a woman of modest pretensions could possibly need," he said with an edge of contempt. "Call me when you are ready and I will personally conduct you to my mother."

A familiar perfume hung on the atmosphere, adding to the stuffiness. Something bright and metallic caught her eye on the bed, making her pulse quicken as she recognised Joanna's white satin gown, its encrusted pattern of stars shimmering in the harsh line of light. It recalled Lady Elliston's veiled allusions to the lady Joanna and his curt dismissal of the subject. Everything within the room was redolent of the beauty of that woman from the subtle fragrance of the perfume that made her feel slightly dizzy to the discarded gown that without her body to transform it was just another length of showy material. The table he had pointed to was stamped with her ownership: bottles of perfume, skin preparations in pots of glazed clay, brushes and combs inlaid with silver, mirrors and numerous other personal adornments. This then was her room as well as his own. Was he attempting to gauge her reaction, or was his own sense of propriety so far removed from conventional moral codes that he blatantly chose to defy them. Sitting at Joanna's dressing table and taking up one of the mirrors, she viewed the image thrown back at her with singular indifference. It certainly did not affect her as it usually did. Mechanically dabbing the smears from her face and brushing her hair until it crackled like the flame of its colour, she decided that she was being markedly foolish in deluding herself that he had allowed her into this most private of rooms with any particular motive in mind. She was after all only a servant, and a lowly one at that. He could not conceivably care what she thought about him or the way he chose to conduct his life. She should have guessed how it was from the things that Annie had told her. It merely confirmed her belief that morally it was no better here than it was in the kitchen. And if his idea was to disarm her, then he could be assured that he would have no joy of it, for in gazing on all this paraphernalia of a mistress she only felt an indefinable sense of resentment. But why? Now she was indeed being foolish. As to Joanna, she was certain she would have been livid had she known that Elliston had allowed her into their private room. With this thought in mind, the shadow that suddenly intervened between her and the one shaft of light made her quickly look round. He was regarding her intently, his figure set in dark relief against the sunshiny prospect.

"Mistress Venners, you have dallied long enough."

"Forgive me, my lord," she replied. "I had not realised I had been overlong."

"You have not," he corrected, "but I am a man not given to patience. Besides, I take it that there is little else you can do to rescue your looks?"

The remark troubled her. Was he merely referring to her crumpled appearance, or was it an indirect jibe at her disfigurement.

"You must not be shy with me," he remarked, seeing her discomfiture. "I speak as I please. I can hazard what you think, but your surmise is a false one, quite false in fact."

Inclined to believe him, she put the brush down and followed his lead, his long determined strides leaving her breathless in an attempt to keep pace with them.

"Quickly now, quickly!"

Once more she found herself in Lady Elliston's chamber, the scene having altered from dimly lit night to bright blinding day, no softening suggestion of shadow to temper the brilliant flood of sunshine that streamed in through the window. Joanna stood idly by the door, her perfect figure draped in deep blue, her defiant type of beauty quite undiminished despite the silver fillet confining her hair. Her eyes were positively fastened on Elliston, demanding his attention, calling out to him her right of possession, while he, deliberately unconscious of her scrutiny, led Catherine to the bedside. Lady Elliston, eyes blinking weakly at the sun, laid propped against her pillows, a wearied and contentious old woman who felt only too keenly the hour of her decline, her shrivelled features showing ravaged and pained in the harsh glare of day. Thinning strands of hair, slowing turning to white, completed the picture of encroaching decay. In comparison, Joanna seemed like some fair bird of plumage ministering to the needs of a ragged old crow. The analogy struck Catherine as grossly unkind.

"Ah, Mama," bellowed Elliston. It was noticeable that he always shouted in his mother's presence, whether to assert his authority or from a vague feeling of fear, Catherine could never decide. What was apparent was his sense of unease throughout the interview. It was simply impossible for them to conduct a rational conversation, without it degenerating into banter, retort, and counter-retort.

"Joanna," her thin voice commanded. "Prop me up. I want to see my son. I want to look him in the face. Then you can leave."

Joanna did as she asked, but not before directing a malicious glance at Catherine who was so soon to take her place.

"And how are we today Mama?" he enquired.

"You know how I am," she retorted. "Why ask."

She gripped at the silken sheets, the rings on her fingers trapping the light and flashing back colour after colour, ruby, emerald, sapphire.

"Out of respect should I say," he countered, "but whatever else you may think of me I have never tried to deceive you. We are what we are mama, are we not?"

"When I look at you and think of your brother!"

"Come now, mama. Tis only eleven of the clock. We have the whole day in which to pay each other compliments. As you see, Mistress Venners has come at your express desire. You would not wish her to be drawn into our domestic quarrels again, now would you?"

He arched his eyebrows at Catherine, but this time she looked at the floor, the trace of a smile on her face which did not escape him.

"Come here Mistress Venners," she charged. "My eyes are even worse in the daylight."

Catherine moved towards the bed, the red of her hair showing like flame in the sun. Lady Elliston had objected to it from the first and she was not one to alter her opinion.

"Tis all wrong," she said, flicking it aside with her fingers. "Where did you get such a colour."

"I believe from my father," answered Catherine innocently.

"Hold your tongue!" came back the rebuke.

Catherine flinched, wondering what it was she had said to cause such disquiet.

"My dear mama," ventured Elliston coming to her rescue, "I believe the remark was made in all sincerity and not with any thought of offence. Mistress Venners assure my mother that you were not being deliberately impertinent."

"I intended no harm, my lady," said Catherine, still unsure what offence she had committed.

The old lady smiled.

"You are innocent indeed," she opined, her eyes squinting up at the sun.

"There mama, you see, all goodness. We are not accustomed to such things. Now do not look puzzled Kate; the fact of your being a bastard is a mere nonentity."

Now she understood. *They* might allude to the fact of her being a bastard, but she was never so much as to hint of it.

"I wanted to see Mistress Venners alone," announced Lady Elliston.

The swift changes of mood with which she was becoming familiar were manifest again, his eyes blazing in a kind of ineffectual anger, his fist tightly clenched.

"I am lord of this domain, and however you abhor the notion I will be obeyed, even in the matter of women to attend to your puerile needs."

"You may be my son," she spoke between her teeth, "but my master, never."

Then just as swiftly his former mood returned, as if nothing untoward had occurred, and taking Catherine's hand he squeezed it hard as if to restore it more fully.

"She is yours as you wish," he said, pointing to Catherine. "She will please you, of that I have little doubt. Yes, Mistress Venners, you will cater to my mother's wants very well. I seem to remember you cured her of her headache. Now see what you can do to extract the venom from her tongue. I bid you good day."

As he left, the room fell in shadow and the old woman, totally exhausted, sank back in her pillows.

"Can I get you anything further, my lady?" Catherine enquired.

"Naught. I shall be better in a while. Ask Joanna to show you the nature of your duties."

Going out into the corridor to look for Joanna, she saw the two of them together, Elliston and Joanna embracing, their mouths pressed together. Her heart hammered inside her. What was it that disturbed her so much in seeing them thus and what was it about Joanna that began to irritate her to such an extent. Tactfully, she waited until they had parted.

"My lady," she said, quietly catching Joanna's eye.

"What do you want?" she replied, testily resenting the intrusion.

"Lady Elliston asked me to speak to you as regards the nature of my duties."

"I thought you would suit. Tis no surprise. You best follow me."

She walked with the grace of a sleek, fine cat, thought Catherine, smoothly, slinkily, every movement graced with a feline self-possession. Adjacent to the apartments occupied by Lady Elliston there were a few smaller rooms allocated to attendants of the family. It was into one of these that Joanna conducted her. It had but a small window commanding a view of the outer ramparts leading down to that part of the river along which she had walked with Annie and her uncle and aunt on their way to Bardwick. It was not so much the view, however, but the room itself which engaged her attention. Was it possible that she, Catherine Venners, was to be granted accommodation such as this for her sole occupation? The furnishings were naturally sparser than those of the Ellistons themselves, but all the same they were still of good quality and the bed was a proper one as opposed to the straw pallet she was used to at home. An oak chest beneath the window looked solid and spacious, the kind Miriam had always dreamed of to put in her own home; there was also one chair and a rectangular table on which lay a half finished piece of embroidery. She even had her own small tapestry of a lady feeding deer.

"This is to be your room," Joanna confirmed. "The embroidery is mine. I will take it with me when I leave."

Momentarily forgetting Joanna's presence, she leaned out of the window, wondering what working of providence it was that had lifted her from the indignity of the kitchen to this unexpected luxury. A haze now hung over the river and the sun was growing weaker. It was very still and an occasional leaf fluttered down to add to the covering of gold, brown and amber fringing the river. The seasons came and went, constant, unchanging, their pattern as fixed as the stars in the sky; for men and women life was never so simple; made in God's image, they were granted free will, given a life-informing spirit and the capacity to reason and feel; it was this that got in the way of Craven's belief in some immutable pattern. As to her own life, where was it leading and what did it mean. She suddenly felt very vulnerable and very lonely.

"I suppose you only have the one gown?" Joanna said, breaking into her thoughts.

"Yes," replied Catherine, still slightly bemused by the change in her circumstances.

"It will not do," stated Joanna, rather to herself than to Catherine. "I shall have to see what I can find for you. Wait here."

While she was gone, Catherine looked in the chest. It was ample, both for her belongings and for the herbal preparations she hoped to store for the coming winter. On reflection, she realised that had it not been for her knowledge of herbs she would in all probability have remained in the kitchen. It was a sobering thought.

Joanna soon returned, a gown of dark green draped over her arm.

"This should enhance the colour of your hair, if nothing else," she gave out. "I can obtain others later if need be, but let this suffice for the moment. Put it on."

"Now?" asked Catherine.

"Why not?"

She had expected Joanna to tactfully withdraw while she undressed, but clearly Joanna was not going to be quite so obliging. Joanna had her reasons. One was her curiosity to see the extent of Catherine's disfigurement and the other to make sure that her choice was the right one.

"Quickly, I have things to attend to," she complained, as Catherine fumbled to pull off her homespun, now acutely conscious of her nakedness and the unsightly scars it would reveal.

"When did you last wash?" she said condescendingly.

"I did not have time this morning. I was ..."

"Save your explanations. You will certainly have to do better for Lady Elliston. She cannot tolerate unsightliness."

The barb cut like a wound. It might have been veiled but it hurt. Also it appeared to be unnecessarily cruel, coming from someone who had everything in her favour. Joanna's gaze seemed relentless, and in fumbling to pull on the gown she was conscious of exposing herself even more. How she loathed being stared at and in this, her weakness, she knew that Joanna had triumphed. A deliberate exercise in mortification had been dealt and she had given into it without a struggle. She fought back her tears, despising Joanna, but despising herself even more.

"Turn round," demanded Joanna, prodding her this way and then the other. "Brush your hair. It is your finest asset. I will call for you within the hour."

Catherine watched her go with a sigh of relief. The promised hour gave her time in which to regain her composure. Forgetting the recent humiliation, she looked at the gown and saw that its colour did, in fact, suit her. If only from reasons of pride, she knew that Joanna would do her best to make her look presentable. She again brushed her hair. Since even Joanna herself saw it as an asset, she was trusting to rely on it to improve her overall appearance.

It was now growing dark and she lit the candle made available for her use and sat on the edge of the bed. Watching the light flicker and wander, she had not anticipated another change in her circumstances to happen so quickly. After all, it was only a short time ago that she had been assuring her family that she was reconciled to working in the kitchen. Now everything was turned upside down again and she was left feeling more mystified than ever.

From thoughts of her family her mind turned to Craven. Confession within the castle brought her no comfort. To begin with its priest was fat and apathetic. He played at things holy, when in truth he was much more concerned with his secular comforts than the spiritual needs of his flock. Now whatever his faults, Craven believed and that belief was implicit. He instilled it in his flock, made them alive to the reality of the soul as much as the bodily cladding it came in. With Craven confession meant something; with this other, it was empty of meaning.

In accordance with her word, Joanna returned within the hour. She had brought some hair clasps with which she pinned back Catherine's hair to pleasing effect, but only some of it, allowing the thicker and wavier part of it to cover the edge of her face. It was a gesture of kindness that Catherine had not expected, but despite it she remained cold and aloof, letting Catherine know in no uncertain terms exactly what she thought of her.

"I do not like you," she remarked after satisfying herself that Catherine looked presentable, "and I doubt I ever will. You are not a lady born and I am, and therein lies the difference between us. Howsobeit, I will treat you as fairly as I am able, but there can never be any friendship between us. I trust you understand."

"Perfectly," Catherine replied, determined to be strong where before she had been weak, "and I shall endeavour to give you as little trouble as possible. I am not slow to learn."

"I see we understand one another sufficiently well Mistress Venners."

The duties imposed on her were nothing like as onerous as those of the kitchen. Joanna was true to her word, all her instructions being curt but precise. Her main duty was to assist Lady Elliston in robing and disrobing, a somewhat tiresome proceeding owing to the lady's indisposition, both of body and temper. Since she rarely left her bed, she also had to be washed and fed, though her appetite was poor. Secondary duties entailed tidying her room, making her bed and preparing a variety of herbal cures with which Lady Elliston remained very taken; she was also called on to read to her and assist her with her embroidery, the old lady's eyes being so weak that she had a tendency to prick her fingers and spill spots of blood on the sheets. In learning all these duties so quickly, Joanna was soon relieved of many trifling chores, and as a result was seen less and less. Where she was, and in whose company, Catherine could easily guess. So could Lady Elliston.

"Gone to my son again," she would say now and then. "Never meddle with men Mistress Venners. Believe me, they bring naught but misery," and from bald statements like this she seemed to find solace in recounting her past, the triumphs and travails of her many years of life.

From such rambling discourses Catherine was to learn much of the family history. How as a girl of fifteen Lady Elliston had been taken to Runnarth as a bride for Henry Elliston without ever having set eyes on him, the great love he had inspired in her which had never wavered however many times he sought comfort in embraces other than her own, and the two sons she bore him, Henry, the eldest, so tall, so handsome, so learned, the kindest child a mother ever had. And then, of course, Roger, the current Lord Elliston, the son she never could love, whether from the pain of a long protracted labour or the knowledge that her husband was spending those hours with some other woman, no one quite knew. But the fact remained that her aversion grew rather than diminished and in time she scarcely concealed it. Unable or uncaring to disguise her preference, his nature took on those traits which she had helped to foster, the sullen, withdrawn and variable temper of a child that is made to feel aware of dislike and indifference.

It naturally followed that the brothers were not close, for while Henry basked in the light of his mother's affection, Roger sank more and more into the gloom of her deliberate neglect. In desperation he tried to vie for her affection, only to meet with contempt and disdain. And so it went on for all of twenty-five years. And then the unthinkable happened. Henry was struck down by the flux which carried him off in a day and a night. Lady Elliston's grief knew no bounds. Even her husband was unable to console her. Now Roger's star, by a mere quirk of fate, was in the ascendant, but it was not an easy transition. For one thing it left the delicate matter of Henry's affianced bride Blanche to consider; custom dictated that she should now become the bride of his younger brother, but prior to Henry's demise Lady Elliston had already predisposed her mind against him by drawing unfavourable comparisons between the two brothers, everything Blanche had heard about Roger being coloured by his mother's distorted descriptions. Thus, the marriage was set on its course to disaster. She was accepting a very poor second best. He was taking on a bitterly disappointed woman. There were quarrels and worse. After bearing him three sons she felt her duty done and the estrangement was lasting. Separate households were formed within the castle, she sitting alone or playing with her children, he continuing his own pathetic dalliances as he had done throughout most of the marriage. But even he had not reckoned on the outcome.

A certain Lord Richard Baring, son of an erstwhile friend of the late lamented Henry, was invited to the castle at the older woman's behest, and finding Blanche more than willing to have him rectify her former neglect the two of them planned to escape with the children. In a peculiar kind of way, Roger was glad to see her go, even if he had in a sense played cuckold to Baring. As to the children, he hardly missed them. As far as he was concerned, they were hers anyway. Conceived in indifference, possibly hate, he tended to treat them as he had been treated, but more with bemusement than cruelty. This left Blanche to have full control over their formative years, a duty which she jealously guarded and which, incidentally, provided her with every opportunity of alienating them still further from the man who had sired them. So John, James, and yet another Henry, the latter named to spite Lady Elliston, who bemoaned the fact that another could never take the former one's place, went willingly with their mother, and being of an impressionable age soon found a substitute father in Baring. It all having occurred eight years ago, there was still no talk of divorce. As for Elliston, he had no great desire to marry again. His pastimes remained as diverse as his humour, reading, riding and women, occasionally interspersed with religion when nothing else served to alleviate his sense of denial and hurt.

CHAPTER TEN

If Lady Elliston could be demanding and exasperatingly awkward, as is the prerogative of old age, there were times when she could also be exceedingly kind and in a good mood even merry. Thus, a bond was struck between the old lady and her servant. In Catherine she reposed her trust and to Catherine she related her life. Of a certainty, it was rather pleasing to bare one's soul to someone who, unlike Joanna, gave the impression of wanting to listen.

The richness of autumn was over. The days were shortening, each lingering frost heralding the onset of winter. Lady Elliston complained of the cold without ceasing, the one thing mother and son appeared to have in common. Keeping to her room, she rarely ventured into the hall which remained virtually unused except on special occasions, Lord Elliston preferring to entertain his own small circle of friends in the privacy of his own apartments. What impressed itself upon Catherine was the divisive nature of the household which only made for constraint and suspicion.

It was the last day of the month and the frost was severe. Warm in her mistress's room, it was freezing in hers, there being no fire to counteract the icy draught that found its way through every crook and cranny. It was at times like these that she almost longed for the heat of the kitchen again. The chill was totally numbing and she dressed as quickly as she could. From her window the river looked so locked in its trapping of ice that only her breath seemed to speak of things quickened. The air felt as keen as a knife and the ewer of water iced over, her hands hurting dreadfully as she broke it to dab the wet on her face and struggled to put the pins in her hair. Lady Elliston had very sensibly decided to keep to her bed with a demand for extra covers. Catherine had made her as comfortable as possible, but decidedly both age and the weather were doing the worst with her temper. Now, at last, the old lady was dozing. Going back to her own room, which was colder than ever, Catherine picked up one of Lady Elliston's half finished pieces of embroidery, but her fingers were simply too cold and she laid it aside. Instead she turned to the book from which she usually read to the old lady. It was a while since she had been able to read quietly to herself and the text soon absorbed her to the exclusion of the weather. But just when she had found a way of spending her time profitably, she was asked to go and see Sir Edward.

Immaculately dressed, the distinctive cap covering his head, anyone unfamiliar with the household might have taken him to be the lord and Elliston the servant. Whenever he appeared, she surmised that she was wanted, either by one of the Ellistons or by Joanna. This time it was Elliston himself who was asking to see her.

She followed reluctantly; the kitchen had been demanding, but this, if anything, was worse.

At least in the kitchen you were guaranteed a set of tasks, albeit repetitive, but within the main household there was no such routine. Called upon one minute and dispensed with the next, it was the very unknowingness of it all that was vexing. Burgoyne was obviously far more accustomed to it than she was, Elliston having dismissed him as soon as he had conducted her thither.

He stood in front of the blazing hearth, his customary position when it was cold. He looked tired and a little drawn in upon himself, the look she had remembered when she had seen him sitting at the window.

"Ah, Mistress Venners," he said, upon seeing her. "You have been on my mind."

"My lord," she answered shivering, this time not from his glance but from the cold.

He saw the situation immediately and asked her to move nearer to the fire. She did not hesitate, but walked close to where he stood and began warming her hands in front of the blaze. They were only a few feet apart.

"I detest winter," he remarked. "I feel the cold, just as you do. I should imagine it is appreciably warmer in the kitchen."

"Yes, my lord."

"But I take it you would not wish to return to it."

"I think not, my lord."

The firelight seemed to play in his eyes. They had an errant, restless quality.

"I asked you here because I wished to enquire into your well being."

He paused, indicating by a wave of his hand that she should answer.

"I am well, my lord," she vouchsafed without elaborating further.

"It is not your health lady, but your welfare in general I wish to be assured of. For instance, how you enjoy your duties."

"I am content, my lord," she replied.

"The devil you are!"

He seemed to find his words telling, for the silence that followed was of long duration and without regard for any feelings she might have. Amazingly, it did not disconcert her, but instead brought a smile to her face.

"I see you find me bizarre," he charged.

"No, my lord."

"No?" he challenged, arching his brow.

"No," she asserted.

For a moment he appeared nonplussed, but soon recommenced.

"My mama is well pleased with you. It seems, therefore, you have achieved what I in a lifetime have never achieved. Is that not so?"

"I am obliged for Lady Elliston's good opinion."

"Tactful as ever. She speaks of me?"

"Yes, my lord."

"She sings my praises no doubt?"

He, more than anyone, must have been well aware of what Lady Elliston thought of him. Again, it would seem he was testing her deliberately. If that were so, then he must be given a deliberate answer.

"No, my lord,"

"You are honest at least," he replied. "What does she say?"

"I think you know what she says, my lord, but then I do not think she understands you," she said, the words spilling from her lips quite involuntarily and stunning her by their boldness.

"As you do, Mistress Venners," he pounced.

"I trust not to be so presumptuous," she readily parried.

"Do you?" he replied, half jestingly. Then his mood changed like the puff of wind that was at that moment blowing down the chimney and into their midst. "Seriously, Mistress Venners," he said, ignoring it, "my mother is difficult, but I see you have patience, as you have just so ably demonstrated. Another question, how do you get on with Joanna."

"She is most civil," said Catherine, deeming this the most

appropriate answer.

"I can imagine. You are hardly alike," he replied, with a multiplicity of meaning.

She could have construed anything from the way in which he said it, but as ever with Catherine it was the mask of which she was conscious, and he noted how quickly her hands went to touch it, as if she was terrified he might catch a glimpse of what was behind it.

"She has impeccable taste and has turned you out admirably," he remarked. "You are a lady in demand Kate. Ah, a slip, forgive me, I should have said Catherine, or perhaps now you do not mind overmuch."

"As you will, my lord."

"Kate it is then," he maintained. "You would not call me an awkward man."

"Not needlessly so, my lord."

"You parry well, Kate. But to continue. As I was saying, you are in demand. I have had your priest here, Francis Craven to be precise. He was, for want of a better word, concerned. Concerned over what we had done, or rather what we had not done. Apparently, we had neglected your spiritual and moral welfare by placing you in the kitchen, so much so that you had renounced your religious vocation. When I mentioned that you were no longer in the danger he suspected and had been elevated to serving my mother, he was not as mollified as I had hoped. He still insisted that it was incumbent on me to release you from the fate that had befallen you, which as you can imagine did not endear him to me. No man likes to be told of his duty. Had he not been a cleric by profession, I might have seen fit to punish him."

"No, my lord, you cannot," she interrupted, totally forgetting where she was and with whom.

"Now you too give me orders! This is rich indeed," he said, stepping dangerously close to her.

"Forgive me, my lord. I spoke without thinking. But Father Craven is my friend."

"And do you defend all your friends so nobly Kate?"

"He is a good man, my lord. I know I have disappointed him in renouncing the vocation he wished me to adopt, but it was a decision I made long before I came here."

"Well defended," he said, "but take care. I like him not. He is too thin and spare, too much soul and no heart."

"He is still a good man, my lord."

"Good because he practises to be good, good because he

pretends to be so, or unconsciously good. There is a world of difference."

"I just know he is good, my lord. He has a great care for the village."

"Which I do not?"

"I did not say so, my lord."

"You implied it."

She was getting muddled, but not entirely confounded.

"The people see so little of you. They do not know you."

"I have my duties here," he replied, almost by way of apology. "Assizes, rent days, these I attend. What more do they want!"

"Then they see you in the role of master, not guardian."

Had she gone too far, but was she not right? Matthew had only seen him once in attendance at a rent day.

"You have some quaint notions of my responsibilities. I see that you think of me as a bad man as opposed to a good one like Craven."

"No my, lord, I do not think that at all."

"What do you think Mistress Venners. Out with it! I promise I will not put your head on a spike! Tell me."

"I think you pretend to be worse than you actually are, my lord," she replied, retreating away from him, whereupon he became silent and withdrawn.

A bell suddenly rang to cut through the silence.

"You see, duty calls yet again," he said, the glimmer of a smile on his lips. "I enjoy our talks Mistress Venners. We will speak further. For once I agree with my mother. You have a well informed mind and a rare degree of tolerance. Come, your hand."

His grip was tight and the ring he wore dug into her palm, retaining its imprint for many hours afterwards.

CHAPTER ELEVEN

It was a month before she was allowed another day's respite. Dense drizzle had taken the place of November frosts, and the two mile walk promised to be a muddy one. Once or twice she looked back at the castle, grey and solitary in its veiling of rain. Return she must, but she had no dread of that return. There was no specific reason she told herself, nothing with which to examine her conscience, but when an overhanging branch caught in her hair and threatened to tear off the mask, it suddenly seemed pricked into being. Unaccountable tears welled up in her eyes and she did feel ashamed.

Miriam, as ever, was full of questions; how was she enjoying her new position; what was Lady Elliston like, was she kind, was she exacting, and what of Lord Elliston, had she by any chance come into contact with him. Just like Joan, she was curious and eager for any titbits on offer.

"We all be so proud of ye," she said, inviting the others to share in her genuine pleasure, though it quickly became clear to Catherine that Rob was anything but pleased. As far as he was concerned his mother was fawning, to the extent that it literally made him cringe, not so much with embarrassment but with hot indignation.

"Leave the lass alone," Matthew said, gauging Rob's mood. "She'll tell us anon. Ye want everythin' all at once."

"I'm only interested," Miriam explained, her look slightly crestfallen. "I've made an apple pie for ye too, special like, and there's a fine leg o' mutton, and those herbs ye gathered they hae dried a treat, and ye ..."

"Kate 'ull be used to finer fare now," cut in Rob peevishly. "Tis not for the likes o' us to compete with the comforts of the castle I'll be bound."

"That is hardly fair Rob", came Catherine's quick retort. "This will always be my home; as for aunt Miriam's apple pies, they are better than any I saw in the kitchen."

This was followed by a long awkward silence. It was the kind of carping she might have expected from Annie, but never from

Rob.

"Are ye not goin' to tell Kate the good news?" Miriam ventured at last, hoping to mend things a little.

"Mary can tell her," said Rob. "I got work to do."

"Tell me what?" asked Catherine.

"Ay tell 'er," sneered Rob, "not that she'll be interested in our puny doins."

With this he rose to go, his face slightly strained and now looking sheepish.

"Where do ye think ye are goin'?" Matthew said, raising his voice.

"Calf needs seein' to."

"Ye'll stay where ye are and apologise to Kate right now. Ye hae no cause to speak as ye did. I'll nae hae bad manners in my house."

Glowering under his eyes, Rob sat down again, the unnatural quiet only broken by the crackling of the fire.

"It does not matter Uncle Matt," said Catherine. "I understand."

"Well I dunna," put in Miriam, her eyes filling up. "It is no like him to speak so. Ye hae spoilt everything Rob, and I had it all planned sae well."

Rob was stubborn and proud, just like his father, but he was man enough to know when an apology was called for. It was just that Catherine was different and he resented that difference. It was new and disturbing and he felt as if he no longer held such a special place in her affection as he had done hitherto; someone or something had sneaked in and stolen it, and that something or someone belonged to the castle and not to their home or the village. Catherine, normally so perceptive, only saw dimly what it was that aggrieved him and blamed it solely on her new position within the Ellistons' household. Like Craven, he was bound to be a little put out by the turn of events, particularly when they were beyond his control, but Rob had no cause for concern. He was still the Rob she adored and nothing would ever come between them.

"Rob," pleaded Mary, taking his hand, "come now."

"I shouldn't hae spoken so," he said at last. "I just couldna stop mysell. Ye are different though Kate, somethin' I canna quite explain."

"Apology accepted," said Catherine, giving him a peck on the cheek.

"If difference there be, it is a good one," affirmed Mary.

"I'd say twere more than that," Rob persisted.

"Well let us not speak of it further," Mary said. "I shall now tell Kate of our puny doins. What say you to being an aunt?"

"Oh Mary," Catherine cried, hugging her close.

Mary's obvious happiness put an end to any constraint and talk of the forthcoming child soon made them forgetful of what had gone before.

"I feel so confident Catherine," she said, but then she always had, thought Catherine, which made it so much worse when things went against her.

"We'll hae a need of you, Kate, when the time comes," said Rob, much more subdued and conciliatory. "Ye'll try to be with us."

She gave them her promise without exactly knowing how she was going to keep it, but keep it she would. In due time all Miriam's questions were answered to her obvious satisfaction, though Elliston himself was hardly mentioned which left them under the impression that Catherine had only seen him very fleetingly and only then in Lady Elliston's presence. Though refusing to believe that their interviews were in any way special, she made them so by her reluctance to speak of them openly. The remainder of the time passed all too quickly. Matthew showed her the new calf which he had unimaginatively named Daisy in keeping with the long chain of Daisies that had preceded it and Rob showed her the place where they had buried her beloved dog Peter, the dog that had played such a significant part in her recovery. Neither was she ashamed of the tears she shed over him.

Miriam brought out the herbs she had prepared and dried in accordance with Catherine's instructions, and Catherine exchanged them for the small number of cures she had been able to make during her time at the castle.

"There's many hereabouts misses ye skills, Kate," she said.

"And far too many turning to Mother Jomfrey for succour," put in Mary.

"I was afraid of that," Catherine replied scornfully.

Mary offered to walk with her part of the way to Father Craven's. Even now, Catherine felt an obligation towards him.

"Are you really content?" she asked.

"Yes, Mary, I am happier than I have been in a long time."

"You did not say much of Lord Elliston. What is he like?"

Whereupon Catherine became noticeably evasive and hesitant. Mary, seeing her reluctance, discreetly changed the subject, but did not fail to notice the slight tremor which passed over her features at the mention of his name.

The land was looking starker than ever, thin streams of light struggling through the overhead cloud to mirror itself in the numerous puddles that impeded their progress. Already the day was beginning to wane and the road was as empty as it had been on the day she was taken to the castle. It did not look as if they were going to meet with a single soul until they spotted the only too familiar figure of Mother Jomfrey coming towards them. She was carrying a stick on which she leant for support, occasionally muttering oaths to herself as it sank in the mud.

"Of all people," sighed Mary. "Catherine, have a care what you say to her. She seems to grow more spiteful with age."

"I will do my best," replied Catherine, "but it will not be easy."

On seeing them, the old woman raised her stick in a peculiar kind of greeting. "Ye are back then Mistress Venners," she remarked, a slight whistling sound emanating from the gap in her teeth.

"Merely on a visit. I am now returning," she answered thoughtfully.

"Ay, is that so? And are ye still your own woman?" she cackled, intent on mischief.

"You do not change Mother Jomfrey, more's the pity," she retorted, losing all patience. "And let your neighbours be. Your potions are as foul and twisted as your person."

Mary put a restraining hand on her arm, but it was too late.

"One day Kate Venners, ye'll hae cause to regret those words. Withered and twisted I may be, but I hae powers, do ye hear, powers!" she screeched, wresting the stick from the mud and waving it in a circling motion above their heads.

"She is evil Catherine, really evil, which is why you must be on your guard."

"My mother never feared her. Neither do I."

The church, as they approached it, became bathed in the last vestiges of sunlight, as if touched by the hand of God. It made Catherine realise just how much she loved it and all that it stood for; God as she saw Him and not as Father Craven would have her interpret.

"Take care Mary," she said, as they parted. "Try to rest as much as you can. Do not needlessly overtask yourself. Aunt Miriam will understand. And I promise to be there when the time comes."

Mary looked at her, this new and confident Catherine. If only Isobel had been there to witness the change for herself.

"And you Catherine, you must take care too. Remember, you

are still very vulnerable and I would not wish you to suffer any undeserved hurt."

Whether Catherine heeded the warning or not, Mary felt obliged to give it.

ꙮ

The door of the church was open and she went inside. Father Craven was kneeling at the altar in quiet prayer, his head bowed in his hands. Aware that someone was there, he paused briefly to finish.

"Catherine," he said, a tired smile of welcome compressed on his lips. "This is strange. Only a moment ago I had a sort of premonition that I had to come into my church."

She noticed that he said "my church" as he clasped his thin fingers together. The sunlight beamed on his gaunt figure, giving him the appearance of some attenuated angel.

"It is good to see you Catherine. Indeed, you are never far from my thoughts. Only yesterday I was thinking of your mother and the trust she invested in me to instruct you in all that was good. I should like to think there are some books of worth at the castle, though I fear the reverse."

"I read to Lady Elliston from her book of homilies, Father."

"I see," he replied rather coldly. "You have felt no change of heart then since we last spoke?"

"No, Father."

"It is never too late should you feel a change of heart."

"I doubt that I shall," she said, trying to soften her answer. "Lady Elliston is most kind and the duties I undertake are nothing like so onerous as those of the kitchen."

"I get so weary of the world, Catherine," he said, more or less ignoring her.

It was obvious that he was not going to refer to his interview with Lord Elliston, which perhaps was as well, his attitude seeming to be one of injured acceptance in the belief that he would influence her by persuasion rather than force. His immutable conviction of the rightness of things as he saw them had not changed at all, the former disappointment only serving to strengthen his ultimate purpose.

"Father," she gently said, recalling him to a sense of the present.

"Catherine!" he exclaimed, "There are times when I long to be done with this life."

And in his features there showed an awful desolation which troubled her, for there was no divining his innermost feelings.

"You labour too hard Father," she said with concern.

"Tis my calling Catherine. Tis what God demands of me. And He will sustain me. You are a virtuous woman Catherine. I fear that your soul is more in peril now than it ever was before. Remember, a corrupt master corrupts his servants."

She knew to whom he alluded, but it made no mark on her mind. Unlike him, she could judge with her heart as well as her head.

"I see no possibility of returning to Runnarth till Christmas is past," she remarked, deliberately changing the subject.

"You shall always be welcome in the house of God, Catherine. I trust you attend confession at the castle for what it is worth?"

"I do, Father, but I still look on you as my priest."

"I am gratified to hear it."

Having confessed her, she left him to his solitary thoughts. The darkness enclosed him, his repressed emotions beating in his brain like a repetitive hammer, so alone, so apart, so driven by desires beyond his attaining.

Those days on which a fair was held at Bardwick were few and far between and for the greater part of the year it wore an aspect of squalid monotony. It had been another such day. Rain had flooded the open culverts and a smell of putrefaction hung on the air. The houses leaned grotesquely, one to the other, obscuring the remnants of light that struggled for entrance between them.

Annie had just got the children to bed. All day they had proved wearisome and she felt both incapable and unwilling to deal with their surfeit of high spirits. Thoroughly spoilt herself, it was hardly surprising that she had little understanding of discipline or the manner in which to achieve it. Slumping into the nearest available chair she stared dully at the flames. The table, still cluttered, showed three discolouring rings. In fact, the whole place had a general air of untidiness, from the heaps of unwashed linen dumped in odd corners to the unswept rushes with their riddling of dirt. Pettishly she kicked at the fire, contrasting her existence with the life he had promised. It was true that they were in one of the better parts of the town, but it was far removed from what she had envisaged. Running her fingers through her hair she desultorily moved to the table where she picked up a half eaten apple, savagely sinking her teeth into it. If this was marriage, then she was tired of it already. Better a rich man's harlot than a poor man's skivvy. But life with any man other than Gerard was simply unthinkable, those nights when they lay together compensating for all the times that he left her alone, and she fed on them with the ferocity of a bird that feeds on its young. The children were merely incidental, an inconvenient result of such passion, and in letting them do as they willed she could hardly complain when they failed to obey her.

The door was suddenly opened, admitting a rush of cool air into the stagnant atmosphere. He held out his arms and she immediately ran towards him. Stirred by the breeze the dying flames leapt into life accentuating the man and the woman in their brief burst of flame. His gypsy appearance was richly glowing and warm to the touch of her mouth. Withdrawing from his embrace as quickly as she had welcomed it, she was peeved that he should see how much her happiness depended on him and him alone. But he knew how to win her. One engaging look at her and her mood of defiance would be charmed away into one of total surrender.

"Where hae you been?" she demanded, determined to be irked by his increasing desertion.

"Working for you ma cherie, working for you, what else?"

His accent was engaging and he knew how to use it to advantage.

"You are glib," she accused, as he looked at her for an explanation of the untoward word. "What have I got to look forward to," she complained, sitting down at the table, her mouth drooping sulkily.

"Annie. Annie," he soothed. "Look at me. Everything I do, I do for you, yes. You must know that."

"All I know is that you are never here when I need you. The childer defy me and I canna control them. What with their unruliness and the house I canna cope," she said, dissolving into tears. It was a ploy that invariably worked.

"Annie I beg you, do not cry," he pleaded, smoothing her hair from her face. "Do you think that I want to be away from you, you who are my 'ole life, yes. Always we need money. What else can I do?"

Raising her eyes to meet his own, she knew that she could not resist him.

"My love," he murmured, taking her in his arms again and caressing her face with his kisses. "Believe me, this is not the life I wanted for you, but soon we make money, lots of it; then, I promise, we live somewhere better, yes."

"Yes," she faintly replied, burying her face in his tunic, which was red and enhanced the swarthiness of his features. "I will get you supper."

"No Annie, you look tired."

Fully aware of her total lack of domesticity, it was his genuine desire that one day he would be able to provide her with a household of servants to do her every bidding. Then she could play the grand dame as she had always desired. In the meantime, he had to accept things as they were and set about replenishing the fire and clearing the mess from the table. Making a hasty meal of what he could find, he gazed at her fondly. At last he had some good news to tell her.

"What is it?" she asked sleepily, slipping into a mood of hazy contentment now he was back. Whenever they were apart, a desperate fear that she would never see him again would take possession of her and make her wretched and irritable until he returned.

"Christmas, I am called upon to take the troupe to entertain the Lord Elliston."

"You call that good news, do ye!" she railed, springing to her feet as if shaken into sudden awareness by this new and unexpected blow. "You sicken me with your good news."

"Annie, please," he pleaded. It was rarely his policy to shout, knowing that he could obtain far better results by gentle persuasion, but there were times when nothing would serve and this was clearly one of them.

"I dunna want to listen. You canna love me if you do this. I hate you, hate you!" she continued to scream until he caught her in his arms and held her so fast that escape was impossible.

"I adore you Annie, hush now. How can you say such things?"

"What about the other women," she charged, fighting free of his embrace like a vixen. This was ever her final resort because it was the only one that ever visibly moved him. With his fine looks, a flirt he may be, but he was no philanderer and loved her with a kind of desperate passion equal to her own. Quickly releasing her he turned away. She was now dreadfully afraid. "I'm sorry Gerard. I didna mean it. Gerard, please. I get so lonely without you. I imagine all sorts of things. I canna help it."

"Come here," he said at last. "I forgive. You are such a child still."

"That I am not. I hae two childer of my own."

"Yes, Annie, also my children. And I have something for them, and for you."

"What?" she asked excitedly.

He drew a strand of yellow beads from his pocket and fastened them round her neck, pressing her to him and kissing her repeatedly until all her chagrin was completely forgotten.

"Annie, Annie, mon amour, mon amour," he sighed.

"And what am I do at Christmas?" she asked, as he finally let her go.

"Why you can stay with your mama and papa. They love you, yes?"

"I suppose so. You might well see Kate."

"Maybe. I had not thought of that."

"You know I envy her."

"Envy poor Kate. I do not understand."

"At least she will be at the castle."

"Ah, I see what you mean. We talk another time, eh. It is late Annie, no?" he said, a meaningful glint in his eye.

"I love you Gerard," she whispered seductively as he led her to bed.

CHAPTER TWELVE

Preparations for the forthcoming festivities were well under way, and if Lady Elliston could take no active part in the arrangements herself she saw to it that her every whim was obeyed. Imperious and demanding, she refused to let anything be put in hand without her prior approval. In her role as grand dame she determined to make this Christmas one they would not readily forget. After all, she reasoned, it might be her last. Contrary to the wishes of her son, she was set on inviting as many guests of equal social standing as she could think of. Revelling in the anticipation of it, he let her have her way. Admittedly it was some years since the rather sombre magnificence of the Elliston stronghold had been seen to advantage; it also kept her occupied, which suited them both.

Rushes were strewn throughout the length and breadth of the great draughty hall, evoking a fragrance redolent of summer to overcome the long prevailing must. The massive central table was polished to its former pristine sheen and all the best silver set upon it. A tapestry depicting Venus and her minions was replaced by another of shepherds and sheep, much more in keeping with Lady Elliston's taste and, incidentally, more in keeping with Christmas. When she was in a rare mood such as this, her enthusiasm was infectious, and despite the extra work there was a keen sense of expectation which helped to take the effort out of toil. Catherine was no exception. Caught up in the bustle and excitement, she responded to the challenge with a zest akin to that of her mistress. It also prevented her from thinking of Christmas at home with her own family.

Before the accident it had been her favourite time of the year, but following it she was not so ready to join in the fun, her disfigurement making her cautious. Isobel had done her best to encourage her former exuberance, but the mask kept it hidden. One Christmas was particularly memorable in making her painfully aware of her difference and the futility of trying to ignore it. She was fifteen and happy to join in the dancing until one lad, more timid than the rest, refused to take her hand, which left her in the singular position of having to dance on alone or lose face by walking away. Proud, she danced on, but it taught her a lesson, that it was wiser to watch than to risk further humiliation. Passivity taught her to cope and how to be of use without being noticed, such as now when she took a delight in transforming the hall from its overall bleakness to one full of verdure and holly. Being able to contribute to the approaching festivities without actively participating was something she consciously welcomed.

No snow had fallen, but it remained bitingly cold with a bright deceptive sun that warmed no one. The water butts froze and so did the extremities.

"Why does it not snow?" Lady Elliston complained. "Tis not Christmas without snow."

She pouted like a small and petulant child, burying her frail form beneath the press of covers. "You will not forget that sleeping draught, Mistress Venners. I must sleep tonight."

"I have it ready, my lady," Catherine assured.

"No doubt, you would rather be with your own kin Mistress Venners. It will not be much fun for *you,* she maintained, the accent firmly on the "You".

"I do not mind, my lady. I shall enjoy watching."

"Watching, watching!" she disdainfully retorted. "I do enough watching from this bed. Christmas I live again, if only for a day or so. Why, I can recall when I was a girl ..."

Catherine sighed. There was nothing for it but to adopt an attitude of interest as Lady Elliston proceeded to unravel her endless chain of Christmases, many of them vague and distorted by time.

The eve of Christmas saw the arrival of the long awaited guests, each one of them deferentially greeted by their hostess who at last was beginning to live her few days. Catherine watched them from a vantage point in Lady Elliston's room. If Craven were to be believed, God had seen fit to place them in a position of privilege and wealth which was seemingly theirs by right of entitlement. They certainly behaved as if it was, their features being stamped with a kind of conscious superiority. She wondered what he would make of them. She had not seen him for days. Seemingly, he was being deliberately elusive until his presence was necessary.

She had put on the new gown Joanna had procured for her. It was blue and trimmed with an edging of fur. She would have preferred something less showy, her sole concern being to detract from the curiosity of the invited. Already later than she would have liked, the feeble tap at the door could not have come at a more inconvenient moment. It was certainly not Joanna.

"Who is it?" she said, quickly tightening her girdle, and feeling both irritated and anxious.

"Kate, it be me Joan," came the rather subdued reply.

She opened the door to reveal Joan, prettier but grimier than ever, uncustomary tears streaming down her face.

"Please I got to talk to ye," she pleaded.

She looked utterly crushed and wretched, not the Joan of her remembrance at all, and from the way in which she mechanically wiped away her tears with the back of her hand this was obviously not the kind of distress that could be cured in an instant. Joan was her best friend. How could she not help.

"You look troubled. Come and sit down," she said, closing the door firmly behind them, for she had discovered that there was just as much tittle tattle in the household itself as there was in the kitchen.

"I know I shouldna be up 'ere, but I dunna know what to do, and I could only think o' you," she sobbed. "I had a job to find ye as well."

"I should imagine you did. Now come, tell me what is amiss. Does Watkins know you are here?"

"Watkins!" she almost spat, jolted from her sorrowful mood into one of defiance. "I can see how tis with ye. Ye dunna want the likes o' me now Kate Venners do ye. A fine friend ye be!"

"I meant no such thing. But it is Christmas and you must be more busy than normal. I take it you have permission?"

"No I dunna! Look at ye in ye fine clothes, and me in mine! Best get back where I belong eh Kate?" she laughed wildly.

"Stop it Joan," she said, trying to shake some sense into that usually very practical head of hers. The harsh mood having been spent, she once again dissolved into tears.

"Joan, trust me. I trusted you if you remember."

And gradually in between the convulsive crying the truth began to emerge.

"I told Tom an' he says twas none of 'is doin'. He says tisna his, but ye know better Kate, ye know."

Catherine held her close. So Watkins denied responsibility. It was not surprising. Baseborn herself, she knew that it was invariably the woman who bore all the shame.

"What am I goin' to do Kate. I canna go home, there's enough o' them already. Anyways they'd only turn me out."

Catherine thought of the guests. They must have assembled by now, and doubtless Joanna would be smugly noting her absence, but Joan needed her and she could not simply abandon her without some word of encouragement.

"If Tom and you were to wed?" she suggested.

"Wed me," Joan scoffed. "Ye be mad to think on it. They dunna tolerate married wenches in the kitchen, let alone married wenches' brats. I was thinkin' o' another way."

"What?" asked Catherine, vaguely preoccupied with the neglect of her duties.

"Ye know Kate. Ye could do it for me. I'd trust ye."

"No, I do not," she replied, wondering if Lady Elliston had yet made her entrance.

"Come Kate, ye are not that innocent surely. Why, get rid o' it."

She forgot Lady Elliston. She forgot the festivities. She was only alive to the reality of the present.

"Ye bein' good with physic like. Ye got to help me Kate," she nervously continued, noting the tongue tied look of anger that was suddenly evinced in Catherine's face. It was true that Catherine could find no words adequate enough in which to express her abhorrence. All her early teaching had tended towards the preservation of life, the strengthening of the tenuous threads of existence, whose cutting off would come soon enough.

"You cannot possibly know what you ask of me, Joan. Believe me, if you were not my friend, I would make you regret that you had ever spoken to me of such a thing."

Joan could well believe it considering her rigidity of feature, the mask stretching over her face like a second layer of skin.

"You are fortunate that my mother did not think as you do, or I would not be here to listen to your repellent suggestion."

The subtlety of the statement was lost on Joan who could only regard Catherine's growing wrath with astonishment.

"Never speak of it again. Never!" she commanded. "This child is yours to care for and love, as my mother loved and cared for me."

"I'm dreadful feared Kate. Dunna ye understand?"

"Of course I do," she replied, gently cradling the girl in her arms, her anger giving way to genuine sympathy. "Leave it with me. I will think of something. Now promise me you will not do anything foolish."

"I promise," she answered wearily. "Tis a sin I hae already committed but twould be worse to kill the wee thing and I should never hae asked ye. Ye mun help me though."

"I will," she promised, without having any notion of what she was going to do. "Now I really must go, Joan."

"Ye look the lady," said Joan, breaking into a fragile smile.

"I hardly feel like one," she replied, leaving Joan to make her way back to that hell of a kitchen from which she herself had so providentially escaped.

Her mind half on Joan and half on her duties, she quickly made her way to the hall where the concourse of visitors was gathering. At first her eyes were dazzled by the brilliance within; the fires had been lit and coronas of candles suspended high above her danced fingers of flame on the table to reflect all that went on as if through a mirror. Thankfully, Joanna was too engaged in fascinating a group of gallants to note her tardiness. The heat from the hearth was intense and made her feel drowsy, and with the babble of voices in the background everything seemed a little too charged for comfort.

A solitary herald appeared in the gallery and a bugle was blown to signal silence. All eyes were focused on the main door, which slowly opened to admit Lady Elliston. Joanna had done her best to create an illusion of youth. Draped from head to foot in gold satin, her head adorned with a jewel encrusted coif, she behaved like the young woman she had been when her beauty was at its height and Henry had called her his divinest mama as Roger had never done.

Roger graciously let her have her moment of triumph before making his own entrance. For once his attire befitted his rank, whether out of deference to his mother or in an attempt to complement her showiness was his secret alone. He was in a mood to be amenable and gauged the proceedings with an eye to enjoyment, even condescending to be attentive to his mother, who was as adept at the game of pretence as he was himself. No one present could have accused them of a lack of affinity.

Joanna left her bevy of admirers and glided towards him, confident that no other woman could rival her. Incomparably lovely, she had no need for the rather pathetic exaggeration of her mistress. There must have been a time, Catherine thought, when Lady Elliston had been as beautiful as Joanna until age had withered her charms and left her an absurd old woman frantically trying to ape a lost youth. To be young in heart and worn in body was life at its cruellest.

The chatter recommenced, the guests circulating freely and showing a special degree of cordiality to their hostess whom they no doubt considered a frightful kind of joke. Elliston guessed their feelings only too well, but was content to let his mother remain blissfully ignorant; he felt it was kinder, and anyway he could play a part as well as anyone else.

Eyes were soon raised to the gallery where a small troupe of musicians were assembling, one of whom was waving a silken handkerchief to attract the attention of the ladies who, readily taken with his good looks and charm, blew kisses to him in return. It was Gerard. Catherine was quite surprised to see him, wondering what Annie's reaction had been when he told he was to entertain the Ellistons at Christmas. Not good, she surmised.

"That gentleman, I believe, is trying to catch your eye," Joanna wilfully whispered in her ear, Catherine having just found a suitable niche in which to lose herself for the evening.

There was no avoiding the fact. Gerard was excitedly waving and mouthing her name with typical Gallic abandon. Adopting a contrived sort of smile, she raised her hand in grudging salutation, when in reality she could have slain him without any compunction. The very attention she had wished to avoid was now focused upon her. She was being stared at and spoken of in whispers, and, without wanting to hear, it was hard not to listen. "Lady Elliston is growing bizarre in her choice of attendants," was one remark, and another, "I hear the old woman thinks well of her since she cured her of her headaches," and lastly but most tellingly, "Why have her here though. Tis hardly the place she would wish to be seen in. Neither should we be obliged to look at her." Catherine began to feel wretched.

"Let the music commence," said Lady Elliston.

It was the best thing that could have happened, for once the music began she was instantly forgotten, the throng eagerly joining in the intricate dance steps of the day. Sat away from it all in her niche, she at last felt safe from all further scrutiny. She thought of Annie and how much more she would have revelled in it; Mary was right, there were times when life seemed very unfair.

The music ceasing for an interval, the banquet began. Lady Elliston took her rightful place at the head of the table, Lord Elliston sitting on her left and facing a somewhat garrulous woman in yellow who talked over loud and over long, continually throwing out her hands as if to give emphasis to the inanity of chatter that gushed from her lips. Catherine sat with Joanna at the far end of the table where she could view the affectations of those assembled with an air of amused detachment. Much of the talk was bold to the point of being unseemly; this, no doubt, was the moral taint of which Father Craven had warned her, but it passed over her like a sprinkling of chaff. In a way it was harmless and she even found herself smiling, not so much at the conversation, but at the strictures of her priest. The dinner seemed to go on without end and her thoughts turned to the kitchen and how they were coping, or rather how Joan was coping. There was a surfeit of everything, including the traditional boar's head, an apple daintily choking its mouth; an elaborate sugar confection of the castle was particularly pleasing to Lady Elliston. The old lady was, in fact, enjoying every moment of the feast, her thin reedy voice distinctly audible in the welter of trivial talk that vied for ascendancy over the clatter of plates. Joanna, much to her chagrin, had attracted the attentions of a corpulent man whose manners at table were as crude as his discourse, but from rules of politeness she had to endure it. As far as Catherine was concerned, she had got what she deserved. For herself she was moderately content; being sat right at the end of the table, the tendency was to shun her altogether, apart from the company of one of the hounds to whom she fed titbits. Several of the guests discreetly left the room to be sick before the meal had finished, others drinking themselves into a kind of semi stupor.

Once the meal was over and its remnants despatched to the kitchen, they sat down to watch a mediocre group of play actors who had to be continually prompted. It was fortunate, therefore, that Gerard's troupe made up for the poor quality of the players. During the interval he sought her out with his usual high spirits.

"Catherine, I am a surprise, yes?"

"Yes Gerard, but then you always were."

"Ah, but you see Catherine, it is my unexpectability which the ladies find so irresistible."

"I think you mean unpredictability," she teased.

"But that is what I meant."

"And Gerard, I beg you not to draw attention to me again. It was most disconcerting."

"You are too conscious of yourself ma cousine."

She then went on to ask him about Annie and the children.

"We are 'appy sometimes, sad sometimes, yes."

Catherine smiled at the accent he effected so charmingly. It also served to disguise what he really felt. She knew she would never get a direct answer, but it was fun to probe him all the same. He was such an engaging kind of man.

"We are like all married couples, yes," he continued.

"Gerard you are incorrigible."

"I do not understand."

She did not enlighten him and he went on to ask her if she was happy and she had to own that she was. From the little he said, it was clear that Annie was making demands, complaining at his absence, becoming bored, craving the things he had so rashly promised to give her, the fine house, the pretty clothes, all so essential, or so she thought, to her very existence.

"Right this moment, Annie, she envy you. Because you are 'ere, I am 'ere, but she is not."

"I can imagine," she laughed. "I would willingly change places with her, believe me. Even so, she adores you Gerard, well as much as she can adore anyone. She is so used to getting her own way, but you must not give in to her always. It is bad for her, and bad for you."

"You are a good woman ma cousine. I try. Soon I shall be able to give her anything her heart desires, of that I feel very confident," he said, drawing her away to a quiet corner. "You can keep a secret?"

"Yes, Gerard, I think you know that I can," she replied, catching at the excitement that was kindled in those dark eyes of his.

"I find ways of making much money in very short a while."

He told her to look out into the night, frosty and lit by a spattering of stars, and then to the blackness of the forest beyond the river. She caught at her throat in disbelief. Was he really so besotted with Annie that caution meant nothing to him. Did he really think that his love would act as a talisman to protect him against the laws of the forest. She only had to look at him to know that he did.

"Gerard, this is folly! Consider the risk."

"I am clever fellow. I never get caught."

"You are a foolish fellow!" she rounded on him, her voice involuntarily raised so that one or two of the guests looked at her strangely.

"Hush, Catherine, hush."

Seeking to pacify her, he sat her within the embrasure of the window where they were well out of hearing of anyone. Her reaction had baffled him. He had always thought her the most reasonable of the family, which was why he had chosen to confide in her, yet here she was taking him to task. "You 'ave a temper I had not thought there," he said, taking her hand.

"Gerard, I entreat you to be sensible. You know the penalties inflicted. You must understand why I fear for you."

"I tell you, I do not get caught."

"Oh Gerard, I sometimes think you more of a child than Annie."

"I make much money. Annie is 'appy. I am 'appy. What could be better."

His friends were signalling to him that it was time for them to perform again, and she had to let him go. Gerard would always find favour and the guests were already clapping in anticipation of hearing him sing, but what if a time came when charm was not enough to carry him through life, particularly now he was taking chances with that life just to please Annie. It was this that made her feel sick at heart. With Joan and now Gerard, any interest she may have had in the festivities began to swiftly evaporate into the brooding blackness of Runnarth forest which up until then had never seemed threatening before. She had not wanted to share in such secrets. Why had he confided in her. Anger and resentment helped to deaden her fear, but who was she to confide in now that her mother and Peter were dead, and who was she to confess to if not Father Craven. In God alone must she trust.

"Mistress Venners, you are not dancing."

Snapped out of her reverie, she looked up to find Lord Elliston keenly eyeing her.

"My lord, I ..."

"In what dark regions are you travelling?" he mused. "You are certainly not here. Again, I ask you why you do not dance. Do not think to evade me Kate. First you are intriguingly engaged in furtive discourse with our most personable musician and then you keep a lone vigil with the night."

"The gentleman is my cousin's husband," she explained.

"I am not interested in your kin Kate. What I am interested in is your lack of spontaneity. My mama has resolved on everyone enjoying her little gathering and it is my purpose to see that they do. Obviously this is not the case with you," he quizzed, never relinquishing the scrutiny of his steady gaze. Not answering, her involuntary thought was how singularly attractive he looked.

"You stare Kate."

"Forgive me, my lord. I am not quite myself this evening."

"Which is all the more reason why you must be drawn out of yourself and forget what irks your soul, that is if you have one."

"My lord?" she questioned. He sometimes said the strangest things.

"I believe we are all supposed to be imbued with such, are we not?" Again, she did not reply.

"My dear Kate, you are too serious," he laughed. "Tis

Christmas, is it not?"

The revellers began the last dance to the accompaniment of Gerard's musicians.

"Come Kate, you will dance once this evening. I demand it."

Gerard was momentarily dismissed from her thoughts when she realised that he actually proposed engaging her as his partner.

"I do not know the steps, my lord," she said hurriedly.

"Nonsense. Follow my lead. I am no dancer, Kate. Just be inventive as I am."

She unconsciously backed towards the window, her fingers gripping the ledge.

"Mistress Venners," he charged, "I pray you to join me in this dance."

She could see he was in no mood to be denied and the music seemed warm and inviting.

"You have no escape Kate. Even you are not slender enough to squeeze through that aperture," he remarked, measuring her frame against that of the window's. "Come," he gently commanded, as if he understood perfectly her reluctance.

She placed her hand shakily in his as he led her away from her self imposed seclusion and into the midst of the festivities. The guests stared at her somewhat askance, but the dancing and the music soon made them forgetful. There was no doubt that his dancing owed more to invention than skill, but surprisingly she had little difficulty in following his lead, her own movements flowing in tune to the music. His ease of manner and ready smile made her forgetful of everything and everyone, even her own marked difference, and she found herself responding with a warmth of heart both new and different.

"You see, Kate," he said, out of breath, at the conclusion, "you are a much better dancer than you give yourself credit for. I thank you."

Joanna eyed her suspiciously as he went to rejoin her. The revels were ended. Lady Elliston was thoroughly exhausted and had to be carried to bed.

Catherine could not sleep. The various incidents of the evening fastened themselves on her mind and made rest impossible. Joan's predicament, Gerard's recklessness, Lord Elliston's marked attention to herself, that more than anything. Reason told her that he had singled her out because he knew that no one else would, but her heart wanted to believe differently.

Sir Edward Burgoyne and his wife returned to Runnarth in January, having spent Christmas at their family home in Durham. Since he had last conducted her to Lord Elliston, Catherine had not seen much of Burgoyne and his wife only fleetingly. Now he assumed a certain ubiquity, often being closeted with his master who appeared to hold his offices in some esteem. Lady Burgoyne was very tiny in relation to her husband and always appeared to be tiptoeing beside him, no doubt in an attempt to complement his stature. This gave her an appearance of condescension of which she was utterly innocent. If truth be told, she was completely in awe of him, looking upon him as a sort of demigod who was deserving of someone much better than she was. She could never quite understand what could have induced him to wed a woman so insignificant as herself when he had the choice of hundreds more deserving. What she failed to grasp was his practical good sense in the matter. All he asked for was a good and virtuous partner free from all womanly guile which in his experience led to all manner of problems. Pretty and provocative women were best reserved for youth, but when it came to the choosing of a wife it was better to stick to the plain and homespun variety. Reticent and undemonstrative, he was well pleased with his Margaret, and if only he had occasionally seen fit to apprise her of the fact she might not have been so lacking in confidence. As it was, she worshipped him in the knowledge of her own inferiority. When she became anxious or muddle headed in his presence he attributed it to her temperament and never to his own exacting high standards. Motivated by a sense of duty both to his family and Lord Elliston, he liked to think of himself as a kindly man, sober maybe but certainly not intimidating. The trouble was that he was virtually a man of no faults, in other words a man without measure.

Catherine found Margaret a little perplexing. One moment she appeared haughty and cool, another highly strung and nervous. "How is Lady Elliston," she would ask in grave rehearsed tones, and before Catherine gave out her reply she would have her next line ready and waiting, invariably ending "It is well," or conversely, "I trust she will be better ere long." These set phrases were a source of amusement to Catherine and of habitual annoyance to Joanna who loathed prevarication.

On a bleak day in February she would get to know her better. Unrelenting drizzle had taken the place of early morning sunshine; there were signs of the coming spring and a few birds were already making nests along the river, but the gathering of cloud soon hemmed them in again and once more it reverted to winter. Lady Elliston had kept to her bed, leaving Catherine to her own devices. Deeply engaged in examining her cures, the sudden interruption had taken her by surprise.

"I trust I am not disturbing you Mistress Venners."

It was Margaret looking rather wary and uncertain.

"No, not at all, Lady Burgoyne," she replied, quickly getting to her feet.

"Please, no ceremony Mistress Venners," she appealed.

Catherine asked her to be seated. It was the first time she had had occasion to study her properly. It occurred to Catherine that she could not be much above thirty, though Burgoyne was nearer fifty. The neatness of her person and her tightly coifed hair gave her an appearance of natural demureness.

"I see you are alone," she commenced. "It is well, but mayhap you have duties to attend to. I could return later if you desire it. Pray, accept my apologies."

Catherine, who had thought to be nervous, was completely taken aback. It would seem that Margaret Burgoyne was genuinely timid and very unsure of herself. Obviously those carefully rehearsed forms of address were a necessary foil to mask her feelings of inadequacy. Diffidence was something that Catherine understood only too well, and whatever she had thought of Lady Burgoyne initially was about to undergo a complete reappraisal.

"Lady Burgoyne, I assure you I am not unduly busy. Is there anything I can do for you?"

"Lady Elliston tells me how beautifully you read," she said with a view to procrastination, her eyes betraying her insecurity in their quick darting movements. "I often read to her too. She says it helps her to sleep."

The ambiguity of the statement struck them both, Catherine's warming smile melting away the woman's affecting shyness.

"How silly of me," she continued. Sir Edward is always telling me to think before I speak. And I really do try."

"On the contrary, Lady Burgoyne, I think you should ever speak freely."

"You are most kind Mistress Venners. No doubt, you are wondering why I am here. Having heard of your skills, I was wondering if you could cure me of a rash from which I suffer on occasions. Thankfully, it is not visible, but a great irritant nonetheless. I have tried other cures with little success. Sir Edward says it is my temperament, and I know I must be an awful burden to him at timcs. He is, as you know, such a fine man, and it is beholden upon me to be worthy of him."

It apparently cost her a good deal to admit to such failings, and made Catherine wonder if Sir Edward had any idea how much he was held in regard by his wife. With Burgoyne one had the feeling that without the slightest touch of vanity on his part he made the kind of unconscious demands that a woman like Margaret would see as intolerable burdens.

"I shall be pleased to help if I can, but first I must make an examination."

This was decidedly distasteful to Margaret, who detested the idea of being prodded and poked.

"Is there no other way?" she asked.

"No, I am afraid not," Catherine replied, though assuring her that she would be as gentle as possible.

"Then I suggest we get it over and done with," she said.

The rash she exposed was red and inflamed, and as Catherine surmised very itchy and flaky. She was confident she could cure it, but sorry that Margaret had gone on suffering so unnecessarily before she sought treatment.

"Take the potion twice daily and use the salve once a day but sparingly."

"You have been very understanding Mistress Venners, and I thank you."

The ordeal over, she seemed reluctant to leave. Her former hesitancy gone, she had need to talk a little and the more she talked the more Catherine came to like her, feeling that protectiveness towards her that had first attracted Burgoyne. She spoke of her two sons with great affection, trusting, of course, that they would take after her husband. At present they were in service to a highly placed family in Durham. She had travelled widely, including France and Flanders, and had once attended on Queen Philippa at Westminster. Moreover, she was an inordinate lover of books, this fact alone being enough to endear her to Catherine, who began to discover how little learning she had attained in comparison. Now completely at her ease, she listened with genuine interest to what Catherine had to say of her own family and the books she had read and those she still longed to read.

"Reading has been one of my greatest pleasures Catherine. I may call you Catherine?"

"Please do."

"You see, Sir Edward is often away and our sons left us at an early age, so books have filled what could have been many a dreary time. I cannot conceive of a greater blessing than the gift of reading letters." She suddenly stopped, blushing profusely. "I trust I have not talked overmuch Catherine. When I become interested, I do not always know when to stop. Sir Edward would tell you as much, so you must not be afraid to bid me hush."

"Not at all, Lady Burgoyne."

"You must come and borrow freely of my books. It would give me infinite pleasure to share them."

"Thank you, Lady Burgoyne. I should be delighted to do so." She got up to go, clutching the remedies to her, and then hesitated by the door, as if she wished to convey something, but did not know how.

"Tis a sad thing you have to bear," she eventually said. "I could not, but then you have much fortitude of spirit, a trait in which I am sadly lacking I fear."

"I would not say so, Lady Burgoyne. I trust you will soon find relief."

"I have every confidence in you, Catherine. Now you will remember to come and borrow of my books?"

"I will."

Back in the seclusion of her own spacious withdrawing room, Lady Burgoyne poured her first draught. She had eaten alone, Sir Edward still being in consultation with his master. Evening shadows gathered prematurely in the room amidst a flicker of candles, the rain buffeting against the walls in great icy streams. She decided to use the ointment later when there would be no chance of any interruption, not that she considered her husband in any way intrusive. God forbid that she should. He was a fine man, utterly dependable. Complain, she should not; no one could have asked for a better husband, always fair, always just, always honest, always, always infuriatingly right. The flames leapt and spluttered as if in accord with her thoughts. Stop this, she reasoned. Then she heard him, his step along the corridor. There was no mistaking it. Immediately she straightened herself, not that she had any cause to.

"You should not have waited, Margaret," he yawned, taking the weight off his legs and splaying them out to the hearth. Even he could dispense with decorum at times. "It has been a long day, too long by far."

"Shall I order supper?" she enquired.

"I have already supped with Lord Elliston. My God, the energy of the man amazes me. We have spent the whole of the afternoon assessing the annual dues, yet I fear there are still discrepancies to be dealt with. If only he would agree to attend for once, I believe it would make all the difference. If he does not, this will be the fourth year in which I have been obliged to act as his representative."

"Tis not fair, the way he expects you to take everything upon your shoulders," she sympathised.

"He is astute for all his apparent unconcern. Where the law is concerned, I doubt there is another man in the land knows more than he does."

"Then if he is so knowledgeable, tis meet that he should be in attendance."

"Maybe, maybe. He is a lonely man Margaret, I do know that, and I would not wish to change places with him, no indeed," and with that he took her hand and pressed it companionably.

"He has no cause to be lonely," she averred.

"Margaret!" he cautioned.

"Forgive me, husband. Tis just that you look so tired, and then he takes you away from me so often."

"Tis always the same at this time of year," he replied with irritating resignation. She knew it would be his reply; it had been for over ten years.

Lying beside her that night, she had told him every detail of her own eventful day, of how the Venners woman had given her a cure for her rash, of the sympathy she had exhibited, of their shared love of reading and of her promise to lend her some of her own books.

"Well," he had said reservedly, "I hope you know what you are about. Mistress Venners, it would appear, has made as marked an impression on you as she has on Lady Elliston, but a word of caution. Do not become too enamoured."

"Husband, I see you object," she said disconsolately.

"My dear Margaret, not at all. If she can cure you of that dratted irritation, well and good, but remember our position. She has no background to speak of. To be blunt, she has no known father, but if you find her company agreeable then I see no harm in it."

"Then I can continue to see her."

"Have I not said so," he yawned. "Now I really must get to sleep."

CHAPTER THIRTEEN

"Damn the blasted wind," he swore as another wreath of smoke wafted its way into the room. Stepping apathetically over the two dogs lying in front of the blaze, he kicked the half consumed wood and stood gazing into the flames.

He had spent the entire week assiduously assessing the annual rents and dues with Burgoyne and now he was heartily sick of it. Though it was unconscionably late, he was unable to sleep. He could have sought comfort with Joanna, but this had long lost its relish. Given time, he thought, there was nothing that did not eventually pall. Nothing whatsoever. His own position, for instance, was scarcely to be envied, though it was clear that his tenants thought otherwise. The feudal days of his forebears, once so sure and certain, were now long past and the slow erosion of the system had already commenced. Burgoyne recognised the fact as well as he did, but pragmatically kept to the system, which was why he made such a trusted adviser. As his mother had so frequently remarked, Sir Edward was far better at the task than he was himself and it frequently occurred to him that nobody would lose overmuch if he were to put the whole damnable place into his hands entirely; yes, why not, let it go to Burgoyne, or let it go to hell. What did it matter. Why should he care. But he did care. Otherwise what had prompted him to spend the greater part of that day in sorting out the petty concerns of his domain. That Burgoyne cared as much as he did also seemed to make it worthwhile. Sober, persevering, at times irrepressibly dull, he was a man he owed more to than most. If only Henry had lived he would not have had such things to weigh on his mind; as it was, he regarded himself as the proxy Lord Elliston, proxy by virtue of the fact that the rightful heir had died, but Burgoyne had been right to remind him, albeit tactfully, that it was four years since he had been in attendance at a rent day. He must attend this next one, duty if nothing else compelling some sort of obligation, but the thought of witnessing that wretched assembly paying homage sickened him. Why could they not understand how he hated their deference, their sham of servitude in case the little they had was taken away from them.

When he was younger and more idealistic he had naively tried to establish some sort of tenuous relationship with his peasants, but it was only too apparent that they could not regard him as anything other than an overlord to whom they were perpetually in thrall. A man of more patience might have persisted, but Elliston was not such a man. Accordingly he looked on his presence at rent days as serving no purpose, for once the business was concluded his tenants would walk away as if he had no other existence for them. It was this that irked him, that they could not see him as another human being with faults and feelings akin to their own. For all the notice they took of him, he might as well have been some heathen god to whom they yearly bestowed gifts to keep away bad fortune, and yet their lives, both his and theirs, were inextricably bound up in the land which they worked to their mutual benefit, or so he had been taught from his childhood. Despite his faults, he was a fair and reasonable overlord who refused to see the necessity for change in the order, but how could it not change when humbler men of vision began to question the values of a system that denied them the right to be free. As for the commuting of service on his land for a payment of money it set his teeth on edge, mainly because he was a lonely man to whom the practice seemed little short of betrayal. In truth, he was arrogant, little thinking that the freedom of his peasants was as vital to them as it was to himself, but it was an arrogance borne of fear more than feeling.

The hound at his feet whimpered as a spark caught its body, then lazily turned over and went back to sleep. The ease with which it slept made him sigh for some similar oblivion, whereas he mithered and mulled in the knowledge that the feudal days of his ancestors were being eroded and he felt powerless to prevent it. It seemed as if he was in danger of being Judas cursed, of being placated by a paltry piece of silver in exchange for a few strips of land, in effect a portion of that precious earth which had sustained both the high and the mighty, the humble and the poor. And what of his own place in the pattern. Removed from his tenants, hated by his mother, estranged from his wife, patronised by his mistress, he was more of an outcast than a supposed man of influence. For all the influence he actually wielded, he might as well have been a prisoner confined in a tower rank with ivy. Such were his thoughts as they drifted into the wavering glow, a cup of half drunken wine held idly in his fingers and threatening to spill its contents at any given moment. The flames were growing weaker and his eyelids were drooping. At the sound of the knock on the door, the cup slipped from his fingers with a clatter. Still half awake, he sat up, waiting to confirm that his senses had not deceived him and that this was not just part of some half forgotten dream, but indeed the world of substance come to plague him once more. Again the feeble sound echoed dimly through the room, the candles guttering forth despondent flickers of flame before the keen easterly wind extinguished their effort.

"Enter," he sighed.

Catherine entered, treading like air across the void, the candle light briefly highlighting the richness of her hair.

"Forgive me my lord, I had not realised the lateness of the hour."

"So it would seem Mistress Venners," he drawled, groping to find the cup, the fire having nearly gone out while he slept.

"Let me see to that," she said, picking up the vessel and placing it on the table. "I intrude my lord. I will leave you."

There being no reply, she was on the point of doing so when he sprang to his feet and motioned her to take his place.

"Pray, make yourself comfortable Kate," he said facetiously. "Is there anything I can get you?"

She could see he was in an errant mood, the wine only having increased it. There was no jest in the game; it was deliberately pungent.

"I perceive it is cold, my lord," she ventured, "and new candles would not be amiss."

"I see I am met with insolence," he rebuked. "You threaten to reverse the order Mistress Venners, a somewhat dangerous proceeding."

"I merely stated what I thought to be obvious, my lord," she replied, shivering, perhaps more alarmed at the icy temerity of her unconscious rebuke than the actual coldness of the room. Anyway, she could not see him properly and that was disconcerting.

"Let me remedy the defects of my sanctum," he said, his heavy outline kneeling before her to rake some life into the fading flames. She smiled at his efforts as another rush of smoke filled the room and made her cough. "To work Kate," he shouted, dragging her from the chair and resuming his erstwhile position. The pressure of his hands on her slight figure rather disarmed her, but the work of putting his demand into effect nerved her for the mission on which she had come. He gave her no indication of where the candles were kept, but she found them, and soon the room was filled with a more warming glow.

She had learned how to coax a fire into flame by watching Joan, and quickly remedied the situation, though all the while her heart thumped in great unsteady beats, knowing he was watching, scrutinising her every action.

"That will suffice," he said, as she knelt back to survey her efforts. "I have proof enough of your superior capabilities in housewifery."

"My lord," she acknowledged, turning to meet his eyes which blazed with the same intensity as the one steady flame.

"You remain cold, Kate?" he asked, almost gently now.

"A little, my lord."

"A little," he scoffed. "Get up. What in hell's name are you doing here anyway. I am tired. State your business and go. You are becoming a might presumptuous."

"I had no intention of presuming, my lord," she replied, flushing.

"I have offended you?" he enquired archly.

"No, my lord," she assured him, touching the mask that gave her the appearance of some ghastly apparition come to haunt him. She felt suddenly weary as well as cold and only too conscious of her disfigurement which sapped her confidence and left her feeling inadequate and of no consequence.

"Stop fingering that damned thing," he ordered. "It unnerves me."

The thought of him being unnerved brought the faintest of smiles to her face. She stood still, not knowing what to do or to say.

"I am listening," he said. "Proceed."

"I wish to speak to you of Joan Barton, my lord."

"Joan," he murmured, his eyes beginning to close.

"We worked together in the kitchen when I first came. There is a man, Watkins."

"Mm, I know of him," he yawned.

"Joan was very good to me, my lord, and Watkins ..."

"Has got a brat on her and will not take the blame," he interrupted. I take it I am right?"

"Yes, my lord, and ..."

"Wait," he cautioned, lifting his hand. "How fierce you are in your friendships Mistress Venners. I do believe you are suggesting that I arrange for him to marry the girl simply because she showed you a measure of kindness. Well?"

"I thought, my lord ..."

"Oh, stop thinking!" he roared, fully regarding her. "You really are presumptuous Mistress Venners. I take it you would now have me know of my responsibilities in the kitchen, let alone my oversights in the village. You are becoming a constant irritant in my flesh that refuses all balm. You are conversant with balms Mistress Venners? I seem to recollect my mother puts great store in you. Ever a misguided woman."

Fighting back the tears that trembled on her lids, she refused to be dismissively crushed by his scathing assessment of her abilities. It was this that really hurt, as it brought to mind her mother and Peter and how they had carefully prepared the herbs and blended them together in order of efficacy.

"I am a tyrant Mistress Venners. I see it in your eyes."

She could not speak and fixed her gaze on the floor.

"You are trembling at my vindictiveness?"

"No, my lord," she corrected, her voice partially breaking. "I am cold."

"Spoken like a veritable martyr," he laughed.

Another blast of wind and yet another of the candles gutted out. Getting to his feet, he swore roundly, stamping and blowing on his hands. Nothing could fight off a north easterly, he thought; it was relentless, like this wisp of humanity before him.

"I will see what can be done Kate. By the way, Burgoyne tells me how well his wife fares after using some concoction you prepared for her."

It was a veiled apology, but an apology nonetheless. Looking up she saw he regarded her with mock hostility, the corners of his mouth twisting into a wry smile.

"Thank you, my lord."

"No gratitude Kate. I am beyond being thanked."

Sinking back into the chair, he puzzled over this singular girl who dared to speak so boldly on behalf of another. Would that he had such friends.

CHAPTER FOURTEEN

She must have overslept. Otherwise, how account for the luminous light. Leaping out of bed, she ran to the window to discover that during the night the east wind had whirled down its late gift of snow, just at a time when everyone had thought that winter was over. It was this that accounted for the unnatural glare which had caused her to wake earlier than usual. It could not have come at a more inconvenient time, as this was going to be one of those precious days when she had planned to go home. Normally she adored the first snow fall. Now she hated it. If she had to postpone the visit, there would not be the likelihood of another for over a month. Cold with disappointment, she looked despairingly on the snowy stillness, the gathering drifts appearing to form a barrier against the hardiest of travellers.

"What a pity the weather has changed so Mistress Venners," Joanna remarked, feigning concern later that morning.

"It may not be quite so hazardous as it looks. I shall go and see before abandoning the idea," she replied, her voice hardly disguising the vexation she felt both with the weather and Joanna who, if anything, looked more lovely than usual. For the first time in her life, she was beginning to experience the indignity of a fierce jealousy.

"I would think it a vain hope at best," she replied, smiling faintly to herself.

Why does she ever better me, Catherine fumed, making her way to the kitchen where she remembered that there were some heavy shoes especially kept for such weather. At least there was one thing in her favour; she would not have Lady Elliston to contend with, for there was nothing like a bout of inclement weather to put her in a foul mood. That privilege would belong to the lovely Joanna!

She welcomed the heat in the kitchen, at the same time realising her good fortune in having escaped it. Joan and Watkins had left, Elliston, true to his word, having found them a similar if less onerous position at Sulburgh, one of his minor estates. Joan had been full of gratitude at the time, the kind of gratitude Elliston waived aside, though Catherine could not help but conjecture whether she herself would have been quite so joyful at the prospect of being tied to Watkins for the rest of her days. Did this gesture on Elliston's part owe something to herself? She would have liked to believe that it did, but her nature would not allow of such an avowal.

She grabbed at the first pair of shoes that came to hand without bothering to ask for permission. Anyway, they were all too busy to notice, apart from Maud who was desperately trying to attract her attention. A thin, cadaverous looking man, the antithesis of Watkins, now appeared to be in charge, though equally capable of exacting the same sort of obedience.

"Is that your new man," asked Catherine, moving to where Maud was employed in cutting pastry. Maud nodded. "Gracious, he is worse than Watkins," she whispered in her ear.

Maud tittered grotesquely, poor girl, clutching at Catherine's hands in obvious excitement, now and then pointing at her gown or touching her hair and smiling, smiling all the time. Like Catherine, she had her own cross to bear, but it was the affecting way in which she dealt with it that moved Catherine deeply. The girl had nothing to look forward to, no especial joy in store, but made the best of the little she had. If Craven's dictum to be satisfied with one's place in the appointed pattern was to be followed, then Maud was a worthy example. She certainly made Catherine feel very humble.

"I expect you miss Joan," she continued. Again the excited nod, the eager face of enquiry pressed towards her own. "I own it is good to see you again Maud."

In response she drew Catherine to her, pressing kisses on the exposed part of her face, tenderly touching the mask with her cheek, employing all the sensations of feeling and touch to make up for her lack of speech. The new man in charge walked towards them. He looked none too friendly.

"I best be leaving," said Catherine, afraid that Maud might suffer from her presence, but the mute appeared loath to let her go. Clutching her hand, she took her to the far end of the kitchen nearest the buttery, a rather gloomy area where many of them had previously slept. A line of roughly made pallets was ranged along the length of one wall, Maud indicating her possession of one of them by sinking proudly upon it. The coverings were coarse, but to Maud they were unaccustomed luxury. Could Elliston be responsible for this too; somehow she had to know.

"Maud, who has done this? Was it Sir Edward, the man who came to take me away?"

Maud nodded her answer. Then it was true. Employing Sir Edward as an intermediary, he must have taken note of what she said.

"It is fine indeed Maud. Somewhere to rest properly at last. No wonder you are pleased."

Maud positively beamed. It took so little to please her. They made their way back to the table without attracting too much attention. Thinking it an opportune moment to leave, Catherine went to the door, turning to wave to the girl as she left. Maud was still smiling.

Much to Catherine's annoyance, Joanna's prognosis on the weather proved only too right. The snow was several feet deep in places and it would have been foolhardy to attempt a walk of any distance. Instead, she read the book Margaret Burgoyne had leant her until late in the afternoon when winter's blood coloured sun faded away to a thin trail of pink, leaving the earth to go on sleeping beneath its blanket of snow. She too fell asleep. She was a child again, a child as she had been before the accident when existence was sweet and there was nothing to mar it.

Further snow fell and the earth was all but hidden beneath it until the last week in March when a great thaw began. Paths were churned to muddy streams and the river kept rising. Heavily laden skies discharged their pent up waters to add to the flood and there were those who spoke of a deluge sent by God. The days were dark and hueless, the rain lashing and slashing its way into the village until its inhabitants were knee deep in water. Rob and Matthew waded into the lean-to where the two Daisies stared up at them, their eyes dilated with fear. Father Craven offered up prayers, but the weather persisted. Loath to leave their homes for higher ground, they only did so when their lives and that of their livestock were at risk, and no sooner had they done so than came the much needed change in the weather. Weak sunlight revealed the devastation only too clearly, their precious strips of earth lying immersed beneath a newly made lake on which floated the bloated carcasses of lost and valuable livestock. But the waters were already receding and it became a matter of salvaging what little they could. Resigned but resilient, the task was done quietly and without complaint.

Capricious nature now smiled on them, sending warm suns to nurture the earth and protect their husbandry. Lord Elliston made good some of their losses and the work went on apace, for as Matthew so often said, "The land were like marriage; ye had to keep faith with it to reap of its benefits."

For Catherine it was a time of anxiety and guilt. Anxiety because the very turbulence of the flood separated her from all news of her family; guilt because within the relative security of the castle she was prevented from sharing their hardship. It was just a matter of waiting and praying, and it was only when Burgoyne was able to confirm that there had been no loss of life that she felt some sense of relief. With the snow, and then the flood, it had been over three months since her last visit.

The fine weather continued until rent day when an ill timed fall in temperature saw the arrival of a flesh cutting blast which caused everyone to shiver, apart from the likes of Maud who had the warmth of the kitchen.

Catherine was returning one of Margaret's books. She was greatly improved, Catherine's physic having cured her of her complaint. She enjoyed Catherine's visits very much, as did Catherine, and the books were becoming almost secondary to their friendship.

"Did you like it Catherine?" she asked.

"Very much. I marvel over the illustrations as much as the lettering. What a labour of love to have created such things. Sometimes I am almost afraid to touch it, for fear of doing some unintentional damage," she said, carefully returning it to its place.

"I am afraid you have all but exhausted my collection," said Margaret looking troubled.

"Then I can always go back to the beginning," she replied, seeing the look of disappointment in Margaret's face lest the lack of further books put an end to her visits.

"Why, of course. How very astute."

It was unbelievably draughty in the large apartment, Sir Edward preferring the minimum of flummery as he termed it. Fastidious in his personal attire, when it came to his living quarters he was positively Spartan. No tapestries adorned their walls to counteract the draughts, much as Margaret would have liked them, but as in all things she deferred to his superior judgement and tried to adapt her tastes to his. Had she told him of her preference, no doubt he would have heeded, but she kept silent, ever thinking he knew best.

"I do hope the rent day passes without incident Catherine. Sir Edward has worked very hard these past weeks. If only Lord Elliston would attend it would relieve him of much of the burden. Tis not as though he has much of import to occupy him at present, though I suspect he prefers other company to that of my husband's."

She paused abruptly as if to check the rash flow of words. Again she had forgotten to think before she spoke.

"I believe Lord Elliston will be present," Catherine replied. "Joanna said as much this morning."

"Does that ...", she hesitated, "woman know everything."

"I believe very little escapes her," said Catherine with a knowing kind of look.

"You are wise beyond your years," Margaret replied.

After Catherine had left she looked out on the windswept day where she could just discern her husband and Lord Elliston riding out to the manor, a small party of retainers in attendance. "Tis a wearisome life," she mused, drawing her mantle tightly about her.

Catherine was met in the corridor by Joanna who curtly announced that Lady Elliston was asking for her. She went immediately. The old woman was tossing and turning in an agitated manner.

"Tis my head Mistress Venners, forever spinning. Can you not do something to ease it."

Her tone was peremptory, the voice dry and brittle like the flesh in which it was cased. Since Christmas the light seemed to have gone from her, leaving but a dim and tremulous spark.

"My lady, I think you should try and rouse yourself. It is bad for you to lie in bed so much."

"Nonsense," she croaked. "It will kill me to get up in this weather. Do as I demand and fetch me some physic. You know the one I prefer."

"I will prop you up a little," she said, gently lifting her. Her arms were withered and fleshless, her fingers like the grip of a claw.

"I am helpless now Mistress Venners, completely helpless, and all he wants is my death. Yes, my death, nothing more," and two carefully rehearsed tears trickled down her cheeks. "You understand Mistress Venners! You understand!"

"You must not distress yourself Lady Elliston. Let me wash you again and re-comb your hair. I am sure you will then feel much better."

"Better," she sneered. "I have done feeling better. Bitter is what I feel Mistress Venners," she laughed. "Bitter not better!."

“Not easy ploughing weather my lord,” stated Burgoyne in an attempt to draw his master out of his sullen reverie.

“I am hardly interested in the vagaries of the weather, Burgoyne,” came the reply, whereupon silence was ensured for the remainder of the ride.

The steady clop of the horses hooves on hardened ground, the vicious caress of the wind on stony faced men and the mist laden sky made for an aspect of unrelieved greyness, dulling the spirit and making talk tedious. Burgoyne knew when to keep quiet. Having served Elliston for many years, he was only too aware of his extremes of temper. But, as Margaret was so fond of reminding him, now that he was over fifty maybe it was time to retire and make way for someone younger. That aside, he was a man of the utmost integrity. He enjoyed his work and found satisfaction in doing it well. He also liked Elliston despite his moodiness. Stretching his tall heavy frame in the saddle, he gripped the bridle and resolved on retaining his position while he was still capable of doing it.

Thin powdery flakes began to descend, and in spite of a weak and watery sun it remained bitterly cold.

“Here we are my lord,” he remarked, as they came in view of the village.

“So it would seem,” Elliston retorted, noting Burgoyne’s lack of gloves and his thin riding garb.

Never eschewing gloves himself, he clapped his hands together in an effort to keep warm. Burgoyne must have warmer blood than him was his thought. Even though he wore thick woollen tunic and hose and was draped from head to foot in a fleece lined cloak, he still managed to shiver. As a child he had always felt the cold keenly, so much so that his mother had accused him of having naught but girlish blood in his veins, unlike his brother Henry who never suffered from such neshness. His eyes showed bright in the rawness, his mouth feeling tight and sore. Dismounting, they walked briskly to the manorial hall where the selfsame rubicund bailiff who had taken Catherine away from her home still sat in judgement.

“My lord, you are most timely,” he obsequiously announced, bowing low before them.

“Stop your twittering Talbot and get on with it,” Elliston charged, sweeping past him into the hall and making straight for the fire. In front of the blaze stood a raised table bearing an assortment of delicacies and wine.

“I thought we would eat first, my lord,” Talbot said, fidgeting before him.

"How considerate Talbot," he replied. "We must not deprive you of your dinner, eh? Your constitution would scarce stand the shock."

The others looked at one another and smiled dubiously, all but Burgoyne who knew when a hearty laugh was called for. Elliston slapped the disconcerted bailiff on the shoulder.

"Quite so, my lord," he tittered like a naughty child.

☙ ❧

In the outlying fields the men had given up trying to plough, the earth refusing to yield to their labours. They were now cold and tired and not in any mood to meet with their bailiff. "God rot 'im," said one. "Take a lot to rot 'im," said another. Then there was laughter. It made everything seem more bearable.

Mary's belly was beginning to swell now and occasionally she fancied that she could hear the kick of her child, notwithstanding Annie's scornful glances whenever she told them.

"Annie, ye look well," remarked Matthew, bent over his bowl of pottage.

"Ay father, so I am."

"Such a beautiful gown too," said Mary, feeling the thickness of the material.

"Ay, ye are lookin' a right lady," Miriam agreed.

"What I'd like to know is where the money's comin' fro," questioned Rob, casting withering glances in her direction.

"If you must know," she pertly replied, "Gerard is becoming quite a gentleman."

"He is getting more commissions?" asked Mary.

"Ay, ye could say so," Annie gave out, rather too obliquely for Rob's liking.

"Ye mean he is singing now at bigger gatherins?" said Miriam.

"Yes, mother, he is. Did he not sing with his troupe at Runnarth Castle last Christmas. I would have thought Kate would have told you."

"To speak truth, we have not seen Kate since before Christmas."

"That does not surprise me," she scoffed, twisting her curls round her fingers.

"What mean ye by that?" Rob challenged.

"Naught, but what I say," she replied tantalisingly.

"Ye know it would hae been impossible for her to get here last February with the weather and that," Miriam put in.

"As good an excuse as any I suppose."

"Ye dunna know when to close ye mouth Annie," Rob charged.

"Enough!" interposed Matthew, asserting authority over his querulous family.

"You should not say such things Annie," whispered Mary.

"She danced with Lord Elliston, Gerard told me," Annie continued.

"Our little Katie?" said Miriam looking astonished.

"Yes, he asked her to. I expect he felt sorry for her."

"Why should he," charged Rob. "She's a fine girl our Kate."

"That's a mite cruel Annie," Miriam chastised.

"That's as maybe. I shall not say another word."

Rob eyed her suspiciously.

"Where is the money comin' fro' Annie?" he asked yet again. "Mind you tis not bad gold sister mine."

"What do you mean Rob?" enquired Miriam anxiously, seeing the look of alarm in her daughter's hitherto complacent features.

"Not to worry mother. I am just giving my sister a little brotherly advice."

"Keep it!" she said, suddenly rounding on him. "Ye be jealous because Gerard is so much more a man that ye'll ever be."

"Stop it at once!" shouted Matthew rising to his feet. "I'll hae no more on it."

Silence restored, they remained quiet until they had finished eating. Mary was going to see her sister Alice prior to Alice's husband Geoffrey becoming a freeman like Matthew. Alice was as excited as she had been over the birth of any of her children and she had a right to be, Geoffrey having saved many years for this moment.

"Ay, tis a good thing to only hae ye own land to think on," said Matthew. "And, mark me, there'll come a time when every man will pay a proper rent for his land and not be beholden for it to any lord."

"That's dangerous talk father," said Rob. "Who is goin' to work the lord's manor lands then?"

"They'll hae to hire labour of course," replied Matthew. "Ay, men who request a decent wage for what we've done for no thanks at all. I've seen such men, free roving men who travel the country demanding such work."

"I canna see it," said Rob.

"Ye are just old fashioned," charged Annie. "I believe he would like to bow and scrape to the Ellistons for the rest of his days."

"I dunna see it, that's all," said Rob, scowling at Annie.

"Ye dunna see anythin Rob!" she replied scornfully.

"Ay twill be a treat to see the look on Geoffrey's face as he hands o'er the money," Matthew intervened, determined to avoid any further squabbles. "Something I'd not miss, especially as I hear Elliston himself will be present."

Annie smoothed her gown. What dull, unexciting lives they led, she thought, when compared with Gerard and herself.

"Ay, the seasons come and go, that's one thing ye can rely on Rob. Ay, nature is a wondrous thing and we hae much to thank God for," Matthew reflected, unable to resist his penchant for weaving words of wisdom.

"Ye'll not be coming mother?" enquired Rob.

"No Rob. Annie and I will hae supper waiting when ye return. Annie, tis time ye saw what those two scamps o' yourn are up to. They've been gone a long time."

"They are hardy enough," said Annie, chewing on her nails. "Sons are best anyway, less trouble."

"I agree with you there," put in Rob, tweaking her ear. "Take care ye dunna come a fall Annie."

Mary's movements were becoming slower now her time was drawing near. Walking as briskly as she could in her condition and taking especial care not to slip, for the path remained treacherous, all her thoughts were of the coming child. The day had a keen and vibrant edge to it, just like the child inside her that would suddenly make her aware that it was alive and longing to thrust its way into the world. She patted her belly and smiled contentedly. Yes, thanks be to God for all of his blessings, even Mother Jomfrey she added, on seeing the old crone emerge from her hovel.

"Good day Mother Jomfrey," she said in an attempt to be affable. "How bitterly cold it is."

"The cold n'er hurt me," she maintained, the glint in her eyes made keener by the blast. "Ye'll be seein' ye sister, nae doubt. I hear Master Frincham hae his money to hand."

"Yes, that is right," she replied, wondering how the withered hag gathered her news with such speed.

"Ay," she laughed, a horrible grating laugh.

"I must be on my way," said Mary, feeling slightly flustered.

"Good day to ye Mistress Thompson. Take care. Ye'll bear a bonny babe ere long, God willin'," she muttered. "Ay, God willin'."

Mary walked on, rubbing her hands in a futile effort to dispel both the cold and the uneasy impression the old woman had left in her wake.

Alice was still in the throes of getting both herself and her husband ready for this most special of days.

"Geoffrey's countin' the money again, just to make sure," she said, lightly hugging Mary, whose condition prevented a fiercer embrace. "Ye've no idea how many times he's gone o'er it."

Mary could well imagine. Geoffrey emerged from the same dingy corner where Isobel had once tended his wife. He looked far less joyful than his wife, sheepishly smiling at his sister-in-law, his apple cheeks scrubbed to waxen rosiness and deepening to scarlet as Alice insisted that Mary take a good look at him to see that she had done her best to make him look bonny as she called it.

"You look very smart Geoffrey," Mary assured, trying hard not to smile, as the poor man fumbled self-consciously with the spotless brown tunic and tried to smooth his flyaway away hair which Alice had insisted he wash.

The five children were equally well scrubbed, the eldest, Walter, having grown into a great hunk of a lad whose strength of body did not, in any way, extend to his intellect. The three girls danced attendance on their mother who was rummaging under the bed to bring out a dilapidated box, the repository of all their worldly goods. The youngest scrabbled on the floor with the dog. Mary was then told to wait while she disappeared behind the partition with the box and her daughters.

"She's gettin' into 'er new gown," sighed Geoffrey in response to Mary's look of enquiry.

"Made it 'ersell too. Well tis what she wanted," he continued almost apologetically.

From the increase in activity going on beyond the partition, Mary began to wonder what to expect, particularly as Geoffrey seemed less than enthusiastic. In between the dressing, Alice kept up a flow of chatter, enquiring after the family one by one and wanting to know all about Catherine and how she was finding her duties at the castle. At last there was a pause.

"Are ye ready?" she said.

"Yes, I am ready," replied Mary.

Mary had never seen anything quite like it before and doubted if she would ever do so again. For a moment she was quite lost for words, as Alice swung round in the billowing tent of colour. Predominantly orange and red, the garish creation appeared more than capable of assuming a life of its own, and to make matters worse Alice had painted her face and pinned up her hair in a bobbing mass of coils. Her eyes were shining with that rare pleasure that happens only once or twice in a lifetime. She was in effect joy personified, the proud wife of a dearly loved husband, and it was not in Mary's nature to spoil her enjoyment. Even in the most perfect of natures there is always room for a little kindly deception and Mary was disposed to practice it now.

"You look very fine Alice, very eye-catching," she at last remarked.

"I knew ye'd like it. Mary always had good taste, dunna ye think so Geoffrey?"

Geoffrey merely nodded. Though resigned, he was evidently concerned as to what his neighbours would think. They still had an hour or more to wait, an hour in which Alice fussed and fretted and grieved that her eldest was so simple minded.

"He'll do," said Geoffrey, beginning to feel that growing anxiety of long pent up hopes about to be realised.

"Talbot, have those benches moved forward," Burgoyne demanded.

Talbot raised his thumb and a dozen lackeys rushed to do his bidding. Shivering visibly they fumbled to move the benches from the far end of the hall where great icy blasts of cold air blew in on them from the partially opened door. Elliston stood in front of the hearth, morosely kicking the logs.

"For the love of God, have this fire attended to Sir Edward."

"See to it," Burgoyne instructed the bailiff whose face was covered in sweat, which seemed faintly amusing considering the nature of the request.

Rows of rolled documents lay in front of them, the remains of the repast having been quickly removed.

"My eyes are not as good as they once were, my lord. Pray what says this?" asked Burgoyne in an effort to divert his master's growing testiness.

"Jomfrey. Fee three fowl, eggs one dozen. A fool could read it Burgoyne. Take care your brain is not getting addled. And, Talbot?"

"My lord?"

"Take that smirk off your face."

"No offence, my lord, I am sure," he twittered.

"But I am not!" he countered.

A few lowly cottars crept in from the blast, their faces purple with cold, their noses dripping.

"Everything would seem to be in order, my lord," said Burgoyne with an air of composure.

"Mm." His elbows on the table he scrutinised these, his lowliest tenants, who eyed him surreptitiously in return, though one or two of the women were bold and their looks far from modest. His like was rare among their kind. Matthew was higher in the scale of things than most of his neighbours, having already bought his freedom and had only really come for the purpose of seeing Geoffrey gain his. Many of them owed payment in kind and brought a variety of livestock which were penned outside in a pound, including frightened cows and recalcitrant pigs which tugged at their tethers. Hens were caged and brought into the hall amidst a cackle of feathers. Sacks filled with the produce of the earth were carried high on the shoulders of the men who had grown them, the women bearing heavily laden baskets as well as keeping an eye on the children. Everyone seemed to know their place in the pecking order without directions from those higher up it.

Geoffrey and Alice were the last to take their place, and for effect Alice could not have timed her entrance better, giving her neighbours ample opportunity to see her in all her billowing glory. Their whispering grew louder as she quite blithely took her place beside Geoffrey who was looking more like a man about to be sentenced than one to be granted his freedom.

"Who in God's name is that?" Elliston said in an aside to Talbot whose mouth was still agape at the apparition. Burgoyne leaned over. "I believe it is one Mistress Frincham," he elucidated, his left eyebrow slightly raised.

"The devil it is. I feel underdressed by comparison. What say you?" he smiled. "Talbot, wake up man," he ordered, closing Talbot's mouth for him, much to the amusement of everyone assembled. Matthew and Rob signalled their encouragement to the Frinchams who sat a few rows behind them with Mary who was looking distinctly self-conscious. "Poor Mary", Rob whispered "I bet she wishes she'd hae sat along with us."

"No wonder," grunted Matthew. "The woman must be off 'er head to come dressed like a common mummer."

Elliston yawned, his eyes growing heavy with gazing at the spectacle of Mistress Frincham's gown. Talbot, slightly discomposed, rose from his chair to formally open the proceedings. A cow mooed its reply from outside giving rise to laughter from the rear of the hall.

"Silence," commanded Burgoyne. "Remember where you are. This is not a fair."

The chatter ceased as he methodically arranged the documents in order of priority. He preferred to deal with the lowliest tenants first, for they were easier to keep a check on and had little to say. Their paltry tributes being deposited, the bigger ones rapidly followed, Talbot having checked the inventory against each item, including the livestock outside. There being no discrepancies, they quickly turned to more pressing matters.

"John Day," called Talbot.

"Ay sir," said a scraggy man springing bolt upright at the sound of his name and nervously fingering his cap.

"I have it here that you omitted to work two days on your lord's domain. Yea or nae?"

"Well sir, it were just ..."

"Yea or nae," boomed out Talbot, his face reddening from the heat of the fire behind him.

"Yea," the man replied looking completely crushed.

Elliston leaned over to whisper something in Burgoyne's ear.

"A moment Talbot," Burgoyne interrupted. "Let the man speak."

Talbot looked clearly put out, but had to abide by the overruling.

"It were like this, my lord," said the man hurriedly, his surprise at being given the opportunity to speak quite unnerving him. Elliston raised his hand.

"Cease," said Burgoyne, whereupon the poor man sat down again.

"Tell the dolt head to speak more slowly and to take his time," said Elliston. "We are in no hurry I take it?"

"John Day, stand up. "My lord requests that you take your time to explain the reason for your absence."

Day gripped his cap more tightly still and began again. "The wife were expecting 'er first. She were taken badly. I couldna leave 'er."

There was a hub of discourse round the hall followed by some unpleasant tittering.

"It was a difficult confinement then?" asked Burgoyne.

"Beggin' ye pardon sir?"

Elliston stood up. "What my learned friend meant to say, only he speaks so clumsily, (now it was Sir Edward's turn to be put out) was if the birth was a hard one."

"Oh, it were sir, I mean my lord." The faint muttering ceased in their growing attentiveness to the richly resonant tones of their lord's voice. He had that rare quality of being able to hold a crowd without having to shout above it.

"And it was so bad that you neglected your duties to me for those of your wife?"

Day bowed his head.

"Well?"

"I couldna think o' anythin' else at the time only 'er, my lord."

"Spoken like a man John Day. What would you suggest as an acceptable fine?"

Day said not a word.

"The man ought to be lashed," grumbled Talbot.

"This is all a little untoward, my lord, if I may make so bold," put in Burgoyne.

Ignoring them both, Elliston continued. "I propose John Day that you work the two days you owe me when you see fit, but within the next month. How does that suit?"

"Very well, my lord. I thank ye kindly."

The tenants were as surprised as Day. If he was going to prove this lenient, they hoped he would come more often. Further hearings followed, those concerning boundaries, the straying of cattle and the encroachment of weeds; Burgoyne meted out fines, Talbot collected them. Consideration had to be given to the seasons, when to plough and when to leave fallow and the days to be allotted to work on Elliston's lands. It all took time and patience.

As the transactions became increasingly drawn out, Elliston noticed an old woman beginning to sway unsteadily on her feet at the back of the hall.

"Burgoyne, cannot that woman be seated."

"Not unless someone is willing to give her a seat my lord."

"If I did not know you better, Sir Edward, I would say you were afraid."

Undeterred, he now demanded that the woman be given a seat, but since she was only a cottar no one seemed willing to oblige.

"I am waiting," he said, eyeing them acutely.

"I will," said Rob in a firm tone, though Matthew was pulling at his sleeve. Matthew had bought his freedom and for Rob to give up his seat for such as a cottar was demoralising in the extreme.

"Good man. Your name?"

"Rob Thompson, my lord."

"Thompson? The Thompson whose cousin works at my castle?"

"The same, my lord."

Burgoyne was a little taken aback. After all, none of this was hardly relevant to the proceedings in hand. He waited, however, while Rob assisted the woman to his erstwhile seat where she collapsed all of a heap next to Matthew, who continued to fume, albeit under his breath. Thereafter, there followed a lengthy debate on matters relating to the land in general as Talbot grew hotter and hotter.

"I think we are about at an end, my lord," Burgoyne intimated, wiping his brow as the fire blazed on behind them. Only Elliston was warm and comfortable.

"Frincham," at last called Burgoyne.

Alice squeezed her husband's arm. "Now ye remember to speak in a good bold voice."

"Ay, that be me," said Geoffrey, fumbling to readjust the neck of his tunic which was cutting horribly into his neck.

"Your dues, please, Frincham."

"Well it be so as I hae a different kind this time, sir."

"Different!" thundered Talbot. "What insolence is this?"

An upstart tenant was all he needed to complete his day. Frincham's neighbours shuffled uneasily on the hard wooden benches, straining to catch each word, for this they must not miss.

"Tis not insolence, my lord," said Alice jumping to her feet and looking like a virago straight at Elliston. Always go to the top for results was Alice's motto. Mary tried to urge caution, Walter sitting beside her like an inert clod of clay.

"What is it, then, Mistress Frincham?" Elliston enquired, brooking no interference from either Talbot or Burgoyne.

"Ye tell 'im Geoffrey," she commanded, promptly sitting down again.

Geoffrey went red and white by turns, and then an awful sickly grey as he stammered out what should have been the supreme moment of his life.

"Tis here, my lord," he said, bringing out the small pouch of coins from his tunic. "I hae saved it for to be a freeman."

"Come forward," ordered Elliston, his face noticeably darkening as Geoffrey walked towards the platform, his hands clammily clutching the purse. "Count it Burgoyne."

Burgoyne counted. The silence was dreadful. Mary looked for Rob who smiled faintly in her direction.

"He has the required sum, my lord," announced Burgoyne "as laid down in your lordship's written agreement."

"Tis an old document, is it not Burgoyne?"

"It is five years since it was written, my lord."

"Then it is out of date, would you not agree Talbot? He knew where to look for support, thought Burgoyne, as the bailiff heaved and sweated out his cringing reply.

"Tis mightily so, my lord," he vouchsafed.

"What do you propose, my lord?" Burgoyne enquired.

"I propose that as of now the sum be doubled."

"Doubled!" was the ghastly response from his tenants. Frincham, devastated by this unexpected blow, could only stare in horror. Why, why, after all the scrimping and saving. It was his day. They were all there watching him. Alice, Walter, Mary, the Thompsons.

Burgoyne had been expecting something of the kind. Now that it had actually happened it would give him the opportunity of trying to reason the matter out with Elliston.

"My lord, this is hardly fair," he whispered. "You cannot make rules in passing as it were. They require to be written down."

"Then have a new document made up," came the forthright reply, which was meant to be heard.

"Pray, calm yourself, my lord."

"I am perfectly calm Burgoyne, only a little tired of the petty obstacles you seem to put in my way."

"If we might discuss the matter in private," he replied, noticing how Talbot was leaning over to hear them. Elliston agreed, leaving Talbot to continue as well as he could.

They walked to the edge of the common where a group of children were playing blind man's buff, oblivious of who they were or what they represented.

"I am your lord and master Burgoyne. You seek to override your authority."

"I am only thinking of your own good, my lord."

"My own good!" he spat out, digging his heels in the earth.

"I speak as your friend and adviser. I know full well your feelings on the matter, my lord, but we have a written law than a man is entitled to purchase his freedom and Frincham is perfectly within those rights."

"And as his overlord, I have the right to raise the fee. Men have always worked my land. It is a tradition and a necessary one. Do I not treat them reasonably? They have holy days a plenty and I do not exactly stint them of food during the term of their labours on my behalf. What more do they want?"

"A precious commodity, my lord. They want to own their own land. Try and put yourself in Frincham's place. Imagine how he must have scrimped and saved for this moment. Years of toil and deprivation."

"Deprivation be damned Burgoyne! You speak like an itinerant rebel. Go waive your pike at the head of the mob. Support them if you must. As you infer, I am defunct, useless."

"Far from it, my lord. I simply acquaint you with the facts. Times are changing."

"For the worse."

"Not necessarily so, my lord. There is such a thing as labour for hire."

"Filth. Scum of the earth. Men of no ties and no loyalty. Would you have me engage such."

"I merely speak ..."

"No compromise!"

"But my lord."

"I will hear no more," he said, swinging round on his heels.

Burgoyne thought a moment and then went in pursuit. Forgetting the iciness of the ground, he suddenly slipped, sprawling to the ground in an ungainly heap.

"My lord, I pray you wait," he cried helplessly.

Looking back, Elliston immediately retraced his steps.

"My dear old friend" he said, pulling him to his feet. "You must not get yourself in such a pother. I trust you have taken no harm?"

Sir Edward, looking slightly mollified, brushed the frost from his mantle and readjusted his cap.

"No, I think not," he replied somewhat crustily.

"My apologies Sir Edward. I am to blame. Pray, continue."

"I have forgotten where I was."

"Hire of labour I believe," he laughed, noting a tear in the sleeve of Burgoyne's sleeve where it unfortunately showed.

"Yes, yes, but putting that aside for the present, you must see that doubling the sum is unreasonable."

"But then when was I ever reasonable."

"Perhaps a quarter of the sum beyond that already collected, my lord?" he hazarded, holding the gash in his sleeve. "Poor man, I feel for him."

"I had noticed Sir Edward. You are getting soft with your increase of years. I will have to watch you. Howsobeit, I will let your superior counsel guide me in the matter. Anything to get out of this cold."

They re-entered amidst a babble of talk which instantly ceased as they ascended the platform.

"Frincham," said Burgoyne in the kindliest manner possible. "As my lord says, the prescribed sum is rather out of date, and as of this day it is proposed that it be increased to a quarter beyond what it was. I shall have a new document drawn up to such effect."

A muted sigh of surprise could be heard throughout the hall.

"Therefore, my good man it behoves you to be patient a little longer. Then, on Lord Elliston's word of honour, the freedom you crave shall be yours. Give him back the money, master bailiff."

Geoffrey, face bowed to the ground, a muffled if impotent protest on his lips, walked back dejectedly to his seat. It would take him at least another year or more to collect the additional amount.

"Tis wicked and them that makes the law are wicked," shouted Alice.

"Who speaks treason!" roared Talbot.

"I did!" retorted Alice springing to her feet before Mary or Geoffrey could stop her.

"Sit down Talbot," Elliston sighed. "You look ridiculous."

Talbot did as he was bidden, feeling humiliated.

"Always speak well of your husband Mistress Frincham," Elliston continued. "Few women do, but I shall not change my mind."

This was followed by a few loud guffaws from the men which helped to lessen the tension.

"We'll hae the money come autumn, my lord," Alice said bravely before resuming her seat.

"Ye'll ne'er get the money," Mother Jomfrey cackled. "Maybe if ye had nae bought that flouncy creation ye would hae had a little more to spare."

"Who spoke thus?" asked Elliston.

"I believe it was that old besom Jomfrey," replied Burgoyne.

"Bring her forward."

Mother Jomfrey was unceremoniously thrust to the front of the hall.

"You have a viper's tongue for a woman of your years Mother Jomfrey. Guard it well. Your outward glee at another's misfortune will cost you a fine."

"I am a poor woman, my lord."

"I agree. Poor in character. Burgoyne see that one fowl is brought to me now."

Orders were given to Mother Jomfrey's son who, cursing his mother, returned with the struggling bird.

"Give it to your mama," Elliston commanded. There was much conjecture as to what would transpire next as the old hag's fingers dug into its feathers. "Mistress Frincham, come forward."

Alice, surprised by the summons, straightened her own vivid plumage, and stood before the platform.

"Mother Jomfrey, give the bird to this noble dame. I trust it will be a lesson to you."

Never was there such uproar at a rent day. No one had ever got the better of the old witch before. It was rare. It was fun. For all his disappointment, even Geoffrey was smiling as Alice took her prize.

CB ED

"Thank God that is over," said Elliston, whipping his horse to a faster pace.

"You were a success my lord. Did you not see it on their faces. You made them laugh?"

"I was ever the man for a jest," he retorted, his face set and stern.

CHAPTER FIFTEEN

Bardwick had been spared the worst of the recent floods, but the legs of Annie's precious new table were tarnished and no amount of rubbing could cure it.

"I will buy you another, Annie," Gerard promised. "Your mother and father, they suffer more I think. We must think of them, yes."

"I do think of them Gerard," she half heartedly replied, gazing at herself in the new gilt edged mirror he had bought her. For once in her life, she had everything she had ever wanted, fine clothes to show off in, elegant furnishings which were the envy of her neighbours and a husband whom she adored in her own selfish way. The boys were not so much of a problem either now she was able to keep them from interfering with her comfort by giving in to all their demands. Of right and wrong, she taught them nothing, but then she had the excuse of knowing so little about such things herself. If she gave any thought at all to the source of their sudden good fortune, she conveniently closed her mind to it, and since Gerard never volunteered such information she chose not to ask him. It was so much simpler to enjoy the present than to think of the future. Much as she wanted to, however, she could not completely close her mind to the fact that whatever Gerard was doing to supply all her wants, it must entail risks. Rob had hinted as much, and she was aware of murmurings amongst her neighbours. Gerard's new found occupation was also nocturnal and occasionally he had arrived home with the smell of blood on his clothes, animal blood it was true, and this in itself was a warning she ought to have heeded, but still she kept silent. Anyway Gerard was clever, he would never get caught, or so she chose to believe. It was true that he was becoming more tense, less inclined to talk and at times noticeably subdued. She no longer feared the threat of other women. The danger inherent in the new work made him want her more than ever, sometimes feverishly so, but once their passion was spent he would become quiet and withdrawn.

"I shall be away again tonight ma cherie," he said.

"Oh, Gerard, not so soon again."

"I am afraid it is so. This new job, it make demands, as you do."

"I only demand that you stay here with me."

"Now you know that is not true," he teased, brushing her hair with his lips.

"Gerard?" she ventured, feeling a slight nip of conscience. "This work you do. It is not dangerous is it?"

"Nothing to trouble your head over," he laughed.

If only then she could have told him that none of it mattered in relation to his safety and the love she bore him and that now she had more than sufficient to make her happy he had no need to undertake any further risks on her behalf, but Annie would never have enough, greed and love of self making her reckless.

When he told her of the necessity of carrying a knife, she did not ask him why, but happily got him one and then insisted that the letter "G" be engraved on the handle to make it more distinctive, and because of his love for her he was willing to take the foolhardy step of engraving it himself, added to which there was a certain excitement in tempting the fates.

☙ ❧

It was after Easter before Catherine was able to return home. She had a lot of news to catch up on, including all the happenings at the rent day and the nature of the fine meted out to Mother Jomfrey because of her viperish tongue. That it was at the instigation of Lord Elliston himself made it of even more relevance, to Catherine at least. But when they turned to sounding her out on Annie's increase in prosperity, she was aware that she had to proceed with caution by pretending to know as little as they did. She hated the deception, but was left with no other choice.

Miriam showed her the cures she and Mary had prepared in accordance with her directions, Miriam always being anxious to make sure that they had done everything properly. In her aunt Catherine recognised something of Margaret Burgoyne, equally able, equally uncertain. She then showed them the more complicated cures she had been able to make up herself, but from what they told her it was apparent that Mother Jomfrey was continuing to exert an unwholesome influence. Being humiliated at the rent day had not improved her character and from some twisted notion she blamed it all on Catherine. But she would always hate Catherine, just as she had hated her mother, simply because they had dared to show her up for what she was. The old hag had now resolved on a new tack of getting her own back. Instead of going out to confront her, as she had done in the past, she would keep a close eye on her comings and goings and strike when Catherine was least expecting it. Anticipating revenge was somehow sweeter. She was watching now as Catherine started on her return journey.

"The vile-visaged bitch," she cursed, as Catherine walked past.

"Why dunna ye leave 'er be?" said her son, breaking into a hollow cough which racked his skeletal frame and brought an unnatural rush of colour to his face. His wife handed him a blood stained piece of rag and pressed it to his mouth. A thin trickle of blood oozed on to it.

"And what good are ye as a son," she whined, loathing evinced in her eyes. "Ye canna do a day's work, and as for her! Where's the grandchilder she promised me. Barren, that's what she be, not that ye be likely to get 'er with child."

Pointing her grimy fingers at them, she took her stick and tip tapped to the fire. Sat still in her chair with a corpse like inertness, she broke into a kind of meaningless sing-song, the steady creak of the chair as it rocked to and fro keeping time to the plaint.

The woman at the table cradled her head in her hands, faintly sobbing. The man, his violent coughing spent, reached out his hand to touch at her hair.

"Ye hae an evil tongue mother. What did his lordship say, a viper's tongue. Aye, that's what ye hae, the tongue o' a serpent. As for ye physic, ye may as well keep it for all the good it's done me."

The woman suddenly ceased crying. Raising her head, wretched defiance in her face, she gripped him by the hand and turned the scorn of her feeling fully on his mother.

"Ye speak truth Luke. She hae no skill but what feeds on fear. Why not ask Catherine Venners for a cure."

Mother Jomfrey continued to sing on as if oblivious.

Made brave by his wife's courage, he pressed out his hands on the table and bore himself up, a breathless choking sound being the cost of his effort.

"Ay I may well do just that," he threatened, staring at his mother.

For answer he was met with a derisory fit of laughter.

"Ay, ye do that Luke," she cackled. "Ye do that and perhaps she'll cure yon bitch too."

The effort had cost him too much. He slumped back in his seat and look despairingly at his wife. Their helplessness overwhelmed them. The fire crackled and the old woman hummed.

"Feeling better already my son," she eventually remarked, turning her face contemptuously upon them.

ᏟЗ ᏋᏅ

She was not disposed to hurry. Besides it was a day made for idling when nature gives of her best and demands to be enjoyed, so she threw back her head and rejoiced in the warmth of the sun on her face. Normally, she would have devoted part of her visit to seeing Craven, but she was not sufficiently in command of her feelings to withstand such an interview. There was simply too much to confess, not only the secrets she was keeping on behalf of Gerard and Joan, but also her own deep rooted secret which she refused to acknowledge even to herself. The possibility that Craven's icy logic might find it out and lay bare her soul was far too unnerving a prospect. Moreover, if she wished to confess or ask for spiritual counsel there was always the accommodating priest at the castle and in effect she need never see Craven again, but she knew that this was merely a means of appeasing her conscience and that ultimately she would seek Craven's guidance.

The castle looked almost serene in the full flood of sunlight. From the courtyard came the sound of horses hard ridden and she guessed that Lord Elliston had taken advantage of the weather. Doubtless sunny hours brought out sunny moods. She wished it could always be so, the window in her room framing the view and likening it unto an illuminated picture she had seen in one of Lady Burgoyne's precious books, all brightly depicted in blue, green and gold. She had collected a few early spring flowers and was arranging them when Joanna entered.

"You have at last chosen a propitious day Mistress Venners," she said, the bold beauty of her features enhanced in the full rush of light.

"Yes, I am fortunate."

"You are indeed," she agreed, a wealth of innuendo in her tone. "It is Lady Elliston's wish to rise on the morrow."

"I shall be pleased to see her get out of that bed. It is not good for her to lie in it day after day. Do you think a few of these flowers might cheer her."

"Maybe," replied Joanna, scanning the blooms with a look of indifference. "By and by they will die, but then nothing of beauty lasts forever, is that not so Mistress Venners?"

"I really cannot say," said Catherine, rather disturbed by the strangeness of the remark.

"No, I suppose not, but then why should you," she retorted,

fixing her brilliant blue eyes on Catherine's masked and distorted features. It was true that the barb was directed at Catherine, but it was also double edged, in that it was equally applicable to herself, and judging from Joanna's expression Catherine gathered that it was intended as such.

☙ ❧

She was awakened early next morning by the clatter of horse's hooves amidst a general melee of raised voices, commands and counter commands.

"I want all ready by tomorrow," Sir Edward's imperious voice could be heard above the rest. "Lord Elliston desires to leave at first light." Leaving. How terribly final the word seemed. Her room not commanding a view of the courtyard, it was futile to rush to the window. She hastily washed and dressed. It was too early for her to commence her duties, and yet it was impossible to go back to sleep. Failing to notice the glory of the newly risen sun, she found herself shivering, notwithstanding the early morning glow that crept into her room and made even more golden the petals of the captive marigolds. Why should the notion of him leaving so perturb her. Was he not her lord and master and entitled to do whatsoever he pleased. If he left forever, it was no concern of hers, she told herself, staring blankly at the sun washed floor.

☙ ❧

"I want to get up this morning Mistress Venners," Lady Elliston announced with some determination.

"Yes, my lady," she replied absently, her usual concentration lacking as she busied herself to little avail.

"Mistress Venners, you are pulling my hair. Do please attend to your duties. You are uncommonly clumsy this morning."

The few sharp words had their effect as she raised the old lady to her feet and helped her to dress. The heavy purple gown hung on her ever thinning frame and Catherine had to girdle it tighter still. Gently combing the sparse strands of her hair, she thought of Joanna, the eventual cloying of all beauty and the futility of the issue in regard to herself.

"Ouch. Do be careful Mistress Venners."

"I am sorry my lady."

"Your day off seems to have had a peculiarly adverse effect upon you. I should refrain from picking flowers if I were you."

This, then, was her gratitude for the flowers; at least, Joanna must have given them to her, although they were nowhere in evidence. Tottering unsteadily to a crimson covered chair, the old lady took up her mirror and stared into it to gauge the effect of Catherine's handiwork.

"I look on my own ghost Mistress Venners," she laughed, but not unpleasantly. "I was once – ah well, that was long ago. A little more rouge I think."

Catherine dabbed it on, trying to make it look as natural as possible.

"That will do," she said, the voice rasping and cracked, but all the nobility of her breeding still intact.

Unexpectedly there was a rush of cool air as the door was flung open to reveal the object of all Catherine's thoughts and, incidentally, the cause of all her apparent distraction.

"Ah Mistress Venners, I see you have done excellently as usual," he glibly remarked, surveying both herself and his mama.

"I can do without your observations," Lady Elliston countered, eyeing him with brittle countenance.

"Quite, that is why I came. I therefore propose ..."

"You propose!"

"Yes, Mama, I propose," he firmly continued, winking at Catherine, "that you sit in your favourite herb garden. I take it that is what you would wish?"

"I wish for you to leave me alone."

"And so I shall, and sooner than you think, for now that the weather has taken a turn for the better I intend to leave for Sulburgh."

"Go by all means," she sourly retorted, smiling grimly to herself, though the notion of a lengthy separation failed to fill Catherine with any similar surge of joy. Rather did it fall as a sudden shower of rain on a sheep shearing, totally unforeseen and blotting out all sense of pleasure at a stroke. Could he see what she felt. She trusted not. At least, she was reasonably satisfied that her features, rigid as they were, betrayed nothing of her inner emotion.

"Mistress Venners, help me into the garden," she requested, choosing to ignore her son who yet lingered.

"Mama, I shall require Mistress Venners to accompany my party. We have need of extra hands, and what is more it will give Mistress Venners a chance to view the sea. You would like that, would you not Kate?" he asked pointedly.

"Mistress Venners stays here," Lady Elliston objected. "I have need of her. She alone knows how to dress me correctly and attend to my ills. I will not be deprived of her services."

Catherine stood aside, little flattered and barely amused as they continued to wrangle over her fate.

"You are unreasonable Mama. Lady Burgoyne can supply you with a waiting woman."

"Lady Burgoyne is a fool! She lets her servants do as they please," she maintained, her hands flying at him excitedly.

"All the better. You can teach them how to behave. Can she not?" he quipped, turning to Catherine.

"It is not for me to say, my lord," she replied evasively.

"Tactful as ever Kate. I have spoken. You shall come to Sulburgh where, incidentally, you have friends I believe."

"My lord?"

"A certain Watkins and his spouse. I take it you remember them, especially since you spoke so boldly on behalf of that spouse." Forgetting her shyness, she smiled up at him in recollection.

"You see Mama, she is pleased at the prospect. A poetic nature should not be denied a glimpse of the ocean. It will please us both."

"Choose Mistress Venners," she cried in frustration.

"There is no choice!" he threw out. "Tomorrow Mistress Venners accompanies our party. I have decided." And with that he left them.

Comfort her as she would, Lady Elliston refused to be placated and what should have been a pleasant retreat to her garden became an arbour of discontent which she vented on poor Catherine remorselessly.

Joanna had told her to be ready by first light, and she spent much of the evening in packing what seemed most appropriate for a journey whose distance was hard to determine, since she had never ventured further that the environs of Runnarth and Bardwick in her life. It was this sense of ignorance, coupled with Joanna's supreme condescension, which threatened to spoil her initial enthusiasm. It also gave rise to delusion and doubt. For one thing, she refused to see his insistence on her accompanying them as anything other than a ruse, and a spiteful one at that, to deprive his mother of her care. If this was true, then she was simply being used and his motives were base. But were they? It was safer to think so, rather than have her vulnerability exposed, which would be akin to having the make-do piece of linen torn from her face and leaving her devoid of any refuge. In a word, she permitted self-pity to colour her judgement.

Joanna draped her gown over a chair and proceeded to brush at her hair with vigorous and irritable strokes. Within the adjoining room Elliston drew on his night robes and waited.

"What took you so long?" he casually remarked.

"I am ready now," she coolly replied, slithering her body beside him. "Why bring the Venners woman?" It was less of a question and more of a charge.

"Why not?" he replied. "Does she not deserve a change of scene as well as you?"

"She annoys me with her wretched face and her ingratiating ways with your mother."

"I do not find her ingratiating. You make too much of it. As for mama, she pleases her, and that is rare."

She reached to embrace him; they kissed hard and long. An obsessive need devoid of tenderness was the nature of the passion that bound them. It was the only kind of love he had known.

Catherine tried to sleep, but her mind was too active for rest. The mask was removed, lying like a dismembered part of her body at the edge of the pillow. Usually it was the one time of day when she was least conscious of her disfigurement. The darkness to her was a friend, an opiate of nature designed to soothe, not to frighten. But that night was different. The moon was a full one, filling the room with a ghostly kind of light, and causing her to cower like a child beneath the sheets. It felt intrusive, like an actual physical presence, from which there was no place to hide. Seeming to be all around her, she began to finger the scars, deriving a sort of vicious pleasure from tracing the extent of the ill disposed pattern until she could stand it no more, and called out on God to forgive her self pity. Intervals of restive sleep brought terrifying dreams in which Joanna knelt at her bedside and railed at the cloying of everything beautiful, but it was not the real Joanna but some dreadful mutation that threatened decay and disease. "No!" she screamed herself awake. A strand of hair was tightly wound round her neck, her body bathed in streams of perspiration.

Afraid to sleep again, she lay waiting for the dawn. When it finally came she was beset by a numbing tiredness that dulled all other emotion as, heavy eyed, she gathered up her bundle for the forthcoming journey. Lack of sleep had robbed her of any sense of anticipation or excitement. A mass of people thronged the place where she stood, but she gazed on it all with an abstraction born of sleepless inertia. Before she could collect herself she was unceremoniously dumped, both body and baggage, on a rickety cart which brought up the rear of the never ending procession. The sudden lurch of the cart at last brought her to her senses, which was perhaps as well as Margaret Burgoyne had come to give her a book to read on the journey. There being no time in which to properly thank her, her gratitude was expressed in a feeble wave of her hand as the tiny figure of Lady Burgoyne receded into the distance. No one else shared the cart, only herself and a mountain of baggage, plus a taciturn driver who only paused to mutter impatient oaths to the horses in his charge. By seven the sun blazed forth to set its optimistic sheen on the party. Feeling more awake than before, she fully intended to take note of the journey, but with the sun in her eyes and the lumbering motion of the wheels she was gradually lulled into sleep, a restful kind of sleep that was only too welcome after her night of unrest. Only the sudden halt awoke her. The driver informed her that they were to rest for an hour, but no more. She had not thought to bring anything in the way of refreshment with her, and rather than jostle for what was on offer along with the others she decided to wander. They were perched on a plain, high above a wooded valley from which they had made their ascent; virtually treeless and covered in broom, its colour blended in with the sun and seemed just as expansive. Careful to keep the distant babble within earshot, she kept to the edge of the path and gazed down on the thickly wooded landscape, half mindful of Gerard as she did so. She had not gone far when her progress was interrupted by the pounding of hooves. Without turning, she knew who it was.

"Alone again Kate?" She half turned to face him, but the sun obscured his features. He quickly dismounted and she saw him very clearly.

"I was admiring the countryside my lord. I thought to see more of it," she explained.

"You have a liking for solitary places, Kate. Well so do I. It must be attributable to the poetic persuasion within you. Like you, I also have an inclination towards the inviolate, the unspoilt."

He looked at her keenly, as if to make her aware that his allusion was not to the land alone. "How like you our progress so far?" he continued, his mood changing to the one of banter with which she was only too familiar.

"I am enjoying it, my lord. I know so little of the outside world and ..."

His sudden laughter hurt, for she realised that her reply had only revealed the extent of her ignorance and that his world and hers were very far removed. Staring fixedly at the ground, she felt humiliated. "One day I will show you the world Mistress Veneers," he said.

"Are you sulking sweet Kate. I but jested after all. I see you are jealous of your learning and think I make light of it, but you should know me better by now. I am regarded as a well educated man, but believe me there are other things far more worth the attaining."

There was an implication in his words that disquieted her. Again she had been given a glimpse of that gnawing isolation which he chose to disguise in a veneer of barbed urbanity.

"Forgive me, my lord. I had no intention of seeming churlish."

"Come, let us walk a little way. Then I can at least make sure of your safe return. I take it you have not as yet eaten?"

"No, my lord. I had not the time."

"There is time for everything Kate," he mildly accused, taking from the horse's saddle a parcel of food and a pouch of fine wine. He then spread out his cloak and bade her be seated. She did as she was told, but remained extremely guarded and a little ill at ease. The food was naturally of the best and he doled it out fairly. Leaving his cloak entirely at her disposal, he sat a little distance away from her. Finding the wine over rich it caused her to cough and it amused him to watch her dab at the spillage that ran down her chin; feeling chagrined and ashamed, she was at least grateful for the handkerchief he proffered.

"Better?" he asked, as she gave it back to him.

"Thank you, my lord," she replied, fixing her gaze on the wood below, simply because she was afraid to meet his own with composure.

"You have deserted me yet again, Kate," he reproved after a while. "I provide you with good food and congenial talk, and in return I am treated with indifference, which prompts me to ask am I not your saviour, Mistress Venners?"

"I have only one Saviour," she charged, without really thinking.

"So be it!" he replied, leaping to his feet and re-saddling the horse. She could not think what had made her say such a thing; it was the kind of rebuke she would have given to anyone who had posed such a question, but no doubt he would see it as insolence.

"I spoke without thinking, my lord," she said apologetically. "You have been most kind and I am indeed grateful."

"Grateful again!" he threw back, but when he turned to look at her any qualms she might have had were quickly allayed by the warmth of his smile. "Best hurry now, Mistress Venners. We still have a fair distance to travel."

Darkness fell before the journey was completed and they had to make camp a mere six miles from their destination. Gazing up at the stars, she soon fell into the restful kind of sleep she was so much in need of. Dawn brought another perfect spring morning, and they set out at once. Refreshed and renewed, she lurched pleasantly amidst the pile of baggage, the driver remaining as taciturn as ever. Less wooded and hilly, they were now passing through fields of newly planted corn where men with ploughs and oxen were working as hard as she knew her uncle and Rob would be working, but here the earth looked richer and far more accommodating. Eventually the land seemed to level out altogether and there was a tang and freshness in the air with which she was not at all familiar. Gulls wheeled and circled overhead, such birds as only came to Runnarth in times of bad weather. And then she saw it, a wide and seemingly endless expanse of water that had to be the sea. She remembered Peter telling her that the river was incomparable to the boundless chain of the ocean, but only now that she was actually seeing it for the first time could she begin to appreciate what he had tried so hard to describe. She was seeing it to advantage too, for the day was calm and the sun made it blue and beguiling. The sand was white and firm at its edge, just as Peter had told her, gradually rising into hillocks of grassy dune that presented a feeble barrier to the wind as it blew in fresh and salt-edged from the water. She could not lift her eyes from it, gazing on it with the kind of rapture a mother reserves for her first born. The cortege was now slowly making its way across the headland to Sulburgh Castle which stood on a rocky promontory with the sea at its base. All the bustle that had attended on the commencement of the journey now recommenced at the end of it, Sulburgh's tiny courtyard being transformed into one of workmanlike efficiency. Names were called and quarters assigned. Naturally, Elliston made his entrance unannounced, Joanna at his side, a wife in all but name. The sight of them together always made her reflective, which was why Joan caught her completely off guard.

"Kate! Kate!" she exclaimed, "let me look at ye," and before Catherine could think any more she was held in a crushing embrace. "I said to Tom I be sure it were ye, but he said ye wouldna come 'ere, but I'd know ye anywhere Kate. Still so thin and lost like."

Catherine gave into the embrace readily. It was what she most needed, a friendly and familiar face, and with Joan it was easy enough to renew old acquaintance. All she had to do was listen while Joan blathered on and led her to the kitchen where Tom, fleshier and ruddier than ever, grudgingly held out his hand. He was content and did not want his comfort interfered with in any way.

"We be so 'appy 'ere Kate," she rambled on. "Not too much to do and near enough in sole charge. Tis grand to spend afternoons by the sea rocking the bairn on my knee," whereupon she whisked Catherine up a small flight of stairs and into a decent sized room, albeit sparsely furnished, in which stood a rough wooden cradle.

"He be asleep the darlin'," she said, peering into it. "Look ye Kate, just look."

Catherine looked. He was not the most engaging baby and, worse still, appeared to have inherited more of his father in the way of looks than his mother, but Catherine made the appropriate noises of appreciation, knowing that every baby was special to its mother.

"And just think," Joan continued, making little cooing noises over the infant, "I should never have had ye Tom or been 'ere but for Kate, should I now." She looked at Kate and beamed with an almost childlike gratitude. "I owe everythin' to ye Kate, and I'll not forget it either."

"It was not entirely my doing," Catherine tried to explain, but Joan was having none of it; as far as she was concerned, Catherine had everything to do with it.

☙ ❧

She had been allocated a tiny room right at the top of the one and only tower with a fine view of the sea. She thrilled to the very sight and sound of it, delighting in it like a child delights in seeing the wonders of nature anew. She would have loved to rush down to the strand there and then, but Elliston had planned a special dinner for the commencement of his stay and all were invited. It was a good humoured affair, but of shorter duration than usual as everyone was tired from the journey.

With the dawn chorus came her first full day at Sulburgh. The weather remaining fine and the sun shining bountifully into her room, Joanna had given her to understand that there was nothing for her to do until noon which meant she was free with a terrifying and boundless freedom. The morning, the day, the world was hers.

The breeze was singing in the rushes as bare footed she stumbled through the soft sanded dunes to the firmer sand of the shore. The tide was out, but she ran towards it, the wind blowing in her face and tossing her hair in a wild auburn stream like the seaweed that swayed in the water. She owned no inhibitions at that moment. She was all spirit with no flesh to bind her. Reaching the edge of the water, she let out a cry of pure delight as the waves washed over her feet. Looking back she could see her footprints clearly outlined in the sand, but beside the shore itself there were others, those made by horses, a double line of them disappearing into the distance, and suddenly her joy was not so complete, knowing that he and Joanna were out riding along her stretch of beach, her edge of sea. Her freak was over as quickly as it came; she was now decidedly more serious. Turning inland, she picked up a jagged piece of stone and kneeling down on the partially wet sand wrote out her own name and his. She then smoothed over her own name and put Joanna's instead. It was all capricious nonsense of course, and with the heel of her foot she quickly erased it. If only life itself were that easy, she thought. The sea, she decided, was making her giddy and impulsive, but she still felt bewitched by it, and in between brief intervals of seeing Joan and the baby, she came back to it again and again. She stayed until the tide had turned and then headed back towards the dunes; it was a beautiful sunset and an equally fine night with a generous underpinning of stars. The sea air had made her tired and she lay down on the grass listening to the waves washing over the rocks. She felt as if she could have stayed there all night, but eventually the cooler air drove her inside. Also, Joan had asked her to supper and she did not want to be late. The corridor was reasonably well lit and she ought to have seen him, but seeming to come out of nowhere he grabbed her by the hand and hustled her up to his apartments above.

"You shall sit right there Mistress Venners," he ordered, all but flinging her into a chair. Now it was cooler the fire had been lit and he was warming himself in front of it. The room in which she had literally been deposited was small and intimate and the atmosphere friendly, somehow in keeping with the rest of the castle which had none of the brooding quality of Runnarth.

"I have been observing you Kate," he said at last, turning to face her.

"My lord?"

"To see the sea is my delight on a brilliant day both sunny and bright," he quipped, almost breaking into song. "This morning! Surely you recall it, or has that first enchantment made you forgetful?"

"No, my lord. I had not thought to be seen," she replied, slightly taken aback that she should have been caught acting like a child building sand castles. Had they been observing her together, he and Joanna, laughing at her naivety. What a pretty picture she must have presented. She bit her lip in undisguised rancour.

"Ah Kate, you must not mistake my jest. I am not making fun at your expense. You were brought here to enjoy yourself and it is right and fitting that you should. Incidentally, Joanna was not with me at the time, if that is what concerns you." That it did concern her he could tell, for she was noticeably pacified to hear him say so. "Come Kate you grow serious with me. It was not always thus."

"You must excuse me my lord. It was just knowing you had caught me so unawares."

"Then I must do so more often. After all, Sulburgh is not Runnarth, which is why you are here, to take advantage of the welcome contrast and enjoy it while you can."

"I trust to, my lord. It is so very beautiful."

She was now smiling, a delightfully genuine smile and full of good intent.

"That is better. Now, why are you here, you are asking?"

"My lord?"

"Do you not require an explanation?"

"I am naturally curious my lord."

"So be it. Joanna is unwell. I am not. I am in want of company. You are here to supply it."

If bluntness be counted a virtue, then he was a virtuous man indeed, she decided, eying him critically.

"Let me guess what you are thinking; that I am lacking in finesse, that I am crude in my dealings. Come, tell me. I will know if you speak truth or not. One thing I have learned about you Kate Venners is your inability to dissemble. I find it rather engaging."

It was impossible to deceive him, for had he not proved time and time again that she was inept in the art; it was like her evasiveness over Gerard, it had only made her family more suspicious. No, she would never lie convincingly.

"I was wondering if such bluntness could be accounted a virtue, my lord."

"Well said," he laughed. "Now you are at ease, the Kate I would have."

No more was said for a while, but she was not embarrassed by the quiet; she was more than content to let be and wait on his humour.

"You know a fair deal about me Kate, I presume," he at last began, looking at her closely, "and now, in the manner of my bluntness, as you term it, I wish to learn more about you."

The request took her entirely by surprise. It was not at all what she had expected, and she was not even sure what he wanted to know, so she spoke of her mother, simply because she had loved her so much and everything about her still remained so vividly within her recollection. But it proved a mistake. Her tone of almost spiritual reverence began to try his patience until he could stand it no more.

"You loved your mother Kate," he accused, cutting into the thread of her narrative.

"Yes, my lord, of course."

"And she loved you?"

"Naturally, my lord," she replied, and then coloured, knowing full well what it was that perturbed him.

"Why do you say naturally, Kate?" he pounced, falling at her feet and gripping her hands.

"Because ..."

"You are naive Kate. You suppose that all mothers love their children through the mere fact of them being so."

"I know that my mother loved me, my lord," she maintained.

"Then you were indeed blessed Mistress Venners, for mine despises me."

"No, my lord," she broke in. "It cannot be, my lord," for it did not seem possible that a mother could hate her own son.

"But it is so, and you know it to be so. I thought you more perspicacious Kate."

She could almost feel his sense of rejection as a physical hurt, and in an attempt to assuage it she bowed her head on his hands.

"I think that underneath all your sparring Lady Elliston does love you, my lord."

"You are kind Kate, but deluded," he replied, stroking her hair. "My so called mama has always despised me. The very sight of me is anathema. It has always been thus. You see she adored my brother. He died. I did not."

"You must not speak so, my lord," she implored with tears in her eyes, her reserve forgotten in her need to reassure and comfort him.

"For all my faults, Kate," he said, rising to his feet, "I remain an honest man. I am not afraid of the truth. Come Kate," he laughed, seeing the honest pain in her features, "you are too intense. You cannot alter a fact merely because you find it untenable."

She asked if she should leave, but he told her to continue and seemed to hang on her every word, or was it her face. The distinction appeared to make little difference. As he had intimated, she was there to fill a void, and she did so to the best of her ability.

"Tell me about this man they called Peter the Hermit," he said.

"Peter, why he was the most saintly man I have ever known, my lord. Even you would have liked him," she tactlessly affirmed. The blunder was out and there was no way of retracting it, even if she had wanted to. His face was a blank, but then a rather questionable smile stole over it.

"Are godly men barred to me Kate? Do I only fraternise with the wicked?"

"Forgive me, my lord. The remark was unintentional."

"You begin to know me too well. It is true I have no particular liking for the clergy, hypocrites for the most part, but this Peter, he sounds a little more to my taste. But Craven, what of him?"

"My lord?" she replied, neither wanting to hear her confessor denigrated nor wishing to speak in his defence.

"Be careful of him Kate, that is all. And what else would you tell me?"

"Nothing that I can readily think of, my lord."

"Indeed. I shall look to the day, Kate, when you will not feel obliged to keep anything from me."

He had noted then her deliberate omission of all reference to her accident and the circumstances surrounding it. She knew that he would. But a private pain is not easily divulged, and the nature of it still made her diffident in his company. He was not wrong in thinking that consciously or not she was using it as a means of preventing all further intimacy between them, that she was dependent on it like a cripple on a crutch.

"You can leave now Mistress Venners. Your apprehension is misplaced. Another time will suffice and then maybe you will not be so dismayed at the prospect."

When she returned to her room, one very bright star was encased in the window. It made her think of the Magi and their journey in search of the Christ child. The book Margaret had leant her lay open at the bedside. She flicked over the pages, but it was not so much the written words as the spoken ones that so engaged her mind. "Pray God, comfort my lord," she prayed, casting the volume aside.

Joanna soon rallied and she saw little of him for days. If she saw little of her lord, she saw much of Joan and the baby, and whenever time, the weather and Watkins allowed they would amuse themselves on the beach, baby Tom gurgling with happiness one moment and then wailing horribly the next. Before long Catherine became as besotted with the child as its mother, dandling it on her knee, cooing over it when it cried and remedying its wet and messy state with matronly ease.

"You ought to hae childer of ye own Kate," Joan affirmed, as Catherine rocked baby Tom to and fro in her arms.

"Mayhap," she replied, almost dismissively.

"I mean it Kate. Ye should be wed by now."

"You know I shall not marry."

"Ye must not think like that. One day, why ye never can tell. Anyways if ye let ye looks bother ye o'er much ye'll never ..."

"I am content as I am," she broke in. "I shall become a doting old maid, who will take care of your children and trust to have them love me a little in return."

"I give up!" she retorted. "Patience ne'er was a virtue o' mine and there be times when ye'd try a saint Catherine Venners."

"I agree," she replied with an under-eyed grin, "but we are friends just the same."

At this, Tom began to howl and the discussion was brought to a close.

☙ ❧

The days when she was not with Joan were solitary and too much so for her peace of mind. She would spend whole afternoons wandering along the sand, only the flight of heedless gulls breaking the flow of her thought, but neither the sea nor the sand could charm away her mood of increasing disquiet. The strength of her feeling was at last forcing her to be honest. It was no longer possible to delude herself into thinking that what she felt for Elliston was merely compassion or the sympathetic feeling one human being had for another. It was much more than that. But that he could possibly care for her in a similar way seemed impossible. It was true that he had been uncommonly attentive towards her, but this she put down to his difficult relationship with his mother and the fact that she was in attendance upon that mother. Then again, as he was never tired of telling her, he found her patient and inclined to adapt to his moods. But what if the underlying reason was nothing more than pity. It was this that really rankled, this that kept her awake at night and made her call on her Saviour to help her overcome a futile fixation.

Towards the end of May news reached them of Lady Elliston's rapid decline and the need to return without further delay. On her last night at Sulburgh she had gone to say her goodbyes to Joan, as it was doubtful that she would have time in the morning. She smothered the baby in kisses and hugged Joan so tight that she scarcely could breathe.

"We'll be seein' ye again Kate. Dunna take on so. Y'ell come back sure enough."

"I pray so Joan. It is just ... I am being foolish," she sobbed.

"Kate, dunna upset yesell."

It would have been unfeeling to tell Joan that parting from her was not the primary cause of her distress and she liked her too much to unnecessarily burden her.

"There now Kate, ye never know I might come back to Runnarth some day."

"God bless you Joan."

"And you Kate. Ye think about getting' wed now."

Such advice only made her more wretched and she was glad to get away before she did or said something she would later regret.

Unable to sleep she walked down to the rose garden; secluded and surrounded by a sheltering high wall, she had often had recourse to it during her stay; she had even given it a name of her own devising, arbour of heart's ease, and on this final evening at Sulburgh she felt compelled to visit it one last time. For all she knew, she might never return again. Rain had fallen during the day and the scent of summer's first roses was heightened, but the sky remained stormy and a hazy moon dipped in and out of the clouds. The wind was keening like a fettered soul, its dull undertone sounding mournfully in sympathy with the wash of the waves on the beach. They must be, as she was, possessed by some indefinable force that would not let them be. The night being starless and the moon fitful, she had to pick her way cautiously between the rose beds, gently parting the branches that threatened to trap her, but when she heard footsteps she began to panic. She wondered who it could possibly be at such a late hour, and then the inevitable happened, a particularly vicious branch sinking its thorns into her gown and pinning her to the spot. Frantic, she attempted to extricate herself and when this did not serve took hold of the branch itself and wrenched at it until the exposed parts of her hands were scratched and bloodied. When she saw it was him, the desire to rip herself free became even more pressing.

"Impaled Mistress Venners," he remarked, catching hold of

her hands, whereupon her blood trickled on to his gloves. "Now I thought patience a virtue of yours," he chided, dexterously freeing her while she waited like a helpless child. The final thorn extracted, he led her to the safety of the main path.

"I am sorry my lord to have caused you ...". She could not speak further, her long suppressed emotion finally breaking into unrestrained sobbing. He drew her to him so that her head nestled against the warmth of his shoulder.

"I would not have thought one capricious branch could cause so much misery," he soothed, "but mayhap there is something more."

"No my lord," she maintained, beginning to regain her self-composure.

"You choose to visit my garden at odd hours Kate?"

Still unsure of herself, she could not answer him.

"All right, I will not tease you," he said, as she pulled away from him. "I will not even enquire why you have chosen to pace hereabouts when I myself stand accused of doing exactly the same thing. You may ask of me if you will."

"It is not for me to ask questions my lord. For myself, the explanation is simple. I was unable to sleep."

"Which has unstrung your nerves and made you not yourself. I take it there are reasons for this insomnia Kate."

Her reply was one of silent appeal.

"Then I shall not pry. Still, tis not a night conducive to solitary musings."

"No, my lord."

"And your remedies on which you place so much reliance, have they proved of no avail either?"

"No, my lord."

"Then your complaint has no common cause."

Seeing her discomfiture, he quickly changed the subject.

"Is it that you like roses?"

"Yes, my lord, I do."

The wind had abated somewhat and the first signs of dawn were visible in the sky. She could now see him better, there being that restive look about his features that made her want to touch his hand and drive the mood from him.

"And which shade of rose is your favourite," he said, reverting to his bantering tone. As always, she began to wonder whither the conversation was leading, for now he was being subtle in a way that was strangely out of character.

"The red, my lord."

"You surprise me Kate. I would have thought the white would

have been your choice."

"And you, my lord, which pleases you," she replied, knowing full well that she was expected to respond in like vein.

"You should know without having to ask, Kate. White, and white alone. You see it is all that I am not, pure and unsullied. Such a flower is rare indeed. You see," he continued, reaching for a perfect specimen of his musing, from which he snapped off each thorn before placing it in her fingers. Now tell me why you have a preference for the red."

There was an intensity in his look that disturbed her and made further speech difficult. She was at a loss what to say, and yet had she had the courage she would have told him so much.

"You will not be drawn Kate. I am disappointed. Wait, I have the answer," whereupon seeking for the deepest, darkest red he held it alongside the white. "There, now you have no excuses. Study it well and give me your answer."

The merest attempt at dissimulation and he would know, of that she was certain. It showed in his eyes, as if the mirror of his soul could be read within them.

"Come, Kate, I will not be denied."

"As you prefer the white, so I prefer the red, my lord," she replied, and though her reply was equivocal he was not slow to grasp the sense of it. She had spoken as he had desired and he was satisfied.

"You speak with candour Kate. I never doubted you would not."

What manner of man was he, she thought, who could overtly attribute character to the shade of a flower.

"I want to look at you Kate," he said, touching the mask. "Close your eyes if you must, but see you I will."

She closed her eyes tightly, and let him unfasten the strings of the linen. The extent of the disfigurement was worse than he had imagined and for a moment he involuntarily looked away. Ashamed of his weakness, he gently ran his fingers down each scar and tried to imagine what she would have looked like free of the impairment, but the more he tried the more he realised that the two sides of her face, both the smooth and the blasted, were in actuality the whole and that it was impossible to separate the one from the other. Almost despising himself for subjecting her to the ordeal, he had to know the extent of her vulnerability if he was to take that hurt upon himself and in some manner heal it.

"Open your eyes Kate."

"I cannot," she replied, afraid to see the effect she had made upon him.

"You can and you will," he commanded.

She did as he asked, relieved to see that there was no visible change in the way he looked at her. He neither looked away as others were wont to do, nor did he stare at her as if dumbstruck. His look was one of simple understanding and from that she drew comfort.

"I trust your senses have not been offended overmuch, my lord?"

"Am I swooning Kate? Am I appalled? You are vain of your looks, just as you are vain of your learning. It is fortunate that you do not think of them to the exclusion of those more pleasing traits in your nature. Do we understand one another."

"I think so, my lord."

"That being so, you will not be afraid to tell me what I wish to know Kate. How and why the accident happened? The time and place are ideal, particularly now you are no longer afraid."

"I was teasing my cousin, when it happened," she began. "It was all somewhat trivial."

"Great tragedies are born out of trivialities Kate," he affirmed.

When she had finished, he gave her back the mask. It was only then that she realised that she had not even thought to put it back on, so at ease was she in his company.

"That is all, my lord," she said, replacing the linen.

"All, Kate?" he replied with a smile. "The word is infinite. Are you tired Kate?"

"No, my lord."

"Neither am I. Tis strange, is it not? I shall be sorry to leave this place. It has always had an air of magic about it," he said, placing the roses in her hand. "I trust you will sleep better ere long."

"You also, my lord."

Joanna was waiting for him impatiently.

"Where have you been!" she demanded.

"Picking roses," he casually replied, which only infuriated her further.

"What sort of answer is that – for nearly three hours."

"I am careful in my choice of blooms," he parried.

"What is the point of my sharing your bed?" she retorted, slithering under the bedclothes.

"None that I can see," he replied. "Force of habit maybe?"

He could be vindictive when he wanted. She shook out her hair, looking daggers at him. He had only confirmed what she had known for a long time.

"I bore you then. Why do you not say it?" she charged, hard resentful tears welling up in her eyes.

"On the contrary, Joanna, I would say that I bored you. In fact, you have borne with me well, but what have we left? Now our passion is spent, very little."

"When do you wish me to leave?" A woman who did not create a scene was not to be lightly discarded and he would see to it that her services did not go unrewarded.

"Sooner rather than later, shall we say. I believe your parents have a marriage in mind for you."

"You can be so cruel!"

"No Joanna, I am practical. You never really cared for me if you are honest. It was prestige that drove you into my bed. It suited us both at the time." Disdainfully she rose from the bed, flinging on her night robe. "You see, you cannot gainsay it," he continued. All the clothes and jewels are yours to keep and rest assured your allowance will be generous."

"And pray, who is to take my place," she enquired like a vixen in retreat.

"You presume."

"Do I? Picking roses is original, but hardly clever."

"You are the clever one, not I."

CHAPTER SIXTEEN

It saddened Catherine to see how Lady Elliston had deteriorated over such a short time. Nervous and aggressive by turns, it was hard to humour her at all now as she lay shrivelled and shrunken in her silken sheets.

"He had no right to take you away from me Mistress Venners" was her repeated complaint. "It was unnecessarily cruel and in keeping with his vileness towards me. You cannot know what it is to be without proper attention, to lie here at the mercy of some ignorant chit of a girl whose manner is both patronising and perfunctory."

Catherine sympathised as best she could, although as ever her loyalties were fiercely divided. How could they be otherwise, feeling as she did towards the object of all the old woman's anathema.

"You know how I like things done Mistress Venners. Tis not the same with you away. I shall not ask if you enjoyed the change. I prefer to dismiss the episode as one of my son's more malicious acts."

If she tried to defend Lord Elliston in even the most guarded terms the old woman became violently agitated and since she was too frail to withstand any undue excitement Catherine wisely desisted. Constantly at her beck and call, every hour of her day was taken up in tending to the needs of her bed-ridden mistress. She washed her body, combed her hair, fed her what little she could eat and dosed her with endless potions.

"Tis humiliating to grow old Mistress Venners. I long to be done with it."

Catherine spooned a few morsels between the blackened teeth, the old woman clutching at her fingers and staring up at her with eyes grown large and piercing from the lack of flesh surrounding them.

"To think I was once the finest lady in Northumberland, and now reduced to this. God has truly punished me! Robbed me of my son and left a thing unnatural in his stead."

She resolutely refused to see Lord Elliston and he tactfully kept away. Caring as she did for both mother and son, Catherine felt herself perpetually torn betwixt the two. Dying was a dread business and the old woman was clearly eking out her days on a diminishing glass of time, while her son waited alone and knew the sting of rejection more keenly than ever. All that Catherine could do was to make her mistress as comfortable as possible and pray for some miracle of reconciliation between mother and son before it was too late. Wearied and worn herself, she would crawl into her bed for a few hours' respite, only to be awakened shortly afterwards with the message that she was urgently needed. It seemed that no one else would do.

"My heart, Mistress Venners, it pains me so. My head, Mistress Venners. God help me, Mistress Venners," she would cry, as Catherine endeavoured to administer something a little stronger until there was nothing stronger left to administer. The signs of decay were too marked, all the potions in the world not being able to ward off the inevitable outcome. Occasionally the old lady, exhausted by the effort of staying alive, would find oblivion in sleep, but it was only the final oblivion that would ultimately give her rest and Catherine prayed for it hourly. She had not seen her family for weeks and the increasing strain was beginning to tell on her own health. Even Elliston himself paled into a dim and misty figure as every minute of every day was taken up in alleviating the sufferings of his mother. It was not that anyone else had not offered to relieve her. Margaret Burgoyne for one would willingly have obliged, but Lady Elliston was still sensible enough to know whom and what she wanted and Catherine remained.

After a particularly trying night when her mistress had fretted herself into sleep and she was just on the point of seeking her own bed, she was interrupted by the arrival of Joanna. If this was yet another demand for assistance she felt she would have to refuse and arrange for someone else to go in her place, no matter how much the old lady objected.

"I thought that Lady Elliston slept," Catherine remarked, rubbing her eyes.

"So she does Mistress Venners. Tis not of Lady Elliston that I wish to speak. I am simply here to bid you farewell."

"Farewell?"

"Yes, I am leaving and shall not return. Shortly I am to be married."

Tired as she was, Catherine sat up to make sure that she had heard this aright.

"Leaving?"

"All things have their term Mistress Venners, and mine here is now at an end. I cannot say I regret it. Lady Elliston is hardly congenial company."

"She is old and ill," Catherine interceded on her mistress's behalf.

"So she may be, but I am not, and while I am still young I intend to employ my time in better ways."

Still proud, still incredibly lovely, thought Catherine. "You know I never liked you Mistress Venners, but then I believe the feeling is mutual?"

"You are at least honest," Catherine replied. "You were hostile to me from the first and it is not in my nature to seek for friendship where none is vouchsafed."

"Hardly a Christian precept," Joanna retorted.

"Christian precepts are necessarily trying, and like you I cannot always live up to them."

A clever thrust, it was not lost on Joanna.

"You were envious of me Mistress Venners. The reason is obvious."

"I freely admit it," Catherine agreed.

"Well you will be free of me now," she said turning to go.

"I wish you well Joanna," she replied. Believe me or not, I mean what I say."

Joanna had no reason to doubt her sincerity, and for this one and only time they were in accord, one with the other.

"Strangely enough, I wish you well too Catherine," she replied.

"No rancour," said Catherine smiling.

"None whatsoever," Joanna replied, returning her smile.

All day the rain had not ceased and the courtyard had flooded. The sound of it swam on the edge of the old lady's consciousness. She clutched at the sheets, her eyes glazed and wildly staring. The physic had brought her no ease and now she lay silent and drained. Waiting. Watching. For whom and for what, Catherine wondered. The Burgoynes hovered uneasily at the foot of the bed.

"I think you had better fetch Lord Elliston," Margaret whispered to Catherine.

Once again, it was Catherine on whom everyone was depending, neither Edward nor Margaret having the courage to approach him at this, the most critical hour. She found him sitting alone and staring into the darkness.

"My lord, Lady Elliston is worse. We think you should come."

He turned, his face livid in the gloom.

"Has she asked for me Kate?"

"No, my lord, but she is a little more at ease. It cannot be long now."

"Then I shall come when she requests me to come."

"But my lord ..."

"No Kate, when she requests. Do you understand?" His features were set, pitiless. How could she leave him thus. Perhaps even now it was not too late. "Why do you remain Kate. I have said all I have to say."

"Lady Elliston is dying my lord."

"So?" he answered. "She never loved me in life. I scarce think it likely she will love me in death, but mayhap you think differently."

"She is still your mother, my lord."

"You loved your mother Kate. I do not love mine."

"Please my lord," she pleaded, falling at his side. "Be merciful."

He did not move or speak.

"You think by this last act some wrong will be righted Kate," he laughed derisively. "You innocent. Hatred does not finish with death; it goes on, into eternity."

"God be with you, my lord," she said, touching his hands and involuntarily pressing them to her lips. Clearly there was nothing she could do or say to move him.

It was now well past midnight. As the rain continued to wash against the windows, so Lady Elliston continued to tenuously hold on to life. The Burgoynes had left, looking to Catherine to inform them of any change. Lady Elliston remained awake, half in life, half out of it, rasping for each hard won breath. Fear and resignation paradoxically dwelt in her eyes, a longing to be free of this world, a dread of the next. The last rites had been administered and there was nothing between her and mortality but a trickle of sand in an hour glass.

"I cannot see Mistress Venners," she wheezed. "Why is everything so dark?"

"Tis evening my lady and the day has been a rainy one. Hush now," she soothed.

Despite the best efforts of those anxious to ease the fear and pain of it, at the last death was a solitary business.

"Do my hair," she suddenly demanded, regaining some of the old spirit and then as soon relapsing into a world of half remembered faces and shadows. Catherine felt it time to fetch the Burgoynes. Sir Edward asked her if she had been to see Lord

Elliston again. She informed him that she had not, but was relying on God's grace to effect in him a change of heart.

"My throat is dry Mistress Venners," she croaked. Catherine forced the cup between her lips, and this time she managed to swallow the contents without disgorging them onto the bedspread.

"Try to rest now, my lady," Catherine said, wiping her mouth.

"Time enough for that," she managed to reply, her acrid sense of humour serving her right to the last. They looked at each other and smiled.

The door was suddenly opened, the candles flickering in the draught. So he had come after all. She thanked God for answering her prayers.

"I believe my presence is needful," he said. Catherine looked at him reassuringly, but her concern went unacknowledged.

"She is sleepy my lord," she explained, as if to make him comfortable at his own mother's bedside.

"No matter. I will sit here where she cannot see me too well."

But he had come, thought Catherine. Somehow she knew that he would.

"Who is it?" said Lady Elliston, straining to catch their words, which came to her like the faraway echoes of a long forgotten dream.

"It is your son Lady Elliston," Margaret explained, as she rearranged the pillows.

"My son!" she replied, a beatific smile transforming her features. "Henry," she called. "Is Henry here?"

"No, my lady, you misunderstand," replied Margaret, looking at Elliston in despair.

"Let her think what she will, Lady Burgoyne, tis kinder," he said.

"She rambles my lord. It is often the way," whispered Burgoyne by way of consolation. Only Catherine remained silent as his eyes sought her own, hard and emotionless with a stoicism born out of years of rejection.

"Tell her that he is here, Mistress Venners, the one she chooses to be here. Maybe he is. Tis said that the dying can see beyond this life and it would be apropos of Henry to turn up at such a time."

Reluctantly, Catherine bent her head to the feverish woman's ears and whispered what she so longed to hear.

"He is indeed here, my lady," she said, tears already stinging her eyes, not for her mistress but for the son of that mistress.

"I knew he would come. Henry, my darling child," she cried,

her voice growing stronger in her excitement.

Sir Edward and Margaret shuffled uneasily, but Elliston himself remained perfectly still, not a flicker of the eyelid betraying his own personal feelings on this, the final act of the drama.

"They took him away from me, but I knew he would return, my only son."

"Perhaps we should leave," suggested Burgoyne.

"If I can remain, so can you!" retorted Elliston.

Catherine stood by the bedside, deploring the dreadful look of happiness that spread over Lady Elliston's face. She felt like striking her, stopping her mouth with the sheets. Appalled, she could not face him and turned away.

"Why you Henry, why did they take you from me," Lady Elliston continued to ramble. "Roger did it. He was jealous because of my love for you. A curse on him! A curse on him!" She threw out her hands in one last gesture and then fell back, her eyes open and staring.

"No Mistress Venners," he protested, as she went to close those eyes. "I shall do that last service." The gentleness of the action belied the bitterness at heart. "I take it you will help prepare Mama," he said curtly.

"Yes, my lord," she answered.

"I now take my leave. I trust you are satisfied Mistress Venners."

Lady Elliston was interred with the rest of her line in the family vault of the castle chapel. The funeral was noted for its lack of pomp, the plain coffin being despatched with the briefest of ceremonies. Catherine was not invited to attend. In the circumstances it was hardly surprising.

Subsequently she saw little of him. He locked himself away, keeping to his room, and when he did emerge it was to take long solitary walks or ride his horses to the limits of their endurance. When they threw him he did not seem to care or even notice. The affliction of soul and heart hurt him far more. Since Joanna's departure he took comfort with any woman who was willing to solace him. Such was his existence.

With Lady Elliston's death, Catherine's position at the castle had become rather anomalous, seeing that now there was no one to wait on. Margaret was willing for her to become her own personal attendant, a solution which would have suited them both, but she could do nothing without Elliston's consent and it was impossible to seek his guidance on any matter at the moment. Having little to occupy her mind, she went over the scene of that terrible death bed again and again. Naturally she felt fully to blame for the outcome, having done everything to persuade him to attend against his better judgement, and better it had proved to be.

The first days of summer were now lost in showery squalls of rain that kept her awake into the early hours of dawn. If the sun did break through its reign was short, great black clouds hovering overhead and reducing the view to greyness again. Tension exuded from the very walls of the castle as everyone went about their duties straight faced and portentously silent. It was the last day of June and she was sat in her room trying to lose herself in the book Margaret had originally leant her when she was interrupted by a young and slovenly looking girl, her face horribly painted, and her mien coarse and insolent.

"Lord Elliston wants ye," she said, giggling through her teeth.

"Are you certain?" asked Catherine over politely, as she put down the book.

"Course I'm sure. He said as I were to ask ye to go to him now," she succinctly explained, arching her eyebrows at Catherine's masked features.

"Then I will go at once."

"He be in a vile temper Mistress. Tis terrible to see," she volunteered as if to gauge Catherine's reaction. "I should look to yesell if I were you."

Choosing to ignore the remark and perfunctorily brushing her hair, she thought herself equal to coping with the extremes of his humour by now, even those resulting from his mother's rejection.

For some days the sconces on the wall had not been lit and she had to grope to find her way. Knocking tentatively and receiving no acknowledgement, she quietly entered. The pervasive fetidness made her feel nauseous, as did the aspect of Elliston himself who lay slumped across the table, an empty goblet held in his hands. So changed was he that she scarcely recognised him. On seeing her he staggered to his feet, swaying awkwardly as he did so.

"Mistress Venners," he slurred. "Prompt as ever."

"My orders were to come immediately, my lord. I merely obeyed them."

"Quite so," he hiccupped. "You must excuse the mess," he continued, gaily pointing a finger at the chaos around him. "I have not been well."

"I am sorry to hear it, my lord. Is there anything I can prepare for you?"

"I have need of more than physic Kate, Catherine, whatever you are called," he threw out, slamming down his fist on the table. "Come nearer, Mistress Venners."

She did as he asked. He looked dreadful. The dirt of days was upon him, dark shadows showing round his eyes which were startlingly blue and unnatural from his excesses. His mouth was slack and moist.

"Not a pretty sight, eh Kate?"

"My lord, you are indeed not well," she replied, anxious to pacify him.

"Talk to me Kate," he whined. "Talk to me."

"I think you should sleep first, my lord. Then we can talk."

"You were eager enough to talk to me once," he said, roughly pulling her towards him. "Point out the way of my duty. You could talk well enough then as I recall."

"Forgive me, my lord. How could I know? It was unfortunate..."

"Unfortunate," he shouted, shaking her hard. "You mince your words Mistress Venners. It was bloody and base."

"What would you have me say, my lord," she appealed. "I regret it is as much as you do. I never thought ..."

"Exactly! That is your trouble Kate, you do not think. You act! Well it is my turn for acting."

He dragged her to the fire, viciously kicking the dogs who growled and cowered away.

"What do you know of passion Kate Venners? Desire of a man for a woman, a woman for a man? Little I warrant, though doubtless you have an opinion on that subject too."

"I know not, my lord," she replied, trying to free herself. "Please let me go."

"All women are harlots Kate. Never giving freely. Always wanting payment."

"I believe my mother knew of love, my lord," she said, attempting to reason with him, though in referring to her mother she realised she had only exacerbated matters.

"Your sainted mother!" he slurred. "How sick I am of having her virtues paraded before me. But what of your father? Let us speak of him for a change. I dare say he has fathered more than one bastard, as indeed I have. You honestly think he loved your mother. You make me smile! He took his pleasure while he could, and it would seem your mother was only too willing to oblige him. I wonder what he gave her in return besides you; a shiny piece of silver, no doubt."

"I will not stay to hear my mother reviled," she charged. "You speak of love without knowing anything of it. Is it not tenderness, affinity, desire without the taint of lust?"

"You see, you do have a view," he laughed, holding her from him as she recoiled from the foulness of his breath. "Desire without the taint of lust. Now that is amusing."

"Please let me go, my lord. You are not yourself."

"I am very much myself! What you see is the genuine Lord Elliston," he said, effecting a strutting attitude. "What is more, I know your secret Kate Venners. You fancy yourself in love with me, do you not?"

An involuntary flush of crimson rushed over her face.

"You see, I am right. Well, Kate, since you love me," he spat, "I can teach you all you ought to know. You will find me more than capable in the art of instruction."

It was then that he began to tear at her like a fiend, pulling her to the ground and pinning her beneath him, his mouth raging down on her own.

Desperately she fought to keep him from her, but she was like a bird about to be savaged by a cat; he was unrestrained, violent, and when she resisted he struck her repeatedly until his hands were stained with a trickle of blood.

"You have desired me for a long time, Kate. Now you have me. You are no different Kate Venners, just another whore for the taking and I will prove it."

"I beg you, do not hurt me my lord! Please! Please!"

He suddenly released her. Stumbling to her feet, she ran towards the door, but before she could reach it he grabbed her again, dragging her towards the room he had formerly shared with Joanna.

"So, you will not oblige me, Kate," he railed, tearing the mask from her face.

One of Joanna's silver backed mirrors was lying on the table and he thrust it in front of her. "Do you for one moment imagine I could make love to that. You, who do not even have the one redeeming feature of a harlot – a pleasing face. Look!" he raged, forcing her to confront her own self-mocking image. Calm no longer, she broke into long repressed sobs, as she tried to cover her face.

"No, you have nothing to fear from me Kate", he said, holding fast her hands. "What a travesty of nature you are. Better you had died than lived to plague the world with such repellence."

Finally letting her go, he threw down the mirror. She was now crying uncontrollably, convulsive sobbing wracking her body.

"Take that and go!" he screamed, flinging the mask in her face.

Clutching it to her, she unsteadily walked to the door. As she groped her way back to her room, she thought someone called to her, but she was far too distressed to pay any heed.

He slumped before the cheerless fire and brooded well into the night, until the last ember flickered and died and the room was left in blackness. "Oh God, what have I done," he cried, burying his head in his hands.

ଓ ଛ

She sobbed unremittingly throughout the long night until she was unable to cry any longer. It seemed terribly cold, but she was trembling from a cause more cutting than the weather. Humiliated and repulsed, she refused to recognise the nature of the hurt, desperately trying to close her mind to all that had happened, letting the hurt drag her into forgetfulness, so that the past, the present and the future became a meaningless void. She was just empty matter, adrift, alone, dead to herself and dead to the world. When dawn came she dragged herself about in the half light. The extent of her injuries was now more visible. Her lip was swollen and cut and there was purple bruising on the exposed side of her face, but that would heal, not so the lacerating words from which she felt she would never recover.

It was Margaret who had called out to her, and guessing there was something amiss it was Margaret who now came to see her.

"Why, you are not well Catherine. How came you by that bruising?" she questioned, full of concern.

"I must have fallen," she replied vaguely. "There has been an absence of proper lighting as I recall."

Margaret felt her hands and found them to be as cold as her manner.

"I think the fall has shaken you badly. Wait here while I fetch you a warm posset. Lie down now," she coaxed, helping her back into bed.

Catherine lay shiveringly compliant until Margaret returned with a cup of steaming liquid which she bade her take without more ado. The potion, strongly spiced, had the effect of bringing some colour back into her face.

"There now, I trust that is better," she soothed, treating her like some sick child in need of comforting.

"Much," Catherine said, the flicker of an appreciative smile on her lips.

She then made her go and sit in the adjoining room where a fire had been lit to dispel the unseasonable weather.

"Now you are indeed looking better Catherine," she said encouragingly as she rubbed her icy hands in her own.

"I feel better," she affirmed, but in that same distant tone, as if the words were not entirely her own.

"I was worried because when I spoke to you last night you did not seem to hear me. Tell me if there is something wrong Catherine, if there is anything I can do to help. It is fitting I repay your kindness."

She was genuinely touched by her concern, but there was little Margaret Burgoyne or anyone else could do to alleviate her misery. It was simply there and had to be endured.

"I thank you for your solicitude Lady Burgoyne, but you must not concern yourself. The fall must have distressed me more than I thought. I do vaguely recollect you speaking to me. Please forgive my rudeness."

She, who had never been able to lie with conviction, was now finding it relatively easy in her unfeeling condition, though to Margaret the explanation afforded was not entirely satisfactory.

"It must have been a bad fall to so unnerve you Catherine. Tis time the sconces in the corridor were re-lit. I shall speak to Sir Edward about it. If only I had been aware at the time I would have stopped you, but because you were crying I thought it a private matter and that you wished to be alone."

A private matter, thought Catherine. Oh yes, very much a private matter.

"A bad fall can quite disturb the constitution. I think you would be wise to postpone your visit to see your family."

Catherine felt her hands clench in realising that this indeed was supposed to be her day off. At all events, whatever had happened, she must see her family. Immediately she got to her feet, but the room swam before her and Margaret had to ease her back into the chair.

"I have to go," she repeated over and over again.

"You are in no state to go anywhere Catherine," Margaret maintained. "I will have a message conveyed to them. They will understand."

Still trembling, she lay back in the chair, exhausted and drained.

"I shall be better in a while. You will not prevent me, will you?" she pleaded.

"Rest a while and we will see."

After Margaret had left, she was able to sleep. When she awoke she felt calmer than she had done hitherto and certainly up to the journey. Margaret made her eat before even considering it, but just as she was about to leave a summons came from Elliston.

"It is not timely," she weakly informed the man who had brought it.

"This is rich," he laughed. "Am I to tell his lordship that you refuse?"

Realising the futility of it, she said she would go, but alone.

The room had been disgorged of its filth of the previous night and he too was renewed in outer appearance and manner, but she could not look at him. The hurt was too raw.

"Mistress Venners, Lady Burgoyne tells me you have not been well."

How ironic of Margaret to unknowingly make things worse, she thought, the strain in his voice slightly disarming her.

"Well?" he repeated when she did not reply.

"I am better now my lord," she replied, her own voice thin and finely controlled.

"I do not think so." He would have said worlds to her if only he could have conquered his feelings of guilt and remorse, but the words went unspoken. She was not his Kate any more. He had lost her. All that had been fine and good between them, he had destroyed. He longed to ask for her forgiveness, but the Elliston blood ran in his veins and he was crippled by pride.

"You are still intent on returning home then?"

"Yes, my lord."

Moving towards her, it wrenched his heart to see how she involuntarily flinched lest he touch her.

"We should talk Kate."

"I thought you had said all that it was needful to say, my lord," she replied stingingly. After all, she was only flesh and blood and he had made her a gift for venting her reproach.

"Drink ever makes liars of men," he said in defence.

"But it also speaks with a truth sobriety denies," she countered.

"Believe what you will. I am too tired to reason, but as God is my witness I intended you no harm."

There was no guile in his statement, and had she not been undergoing that tearing hurt she would have known it.

"You do not look at me Kate. Do you find me so contemptible that you cannot raise your face to mine?"

The answer she gave him was barbed and bitter and allowed of no forgiveness.

"I thought you never wished to look on my face again, my lord."

Never had he seen her so implacable. What he had lost in a moment's insanity, he might never regain in a lifetime. The time was not opportune and she was anxious to be gone. It was all a tragic waste.

ന്ദ ജ

As Margaret had said, the day was blustery but dry, but she was too preoccupied to notice it. It was all very well him saying that he had intended her no harm, but he had harmed her and irrevocably so. But why? Because he had discovered her love for him. Surely a groundless reason, for he ought to have been flattered if not amused. She must not think about it for fear of going mad. The strange thing was that her feelings towards him had not really changed; if anything her love for him was stronger, purified even. That it was a misplaced affection was only too apparent in his cruel and humiliating rejection, but the fault had been hers to imagine that any man could possibly care for her, let alone a man like him.

She was looking on her home as a place of refuge, but it proved nothing of the kind. Once there, further explanations were demanded of her, notably from Rob who as ever was anxious to get to the truth.

"Ye couldna get bruises like that fro' a fall Kate," he charged. "someone's been beatin' ye Kate, and I want to know who it is."

"You are getting too inventive by half," she quickly replied, shrugging off his anger and weakly smiling at Mary who guessed that there was more to it than Catherine was willing to admit, though she herself had no intention of pressing her as Rob was doing.

"Dunna I get a moment's peace in my own home," Matthew complained. "If the lass says she's had a fall, then a fall she's had and let that be an end to it."

"She must think we're simpletons," Rob persisted. "If ye be shieldin' someone Kate I want to know why, and if ye be afraid then ye hae all the more reason to tell us."

Mary looked to him to keep quiet. It was obvious that he was only upsetting Catherine further, but once his temper had flared there was no restraining him.

"I tell you I fell," she maintained. "Uncle Matthew believes me. Why cannot you."

"Because he's stubborn like his father," Miriam remarked, looking at Matthew under her eyes.

"If I find out who tis, I'll break every bone in their body," Rob threatened.

Catherine had to admire his spirit, an involuntarily smile

playing about her lips at the notion of Elliston locked in combat with Rob. It would appear that even in the most wretched of circumstances there was often a glimmer of humour.

"What is so amusing?" he questioned, his unruly hair enhancing his livid appearance.

"You are Rob. You get so excited over naught."

With the aim of putting an end to the rumpus, Miriam announced that dinner was ready. The table was spread with all the good things of old to tempt her appetite, oat cakes, barley bread, hunks of salted mutton and a variety of cheeses.

"I hope ye be peckish Kate," said Miriam filling her plate.

"She would be if she worked on the land," Matthew put in.

"Ay, as ye say Matt," sighed Miriam, wishing he would occasionally forget his precious land.

"Healthy life workin' the land," he resumed, falling to on his heaped up platter.

"Tis not for all of us though," Mary bravely defended.

"No," agreed Miriam, "and some o' us like Kate had no choice."

It was an unexpected barb which made Matthew think; it certainly made him change the subject.

"So Lady Elliston is dead at last," he began, his teeth chewing on the toughened meat and spitting it out when he had done. "I thought she were bloody immortal."

"Matt!" Miriam rebuked.

"Well tis true. There seemed no gettin' rid o' 'er, but fro' all accounts he tried hard enough."

"Ay," Rob agreed. "I hear there were no love lost between 'em. Anyways, tis said he be goin' to the de'il fast enough himsell."

In listening to their ill judged conversation Catherine grew noticeably quiet, though Mary was quick to perceive the tears that threatened to spill from her eyes.

"Puffed up pigs' bladders, that's what they be," Matthew said, his mouth full of mutton. "Too much time and not enough toil. What they could do with is a term workin' on their own blessed land instead o' keepin' men in serfdom to do it for 'em."

"Matt, the way ye speak," Miriam cautioned. "And mind now, Kate hae a care o' the old lady."

They looked at Catherine for further explanation. After all, she was bound to know what went on better than they did.

"I tended Lady Elliston during her last days," she ventured. "She suffered greatly and tis hardly kind that you should speak so harshly of someone you did not even know."

"Bah!" put in Matthew.

"No, she is right," said Mary. "It is wrong to speak ill of the dead, but how will this affect you Catherine?"

"It is possible that I may obtain a position in the household of Lady Burgoyne."

"Oh, that is bonny," said Miriam. "Tis right that ye should hae a good position after all ye trouble with the old lady, and as long as Lord Elliston be agreeable I canna see any reason why ye shouldna be happy."

"I wouldna think he cares what she do," said Matthew. "From all the rumours flyin' about he only cares for 'is own pleasures if ye can call 'em such."

"Ay, lewd in thought and deed," Rob added.

The tirade against Elliston continued unabated until Catherine could stand it no longer. Mary, seeing how it was affecting her, tried to turn the conversation but with little success.

"Tis not so!" Catherine suddenly rounded on them. "Again you speak of those you do not know. Lord Elliston is not what you would have him to be and you do him a grave injustice to criticise him out of hearing. His motives are often misunderstood. I know!"

The clatter of knives was abruptly suspended. Sitting back, they stared at her in amazement. It was so totally unexpected. Even she had not anticipated that she would spring so readily to his defence. All things considered, she had no cause to defend him, but despite the abuse she had suffered at his hands she felt bound to speak out.

"Well, well Kate, ye do surprise me," Matthew said at last. "I dunna think ye would hold wi' the doins of such a man."

"I do not condone Uncle Matt. I am simply saying that you are misinformed."

"Well ye know best lass," said Miriam, "and tis not for us to believe everythin' we hear. Things often get twisted in the tellin'."

Mary, smiling sympathetically, had nothing to add. She knew, instinctively, that whatever had led to Catherine's outburst was connected with the man she had just so nobly defended. She had always known it, ever since Catherine had first refused to discuss him.

Tacitly agreeing that enough had been said of the Ellistons, they confined themselves to less inflammatory topics like her visit to Sulburgh and her first sight of the sea which was as unknown to them as it had been to her. The way in which she described its vastness seemed incomprehensible, but because she counted every one of her days at Sulburgh as precious the narrative gained in the telling and was vivid in depicting the dream-like charm of a place rich in lost association.

She stayed with them longer than normal, the prospect of having to return making her increasingly reluctant to leave. When Miriam reminded her of the time, she made excuses, assuring them that another few minutes would not make any difference. They guessed that her unwillingness to return had something to do with her so called fall, as prior to this she had always been anxious not to be late.

"Best be goin' lass," Miriam reminded her.

"Yes, yes, I must," she replied hastily, her whole nature recoiling from the idea. Rob did not help matters by reminding her that Mary's time was now drawing nearer.

"You will be here for her?" he asked yet again.

"Have I not said so a thousand times already!" she snapped in reply, her nerves stretched to the point of breaking before she was able to stop herself. "Oh Rob I am sorry. Please forgive me."

"You should not press her so Rob," Mary gently chided, ever sensitive where Catherine was concerned.

"Ay ye'd try the patience o' a saint," Matthew threw in.

When she finally left them it was well past her usual time.

"There is summat amiss with the lass Matt," Miriam remarked.

"Ay, maybe, but what can we do if she dunna say."

"Naught," said Rob. "She shuts us out now. She's part of their world, not ours."

"That is not fair Rob," Mary said. "There are some problems that cannot be shared."

"What sort o' problems?" asked Miriam.

"It is not for me to say."

"Ay, well, I think the lass hae good sense," said Matthew. "There's too many damn problems in the world without lookin' for 'em, and I seem to hae more than my fair share."

Their hostile looks did not bother him. Used to being thought unfeeling, he deliberately invited the impression, even if beneath the crusty exterior there was a man of some emotion. He liked to have them think him hard headed, the Matthew Thompson all his neighbours looked up to, tough, resilient, master over his own home and land.

The sun was already low in the sky, and if she was going to get back before nightfall she would have to hurry, instead of which she dawdled, so that she was only half way there before the drawbridge was raised and the portcullis brought down for the night.

"No, my lord, Mistress Venners has not returned," said Sir Edward. "Do you wish me to have the horses saddled?"

"Do it at once. Mistress Venners has not been well. I am concerned for her welfare."

"So my good lady informed me, my lord. Howsobeit, do you not think something may have caused her to stay. I believe her sister-in-law is near her time."

"No I do not. I need to know she is safe. I need to know!"

Burgoyne thought the whole venture foolhardy in the extreme, it being beyond him why he was making such a fuss over Catherine Venners unless she meant more to him than a mere lady's attendant. Perhaps Margaret was right and there was more to it than met the eye. When it came to things of this nature, he had to confess that the weaker sex invariably had the advantage.

The horses having been saddled, Burgoyne watched him closely. He seemed like a man demented. Never, in all his years of service, had he seen him in the seething mood that was upon him now. He raved and called her name, savage and tender by turns, his eyes swimming with tears of remorse and self-pity.

She did not hear him. Her senses were dulled to everything and the sensation was sweet. Unutterably weary, she longed to sink down and rest. It was growing dark and the sky was empty of stars. Nothing seemed to matter any more. She was slipping, slipping, slipping away ... He found her shortly afterwards. Leaving the horses in charge of Burgoyne, he ran to where she had fallen.

"Kate, Kate," was all he could say.

She was blissfully unaware.

"Thank God," he said looking at Burgoyne.

Burgoyne watched in silence, wondering on this strange outflow of feeling for the girl. Margaret was right. Catherine Venners was no ordinary woman.

The next morning she awoke in bed to find Margaret Burgoyne at her side. She stretched and yawned.

"What time is it?" she asked drowsily.

"Mid-day Catherine."

"Mid-day!" she exclaimed. Never since her accident had she been abed at such a late hour.

"Calm yourself Catherine. It was fortunate that Lord Elliston and Sir Edward found you; otherwise, you might have taken a chill. As I feared, you should never have attempted the journey. Lord Elliston was most concerned. He values you highly

Catherine. You must know that."

The remark went unheeded, Catherine turning her gaze to the window which admitted a strong ray of light. Dear Margaret, she thought. Burgoyne was indeed fortunate. Feeling sleepy again, she slid beneath the covers. Affectionately pressing her hand, Margaret left her to rest. She felt detached, remote from everything around her. It was as if she was not the real Catherine Venners at all, but only her wraith condemned to exist in a world far removed from the one she actually inhabited.

He entered unobserved and sat silently by her side as she slept on oblivious of his presence. Smoothing her hair, he luxuriated in its silken touch against his skin. At last she opened her eyes. His smile was one of tender concern, but she could not return it as she once would have done.

"Kate, you are feeling better?" he tentatively enquired.

"Yes, my lord," she said. Her reply was finely controlled, taut like the string of a bow. "I thank you and Sir Edward for my timely deliverance."

"The honour was mine," he quietly said, but there was no hint of sarcasm in the statement. It was an expression of sincere and genuine regard. Only the constraint of things left unsaid raised an insuperable barrier between them.

"Your happening to be riding that way saved me much discomfort, my lord."

A quick tremor passed over his features, but his eyes were bright with indignation.

"Happening!" he raged. "Did you not hear me call you by name over and over again until my throat nigh bled with the effort."

"My remembrance of the episode is not what it should be my lord," she hastily replied, taken aback by his sudden vehemence.

"Do you then place so little value on my regard for you that you think I would not be concerned for your welfare. Be reasonable Kate. You who I care for more than anyone else on earth."

Confused and afraid, her body rigid, she averted her eyes.

"Kate, you will hear me out! I am not like you. My feelings will not be denied, perpetually chained like a dog on a leash. I know your love for me. Know then mine for you. Look at me Kate. For sweet Jesu's sake, look at me!"

She at last turned to face him. He was kneeling beside her, covering her hands with his own, not retentively but lightly as if he was in fear of being repulsed.

"Kate, you can read me better than anyone. My very

countenance must betray me. Anything that is good within me is yours Kate. Yours."

How she longed to believe him, but reason alone precluded the impulse.

"You delude yourself my lord. You cannot care for what repels you," she said, tearing the linen from her face. "Now say you love me!"

There was no pity or abhorrence in his look. Rather did he feel sufficiently confident to take hold of her hands and prevent them from attempting to shield that all too inhibiting flaw.

"Vent your reproach, Kate. You are, after all, entitled to do so, but listen to me first. For days I had brooded on the manner of my mother's death, how even in her last hour she had reviled me. It is true I blamed you in part, but the hurt I felt at that time was unendurable. I had need to express it. This was my means", he explained, gently touching the scars with his fingers, "and, of course, your weakness. You had found a way into the very heart of me, but I had to know if you genuinely cared or were simply like the other women I had known, my mother, my wife, Joanna, every painted harlot and whore. All had used and abused me as I in turn had used and abused them. You are different Kate, the first woman who has actually cared. Do you now understand?"

"I understand," was all she said, her hair brushing against his cheek.

"And forgive?"

"There is nothing to forgive, my lord. As I said, I understand."

Taking her in his arms, he caressed her face with his lips as if he would make whole the scars with his kisses. "You are beautiful Kate," he murmured.

"How can you say so, my lord," she replied, wresting free of his embrace.

"Because you are, and I will make you believe it. I see no blemish in you Kate, but if imperfection there be then it is part of you and has helped to make you what you are, and I love you because of it."

They kissed lovingly, longingly, her fettered emotion finally freed.

"You will come to me Kate, be as a wife to me?" he pleaded, still holding her to him. Those words suddenly cut through her bliss; to the world at large their love was a forbidden love, liable to censure by both God and man.

"You have a wife, my lord," she said, drawing away from him.

"No Kate, she is as dead to me as my mother. A loveless marriage is no marriage at all. I have loved but once, Kate. I beg you, do not reject what is yours and make me baser than I am."

"There is no baseness in you my, lord," she assured. "Let God be our judge."

"Then you will come Kate."

"Yes, I will come."

Taking her hands, he made a solemn vow.

"My heart is yours Kate. May its bestowal never cause you pain."

Her hair of flame caressed his face. His hands tangled themselves in its strands as he wound it about his fingers and drew her yet closer. She was his. Heart, body and soul, completely indivisible, joined in a rapture as old as Adam and Eve.

A thin stream of light lay across the bed, waking him from sleep. He reached out for her, but she stood at the window. Recent rain had washed the earth and the sun was bringing its colours brilliantly alive again. The unexpected resurgence showed in everything, transforming the scene into an illusory world of sweet calm and contentment, the sort of Eden it should be and so rarely is.

"How beautiful the day promises to be, my lord," she said, turning to reassure him that she had not flown so soon, even though every bird beckoned her with its song. She let him take her again, his mouth closing on hers before she could speak another word.

"Nature acknowledges our love Kate. Witness the very change in the weather. Not a cloud in the sky to mar our day."

"You talk like a poet, my lord."

"But of course," he wryly remarked. "Do you not recall a certain rose garden?"

He held her closer still.

"You are happy Kate?"

"I love you, my lord, so how could I be otherwise."

"I merely ask because you seemed so vulnerable when you came to me."

She ran her fingers over his face, the slight disquiet in his attentive gaze drawing forth the tenderness she felt whenever she saw that restless mood coming upon him.

"I was afraid I would not please you, my lord. I was all too conscious of my defects and the fact that there were ugly scars that you had not seen before."

"Kate, Kate," he gently chided.

"I also thought of the many beautiful women I had supplanted and could not help but feel at a disadvantage."

"And now?"

"Now I know differently. I was foolish."

"How could you doubt me Kate. How could I compare those women to the one I love."

He was making plans as to how they would spend their day like a small child who has found joy immeasurable in the possession of a favourite toy or pet. There was nothing he would not do to retain his prize, so afraid was he of losing it. She could read his every thought and was both amused and humbled to realise how insecure he actually was. Her love would be his reassurance. Of that she was certain. He had arranged for the hall to be adorned in red and white roses, thus evoking the fragrance of Sulburgh.

"I thought we would have our favourite flowers to attend us," he said, eyeing them casually.

They walked along the river, throwing stones into its surface. She pointed to various plants along the way, careful to instruct him on their names and various healing properties. He silently listened, intrigued by her learning and the faith she expressed in them. There were so many things to do and say and their time together was never enough, but if the days were not wholly theirs the nights were; those beautiful languid nights of lovemaking and quietly spoken thoughts.

He taught her how to handle a horse and she was eager to learn so that they could ride out together just as he and Joanna had been wont to do in the past. She sat by his side for the first time at formal receptions given in honour of neighbouring gentry or important and officious looking visitors from the capital. And Margaret proved her worth by setting her mind at ease and instructing her as to the necessary procedures to be adopted on such occasions. Even Burgoyne seemed content with this new and, to him, mystifying change. He was right, in that Margaret had understood the situation long before he had.

"Tis beyond me," he would say, "but I own tis a change for the better. We might have less trouble with this one."

"And what is more to the point, so should he," came Margaret's reply.

CHAPTER SEVENTEEN

Meeting and seeing her lord's contemporaries over a number of days, she gained in confidence. At first, they too were diffident, but once having adjusted to her obvious difference they found her both courteous and modest, her facial flaw being more than compensated by her informed and reasoning manner, quite a pleasing change from his usual choice of women. Where possible, they brought her into the conversation in deference to Elliston's wishes. Despite her doubtful background, they were inclined to approve, but whether she was capable of retaining her position gave them cause for concern. They were wily men, these Northumbrians, judicious and sparing of praise. As for their wives, they accepted Catherine Venners new role as yet another facet of Elliston's intriguing personality. Some would have given anything to have been in her shoes.

Having more time at her disposal, Catherine was determined to put it to good use. It was not enough to tend to the bodily ills of the people. She wanted to tend to their education as well, but she had to move slowly; to coerce him into acting on her whims would be a retrograde step and she loved him too well to admit of irksome demands which would only serve to sharpen his temper.

"You are my lady, Kate," he would remonstrate, pacing to and fro.

"And happy to be so," she would affirm, "but I am not your cipher. I want to assist you to the best of my ability, and it is natural that I should do so through the village and its needs."

"I can see to its needs," he would throw back at her, "but mayhap I am not so conversant with them as you are?"

When she did not answer he dissolved into peals of laughter.

"I see you think not my sweet Kate. Do as you think fit, but remember I would be made party to such plans."

"I have your interests at heart, my lord."

Their relationship of charge and counter-charge had only altered in their growing respect and mutual affection. It was a rare relationship based on love and trust and an incredible amount of good humour.

If the village was to be her priority, it was also to be her problem. What would her family and neighbours make of the change in her circumstances. No doubt, it was common knowledge by now. Shame did not enter into it. As far as she was concerned, there was no shame in her love, but would Miriam, Rob and Mary see it that way, let alone Matthew. Should she expect their understanding, they who had given her so much, a home that was hers should she ever need it, and a bond of love and affection that had only been surpassed by her love for Elliston.

She found them strangely reticent, which she felt put her at a greater disadvantage than if they had openly condemned her. As for her neighbours, they were more circumspect; it put her in mind of the months immediately following her accident when they were awkward and unsure as to what was expected of them. If Elliston had taken an agreeable looking wench from amongst them, they might have understood it better, but not the Venners' girl with her glaring disfigurement. True, they recognised her kindness and compassion and, of course, her intellect which was way above theirs, but men did not choose women for these qualities alone. Clearly, there must be hidden depths to Mistress Venners, strange beguiling traits inherited from her mother who had always been a singular woman. It also made them reflect on the future. In a word, what effect this vagary of their lord's might have on their own lives. Until this unforeseen event, they had not fully appreciated just how much they relied on Catherine to treat their ills and alleviate other minor ailments which might interfere with their livelihood. In her new and elevated position, she would probably disassociate herself from them altogether. With anyone else, they would have taken it for granted, but the Venners' girl was an enigma just like her mother before her. She tried to put them at their ease by behaving as if nothing exceptional had happened, but it had and they all knew that it had.

Only Mary was free from restraint, but then Mary's first concern was for her unborn child. Looks of relief showed on their faces when she told them that she could stay as long as was needful, which implied that Elliston was being generous with his favours, and for this they were thankful.

Clearly, they were as bemused by it all as their neighbours, though Mary had guessed all along. Only Rob was really put out, fearing that Catherine was being used as her mother had been used; also, she was still his little Kate, vulnerable and in need of protection, and Elliston could be assured that if ever he were to harm a hair of her head then he would have him to reckon with. But Rob had even more pressing matters, that of Mary and the safe delivery of their child. Perhaps he should be grateful to Elliston for allowing Catherine to stay.

The first nights away from him Catherine hardly closed her eyes, her thoughts revolving solely round him and whether he missed her. If she could have witnessed his feverish activity during the day and his irritability in the evening she would not have wondered. With his permission to tend Mary without the added anxiety of having to leave her at a crucial stage of the pregnancy put her mind at rest, but at the same time she hoped that the birth would not be a protracted one as she hated being away from him.

Within the third day of her arrival Mary's labour pains began. The birth was long and difficult, making Catherine and her aunt fearful of the outcome. Though it was not in Mary's nature to complain, they knew that she must be in terrible pain, yet for their sakes she tried not to show it, but there came a time when she was unable to endure her agony any longer, her cries beginning to bear down on Rob like the sound of an animal caught in a trap. It was at this point that his father thought it prudent to take him out for a walk.

"Leave it to the women, eh lad?"

"Tis all my fault," he replied, his mouth quivering violently as they ambled nowhere in particular.

"If men did not make mistakes, twould be a strange world I'm thinkin'," said Matthew philosophically.

Miriam trundled in pans of hot water, leaving Catherine free to attend to her patient, but in the end it was all of no avail. The still born child was wrapped in a sheet and given to Miriam, enabling Catherine to concentrate on the living, if Mary, haggard and spent as she was, could be termed such.

"My baby does not cry," she managed to speak, looking tearfully at Catherine.

"Mary, dear Mary," Catherine replied. "We did everything we could."

Shaking her head in wan acceptance, she looked for Miriam who had just returned from the pathetic task of laying out the scarcely born scrap of humanity.

"What was it?" Mary asked.

"A boy," Miriam sobbed. "A boy."

Rob took the news like the man that he was, vowing never to

get her with child again, Catherine having given him to understand that unless her health greatly improved it was doubtful if Mary would withstand another such pregnancy. Catherine stayed longer than she had intended, anxious to look after Mary until she was properly out of danger. Father Craven saw to the burial of the child, but only Rob and Matthew attended, Mary still needing the care of the women. For days afterwards she remained weak and listless, but, faithful to the will of God, and patient in adversity she at last began to recover. Rob had hardly left her side, but now that she was feeling better she insisted that he go and help his father in catching up on the press of work that had accumulated during his absence. It was her way of keeping him from brooding on what could not be mended. Alice and Geoffrey were regular visitors, as were her neighbours, all of whom helped to divert her mind from the tragedy of her loss. Their reaction to Catherine remained wary and uncertain, and would have continued as such had it not been for the Frinchams' youngest coming out in a rash which she was able to cure. That night she thanked God for Frinchams' youngest.

"No, the lass has nae changed one bit," Geoffrey Frincham proudly proclaimed. "She's all right Kate. She'll take our part, ye mark my words."

Mother Jomfrey merely cackled, but the others were much reassured.

At last it was safe for Catherine to leave. It was now over a month since she had seen him, and during the whole of that time, which seemed like an eternity to her, she had only received one hastily written note, begging her return as soon as it was prudent and then as an afterthought adding his commiseration on the loss of Mary's baby. She smiled to herself as she read it. It was so very like him; wanting to do the right thing, but loath to do it when it interfered with his own desires.

On the day of her departure it was Matthew of all people who alluded to the change in her circumstances by stating in guarded terms that if things went ill with her she could always be assured of a welcome from them.

Mary hugged her fiercely.

"You are happy now, Catherine?" she asked.

"Yes Mary, I am very happy."

"Then you have my blessing. You deserve some happiness. I trust he appreciates your love. Tis too precious to squander."

"Oh Mary, what goodness is in you."

She had not let him know of her return, wanting to surprise him. The day was beautiful. A stillness hung in the air, a sure sign that the year had reached its zenith and would soon decline into the lazy fullness of autumn. A few more days and they would be assured of a good harvest. The sun dappled her face and her steps refused to keep pace with the longing in her heart. Like a child she wanted to creep up on him unexpectedly and see his reaction. Surprise him she did. He had fallen while out riding and was full of curses and ineffectual wrath. Ordering Burgoyne to fetch a physician he had slammed the door and limped to his bed. She slipped in quietly, hiding behind the tapestry.

"May I not examine you?" she teasingly called.

He hobbled towards her voice, catching her to him. Carrying her to the bed, he awkwardly dragged himself astride her.

"My lord, I think I had better tend to your welfare before you do any further damage."

Falling at her side, they both began to laugh. There being no need of a physician, Elliston was able to enjoy the luxury of an exaggerated pain as she tended to him personally. Peace was restored, not only to the household, but to the Burgoynes, who were now relieved to find their services of secondary importance.

Their summer was everlasting and glorious, each day seeming to have been made especially with them in mind. Could he have had his own way, he would have kept her exclusively to himself, but since there were others who had a prior claim on her affection she was allowed to visit her family whenever she felt the need. In a good mood he was prepared to listen to any suggestions she had for improving the village and, coincidentally adding to the creature comforts of its inhabitants, but she never heckled him. He was no fool, but if he saw sense in the matter he was willing to undertake what she proposed. Thus, over time the villagers found that Kate Venners was an influence for their good. Initially, they supposed that only Matthew would benefit, but he had made it plain, both within their hearing as well as Catherine's, that he desired no special favours unless they were shared by his neighbours. In this, he and Elliston were of one mind.

What Annie thought was quite a different matter. Having determined to be the envy of her neighbours, particularly those dull, plodding blockheads she had left behind in Runnarth – she seemed to overlook the fact that her father was one of them – it would now appear she had been robbed of her triumph by her ill visaged cousin who for some inexplicable reason had taken the eye of Lord Elliston. Convinced that she must have used black arts to get him, for no man worthy of the name could possibly have been interested in her otherwise, she laid the blame on Isobel for having taught her other things besides herbal lore.

Poor Annie, just when she felt everything was going in her favour her wings suffered such a clipping that she fell down to earth with a veritable thud. She soon got over the ruffling, however, smug in the knowledge that she was not a light of love but a proper wife and mother.

Gerard's view of the matter was far different. It gave him pleasure to see Catherine happy. He was also conscious of the great debt he owed to her silence and felt the delicacy of the situation all the more keenly. Time and again she stressed the untenable position in which he had placed her, using it as a means to strengthen her argument and make him see sense. For answer he smiled or made shallow excuses, relying on her to intercede with Elliston should anything happen. His superficial gaiety did not deceive her and at times she was tempted to reveal everything to Elliston. Only fear kept her silent. She was also aware that he had a reputation for adhering strictly to the law as laid down. Meanwhile, Gerard continued to entertain at the castle, his natural charm never overstepping the bounds of propriety as his wife's would have done.

It was a difficult time for Mary and Rob. She was still far from strong and Rob was becoming increasingly anxious. He had intimated to Catherine that he had thought of taking her south where the climate was said to be milder, but he had his father to consider. How could he leave him. Catherine, unwilling to precipitate matters, understood his reluctance to broach the subject, but for Mary's sake she felt he had to do it sooner than later.

CHAPTER EIGHTEEN

Confession within the castle would never satisfy her. Instinctively, she still looked to Craven, he alone and no other. It was only Craven who could absolve her from sin. Elliston's priest was far too complaisant, perhaps out of deference to Elliston himself. It was not that she regarded her love for Elliston as tending to moral corruption, but she was in need of the kind of spiritual guidance that Elliston's priest was unable to give. Elliston had mentioned divorce, but it was such a lengthy process that she felt he did so simply to put her mind at ease rather than with any real hope of prevailing. For himself he was content, but recognising her vulnerability he was anxious to take whatever steps were necessary to protect their relationship. In many ways, Catherine was a paradox to herself, desiring to be both punished and absolved at one and the same time. Meanwhile, Elliston tried to be patient. Never having greatly concerned himself about his own spiritual welfare, he found it a little trying that she should feel so strongly on the matter. It was the one thing he did not understand about her, this need for reassurance of a caring God. Not that he did not believe; he did, but not with the same sense of fervour. Revelation would come soon enough and until such time he could wait. But because he was indirectly the cause of this conscience pricking he was determined to prove that his love was more than compensatory for any misgivings she might have as to the state of her soul. Of one thing he was resolute, that neither God nor man would come between him and the woman he loved.

The day had been humid. There was the threat of thunder in the air and she could not sleep. He lay beside her, unaware that she gazed at him, her eyes brimming with tears. Again she told herself that their love was a good thing, pure and free from all taint. As the first flash of lightning lit up the room, she drew closer to him and then fell asleep, but she dreamed and the dreams were full of Craven exhorting her to step back from the abyss. The horribly gaping mouth of something monstrous was sucking in the souls of the wicked and she had no power to withstand it; like a vortex it was taking her in. When she awoke he was holding her tightly and bathing the sweat from her hair.

"Twas only a dream Kate," he soothed. Clinging to him, she at last fell asleep in his arms.

A drab and grey morning followed the storm and she continued to lie in his arms.

"Kate, I have been thinking," he began, determined to banish the nightmare from her mind.

"My lord?"

"Precisely. That is it. All this my lord. Is it not time you called me by name? I do have one." His good humour did not cheer her as he had hoped, all her thoughts still being concentrated on the nightmare. "You should know what it is," he continued. "You heard my mother say it only too often. That is probably why I dislike it so, but coming from your lips may improve it."

"My lord?"

"Kate, you are not listening. My name Kate." It was such a simple thing he requested, and yet she could not accede to it with equanimity.

"Roger," she whispered.

"Louder," he teased.

"Roger!" she screeched, her hands clenched in the effort.

"Gently Kate," he coaxed. "A name should not disconcert you so." He had no intention of referring to the real cause of her anxiety.

"Forgive me, my lord. I am not myself."

"Tis the weather Kate. Call me what you will. It matters not."

The weather did not allow of any outdoor activity and her nerves were stretched even further. She could not dismiss Father Craven's recriminatory look from her thoughts or the monster that had threatened to engulf her.

Next morning she went to see him. A dampness hung on the air, reminding her that summer was nearly over. She had left Elliston asleep, and having taken no nourishment the chill cut her through. The river companioned the sky, leaden and lifeless, no life reflecting image on its moribund surface. No birdsong broke the spell of the brooding monotony, the sun remaining ghost-like in the greyness above. A few figures moved lethargically across the landscape as if the weather had deadened their senses and left them unequal to the task. Despite the recent storm, the harvest still promised to be a good one.

She deliberately avoided her home, determined that nothing should deflect her from her purpose. A thin veil of mist lay over everything. Enveloped in its shroud of low cloud, the church looked as soulless as the rest of the village. The door of his dwelling was open, but he was not present. A platter of half eaten bread lay on the table and the fire had been lit. All her resolve suddenly left her. She wanted to flee, back to safety, back to *him,* but her will was not her own and she stayed where she was. At length he returned, more as a presence than a flesh and blood entity.

"Catherine," he said, his voice betraying no surprise. "A fire is needful on such a day. How soon the summer leaves us."

Nothing about him had changed, his spare frame, his fair hair, the translucent quality of his skin, nor the look in his eyes, so searching, so exacting.

"I hoped you would come," he intoned like some distant yet solitary bell that cannot be muffled.

"I need to confess," she said, her own voice hurried and unnatural as once her mother's had been. Why was it, she wondered, that although she obeyed her mother in everything else, when it came to Craven she was not minded to listen. Whence came the source of his influence? From God?

"I have been patient," he said. She could imagine his being patient, knowing the extent of his influence and how to effect it. Was he genuinely Christ-like? The Lord thy God is a demanding God crept unbidden into her mind. She looked away, suddenly humbled.

"You have much to confess Catherine."

"I need your guidance Father."

"You need the surer guidance of God. He too is patient."

He led her into the garden. She glanced at the roses, overblown and already dying. It was not as cold or gloomy inside the church as she had anticipated, the brilliantly painted walls lending colour to the day. His long thin fingers, like tapers of wax, made the sign of the cross.

"I am listening," he said.

Elliston knew instinctively where she had gone and immediately went in pursuit. No one and nothing was going to separate them now, of that he was certain. He ought to have heeded the signs better than he had. Honest and good, she had a consciousness of what was acceptable deeply embedded within her, and it was this sense of right and wrong that Craven would eat away at as only he could.

The overall greyness kept its hold on the day and the sky retained its hue of depressive neutrality. It was the absence of colour that lowered the spirit and made conscious effort a burden.

Like Catherine, he was aware of a growing sense of oppression. The great open fields wore a similar dull aspect, a few labourers wielding slow swishing scythes, their strength seemingly worn down by the lack lustre day. Who was this man Craven anyway that he should have such a hold over the woman he loved. He had met him but briefly, but enough to know that he represented everything he most distrusted in the clergy, that professed sanctity of his wrapping itself around him like some divine mantle that allowed of no error. He was full of faultless faults and God alone was fit to judge him.

A few wretched crows squawked ominously overhead as he drew near the portal of the church. From within came the sound of subdued discourse. In recognising her voice, he was tempted to break down the citadel there and then and drag her away. A man of quick impulse, dogged reasoning did not come easily to him, but in order to win any ascendancy over Craven he knew he would have to employ it to the best of his ability. If he gave way to anger now he would only play into the hands of the priest and see Catherine trapped in a tightening net of rigid morality. He was not a man given to prayer, only resorting to God when nothing else served and what he prized most was endangered.

The door admitted him quietly and he was content to stand in the saving gloom and listen. Catherine and her confessor were central to his view and he had no difficulty in seeing or hearing. She was laying bare her soul, pleading for him to intercede with God and have compassion on her sin. He remained unmoved. His God allowed of no mercy. His God was a demanding God who exacted and never forgave.

"Do you think of your mother Catherine?" he said.

"Often Father."

He was using subtlety as a scourge to whip up her conscience, and given a choice she would rather have subjugated her flesh than suffer the torments of his carefully chosen words.

"Was not she too beguiled by such a man?"

"My mother was a good woman," she charged, for not even he would be allowed to condemn her mother with impunity.

"I never said otherwise Catherine. She was indeed a virtuous woman, but tempted by a promise of things that could never be.

You too are virtuous Catherine, which is why like your mother you will ever be tested and tried. She failed in that test, but with God's help I believe that you can overcome such temptation. Resist it now, Catherine, while you still can. I beseech you to leave this man before he leaves you as your mother was left."

"I love him Father Craven, as he loves me. There is no baseness in the feeling we share."

"No proscribed love is innocent," he admonished. "The taint is ever about it. The love you speak of is accursed Catherine."

"No, Father," she denied, hot tears running down her face as she tried to make him understand. "If only you knew, you would not speak as you do."

"I only speak the truth Catherine. Bitter it may be, but your own conscience must tell you that I do not lie. This feeling you speak of is an illusion, a trick of the devil to turn your face from God. Do you not see that in persuading yourself that this man genuinely cares for you, you are simply deluding yourself. When he tires of you, which he will, he will discard you as he has the others."

She had no words with which to fight off the relentless tirade. They all sounded empty compared with his own. Her love was her defence, but he was tearing it down bit by bit.

Elliston had not reckoned on the calculating tenor of the priest's persuasion. Unusually hot, he had to wipe away the streams of sweat that ran down his face. The invective against himself did not move him. What did rankle was the subtlety of the argument. Not only was Craven convincing, he was disturbingly devious. When she had tried to speak in defence he could not help but notice how irresolute her own words were; it was as if she began to doubt their own conviction and was already wavering beneath the growing authority of his. She was, after all, only flesh and blood and he had to ask himself whether she would be sufficiently strong to withstand the calculated assault upon the love she had owned for him. He was growing impatient. This was the first time he had been into the village church and the crudely depicted wall paintings increasingly drew his eye. Crude they might be, but they had clearly been executed with a simplicity of faith that made divinity unquestionable. Matched against the complexity of the priest, they were strangely comforting and made him hopeful of the outcome. Had God truly heard him. Was it possible that He would view his appeal with the compassion every genuine believer attributed to Him. Would God tell him when to speak and when to keep silent.

"I know he loves me," she was saying yet again. "He accepts me as I am. What man would be able to do so unless he genuinely cared."

"Your reasoning is one of sophistry Catherine. You cannot test the truth of his regard by attributing it to his indifference to your disfigurement."

"Not to that alone," she countered, her patience tried by his reluctance to acknowledge that she was entitled to know love as much as anyone else.

"His instincts are those of the animal Catherine. It cares not who it mates. The mere fact of your being different is probably the novelty of his choosing you. No doubt, fair features may pall when there is nothing else to enhance them. All these women have been somewhat similar to himself, shallow, sensual, but you Catherine are none of these things. Do not think to retain your innocence for long though. The taint of corruption will soon be upon it and then you will become as they are. Repent now Catherine, and go to Christ as it was meant from the beginning."

He laid his hands upon her head and she felt the iciness of his touch begin to crush her.

"I love God and I love Lord Elliston," she maintained, though her courage was failing.

The time had come when he had to speak out.

"Enough! I have heard enough." As ever, his voice was warm and impassioned, resonant, forceful.

Craven turned and looked towards the door, where thc object of all his abuse stood firmly regarding him.

"You, in my church!" he accused.

"God's church, Craven, God's church," he corrected, his determined tread echoing throughout the length of the dimly lit aisle. "No doubt, you would wish it were otherwise, but fortunately tis not."

"Take not the Lord, thy God's name in vain," he rebuked.

"Look to yourself sir priest."

Catherine rushed to his side.

"My lord speak not harsh words here," she begged.

"No, Kate. I will not. Your fatherly friend has excelled himself enough in their usage for one day."

"Heed him not Catherine," urged Craven. "You now see him as he is, the devil's guile in every syllable he utters."

"Would that you were in ..." Elliston began, his hand held loosely on the haft of his dagger.

"Hell?" replied Craven, finishing the sentence for him. "We are all in danger of that, some more than others. My only concern is for Catherine, and that her innocence be preserved."

Elliston laughed softly, Catherine putting out her hand to restrain him further.

"Rest easy Kate. He has had his say. Let me have mine. Mark him well Kate, how he turns my love for you to ridicule, how he would have you think I am the devil's instrument, nay the very devil himself."

Craven made as if to stop the flow of rhetoric, but Elliston pushed him against the wall. "No, Craven, you will hear me out, and in God's church, not yours. Kate is mine. In her is my salvation."

"You talk like a man possessed," Craven replied. "Catherine, you only have to listen to him to know what manner of man he is."

"I pray you cease," she implored, as Elliston released him.

Craven walked towards the altar, knelt down at it and began to pray. Elliston looked at her keenly, but she was looking at Craven who, having concluded his prayers, was far more composed.

"The way is yours to choose Catherine," he said. "I can say no more. I have known you since you were a child. I knew your mother. I have a care for you. If you sincerely believe in Christ Jesus, the Blessed Virgin his mother and all the saints your conscience will guide you to do what is right."

She turned to Elliston, who was scraping the floor with his foot and wishing he had not spoken so rashly lest it lower him in her esteem and give Craven the advantage.

"Kate," he said gently. "I do not have your priest's moral rectitude, his fineness of soul, but I have a heart Kate, and for what it is worth it is yours."

Craven looked at him and despised him. He wanted him out of his church and away from Catherine Venners. Elliston knew it and turned to go. He was convinced he had lost her. She had not moved, although he waited a moment before closing the door behind him.

"I knew you would see reason," Craven said, reaching out his hands to her.

"Reason?" she questioned, all her love for Elliston suddenly flowing back the moment she had caught the anguished look in his features. What had reason to do with it, she thought, remaining unresponsive to his gesture. She was seeing him as her mother saw him. There was no blood in his veins, no warmth in that fineness of soul. "Father Craven, I respect you, I always will, but I cannot stay. I cannot."

She ran to the door and out into the sudden rush of sunlight that momentarily blinded her to his departing figure.

"Wait, my lord, please," she cried. "Roger, please."

He turned from saddling the horse and ran back.

"I love you," she sobbed as he gathered her to him. "I will never leave you."

"Never?" he teased, smoothing back her hair.

"No, my lord."

"You know that you called me by name."

"Did I? I had not realised," she replied. "It was not deliberate I assure you."

They had not ridden far before she asked him to set her down.

"Why here?" he asked, as she led him by the hand to a remote part of the river.

Unmooring the boat, she placed the oars in his hands, and without enquiring further he rowed her across.

"I wanted you to see Peter's grave. I think he would understand as Father Craven never will. You see he also had a heart."

She showed him the cave and the rough altar, and he began to appreciate her need for a caring God, even if he did not fully understand it himself.

Left alone in his church, Craven gazed around at the wealth of biblical instruction as Elliston had done, but what comforted Elliston did not comfort him. What had he done that God should try him so. Consoling himself with the precept that the closer one drew to one's Saviour the greater the burden, he closed the door behind him.

CHAPTER NINETEEN

Matthew was right. Not for years had there been such a bountiful harvest, a miracle of God considering the harsh winter. It seemed that just at the time when they needed it most, the late autumn sun put a protective band of warmth upon the land, resulting in a rich reward for their labours. Taking advantage of their rare good fortune, they worked late into the evening, reaping both physically and mindfully the abundance about them. Women and children helped in the task of binding the sheaves and everyone prayed that the weather would hold. Their prayers were answered, neither God nor the weather proving contrary. Now was the time to sit back and drink in the success of their toil, nothing being left in its wake but a quilt of burnt stubble over which a few scavenging birds hovered, it proving hardly worth their while to investigate an earth thus cauterised and bled.

God had been good, and Father Craven held a thanksgiving service in recognition of the fact, memorable for its cautionary words that they must not look on their gift as a blessing for labours hard won, but rather as a bounty deserving of greater devotion to God, who saw all and judged all.

"We mun work 'arder still, I reckon lad," Geoffrey Frincham chuckled, nudging the vacant Walter who beamed an empty grin, his brain retaining shadowy impressions and precious little substance.

"Ay father," he replied, gazing up at Geoffrey with utter devotion, rather like a dog that dotes on its master. The simple trust he had in his father was touching and whatever tasks were within his limited ability he performed out of love as well as obedience. Alice walked between the three girls who were all as pretty and bright as Walter was dull. The other boy sauntered behind making faces at the little girls who were quick to retaliate. At the age of ten he had sufficient guile to more than compensate for the slowness of his brother. Geoffrey often regretted that he was not the eldest, but being soft at heart he reserved a special love for Walter who always did as he was told and in many ways was far less of a burden than the other four put together. Moreover, with God's help, he reasoned the senses that were dimmed in his son might be put to rights when he came to inherit, for Geoffrey still looked to the day when he could proclaim to the world that he was free and beholden to no man, and with the encouragement of Alice how could he fail. Her finest quality was her unfailing belief that all would be ultimately well, and when bad things happened, as happen they will, she felt too keenly the bite of the poison. She was intrinsically good and kind, having a pride in her family and home that could not be equalled, virtues no doubt tiresome to her neighbours who had not forgotten her foolishness at the rent day and still made sly comments about it behind her back. All in all, Alice Frincham was a character and a jolly fine one at that, and characters were popular, even the likes of Mother Jomfrey.

Matthew and Rob had just finished supper and Matthew was reflecting on the harvest with his usual circumspection.

"There will be no another the likes o' that for many a year I'm thinkin'," he said. "Ay, I hae nae seen a harvest like it since I were a lad, but I can well remember we were thwarted for three year afterwards. Tis nature's way. She's a tetchy besom. Gives with one hand, takes away with the other."

"Get away wi' ye Matt," said Miriam, flipping her hand teasingly across his head. "Ye be a Job's comforter, that's what ye be. Ye went to the supper at Baillie Talbot's bright enough, singin', dancin' and drinkin' ye fill, and now ye be maudlin' o'er what ye might hae' to pay for one good crop, why shame on ye."

"Ay, mayhap," he agreed, "but ye know it canna be bettered, that's what gets to ye."

Rob nodded his assent, though his thoughts were more with Mary who sat still and listless. The prospect of another winter to come like the last one made him more anxious than ever. Miriam feared for her too. Neither had Catherine's herbal remedies served to break the pattern of lethargy and weakness.

"I worry about ye Mary," he remarked.

"Ye have no cause Rob. I am getting stronger all the time, I assure you."

But they all had their doubts, even Matthew who kept his thoughts to himself.

November came and she was no better. Seeking Catherine's advice, he at last came to a decision. He would take Mary south. Leaving his father would be a bitter wrench and he did not know how he was going to tell him. Matthew was getting older and his going would break his heart. Catherine recognised his dilemma well enough, the conflict of loyalties, the urgency of a problem not mended by delay. He had already broached the subject to Mary, who discounted it at once, assuring him that once the spring came she was sure to improve, but Catherine, having seen her, told him that the signs were not good and promised to give him all the support he would need.

Naturally, Elliston was intent on seeing matters concluded as quickly as possible; anything that unsettled Catherine unsettled himself. In his mind he had already resolved things. Both Rob and Matt would need money and he was there to dispense it. Catherine could be the bearer of his good tidings. Nothing could be simpler!

Rob could not have chosen a more unpropitious day on which to make known his decision. Fog lay all across the earth, reducing visibility to the measure of a man's footstep and making it impossible to do a day's work. Matthew was already in a foul mood, his irritability evincing itself in the indistinguishable mutterings he addressed to his dish which he held but an inch from his face, the spoon forcibly feeding his mouth like a trowel. Scraping it clean, he spun it towards Miriam for another helping.

"Ye can wait, there be others aside ye," she admonished.

Serving Rob and Mary first, she then ladled out another portion to him which he nestled miserly under his chin. The fire was crackling and spitting, emitting a cloud of smoke which resembled the fog. Rob was more silent than usual, stirring his spoon abstractedly, and gazing doubtfully at his father. Much as he would have preferred to delay the announcement until Matthew seemed in a more receptive frame of mind, he had promised Catherine to tell them before she arrived later that day. Mary looked at him enquiringly. She did not like the hesitant tone of his voice or the way in which he avoided looking at her directly. Surely he was not going to say anything now, she inwardly reflected, knowing full well that he had all the intractability of his father when he was set on a thing.

"Father," he began tentatively.

Matthew still held the dish close to his chin, expecting nothing more than some notion afoot for winter ploughing.

"What be it?"

"I am going to take Mary south."

"South?" he repeated, a little whistling sound emanating from a gap in his teeth.

"What do ye mean Rob?" asked Miriam, who was always in a state of perplexity at these sudden crises in her family.

"He means nothing mother," Mary quickly intervened, gesturing to Rob to keep quiet.

"I mean all I say!" he flared at her, "and ye can hold your tongue and be the dutiful wife ye promised to be."

Unexpectedly cowed into silence, she looked appealingly at Matt and Miriam who were equally dumbfounded, he never having raised his voice to Mary before, not that they could think of a time when she had merited correction.

"She's not well and we are goin' south. London maybe. Tis warmer and I see it as the only way."

"I will not go!" Mary tearfully protested, pushing her stool away and seeking sanctuary in the kitchen. Miriam flopped herself down upon it. Matthew's half raised spoon plummeted into his dish.

"Ye are leavin' for good. Is that what ye are sayin'? I canna credit it. Do ye hae any notion o' the work I've done on your behalf. All this land is yours when I'm gone. And ye sit there and tell me ye are leavin' as if it were naught. What sort o' son have I raised!" he said, staring at Miriam in disbelief.

"A son who puts his wife afore all," Rob replied. "Mother, ye can see she's nae better. She dunna eat. Look at her dish. She has scarce touched a spoonful. Why she be no stronger than a reed, one puff o' wind and she'll break."

"Ye'll leave ye birthright for a woman!" Matthew railed.

"Nae ordinary woman father. My wife. If mother were ill, ye'd do the same?"

Judging by the heavy pause and the rigid compression of his lips, Miriam knew that he would do no such thing. Not that she was unnecessarily upset. She understood him too well for that. As she had often remarked, he was far more wed to the land than ever he was to her.

"Tis not the same," he eventually replied.

"I'll not change my mind father. I trust to come back in a few years' time when God willin' she hae improved. Try to understand father, I dunna want to leave, I have to."

"Dunna ye bother to come back Rob! Ye bloody ingrate! Dunna bother, do ye hear!" he railed, catching him across the face with his fist.

"Stop it!," Miriam pleaded as Rob was about to return the compliment.

"He hasna the guts," Matthew goaded.

It was to Rob's credit that he resisted the temptation and

dutifully turned the other cheek.

"Dunna ye worry woman," said Matthew. "I hae the measure o' him. I'll ne'er strike ye again Rob. Ye not be worth it. Take yon bitch and get out!"

With this he got up and left. Once alone, he almost wished he had not been so hasty, the heat of his temper quickly evaporating into the mist. He huddled beneath his jacket, lamenting the fact that his thickest hung behind the door and not on himself. His thoughts were a jangle. Rob was at fault, not him. Even so, he had to acknowledge that the lass was clearly unwell, but then again that was no doing of his. Rob should have wed a lass of sounder constitution, not a lath of a creature. That aside, he had chosen well. She was amenable and hard-working when she was able, then why in God's name could she not be hale too. "Blast, blast, blast!" he cursed. With the fog swirling thickly, he had to seek shelter, sympathy too if he could find it, and where better than with the Frinchams. Geoffrey would assuredly soak up his troubles and Alice turn them tearfully to account. As for the rest, let them go hang.

❧ ☙

It had been Catherine's intention to arrive that same morning, but Elliston had rightly prevented her until the fog should have lifted. By mid-day the sun had dispersed it a little and he agreed to let her go. She would have gone earlier and deplored the delay.

When she arrived she could sense the atmosphere immediately. Mary and Rob were determinedly sitting apart as Miriam busied herself with the housework, two hectic patches of red accentuating the fullness of her cheeks. Matthew was noticeably absent.

"Kate, I thought ye'd never come," he said, nervously clasping her hands.

"I see you have told them," she whispered, half-smiling at the scene before her. A death in the family could not have evoked more misery.

"Catherine, you knew of this?" Mary asked, a note of disdain in her voice as she anxiously played with the ring on her finger.

"Yes, I knew, and approved of it Mary. Come nearer the fire and I'll tell you why."

"Why? Just to ease your conscience?"

"My conscience is clear Mary. Whatever I have done was only with you in mind. Please, Mary. Such petulance does not become you. Tis not in your nature."

"Catherine, it is unforgiveable," she replied, her tone decidedly more moderate as she sat beside her. "We cannot leave. You know that."

"All I know Mary is that a change of climate might make all the difference to you."

"But you can make me well again Catherine. I know you can."

"That is where you are wrong. I cannot. In the south it is milder and the winters less cruel. Rob will find work there and you will grow strong and bear healthy children. Is that not what you want?"

Miriam agreed with a nod. She had made some mulled ale and was now handing it to them.

"What will father do?" she sobbed. "Rob must not leave him thus. This is our home Kate. We will be foreigners in the south".

"Make her see sense Kate," Rob sighed, wiping the wet from his lips.

"Catherine is right Mary," Miriam added, her voice thinning with emotion. Matt and I must manage as best we can. Ye mun go. Tis your duty to obey your husband and there is no finer man than our Rob."

Mary could no longer resist. Worn down, both mentally and physically, she sobbed on Rob's shoulders.

Matthew sauntered back bemused. Having indulged Rob's ingratitude to the full, he had not received the response he had expected from the Frinchams. There was something wanting in their sympathy he had not reckoned on. Alice had seen for herself the marked deterioration in Mary, and though she did not want to see her go, it seemed better than she be lost to the mercy of London than the mercy of heaven. She reserved her opinion for Geoffrey's ears alone, informing him with the same indomitable spirit she had shown at the rent day that Matt Thompson had no right to come between man and wife and that Rob's first duty must be to Mary who needed the laughter of children to bless their union which was the natural desire of all women, as witnessed by her own happy brood who had been a solace and a joy to them both, though he would never own to the fact, but should he do so he would see that what she spoke was veritably true and ordained of God and therefore indisputable evidence of the rightness of things, whereupon she dissolved into tears and sought for comfort in the arms of the father of that happy brood. Alice, as ever, was never sparing of speech.

Matthew scarcely hurried back. In a word, he was confused, the unpleasant thought occurring to him more than once that maybe he was not entirely the wronged man he assumed himself to be. Pointedly rattling the latch, to leave them in no doubt that the head of the household had returned, he made his entrance like some bear about to be baited.

"And where hae ye been?" asked Miriam, his presence in no manner disturbing her new found composure.

"Geoffrey's," he mumbled.

"I might hae guessed, and I suppose he agreed with everythin' ye had to say."

"Hush ye woman," he cautioned, catching sight of Catherine. "Trust Isobel's brat to hae a hand in the business."

"I have something to tell you Uncle Matt," she commenced, tactfully vacating her chair, which he slumped into without a murmur. "In fact, something to tell you all, but it would have been improper to commence without you Uncle Matt."

It was a brave attempt, but Matthew was in no mood to be patronised. She told them of Elliston's suggestion, and of how he was prepared to pay a labourer to assist Matthew and also to provide Rob with a small pension to get him started in London. Their response was what she expected. At least father and son concurred in their mutual hostility to the proposal. Mary had listened impassively throughout, and as it was she who was at the centre of the argument she felt that she too had a right to be heard.

"I think Rob that you and father should accept Lord Elliston's offer ..."

"Never!" came the quick retort of both.

"Listen," she appealed. "Rob, take the money as a loan which you can repay once we are settled. And you, father, take on the extra labour promised and accept the generosity of Lord Elliston with good grace."

"Ay, maybe tis best," yielded Rob, taking her hand.

"Well it maybe for ye, but I'll ne'er be beholden to no man, least of all because he's my niece's ..."

"Enough!" Miriam interrupted to the astonishment of them all. "Matt, do this for me, if not for them. Tis such a small thing and will make everyone happy. I have ne'er asked ye for much in our marriage, but I beg ye to please me in this."

"It will be done with discretion," Catherine assured. "No one need know."

"I will know!" he countered. "Anyway, what is it worth? I gain a labourer and lose a son. Is that a fair bargain?"

"He will return," Miriam affirmed. "Has he not said so, and ye can ever depend on Rob's word."

"Ay, when I'm gone fro' this troublesome world," he droned

pathetically. Taking off one of his shoes, he spat on the leather and began to rub at it vigorously. There seemed no moving him. Then he looked at them hard. "When will ye be leavin'?"

"I thought after Christmas," answered Rob, holding out his hand in a conciliatory gesture. All will be well father."

"Maybe lad, maybe," said Matthew, pressing it warmly.

CHAPTER TWENTY

Because it would be their last Christmas together, Miriam, like someone about to be dispossessed, was determined to make the occasion special. Everyone was to be invited, and that included Catherine, though she could hardly expect Elliston to be sympathetic when he had been more than generous to her family already.

"Go to your damned people," he raved like a spited child.

"If you could compromise my lord," she suggested, feeling it inappropriate to call him by name.

"You ask me to compromise!"

"Very well I will stay with you. As you say, you have done more than enough."

"And then you will brood and feel guilty at not being with them, which in turn will redound on me, and together we will act out a joyless day and there will be no memory but a miserable one. It seems I shall have to let you go; the day can be theirs, but the night shall be mine."

"Thank you my lord."

"Am I not a good man, Kate?"

"Incredibly so," she vouchsafed.

It was a far different Christmas to that she had spent at the castle, and if she was sorry at being separated from him, she had to own she was pleased for her aunt's sake. Lacking in the formality and trappings of Lady Elliston's last Christmas, it more than made up for it in good cheer. Nearly everyone in the village was invited, for Miriam was noted for her hospitality and the fullness of her table. They wore their best too, holes in tunics and hose conspicuously patched, faces shiny from uncustomary scrubbing. The cold might make them shiver, but they were all warm of heart. Even Annie seemed less provoking than usual. One look at Catherine made her less jealous. For prettiness there was no one her equal. She only had to look around her to be convinced of the fact. She was also the best dressed which added to her feeling of self-satisfaction. If she was the most fetching of women, then Gerard had to be the most attractive of men. All this kept her cooingly complacent and in a humour to be sweetly demure. Gerard was hers, utterly, completely, disturbingly hers. As for Catherine, she convinced herself that Elliston would soon tire of her anyway. Touching the softness of her own cheek, she wondered how he could possibly caress the blasted face of her cousin unless he was prone to a taste for the unnatural which must be the most likely explanation for a liaison that was beyond her limited reasoning. Conversely, what Elliston did have, and in too great a measure for her liking, was wealth and influence, all the things she craved and would never quite possess. If only Gerard could have been Elliston, she conjectured, life would be perfectly blissful.

"What are ye thinkin' lass?" asked Matthew, cramming a pastry into his mouth.

"Naught in particular father. How ordinary Kate looks. I thought to see her in something a trifle more becoming now she has risen so high."

"Kate is all right," he spluttered through the mouthful of still steaming pastry. "Anyhow ye would nae want competition now, would ye Annie, ye being the best lookin' of the lot of 'em."

"You are prejudiced father," she pertly responded, lapping up compliments as he lapped up crumbs.

"Well, ye are not goin' to gainsay it Annie, are ye?"

"No, father, why should I?" she replied, smiling archly. Matthew basked in that smile. He still adored her, despite all her faults.

She looked at her boys with pride, if not exactly affection. They had inherited their father's good looks and vibrancy of spirit. He had a liking for children which she did not; they certainly idolised him which at times made her jealous, but then anything that came between her and Gerard made her feel insecure. She edged her way to where Catherine was sitting talking to Mary.

"Say what you will Catherine, I remain apprehensive," Mary was saying, her fragility accentuated by the dark shade of blue she was wearing and the wistful way in which she was viewing the gaiety going on around her.

"You must not be faint of heart Mary. Think of London as the capital of the world, for in truth Lord Elliston has said as much and I do believe it to be so."

"But your capital of the world will take me away from all I love best."

"But not from Rob," Catherine quickly replied.

"I know, but you still cannot cheer me."

"I can try," she jestingly replied. "It is Christmas after all."

"It is indeed," announced Annie, sidling up to them.

"Annie, you look lovely, does she not Catherine," Mary remarked.

"Indeed she does," Catherine readily acquiesced; her reply genuine and unfeigned, despite Annie's narrowing looks. Whatever did Elliston see in her, she silently mused, when deep down she knew precisely the nature of the attraction did she care to admit it. Secretly, she envied Catherine, had always envied her, not only for her learning and patience, but for the way in which she had seemingly turned the disadvantage of her disfigurement into a positive asset, or so it seemed. Without it, she would just have been another ill gotten bastard. With it she was something different, cultured, dignified, inveigling herself into the affections of others through the offices of that detestable mask, that wretched contrivance which was far more indecent than the scarring beneath it. In the latter surmise for once she was right.

"Gerard bought the material in Newcastle and had it made up for me," she said, preening herself like a bird preens its feathers. This time there was no likelihood of her wings being clipped.

Mary did what was expected of her by feeling the thickness of the cloth, but Catherine was reluctant to indulge Annie more than was necessary.

"You feel it Kate?" she insisted, forcibly smiling.

"I take your word for it Annie. It is most becoming and worthy of Gerard's regard for you."

"I gather you would willingly go to London, Kate?" she pointedly asked.

"I would Annie."

"So would I, but unfortunately I have neither the time nor the money for contemplating such a journey at present. For Mary, it is different of course. She goes for the sake of her health. Others, of course, can go for mere pleasure."

Ignoring the remark, Catherine turned again to Mary while Annie hovered, intent on causing mischief. They were watching Walter, his face set in a vacuous grin, mutton fat dripping down his chin and on to his tunic. Alice was tapping her feet to the music. She was wearing her rent day dress and seemed as colourfully humoured as the shades of her gown, but nobody minded, for they were all too tipsily content to care what anyone thought or did. Annie gazed on the goings on with contempt.

Once again, she was set on trying Catherine.

"He has a liking for green then, our high and mighty lord," she began, desultorily casting her eyes over Catherine's gown.

"It is a colour which pleases him," Catherine replied.

"Ye are a sly one, Kate," she said, her voice losing all its initial smoothness of pitch. "I hope he rewards ye well."

Mary coughed nervously, looking for Rob to come to their rescue.

"I am rewarded as you are rewarded Annie, by the regard of the man I love. There is none other that I know of."

"I am wed to my man!"

Rob intervened before anything else was said. He had come to ask Catherine to dance. Mary nodded anxiously and Catherine was relieved to accept.

"I take it she's been aggravatin' ye again," he enquired, holding on to her as if she was an unwieldy sack of corn. Poor Rob, he was a fine ploughman, but no dancer."

"Nothing that I cannot deal with," she smiled.

"She gets above 'ersell worse than afore. Marryin' the Frenchy hasna improved her none."

"Rob, you are prejudiced against the man. You never even try to talk to him."

It was true. Just like his father, Rob had no time for foreigners, especially dainty mannered ones like Gerard.

"I dunna want dealings with 'im. He will bring nae good hereabouts. I know that."

His remark made her anxious and look towards Gerard who was playing the recorder and displaying all his Gallic charm. He caught her looking at him and blew her a kiss. She recalled his gaiety last Christmas and how he had made her the focus of unwanted attention; that Christmas of disquieting confidences, that Christmas when *he* had danced with her and for a moment nothing else had mattered. Perhaps he was enjoying his day despite her absence. No, he could not. Surely, he must be missing her as much as she was missing him.

The clapping and stamping was getting louder, at times drowning out the sound of the musicians altogether. It was then that Matthew did what no one expected of him. The ale had made him feel young again, and putting his hands round Miriam's waist he led her out into the centre of the room.

"Come on lass. Come on," he begged, a rare glint of joy in his eyes. She had not seen him thus for many a year. She placed her hands on his waist and looked at him coyly. The years began to slip away, the Matthew of dour aspect becoming the bright eyed youth she had married, the lad who had promised her the world for her portion at a time when she had been rash and young enough to believe him. Not that she regretted her lot, far from it. She may not have gained the world, but she had sufficient to make her envious of no one. It was true that he was not the easiest of men to live with, but she still had a care for him, and if the desire of their youth had long burned low there yet remained a flame that would continue to warm when many another more feverish had flickered and died.

The crowd parted, making a space just for them.

"Faster, faster!" they roared, as the two of them wove a tangent across the floor, hopping and skipping with all the agility of their youth.

"Tis unseemly," Annie scoffed as the mad caper came to a close.

"On the contrary, I think it is laudable," Catherine replied. A fitting end to a perfect day."

Annie brushed past her, increasingly resentful. Although she had never liked Catherine for a number of reasons, not until now had she consciously hated her. It was not because of Elliston, not because of her affinity with Gerard, not because of her ravaged looks, not specifically for any of these things, but simply because she was Catherine. She frowned disapprovingly at Gerard who, having just enjoyed the unexpected antics of his father-in-law as much as anyone else, had come to the conclusion that he would never fully understand the English.

"Annie," he engagingly smiled, as she handed him a measure of ale. "Your mama and papa, they enjoy themselves, yes."

"Tis foolish!" she scoffed.

"No, Annie, tis good. A little fun, yes. What harm," he replied, guessing from the fraught tone of her voice that something had upset her.

"Kate is so smug," she continued. "Just because Elliston has bedded her, she flaunts her position and thinks hersell better than women who are properly wed."

This last sentence, purposely raised above a whisper, hardly caused an eyelid to flutter, they having no cause to complain of a liaison which had brought them much good.

"Annie, Annie."

The day was drawing to a close. The laughter of the guests trickled away into the cold of the evening. There would never be such a gathering again. A night of velveteen blue nursed the stillness. The man Elliston had sent to collect her was impatiently stamping the ground and blowing on his fingers. He had clearly waited longer than anticipated. She apologised, and though he said it was of no account she could see he was vexed, and if he was vexed what of Elliston.

She had expected to find him in truculent mood. Instead he sat in the darkness, shivering in front of a dying fire. He heard her enter, but chose not to acknowledge the fact, and she in her uncertainty stood in the shadows.

"Kate," he said at last. "Come here."

She obeyed submissively, kneeling at his feet in an attitude of seeming penitence.

"You see that last flame Kate," he said, touching her face.

"Yes, my lord."

"I vowed that if you had not returned before it was extinguished completely, I would go to our room, lock myself within it and conveniently forget you until the eve of the coming year, but as ever you have managed to outwit me, more by providence than judgement I take it."

"Then I must thank providence," she replied, "for had I not arrived in time I would have grieved myself into my shroud before the advent of the New Year."

She took the coldness of his hands and pressed them to her lips.

"A honey coloured speech Kate, but I suppose it is one I have to accept. I suspect that naught detained you but your goodness of heart, which is less of a virtue when it interferes with my desires."

She did not reply. He looked at her lovingly, longingly, with an air of gentle possession, touching the silkiness of her hair and lifting the mask from her face.

"We still have a little of the day left, Roger."

"Indeed, and I intend we make the best of it."

She was about to rise from her kneeling position, but bidding her remain where she was he asked her to put out her hand. "No, your left," he corrected impatiently. From his tunic he took out a ring, gold and intricately patterned, and placed it on her finger. "I was apprehensive that it might not fit. Tis such a narrow band, but then your finger is as slender as the rest of you. It is my gift to you Kate, a pledge of my regard and affection. Though it is not given with the blessing of Holy Church, it is given with mine. In time it may tarnish. It is very old, but the love that it symbolises never will. I swear it." He pressed her hand to his lips, sealing the oath in a kiss of singular chasteness.

"What must I say, Roger?" she said, her eyes brimming with

tears.

"Naught Kate, naught. There is a story surrounding the ring. It belonged to a distant ancestor of mine who, unlike the majority of my line, was said to have enjoyed a felicitous marriage. As far as I know, it has not graced the finger of anyone else since the death of this woman. Now it graces yours."

"I will treasure it. Always."

☙ ❧

In early January Rob and Mary set out on their journey south. Catherine was there to see them go. The first snow was yet to arrive, but the sky was full of its promise.

"Mayhap London will be as fine as you say it is, Catherine, but places are not people."

"Ay," Miriam replied, her assumed cold giving her an excuse for occasional sniffs into the wet rag she held.

"Ye'll hae me Mary," Rob confidently asserted, putting his solid arm around her.

"I know it to be true, and I would always be with you," she replied, nestling against him.

Matthew looked up at the sky, whistling nervously. He was hating it as much as the rest of them. "Whither thou goest, I go," he suddenly said, his penchant for biblical sayings coming to his rescue.

"And Mary can write," Rob reminded them, viewing his wife with obvious pride, she being the only one of them versed in such besides Catherine. Mary tried to smile encouragingly, but like Miriam she was too full to speak. The final partings were long and protracted. Even Matthew's lips puckered as he hugged his son close. And then they were gone.

"Come along now," Matthew said tetchily. "I hae work to do."

He would not look back. Had he done so, he would have wept and spoiled his reputation for hard headedness.

CHAPTER TWENTY ONE

"Mon Dieu, Mon Dieu," he mouthed, the pain of running constricting his breath, but what was his pain compared to that of the man he had killed. He could still hear those last cries, the dreadful agony of a man dying unshriven, the crack of the ribs against the blade, the clawing desperation of the hands that had tried to fend off the blows. Beside the dead man, he had left the dead animal. Both were still warm. The blood of the man was upon him, its stickiness clinging to him like the suck of a leech. He had not meant to kill. In his panic he had hardly known what he was doing until it was over and the man was lying prone at his feet. It was horrible to witness, but more horrible still to know that he was to blame. If only it could have been a bad dream, a grisly tale with which to frighten the children. He thought of them now, his children, so young, so innocent. A father of children like his would be incapable of the savagery shown by such a man, yet he was that man. He made the sign of the cross repeatedly. Holy Mary, Blessed Virgin, Mother of God, he was that man!

Twice he stumbled and fell. The lights in the town were infrequent and he was guided by instinct rather than reason. If only he could reach Annie and the children, all might seem normal again. The blood of the man had trickled on to his fingers and he tried to lick it away; the taste was of salt.

She was wearing the new blue gown he had bought her, and once she heard the click of the latch she swung round provocatively to greet him. On seeing him, her mouth fell agape. He was spattered with blood.

"Christ Jesu!" she cried out, flattening herself against the wall as if he were an intruder and not her husband at all. The pain in his eyes confirmed what she already guessed. He reached out his hands to embrace her. Never had she looked so appealing as she did at that moment, the flush on her skin, the fear in her eyes, the tiny swallowing motion at her throat that roused all his loving concern and made him momentarily forgetful of what he had done.

"Dunna touch me," she cried.

"Annie," he pleaded, almost incoherently. "Annie, please."

"What hae ye done!" she screamed, pulling the purity of her linen tightly about her lest it should come into contact with the foulness of his.

"Annie, Annie," he entreated, sinking down on the floor and clutching his head. "You know Annie I can tell. I did not mean it. Never, never," he wailed.

"Stop it Gerard. I canna bear it!"

But he could not stop. He had to unburden his soul to someone; that it should be Annie only lent irony to the confession.

"He catch me. I, how you say, panic? Yes, I panic. We fight. He is a big man. Strong, yes, strong. I fear he will win. I take out the knife, your knife Annie, the one you buy me. I begin to strike him. I cannot stop. He cries out, again and again. I cannot bear those cries. At last he grows quiet."

He was now crying piteously, his tears mingling remorsefully with the blood of the man on his fingers. Utterly beside himself, he fell on his knees and started to crawl towards her.

"Everything I do was for you Annie. For you! Love me Annie. Love me."

"I didna ask ye to kill for me!" she retorted scathingly.

He tried to cling to her legs, but she pushed him away, the blue linen where he had touched it stained to the colour of bruising.

"Ruined!" she cried, "Ruined". But whether her concern was for him or the gown he was unable to tell. Leaving her alone, he went to the water butt, discarded his tunic and tried to wash the blood from his clothing. The red gushed away in faint pink streams, turning the water in the tub to the colour of wine; he watched it with a kind of morbid fascination. Finding him thus engaged she changed her own clothes, returning with the soiled blue dress held between her thumb and her finger as if it was noxious to touch. He took it from her and flung it into the water with the other, violently agitating the water with a stick. Tangled together, they looked what they were, one miserable mess. The blood having all oozed out, he hung them up to dry well away from her notice. Ever mindful of her, he had left her a basin of water to wash in, which he used himself when she had finished. They did not speak until the whole thing was done and his body felt raw from its scrubbing.

"Annie," he said in a whisper, thinking of the children who

were asleep in the next room. "We must try to keep calm, yes.

"Say you still love me, Annie, please."

"Yes," she answered somewhat unconvincingly.

"Then let me hold you."

She did as he wished, but her whole body was shaking with fear, both for him and herself. She was not lying when she said that she loved him, but she had no desire to examine her conscience too closely for fear of what she might find there. As she had so conveniently pointed out, she had never asked him to kill for her. His wanting to give her things had been solely his own doing, though it was true that she had never discouraged him. And what was wrong in wishing to better oneself anyway; nothing whatsoever. That it had all gone awry was his fault in thinking he could go on as he had without getting caught. No, she was not to blame for any of it. She had not forced him to continue. It had been his choice and his alone. For all she cared, he could have stopped any time he had wanted. Why then did every new and shiny thing, right here in this house, appear to silently condemn her and make her feel uncomfortable. And why did that lost and agonising look in his eyes fill her with more than a twinge of remorse.

"Gerard, what are we to do?"

"I do not know Annie. I do not know."

"Where is the knife?" she asked, suddenly remarking its absence.

Feeling for where it usually was, he felt sick to the pit of his stomach.

"In my haste, I leave it, I forget!"

"Sweet Jesu, what were ye thinking o'?"

The absurdity of the question stunned him into silence.

"Ye must go and get it now, or we are lost," she continued, becoming more alive to their predicament with every passing minute.

"Not now Annie," he begged. "Please, not now. I cannot. A few hours, please, and then I will go back."

"Before daylight Gerard."

"I promise," he replied, wearily bowing his head. "Then maybe we go from here. Start again in another place, yes?"

Empty at heart, lost and afraid, he clutched at anything that would take the nightmare away and give him hope.

"Twould only draw attention to us. Best stay and behave as if naught had happened."

He drew her to him, wiping the tears from her face with his fingers.

"As always, my Annie know best."

"But I dunna Gerard, I dunna," she sobbed. "I never have, and now it is all too late."

"Hush now Annie. You must not say such things. A good wife to me you have always been. Come, let me hold you to my heart. Hear how it still thumps when it is close to yours, yes." She ruffled his hair and clung to him as a terrified child would cling to its mother.

"I love you so Gerard. Nothing will come between us, will it? They will not take you away from me."

"No Annie," he assured her, but as he stared into the darkness he saw a man lying crumpled on a blooded bed of bracken, a man who had not deserved to die.

*

Snow was yet to fall, but the air felt full of it as the horses were saddled for the first ride of the day. She was growing more proficient by the hour and liked to try and outdistance him. Returning, they felt exhilarated and content, but Burgoyne was waiting for them and his bearing was serious. He whispered something to Elliston, whose mood immediately changed.

"What is it, my lord?" she enquired.

"There has been a killing," Burgoyne explained. "One of my men discovered the body. Tis a bad business."

"Do not mince your words Burgoyne," he fiercely interposed. "Twas barbarous, cold blooded and brutal."

Catherine felt herself blanch. Burgoyne looked at her with some concern. He liked the girl and could see that she was as disturbed by the news as his master, but it was not so much the description as something else that alarmed her, the notion that Gerard might be involved.

"My head verderer viciously murdered," Elliston railed, only too readily confirming her fears. "Twenty-three wounds that drained the blood from him as a fountain gushes forth water." The description caused Catherine to sway unsteadily. He caught her to him.

"Clearly Mistress Venners is distressed by the circumstance," said Burgoyne.

"Clearly," reiterated Elliston, somewhat puzzled by her reaction.

Having dismissed Burgoyne he kept referring to the event for many hours afterwards. It was natural that he should, but when he spoke of it in terms of the law and what it exacted she felt she could stand it no longer and asked to be excused. He also kept fingering the knife which had been found by the side of the body.

"I am not feeling well, my lord. Maybe I need to rest a while."

Elliston looked at her curiously. That her indisposition seemed to coincide with what had happened made him wonder.

"As Burgoyne noted, this news has clearly affected you? More than I would have supposed, considering the victim was unknown to you, or at least I assume that he was."

"He was not known to me, my lord."

She said it with conviction, but he was not satisfied. He knew her too well. He picked up the knife and ran his fingers along the edge of the blade; the sun darted off it making her blink. When he laid it back on the table she saw the letter G on its handle.

"You know something of this Kate?" he said, noting the violent tremor that passed over her face.

"No, my lord. The sight of it unnerved me, that is all."

"You lie Kate!" he accused.

It was true. Gerard had peeled her an apple with the very same knife at Christmas; in fact, he had been proud to show her the letter G engraved upon it to please Annie. That he would be so foolish as to actually use it had never occurred to her.

"You cannot gainsay me Kate. I know you too well. Deny it thrice and you will be more wretched than the blessed St. Peter himself. Come now, the truth."

"Please, my lord, I find this more than distressing."

"You find it so, and what of myself. Does not your reluctance to speak impute a fault I had not thought to find in one whose nature seemed above the fecklessness of other women. It appears I was mistaken. You have the weaving, winding ways of all your kind. Kate, I am disappointed."

Despite his inflammatory invective, she refused to be browbeaten. Gerard was her friend. In her he had placed his confidence. She would never be drawn. "Kate, I appeal to you as one who believes in a saving Christ to confess to me what you know of this matter. It is not only your duty to me, but to Christ himself."

All the tenderness he felt towards her was forgotten in his anxiety to find out the extent of her involvement. He held her by the shoulders and began to shake her violently. That she could be involved in some way was abhorrent to him.

"I know naught," she maintained, half tearful, "and I refuse to be coerced."

"Then you admit you are in some manner implicated."

"Yes, I mean no ..."

She faltered, visibly shrinking under the impact of her involuntary admission. He let her go. He had never intended to cause her unnecessary anguish; rather did his own make him forgetful of his unmannerly bearing. She sat down, breathing hard to regain her composure. Seeing she was still in some distress, he put out his hand to reassure her that his love was still intact. She clasped it to her breast and began to weep.

"Kate, I should not have pressed you so. You do not feel badly towards me?"

"No, my lord," she barely replied.

"Then speak to me. Trust me."

The intransigent mood had given way to one of gentle persuasion, and looking at him she realised that his concern was for her and her alone and that she was to speak in the knowledge of that concern.

'Kate, sometimes I think you do not know the extent of my care. Whatever grieves you must grieve me. Is that not what love is? That tenderness and affinity you spoke of yourself. Do you not recollect?"

"I do," she answered.

"And yet you will not speak?" he reasoned, a hint of impatience in his voice.

"I cannot."

"Or will not?"

He perused the knife again and saw the G on its handle. Why had he not considered it previously. It was all suddenly clear.

"I have it!" he cried, springing to her side. "My powers of perception must be growing dim not to have seen it before. Condemned by his own personal mark, Gerard Duval, smooth tongued Frenchman of the engaging manners and sweetly sung ballads. Sweet turned to sour. How long Kate? How long have you known of this new trade of his? Before our liaison? After? I would know. I have a right!"

"Before my lord. He confided in me over a year ago, the last Christmas your mother was alive."

"And you have kept silent until now, or should I put it another way and say you have knowingly deceived me?"

"I would have spoken my lord," she pleaded, "but I still thought to dissuade him and ..."

"Shield him more like!"

"As you will, my lord, but he is my cousin's husband and through reasons of kinship alone I could not betray him. I did not ask for his confidence. Many times I have wanted to open my heart to you, rely on your regard for me to incline you towards compassion."

"You grow tiresome with your importuning Kate. You talk of my regard for you, but what of yours for me?"

She looked away, knowing that he spoke with an exactness that hurt. He was right. She ought to have spoken months ago. As it was, by remaining silent she had invoked his censure and Gerard had committed a crime that allowed of no clemency. She was doubly punished and deservedly so.

"Have you anything else to say to me Kate? Some other secret you would keep from me? God alone knows Kate, for I do not."

All he could see was her betrayal of his trust, his care, the love he had avowed and almost made sacred for her sake.

"Roger," she appealed. "What you say is true and I am now suffering for my injudiciousness. How misguided my motives were has now redounded in full measure, but be merciful I implore you, if not to me, then to Gerard."

"Such mercy as he showed to a good man, I will reserve for him."

He spun the knife round on the table, staring at it as if he was loath to touch it again. There was only one course of action open to him and he had to perform it, no matter how distasteful. He did not wait long. Burgoyne was sent for and the order given. Shortly afterwards she heard the sound of pursuant horses.

"I had no other recourse Kate," he maintained, almost apologetically. Already he sensed her withdrawal. How simple it would have been to retain her affection could he have dispensed with the dictates of justice and surrendered them to the cause of self interest. To do right and lose. Wherein was the merit of the sacrifice. "I will return when you are in a more receptive frame of mind."

She looked at him sadly. She did not want justice. What she wanted was Gerard absolved, Gerard forgiven.

"My lord," she said by way of detaining him.

"Kate."

"If you still love me, and you say that you do, then be merciful in your judgement."

He took her in his arms. For once he had no words with which to reassure her and the knowledge of it hurt, keenly, more deeply than she would ever know.

"I will be dispassionate Kate, whatever the cost?"

She broke free from him.

"And I will be compassionate my lord. Tis far the better virtue of the two."

"Kate," he helplessly appealed.

"My name is Catherine!" she retorted, running from him.

For the first time they slept apart. To both of them sleep was denied. The morning broke dull and grey veiled, the sky heavy with the threat of snow, tiny flakes of it dancing in the gloom like heralds of the forthcoming flurry. Without his warmth she had been cold and shivery, her body aching from the effects of both physical and mental fatigue. She knew Gerard had been taken; the returning horses told her so.

He had breakfasted early to avoid the necessity of having to go into detail over the measures he had put in hand for the retention of the captive. He also thought it would give her an opportunity of seeing the matter more dispassionately, though he thought it unlikely. At a loss what to do, in a fit of impulse she decided to visit Annie, on the basis that if Gerard was beyond her help, Annie was not. She also had an urge to do something when the situation was such that there seemed nothing to be done. She suffered too in the knowledge that he had right on his side, and that if anyone other than Gerard had been involved she would have had no compunction in condoning his actions.

By the time she reached Bardwick the snow was falling thickly. Already an inch or so covered the ground and she began to wish she had put on thicker soled shoes to contend against the numbing wetness that penetrated through to her toes and made quickness of pace a necessity. The gloves she had put on were not warm enough and only by repeatedly blowing on her fingers could she sustain the painful sensation of blood reawakened. Bardwick appeared strangely quiescent under its fleece of soft snow, the grime at its surface deceptively hidden. Also towns' people were notoriously late risers as every countryman could vouch for. Under the snow Annie's house wore the same featureless aspect as all the others. Standing before it, she was tempted to turn away. Excuses for doing so, and she could think of many where Annie was concerned, quickly sprang to mind, but then she remembered that her visit had been prompted by Gerard and that he, and not Annie, would appreciate her concern. Annie took her time in opening the door.

"What hae ye come for?" she droned. She looked slatternly and unkempt, even though she flicked back her hair to create an effect.

"I had to come Annie. You know why."

Without being asked, Catherine followed her inside. The room presented an atmosphere more coldly hostile than that from which she had come, an untidy mess of ashes lying in the unlit hearth. A smudge showed on Annie's face where she had attempted to remove them. It was only recently that Gerard had been taken. He had gone unresistingly. It was she who had screamed and tried to prevent them.

"Let me do that," she said as Annie sank on her knees and delved into the ashes, her ineffectual labours sending a column of dust into their midst and reminding Catherine of the time when Joan had come to her own rescue.

"I dunna want your help. Can ye bring him back to me. No, ye canna," she charged before Catherine had time to reply."

Resuming her task as if it were some self imposed penance, she fiercely resisted Catherine's offer of assistance.

"Where are the children?" Catherine ventured after what seemed a fitting interval.

"Mother's taken 'em," she grudgingly replied, scooping the ashes into her gown and shaking them into an overfull bucket. Her task imperfectly finished, she lurched to the table and slopped out a measure of ale. There was nothing else upon it apart from a couple of dirtied platters and a covering of crumbs.

"Ye think I'm drunk Kate Venners," she giggled, fondling the jug to her lips, "well I'm not!"

"You ought to take some nourishment Annie."

"What bloody for," she yelled, jerking the contents down her chin, "When everythin' I ever wanted is taken away from me. Ye answer that."

Catherine could not. Annie put down the jug, fingering the pools of spillage to form globular streams, faintly smiling to herself as if at some private amusement.

"Why hae ye come Kate? Not on account o' me, I'll be bound. For Gerard? Maybe. He always spoke well of ye, or hae ye come for the sake of ye conscience? Lost ye tongue Kate. Naught to say in reproof?"

It was not so much the words that hurt. She had fully expected them, but the manner in which they were spoken, but then Annie could measure her scorn as she measured her ale, liberally and without forethought of anyone else.

"Annie I know your feelings towards me, but anything I can do I will. Gerard, if no one else, would expect it of me. And the children, Annie, you must remember the children."

"And ye know all about childer. Well I suggest ye wait till ye own belly be fattened afore ye tell me o' my duty," she replied caustically. "Kate Venners, Lord Elliston's whore! I thought it surprisin' at first, but tis not, when ye think o' ye mother."

Tittering at the cleverness of her invective, she scowled in defiance at Catherine, goading her into the retaliatory wrangle she sought as a right.

"Annie, spite me all you like, but never spite my mother," she retorted, dashing the jug from the table where it rolled on the floor, chipped but unbroken. "I came to comfort you, but I see it is of little use."

The vehemence of the rebuke had a strangely mortifying effect on Annie, whose surface contempt dissolved into dog-like howling that reverberated throughout the chillness of the room, causing Catherine to flinch from the sheer hopelessness of it. She caught Annie to her, and let the girl sob without pause.

"Annie, I am sorry, but you provoked me. I have pleaded with Lord Elliston and will continue to do so, but you must appreciate the seriousness of Gerard's crime."

Her crying at an end, she intuitively thought of Gerard, her only acceptable comfort and solace, but Gerard was gone, and all her tears only served to exacerbate her remorse and despair, and the look she turned on Catherine was savage.

"Dunna think to console me with fine words," she railed, pulling away from her. "Ye'll not save Gerard. No one can. Ye think ye can twist Ellison round ye finger. Well, let me tell ye somethin', ye nor nobody else 'ull move 'im. He'll have his miserable justice will Elliston."

"I can but try Annie."

"Ye be mad to think it!" she cried hysterically.

Taking no heed, Catherine picked up the jug and set to clearing the mess from the table. What little food she found was stale and inedible; either Annie had not bothered or could not hazard the looks of her neighbours, a reluctance which Catherine could well understand. She at last found some pottage which she warmed up and set before Annie who ate it desultorily. When she had finished she moved nearer to the fire which was now burning brightly. Whereas previously the ale had made her refractory, it now made her maudlin.

"Nothing is left," she moaned, hugging herself. "Nothing. Nothing. Gerard, dunna leave me. Oh, my darlin' dunna leave me."

While she thus lamented, Catherine set the house in order. Annie was right. Of what use was her concern. She could not expect Elliston to be compassionate when the law demanded otherwise. He had to remain scrupulously detached even if it threatened to estrange them completely.

"Why dunna ye go," Annie whined, stumbling to her feet. "I told ye I didna want ye here, but if ye should ..."

"Yes, Annie?"

"I was goin' to say if ye should see Gerard, but what is the use."

"I will do my best."

"Best, best!" she spat out. "Ye hae done well enough for yesell anyhow. What need hae ye to worry."

Catherine, fearing further abuse, moved towards the door.

"Anxious to be gone now are ye. Canna stand plain talkin' What do ye do to please 'im?"

Her look was venomous, all the hurt and self pity poured out in denigrating waves over Catherine.

"It canna be for ye looks, that's for sure. Maybe ye hae ways in bed of pleasin' 'im I know naught of. Let me know and I'll use them on ..." She stopped and began to shriek. "Get out! Bastard, strumpet, whore! Get out!"

"I pray God protect you," said Catherine.

"Damn ye and damn ye God."

Burgoyne had more patience than most, but even he had reached the limit where forbearance was difficult to maintain. The persistent and oft repeated enquiries of Elliston were of the kind to try the most unflappable of dispositions, and only by dint of perseverance was he able to sustain his calm veneer.

"No, my lord, Mistress Venners has not returned," he informed him yet again.

"You have the prisoner closely confined? Have you seen him? How does he seem?"

"Remarkably composed, my lord," he affirmed, "which is more than can be said of us he inwardly appended."

"It is said that that those who are about to be executed are at peace with the world and its ways. Where is she Burgoyne! Where is she!"

To ease his restlessness, he went out riding. When he returned, she was back, and yet he could not speak his relief on finding her so. The very reticence of her manner informed him that she had refused to come to terms with the case as it undeniably was. For her part, she could see that he was not open to persuasion. They knew not what to say to one another, and in an attempt to break the cloying silence she poured him some wine.

"Where have you been?" he requested, draining the cup and pouring another.

"I went to see Annie. I felt it to be my duty."

"An unwise proceeding I would think."

"Oh wise is he who is solely wise," she retorted, "for no feeling can unsettle his petrified blood, but I have a little of the fool in me, my lord, and I am thankful for it."

He did not reply to the charge, and for some interval they both remained silent.

"Can you not look at the matter as others see it Kate," he began. "Consider the victim, a man of the utmost integrity, a man who leaves a widow and five children. He has apprehended offenders before, but none have resisted with the barbarity of this Gerard Duval. Incidentally, all came from Bardwick and all were summarily dealt with."

"Summarily?" she threw back at him.

"Aye Kate, summarily. They had one of two choices. The payment of a fine, which I admit was substantial, or that of being outlawed."

"And that is your justice!"

"It is!" he retaliated, "and far better than they would get elsewhere. At least I have never resorted to mutilation as a deterrent unlike some of my less enlightened contemporaries. You veer from the point at hand, Kate, and make me lose my temper."

Knowing he was in the right only made her more querulous and desperate.

"Kate, there are no mitigating shades, believe me. The act cries out to be avenged."

"Roger," she entreated, kneeling at his feet. "I beg you, be merciful. Punish him Roger. It is right and fitting that you should, but withhold the ultimate sentence, I implore you, if not for Annie's sake, then for mine."

He drew her up and held her close. He longed to do what she asked of him, but he knew he could not.

"There is nothing in the world that I would not do to pacify you Kate and know your love for me unalloyed, but the same law applies to all and I cannot alter it to please the woman who I have taken to be my ..."

"Whore?" she interrupted. "Do not hesitate my lord. I am not so dainty as you think me, and it is the truth after all."

Their natures were strangely reversed, his delicately controlled, hers unrestrained passion.

"Such words do not sit prettily on your lips Kate. You are overwrought. It is understandable, but I will not be moved."

She flicked back her hair, as Annie would have done. Indeed, it was as if Annie guided her every action. The affectations she so deplored in her cousin she was now using as her one remaining weapon, and because they grated against her very nature she had perforce to play her part marvellously well.

"It is true," she stated. "Otherwise you would not hesitate to grant what I wish. It is now clear to me why your mother despised you so. You have no heart my lord. You are barren of feeling."

This was not the Catherine he knew, but some terrifying stranger intent on wounding him where he was weakest. Her rantings made him raise his hand, if not to strike her, then to stop her.

"Why not?" she taunted. "Hit me! It will not be the first time."

His hand dropped to his side. In response, she struck him hard with her own. It was the final act of a desperate woman.

"It is finished!" she cried, running from him.

There was little force behind the slap, but the sting of it lingered on his face for long afterwards. On the ledge of the window the snow had formed a thin rim. He scooped it up in his hands and crushed it on the spot where her hand had smarted him only a moment before.

It now seemed that they were permanently estranged. Gerard's trial was to take place at Newcastle, far enough away from Bardwick to cause the minimum of hurt to his family. Burgoyne informed her that Elliston was agreeable to her seeing the prisoner before he departed.

Gerard was confined in the tower of the Good Lady Eleanor. Who Lady Eleanor was and why she was good was long lost to memory. The gaoler in charge reminded her of Watkins, huge and pock marked, and like Watkins taking immense pride in the job afforded him. Having been warned of her arrival, he immediately conveyed her to the prisoner who was confined on the first storey of the tower. Though it was daylight, he still needed a torch.

"A visitor for ye," he said, amidst a rattle of keys.

The room was larger than she had envisaged. A barred window too high to look from admitted both air and light. There was nothing in the way of heat, but the pallet on which he sprawled was well provided with covers.

"Gerard," she almost whispered, "It's Kate."

He raised himself and looked hard at her, as if adjusting his eyes to see through the gloom.

"Catherine, is it really you?" came the familiarly rich

intonation. "Here, over here."

He got up and warmly embraced her, kissing both sides of her face in typical Gallic fashion. They stood thus for many moments.

"He let you come, Catherine. This I know he would do."

Far more composed than she was, the hand that trembled against his cheek was her own. He smiled in that inimitable way he always did. He had lost weight, his olive skin had sallowed, but the eyes still retained much of their sparkle. His hair had grown, falling untidily if fetchingly beneath his shoulders; its soft waves would still have been the envy of many a woman, and the growth of beard leant him an addition of years that suited him. Gone was the boyish vivacity and in its stead a maturity all the more marked for its previous absence.

"You do not change mon cousin. I see you feel too greatly on my behalf, yes? There is no need."

"I love you Gerard. We all do."

He moved close to her again, winding a strand of her hair in his fingers as Elliston was wont to do.

"I am glad to see you Catherine. You will not reproach when too easily you could. What is that English phrase, "I tell you so, something like that eh?"

"Something of the kind," she replied.

"You are the brave one Catherine, always strong, whereas Annie and I. Ah well". His lips quivered. "You have seen my Annie?"

"Yes, I have seen her Gerard. She loves you as much as ever."

He sighed. "We love too strong I think. Tis both a blessing and a curse, this love. And my boys, you see them?"

"No, they are with Aunt Miriam. It is better for Annie."

Her visit to Annie still rankled, and she was loath to speak of it lest she said something less than kind of the woman he adored. He scrutinised her for some time before speaking again, and whereas the guarded look in her features would once have eluded him it did not do so now.

"You have bad words Catherine. I see it. She call you names, no."

"Yes, Gerard, but tis of no import. She is naturally overwrought."

"You must excuse her Catherine. She ever speak and not think."

"She is all solicitude for you Gerard, and I can readily overlook a hasty word."

The silence that followed was full of unspoken thoughts, and better by far for being so.

"I can see what you feel Catherine, but I am, how you say, ready to receive my punishment."

"No, Gerard, I will not let it happen. I will not!" she maintained, her voice breaking with emotion.

"Ah Catherine," he said, holding her close. "You cannot fend off fate. Tis meant. I do not have the will to live. I see that man before me too much. He never 'arm me Catherine. I behave like an animal. When I find out he have children like me and a wife, it grieve me more. Catherine I feel nothing but ... I cannot explain ... the right word, say it, please."

"Remorse," she whispered.

"Yes, yes, that is what I feel. I am always too strong of head, Catherine."

"Headstrong," she corrected, half laughing, half sobbing.

"The laughter now, that is better, it help me."

She asked him about the conditions of his confinement and he was eager to tell her. He pointed to a trestle table, probably borrowed from the kitchen, and assured her that if he stood on it and stretched himself fully he could just about manage to see through the window. To demonstrate, he leapt upon it and caught a handful of snow from off the bars.

"You see," he said, springing down before her. "Clever, eh?"

"Yes, very," she laughed in an effort to oblige him and keep up his spirits.

"But it must be dreadfully cold, Gerard."

"No, no. I cover myself well," he maintained, clutching the blankets up to his chin. "And then I have a candle which is lit every night. The Lord Elliston, he treat his prisoners fairly good."

She felt herself shudder, a grimace replacing the smile. She did not want to hear Roger praised.

"I say something wrong?"

"No Gerard, nothing. Let us not talk of Lord Elliston."

"You quarrel with Lord Elliston. I am the cause, yes?"

She turned away from him, unwilling to discuss the matter.

"Ah, Catherine, I begin to see, I think. In your goodness you plead for me, and he refuse, yes?"

"Yes," she acknowledged. "And let that be an end to it. I do not wish to speak of it further."

"But I do. Tell me what he say."

His mood was so calm and accepting and so totally at variance with her own that she had no desire to recall what had happened between her and Elliston. She was hesitant and constrained at first, but also surprised that the condemnatory tone she had proposed to adopt was lacking in conviction. Gerard hanging on every word only made her feel more awkward, for he was listening with that rare intensity that knows the truth despite the absence of plain speaking.

"I did it for you Gerard," she concluded.

"Then I am not thankful. Elliston is just. I deserve no pity. Myself I show none. I am not deserving of his favour. Because of the ties we have, you think to turn him from what he and I know is, how you say, just?"

"This is not justice!" she cried out.

"Ah but it is. It is not like you to shout, Catherine. I think it is because you know you are wrong, yes? Unfair is maybe a better word."

"Unfair!" she sobbed. "I do not care about such things where you are concerned. I would do anything to save you Gerard. You are my kin."

He made the sign of the cross and looked at her hard.

"You speak like my Annie," he averred, "thinking only of yourself. For once in my life I am strong. Always I am weak Catherine. I bring no one good, and cause misery to many. In my death I shall have no fear."

"Stop it Gerard! You are not going to die."

"Catherine, I am not afraid to die. Perhaps the manner of it, yes. I am deserving of the worst, that I know. But God is good, even to sinners like me if they truly ..."

"Repent," she interjected, her eyes speaking with all the conviction that had been lacking in her condemnation of Elliston.

"Catherine, I am so glad you come. Now you will promise to do something for me?"

"Anything, Gerard."

"Your 'appiness means much to me Catherine. I always have this special liking for you. Lord Elliston, he makes you 'appy, this I know. Go to him, be reconciled for my sake."

She had not expected such a request, and even to please him she did not feel disposed to accede to it.

"If Lord Elliston genuinely cares for me, he will not let you die Gerard."

"He can do nothing else, Catherine, even for you. Now promise?"

"I will try, Gerard, but I cannot promise."

"It will not be as hard as you think. Pray for me Catherine. Pray for me."

They embraced briefly before parting. It was better so.

The snow now only came fitfully. The day was nearly at an end and the faint outline of a new moon hung in the sky.

She must have slept late and long, for when she awoke the sun was high in the sky and the steady drip of thawing snow ran in reedy discord down the gutters. She fingered the crucifix at her neck, the roughly carved wooden cross that Peter had left her all those years ago when she had been too young to appreciate it fully. She still had the rosary he had left to her mother, and apart from Elliston's ring she would rather have parted with every material possession she owned than lose these two treasures.

Later that morning Burgoyne brought her a letter. Looking old beyond his years, she realised that the present circumstances could not be conducive to his peace of mind, though she was also aware of the extent of his loyalty to Elliston. In thinking of Burgoyne's loyalty, it made her question her own. Matched against his, hers seemed but a shallow and vacillating vessel, liable to crack at the first hint of discord. The notion was hardly comforting, and the more she felt at fault the more susceptible she became to Gerard's entreaties.

"I must seem unbelievably tiresome Sir Edward," she said, taking it from him. "Tis unfair that you should suffer in consequence."

"It is not for me to form opinions Mistress Venners. I merely carry out the orders of my master. I would only say one thing, Mistress Venners, he thinks very highly of you and is uncommonly distressed by this turn of events."

"Thank you, Sir Edward. Thank you."

Not waiting for an answer, he quietly withdrew. Whatever the letter contained, he prayed it would bring some positive result, for as she had implied it was damnably trying.

Her hand shook as she opened it. It was a concise and tersely worded note to the effect that Gerard had been removed to Newcastle earlier that morning. He trusted that she was in good health and that did she wish to speak with him she only had to inform Burgoyne. There were no words of tenderness and he must have thought twice in signing himself Roger as it had hastily been scratched through and over-written "Elliston".

Unable to rest, she took to walking along the edge of the river. The fitful showers of snow did not worry her. If she grew cold, she was not even aware of the fact, but when the sun occasionally troubled the water she fancied a face resembling Gerard's rise up to its surface, Gerard as she had last seen him, mature and resigned to his fate. She thought of what he had asked her do, and her failure to do it. Even now she refused to believe that Elliston would let Gerard die. That Burgoyne and everyone else knew differently, even Gerard himself, only served to make her more obdurate.

Two days later Margaret brought her the news she was dreading to hear. All nervous solicitude, she fidgeted with her brooch and hardly knew how to begin.

"Catherine ...."

"Gerard is dead," Catherine said matter of factly, relieving her of the necessity.

"I am sorry," she replied. "The sentence was carried out yesterday morning."

Catherine shivered. On that day his face had been exceptionally clear in the water.

"Shall I continue," Margaret ventured, seeing how deathly pale she had become.

"Please do. I am quite composed."

"Sir Edward attended at the request of Lord Elliston who commuted the sentence to hanging. I have it on Sir Edward's authority that he died well and in the knowledge of God's forgiveness."

"It is what he desired Lady Burgoyne. He had become more of a man during those weeks of captivity. He was not the Gerard I knew, but he is the one I would remember."

Her body began to tremble violently and then the tears came.

"On the day before he died," Margaret continued, "Sir Edward tells me he was resigned and calm, speaking of his wife and children with great affection. He also mentioned you and besought you to do what he asked. He said you would know what he meant."

"I do," she sobbed uncontrollably, "but how can I now that Gerard is dead."

"Perhaps you would prefer to be alone," Margaret said, handing her a handkerchief.

"No, please stay. I have been too much alone."

Throughout the whole episode, Sir Edward had kept his wife well informed. She had observed with anxiety the tell-tale lines that marked his brow and kept him wakeful by her side, and if Catherine was ready to talk she was more than ready to listen.

"Advise me Lady Burgoyne. I know I can rely on your good judgement."

"I think you know what you have to do without my having to advise you. And Catherine, please call me Margaret, I think the time for formalities is over."

"I am afraid. I spoke such harsh words to him that I fear he may not forgive me."

"And has he never spoken harshly to you? Is it not those we love best whom we hurt most, simply because we know them so well. He loves you Catherine. When you see him you will know what to say."

"Thank you Lady ... I mean Margaret. You cannot know how much you have helped to reassure me."

"Not at all Catherine. I have only said what you know to be true."

ଓ ଚ

He stood with his back to her, idly thumbing a sheaf of documents which Burgoyne had left for his perusal.

"My lord," she said falteringly.

He turned, slowly creasing the sheets in his fingers. How drawn and tired he looked.

"Forgive me. I spoke unkindly. Gerard himself said as much. I was at fault Roger. I love you. I ..." It was impossible to continue.

His own eyes blurring, he held out his arms.

"Come to me Kate. Come to me."

The papers scattered on the floor. She was safe, indescribably safe.

"And I thought I had lost you," he cried. "I have been so alone, Kate, so wretchedly alone."

His mouth on hers, they did not speak further.

The separation strengthened them. Never again would they take their love for granted. Out of an unwanted experience was born a tenderness and regard that would be proof against all future pain in whatever guise it might come. To know this was enough. They were blissfully, joyfully happy.

CHAPTER TWENTY TWO

It was spring and the earth was growing warmer. With the pain of recent events, Matthew preferred to be outdoors. There he could mull over his troubles, dig them deep in the earth, or let them sift with the soil through his fingers. He had not expected much of the Frenchman, but that it would end quite so badly weighed heavily with him. Naturally he blamed it all on Gerard, it never occurring to him that Annie had played her part. The Thompsons were well liked; their neighbours were sympathetic but guarded, though amongst themselves they had plenty to say. They were of one and the same mind regarding Elliston. He had to do what was right, despite his involvement with Kate Venners. To do otherwise would have shown a lack of good judgement.

It was Catherine's first visit since that last Christmas they had spent together as a family. Then Gerard had been so alive and vital. Now Gerard was no more.

Miriam was tending her precious bee hives when Catherine crept upon her unnoticed, shading the tallest hive with her presence.

"Well I'll be ..." Miriam suddenly jumped.

Catherine put her fingers to her lips, just in time to prevent the oath from escaping. "Ah, tis good to see ye lass," she said, quickly pulling off her gloves and throwing her arms about her. "Come now, I'll get ye a bite to eat. Ye look nae fatter I'm thinkin'." She smelt of stored apples and tallow, the comforting smells of home. Inside there was the aroma of freshly baked bread.

"Now sit yesell down Kate. I'll be wi' ye presently."

She bustled to and fro, singing wordless ditties to herself as if afraid of the silence. At least in the garden she had had the hum of the bees and the sunlight. The loaf cut and the ale poured, they sat together without speaking, and then both spoke at once. Catherine let her have her say.

"Ay, tis a bad business. I had a care for the lad, for ever a lad he seemed to me. Ay, the way he used to tease me, and ye for that matter. I canna understand 'im doin' such a thing," she said, squinting back her tears. "I'm thankful though to know he were repentant and trusted in the Lord. We've all had a sad time of it, ye too nae doubt, but *he* had to do as he did, Kate, hard though it was."

"I know aunt, I know. How is Annie?"

"I wish I knew. It do worry me so. She has become sae hard and headstrong (Catherine smiled at the word in remembrance of him who was no more). She dunna want me nor Matt, no one, not even her own childer. We still be lookin' after 'em. She's not fit see. They be with Alice at the moment, such good lads too and sae bright."

"You must try to be patient Aunt Miriam. She loved him so much."

"Ay, but we love her too. She be our daughter. It goes 'arder with Matt than me. He dunna say much but I can tell."

"I went to see her after Gerard was taken. Did she tell you?"

It was clear she had, for Miriam looked awkward and abashed, as if she knew not what to say.

"Kate, ye must not blame her if she seems unkind. I know she be dreadful down on ye."

"As I said, we must be patient."

"Ye'll stay till Matt be back? He'd be sorry to miss ye. Ye know how tis with 'im and Annie. She always was 'is darlin', and when she treats him distant like, well it goes badly with 'im. There be rumours too."

"Rumours?"

"Ay, things I scarce like to speak on. Men and such like. Tis said she flaunts 'ersell. Make allowances for 'er if ye will, but it canna continue. *He* will not mind ye stayin' for a while, will *he*, Kate."

"No, he will not mind," Catherine replied, smiling faintly to herself.

Matt arrived in time for supper, his hands brown and sore from his labours.

"Matt, look who be 'ere," she said, relieving him of his mud stained boots.

"And always welcome," he acknowledged, wearily seeking his chair. Catherine could see what Miriam meant in that he had taken it badly. He had lost weight and his eyes were heavy and sunken, but more marked still was the way in which his head had a habit of violently nodding against its will. Miriam's care and worry were revealed in an excess of attention which he found more of an irritant than a comfort, for she insisted on treating him like some sickly child.

"Now put these shoon on," she exhorted. "There's no knowin' what he'd be without me beside 'im Kate. Goin' about in wet feet and ne'er a thought for the consequences."

"Will ye stop ye blatherin' woman," he retorted, his patience sorely tried. "I'm no in my dotage yet." Reluctantly he let her pull the wrinkled leather on his feet."

"You look tired Uncle," Catherine remarked. "I trust you are allowing the hired man to do his fair share of work."

"As needs be," he mumbled, looking under his eyes at Miriam.

"That's just it," she said. "He won't let the lad do as he ought to. A strong lad too, and more than willin', but no Matt hae to go proud footed and do the bulk on it 'imsell. Twas not so with Rob."

"Rob's my ain! I'll hear no more on it."

Sensibly, Miriam desisted. He might openly lament Rob's absence and talk of having need of him, but it was Annie of whom he was actually thinking. It was a pity she had ever met the foreigner, let alone married him. Had it not been for him, she would not have got into bad ways and become alienated from her family, but he did not wish to speak of it more than was necessary. A wrong had to be righted and Elliston had seen that it was done. That was all there was to it. He said as much to Catherine and she was grateful that he should take pains to reassure her that he bore no ill feelings towards Elliston himself. That said, he wished to say nothing further. Moreover, by way of a change he had something of good news to tell them. At the thought of it, a smile softened his features.

"What be humourin' ye?" asked Miriam in some amazement.

"Naught," he evaded, a rare twinkle in his eye as he pressed his hand inside his tunic and brought out a crumpled looking note.

"What hae ye there?" Miriam chided.

"Somethin' o' little use to them that canna read, but much to them as can," he said, looking purposefully at Catherine. Giving it to her, she immediately recognised Mary's ill formed hand-writing. "Got it fro' the tranter hereabouts. I knew it were for us cause I'd taken note of the way ye wrote our name."

"You had Uncle Matt?" said Catherine in amazement. "I took it that you were not in the least interested."

"Canna always go by what a man purports to be lass."

"Stop ye blatherin' Matt. What is it?"

"It is a letter from Mary," Catherine explained.

"A letter fro' Mary?" she repeated, her face a study in wonder and anticipation. “We mun hear it Kate, we mun hear it.”

Mary had received but minimal teaching in letters, but allowing for the formal opening which read like the preamble to one of her lord’s documents the letter read easily enough, the contents more than compensating for the inadequacy of the style. Matthew and Miriam, touchingly attentive, hung on every word.

‘To our dear parents, greetings. We trust to find you in perfect health, as we ourselves are, and send warm greetings likewise to all our family and friends.’

“There’s enough of fancy work in it,” Matthew interjected.

“Hush now!” said Miriam.

Catherine paused a moment before continuing.

‘Let it be known that Rob has taken lodgings in Southwark and become apprenticed to a butcher.’

“A butcher!” Matthew spat. “What kind o’ trade is that!”

“A good one,” Miriam maintained.

Once again Catherine paused. From the look of consternation on her uncle’s face it might have been supposed that Rob had become a tightrope walker or something equally incongruous.

‘The lodgings above the said shop are ample to our needs and pleasantly positioned.’

Catherine wondered. The phrase ‘pleasantly positioned’ could mean anything and it would not be in Mary’s nature to worry them by giving a more detailed description. At last came an item of news that defied contrivance of expression.

‘Dear Mother and Father, we are full of joy to tell you we are expecting a child and Rob is all solicitous for my well being. We are both so happy, and trust you are too.’

“God be praised!” said Miriam, hugging Catherine. “We hae need o’ such news.”

“Ay,” agreed Matthew “Tis a fine thing to be knowin’.”

“Now where was I,” Catherine resumed. “Ah yes,” ‘as we trust you are too, also Annie and Gerard, Geoffrey and Alice, all the children and dear Catherine. Pray God watch over you all. In love and fond affection. Rob and Mary.’

“Ay, tis bonny,” wept Miriam, as Catherine gave her the letter.

Catherine promised her aunt that she would write in reply if Miriam told her what to put down, but this was easier said than done, the sight of the quill poised over the page seeming to have an intimidatory effect upon her aunt, almost as if the quill bore some strange magical property which enabled it to write of itself, everything she so wanted to say being stayed on her tongue.

“Come along Aunt Miriam,” Catherine encouraged.

"I canna speak like Mary. It seems there be an art in letters like."

"There is no art," Catherine laughed. "Just speak as if Rob and Mary were here in this room and you conversing with them."

"I dunna know Kate. I canna think what to say."

"For the love o' Christ, get on with it woman," Matthew remonstrated. "I've never known ye lost for words afore."

Almost whispering, Miriam tentatively began, her eyes furtively following the scratch of the quill as it wrote. Catherine asked if Matthew wished to add anything.

"Ay, tell 'em I be pleased and that Geoffrey hae bought a fine cow."

"What kind o' news be that?" said Miriam slightingly.

"As much as I can think on."

Catherine undertook the difficult task of writing an additional letter informing them of the manner of Gerard's death and all that had happened in the interim. It was painful but necessary.

"Tis marvellous neat Kate," Miriam remarked when she had finished. "We hae kept ye longer than usual Kate. I hope ye will not suffer through it."

"No Aunt Miriam. I was pleased to be able to do it."

Carefully folding the letter, she tucked it in her bodice. It was now growing dark and Matthew offered to accompany her part of the way, but she declined in the knowledge that Elliston would have sent an escort. Instead he had brought himself.

"Where have you been?" he charged, swinging her unceremoniously into the saddle.

"I had to write a letter for Miriam and Matthew. They have had news of Rob and Mary."

"Damn their news. Your place is here beside me, not pandering to the whims of others. Craven can write such letters. I will not have you playing the lackey."

"I am sorry to have inconvenienced you my lord, but you too did not have to play the lackey. I did not expect you to personally collect me."

"I do not collect Kate. You are not a piece of baggage."

"Then stop treating me as such."

It was all in play and they laughed accordingly.

When they had returned he was more receptive to her news, though she could not help but notice how he passed over Mary's pregnancy as of little consequence and his indifference somewhat troubled her.

"Let me look," he said, snatching the letter she had written in reply. "You write better than I do. I will not brook competition

Kate."

"You are envious, that is all. What is more, I would surpass you in all things."

He drew her violently to him and tugged back her hair.

"Unsay it!" he threatened mockingly.

"No, never!"

"Then know this Kate Venners," he said releasing her. "My love surpasses any man's."

"And mine any woman's," she countered.

"Do you have an answer to everything I say."

"Invariably, it seems."

Summer overcrept its season into autumn and the days were long and glorious. Insufficient rain prevented a harvest comparable to that of the previous year, but as Matthew was given to saying, receiving the bounty of God two years in succession was not to be looked for. Winter brought its toll of illness and death. Mother Jomfrey's son died on the eve of 1346, his stricken wife caressing his coldness in her arms. The old woman glowered at her. Now that her son was dead she would probably have to forfeit her few paltry strips of land to Elliston. The younger woman, seeing what she felt, only clasped him the closer.

The annual rent day came and went. Geoffrey was still in want of the necessary sum that would make him a free man, but vowed by all the saints and, of course, Alice, that the following year would see him obtain his reward. His neighbours mumbled something to the effect about next year being a long way off, but in no wise was Geoffrey discouraged. Little outwardly changed. Baillie Talbot increased his girth, Mother Jomfrey her rancour. That Elliston had now attended the rent day two years in succession and was being increasingly lenient was further proof that Kate Venners was bringing her influence to bear.

"I know these people, Roger. Pray, give them your trust," she would entreat him. "If I prove wrong, then you may upbraid me."

Her efforts to assist him were too endearing to be cast aside and he was content to let her guide him.

"Tis you whom I trust," he would softly reply, "you who are my life, my love, my salvation."

"You should not speak of salvation in such paltry terms," she gently corrected. "You forget that Christ alone is our salvation."

For answer, he laughingly stroked the stands of her hair, the coppery gold he loved so much.

"Roger, never leave me!"

"Never?" he quizzed, kissing her forehead. "I seem to recollect you making some such similar request on the day I nearly lost you to Craven. But I am older than you, and the day may come when I have no choice in the matter."

"Then we will die together," she replied vehemently if childishly.

"Kate, the world is not so romantic as you would have it, and I would wish you to live on after my demise."

"I would have no will to live!"

"You would Kate. I would will it from the grave. Life must go on. Twas ever thus."

No more was said on this occasion, but it made him reflective. Better think on hell and its terrors to appreciate the salvation of heaven and its promise of eternal life.

During the early days of June when the air was fragrant with late flowering blossom, they would go riding far beyond the castle and all its cares. He introduced her to the place he referred to as his secret Eden which he had come upon as a boy when he was feeling more keenly the sting of his mother's rejection. Its beauty was in its seclusion, a hidden valley of woodland and streams; it was the sound of rushing water after many days of heavy rain that had first led him there; on a normal day these unseen streams could hardly be heard for their covering of trees. No one knew of it even now except for Burgoyne, so careful was he to safeguard it from common knowledge. If it had not been for the business of Gerard, he would have taken her previously. Now, at long last, he was fulfilling his promise. She had resolved to like it for his sake, that she liked it for her own was doubly pleasing. He watched with delight as she played like a child in the water. That was part of her appeal, that she was so much a child and so much a woman.

"You like my retreat then Kate," he called.

"You know I do."

"I determined to keep it to myself, despite a thrashing from Mama. You cannot imagine what it was for a small boy to have such a secret, a boy, that is, who had known scant affection and little companionship."

"I can," she affirmed, coming out of the water towards him. "What is more I would be your companion until the day I die, did you so desire it."

"Kate," he said, catching her to him. "I have brought many women here, but none like you. You alone have seen it with my eyes and transformed it into the Eden of my boyhood."

Radiant in his praise, she expressed the wish that they return to it whenever opportunity allowed. Brushing a bee from the nape of her neck, he promised that nothing would prevent it. The afternoon grew unbearably warm and they were glad of the shade. Watching the midges spin in frantic effort across the water, she thought of Matthew tending his crops and shielding his eyes from the sun's savage glare, of Miriam drying her herbs and renewing the rushes on the floor, of Annie, resentful and grievously bitter, of Rob and Mary and the baby that hopefully still grew inside her. She thought of those far removed from this life, of her mother and of Peter, and lastly of Gerard who had redeemed himself in dying. Life was indeed short, she reflected, her head resting against his shoulder. It was a moment of utter contentment which she would always remember and far too perfect to last.

It was Burgoyne who broke on their idyll, a flustered and breathless Burgoyne.

"This better be important Sir Edward," Elliston said, getting to his feet.

"Messengers from the capital my lord. The matter is most pressing."

"Look to my lady, Sir Edward. I will ride on ahead. Kate, I am sorry."

From that moment on she noticed a change in him. He told her it was a matter that need not concern her as he had it well in hand, but that he was troubled was easy to see. The following day he partook in a joust; ever conscious of the dangers involved she hated such pastimes, but he loved the thrill and excitement of them for the very same reasons. On this occasion, however, he did not excel. Clearly, he had more weighty matters on his mind. From the Burgoynes she could learn nothing. It was obvious that Margaret was deliberately avoiding her for fear of disobeying her husband and blurting out what she had been told to keep secret. Now the weather broke, those first perfect days having given way to wind and rain which prevented her from sitting in the rose garden they had made together in memory of that at Sulburgh, so that she began to feel like someone wrongly imprisoned, unaware of her crime and for what she was being punished.

Forsake their bed he did not, but they seldom made love and when they did it was markedly devoid of sentiment. She could have been any woman, he any man. If she woke in the night she would find him sitting abstractedly at the window, often with his head in his hands, but her concern only put him out of humour.

She had resolved to be patient in the hope that he would eventually confide in her. When he did not, she felt she could bear it no longer.

"My lord," she said as they were preparing for bed, "I would speak with you."

He did not answer. "Of late you have grown cold towards me, and I would know the reason why."

"Nonsense Kate," he dismissively replied, motioning her beside him. "Have I not shown my appreciation in numerous ways."

She was cold and shivery and her nightgown did not warm her. It was him she needed.

"My lord tis not so. Ever since you heard from London things have been different between us. Tell me Roger if I am in any way to blame?"

He did not want her questions. He wanted her and clasped her violently to him.

"No!" she said, wresting herself free. "It will not do. I would have my lord's love."

"You begin to talk like Craven," he complained, pushing her from him. "I trust he has not been infecting you again with his twisted logic."

She moved from the bed and stood trembling at the open embrasure, her hair blowing softly in the breeze. Immediately he went to her side, his breath feeling warm on her shoulders. She took his hand and pressed it tightly to her breast.

"What is amiss Kate?" he soothed, his manner altogether different.

"Nothing is amiss with me Roger," she said, turning to face him, her eyes filled with tears. "It is you who have changed. You will not speak to me of what troubles you. It seems that everyone shares in your confidence but myself. I love you Roger. I beg you, do not shut me out."

"I do not know what you mean Kate," he laughed feebly.

"You do Roger. You do. How can you deny it! We do not speak any more!"

"You are imagining things. The summer air has affected you."

"Would that it had Roger, but I see very clearly. We promised never to let anything come between us, particularly after Gerard. If it is something I have done, tell me now. Is it my reforms in the village, the enlargement of the common land, the felling of trees in winter?" she said, quickly seizing on a possible explanation for his coolness. "Say if they have not served you well?"

"Would it were that simple," he sighed, looking at her fondly.

"And yet you will not unburden yourself to me, whose care for you is infinite. You forget too easily how my silence over Gerard caused us to suffer. Should we not have learned from such a bitter lesson? I would share in your griefs Roger as well as your joys. Speak to me now, I implore you."

For reply he carried her to their bed and laid himself upon her.

"No my lord, no!"

"You deny me!"

"Your love I have never denied, my lord, never."

"Maybe you will think better of it when we part!"

"Part?" she mouthed, her voice silent beneath the impact of the word.

"Tis so Kate, tis so," he said, turning towards her, stroking her hair across his face. "Attribute all my brutish behaviour to this fact alone. In my muddled reasoning I thought to lessen the ties between us, make us less dependent on each other for happiness, but like the fool I ever was I have only created a wedge that has caused you unnecessary sorrow. Believe me, Kate, I have never changed in my feelings towards you."

"Then I have not offended you?" she said, half relieved, half afraid.

"Kate, Kate," he assured, kissing her face. "Now I will speak, I promise. You will know of the wars with the French?"

"Yes, my lord, but ..."

"Listen," he gently rebuked. "You also know how entrenched I am in my aversion to change. It seems I have inherited the trait from my father, though God knows I saw little enough of him in my youth. Most of my compeers have commuted their service to the king by raising private armies to serve in their place and I should have followed their example, instead of which I am bound to serve fealty myself. Clinging to the old ways has been my undoing."

"Why did you not tell me sooner, Roger."

"Because I am so damnably wretched about it!" he raged. "Not long ago I would have welcomed the order, embraced it with becoming zeal, but not now, not now. If I could rectify the matter I would, but tis too late and I could not even raise the necessary tax to arm a trained levy."

"Will it be for long?" she naively enquired, fearing to hear his answer, yet needing to know it.

"I have no way of knowing Kate. That is what grieves me."

"When do you leave?" she asked.

"In ten days' time."

"So soon!" she sobbed.

"Oh Kate. Kate."

"Then we must make these days so special that they will outlast our severance," she cried. "We will! We will!"

It seemed that to love without pain was not to love at all, an adage which applied stingingly well in their case.

Burgoyne was to be made titular head in his absence, Margaret continuing in her role as head of the household. Catherine was to have special responsibility for the village, a calling which pleased her immensely as it confirmed his confidence in her ability. A retainership of fifty would be left behind, a paltry number should any unforetold problems arise, but the rest were sworn to fealty as he was. It was going to be a formidable task for Sir Edward who was now over fifty, a fact which Elliston refused to take into consideration. Margaret was clearly vexed at the extra responsibility devolving on him and poured out her fears to Catherine, but Elliston stuck fast to his plans.

They did none of the things they had planned. A shadow bore down on their pleasure as the days drew nearer to the hour of their parting. She had determined to be cool and calm, but when the actual day came she was unable to hold back her tears. They lay silently together, the sun flickering over their faces. Dreamily he whispered her name.

"I am here, my lord," she quietly said. "The morning will be a beautiful one and there is much to do."

"Much," he flatly jested, turning his gaze on her.

She buried her head on his breast and wept. "I had meant to be so brave for you Roger."

"Kate," he gently coaxed, kissing her mouth. "If you had been otherwise, I would have thought you unfeeling."

"Unfeeling my lord. Never impute to me that fault," she enjoined, her temper rising at the charge.

"I did but jest," he said, kissing away her wrath. "The memory of our last night together I shall carry here," he continued, touching his heart. She would remember it too. Always. She clung to him more fiercely still.

"Better?" he asked.

"Yes", she replied, her eyes an unbecoming red. "I was thinking."

"You were?" he laughed.

"I was thinking of Peter and how he used to speak of Holy Island and the blessed saints, Cuthbert and Aidan."

"If this is your way of telling me that you are going to cloister yourself up in a convent and mourn my desertion until you are old and feeble and I am plagued by contrition, I do not think I wish to hear any more," he said mockingly.

Not being able to resist such banter, he had merely thought to raise her spirits, but only made her cry again.

"Forgive me Kate. Tis no time to jest, I agree. Now what of Holy Island?"

"I dreamed of it last night. And Peter was there to guide us. I knew it was the island he spoke of, although I had never seen it before. It was so clear Roger. Do you think it of special import?"

"You and your dreams Kate. I seem to remember one about Craven. Suffice it to say, Kate, that on my solemn oath we will go there when I return. Its name suits it well, for it is a place apart. Maybe I am too wordly for such spiritual refinement."

"Is it very distant, Roger?" she asked, ignoring the latter remark.

"From Sulburgh but a few miles. Had I known of your desire then, I would have taken you there."

"I thought it much further," she replied. "You must think me very ill informed at times."

"I think you sublime," he corrected, kissing her yet again, "and would to God I did not have to leave you."

The next few hours were all bustle and haste, the horses being brought out for inspection and the cavalcade drawn up. What a small contingent it looked Catherine thought, and what could it possibly contribute to victory in France. King Edward must indeed be acquisitive in his thirst for power if he had need of such.

Breakfast was a miserable affair. It was taken with Margaret and Sir Edward, the latter being given a string of last orders in addition to those he had already received.

Suddenly there seemed so much to say and so little time in which to say it. Surely the formal farewell he had dispensed to the others was not to be her measure too. It was not. Taking her to their rose garden, he removed the inhibiting mask and ravished her face with kisses.

"This is bitter Kate. How will I fare without you."

It was she who was calmer, she who sustained him. "Come back to me Roger, that is all I ask of you."

She then took the wooden cross from her neck and placed it round his own. "Wear this for my sake. It once belonged to Peter.

Promise me."

"I promise," he said, brushing the roughened wood with his lips. An insistent bugle now summoned him.

"I have to go, Kate."

"Take care my lord," she said.

"You more than me Kate, you more than me. I will write, as you must."

"With all my heart," she assured him. "Pray God be your protector and Providence your guide."

One last, hurried kiss, and he walked away. If she ran quickly enough she would see him at the head of his men, along the winding river, on to Bardwick, and thence no more. He did not look back, keeping his eyes firmly on the road ahead. His face was set, like flint. No one dared speak to him.

CHAPTER TWENTY THREE

In work she found release and a salve to ease her misery. Burgoyne was hard pressed to cope with all the suggestions she made and Margaret did her best to engage her in diverting talk.

If, during the day, the duties she imposed upon herself restrained the natural impulse of her thought, her nights were very different. Wretched nights of sleeplessness when she knew the meaning of desire unsatisfied. Longing for his nearness, his touch, his voice, every prayer in her heart reaching out to him wherever he might be.

He had been gone a little over three months when she knew she was carrying his child. The condition neither pleased nor alarmed her. In truth she was not sure what she felt. Remembering his lack of enthusiasm when she told him of Mary's pregnancy, she felt bewildered. His own children had been little more than strangers to him, and if he had not entirely forgotten them, neither did he choose to speak of them. Of his wife, again he said nothing. His reluctance to speak of a past which was obviously painful kept her correspondingly silent. Confused and uncertain as to his reaction, she decided not to write to him of her condition until nearer the time. Neither did she inform the Burgoynes or her family. By the commencement of the fourth month she realised that something was wrong. She was bleeding and vomiting and Margaret sent for a physician. In private conversation with Margaret he shook his head discouragingly. The dead foetus was delivered shortly afterwards, and only then was she brought to an awareness of what she had lost. Never had she felt quite so alone, quite so utterly wretched.

"Catherine, why did you not confide in me?" Margaret asked sitting at the bedside, her features a mixture of deep concern and mild reproach. "Am I also to assume that you have not written to Lord Elliston or apprised your own family, the very people that have a right to be informed. Tis not like you Catherine."

Catherine reached for her hand and pressed it lovingly. Margaret was justifiably aggrieved. She ought to have spoken much sooner, spilled out her doubts and fears into someone's sympathetic ear. Now that the gift of their love was gone, she could not help but feel partially to blame. Turning away from Margaret she buried her head in the pillows and sobbed.

"Forgive me Catherine," Margaret said softly, her voice ruffled like the breath of wind on water. "I should not have spoken so unfeelingly. It is just that I have been so concerned for you. There will be other babies Catherine, of that be assured."

Catherine rose to look at her. She needed such assurance.

"I sometimes think I shall never see him again."

"You will Catherine, you will. God will put all aright in his own good time."

"I was afraid to impart my news to him, Margaret. When I told him of Mary's baby he hardly referred to it. Then again, his reluctance to speak of his own sons, all this and more conspired to make me doubtful."

Margaret smiled in wonder at her. Until latterly, she had found it hard to see anything of particular merit in Elliston, but since Catherine had arrived even she discerned the makings of a better man.

"Oh Catherine, he would so have wanted your child. He genuinely loves you. Tis good for a man to have children. I delight in mine, as does Sir Edward. The pity of it is that we see so little of them."

"You are always so kind Margaret, so understanding."

"And will you tell him now Catherine."

She thought a while before answering, but already she had made up her mind.

"No Margaret. Tis best he does not know. It will only unnecessarily burden him. Besides, tis a matter beyond mending."

"As you think fit Catherine. No one need know besides Sir Edward and myself."

"Will you help me to dress Margaret. I still feel unsteady on my feet."

"You have been ill Catherine. Gently now."

"What was she like Margaret?"

"Who?"

"Why. Blanche, of course."

"Why do you ask?"

"Because I am a woman and naturally curious."

"She was nothing like you", Margaret replied abruptly.

"Come Margaret, I think you can do better than that."

"I hardly think Sir Edward would want me to vouchsafe an opinion on such matters."

"Please Margaret. He never mentions her and I feel I have a need to know something at least."

"I liked her very well Catherine. She was a handsome looking woman. Like Lord Elliston, she was restless, always wanting to be experiencing life as she termed it. Catherine, is this really of so much importance to you?"

"It is. Pray continue."

What she heard was very much as she had heard previously from Elliston's mama, but tempered by Margaret's own view of the matter.

"It was a bad marriage Catherine, arranged from motives of expediency and little else."

"And the children?"

"She loved the children Catherine. They were a comfort to her. That is why I think I tended to take her part. Fine boys they were, the eldest musical and, like you, devoted to his books, the middle one more keen on the chase; as for the youngest, well he was his mother's especial favourite and, dare I say it, mine too. Lord Elliston amused himself with his ..."

"Women?"

"Yes, women. But she ought not to have kept the children so close, influenced them in her favour, but then he did nothing to prevent it. Had he shown a father's interest, things might have been better. As it was, he left it too late. Catherine, believe me, there is nothing so sad as a grown man trying to convey his love to his children when they have already gone from him. Tis only since you came Catherine that I have learned to see the good in him, to learn to be impartial. Neither Blanche nor Elliston were wholly to blame. A biased mother had sown the seed of discord and they had perforce reaped its harvest. It is you Catherine who have meant more to him than anyone else."

"Thank you Margaret. Thank you."

☙ ❧

It was harvest, not over bountiful, yet not sparsely deficient. Both she and Burgoyne were confident that Elliston would be well content with the way in which they were overseeing his domain. By the end of October his first letter reached her; it told of a glorious victory at a place called Crecy, wherein the Prince of Wales had greatly distinguished himself. The rest was hastily skimped over to reaffirm his love and concern for her. He assured her that Peter's cross was proving a beneficial talisman, and that thus far they had only suffered the loss of two men. Never doubt, he said, that come the spring she would see Holy Island. Again and again she devoured the words of tenderness until the document became yellowed through usage.

Following upon Crecy their own security was threatened by the Scots who, having taken advantage of the wars in France, crossed the border into England under the leadership of their own King. Burgoyne made secure the castle with the few resources to hand. In the event the conflict never reached them, the English, in the absence of their king, having rallied under the banner of their queen and won a decisive victory at the Battle of Neville's Cross. Some of Scotland's finest blood was spilled and their king taken captive.

It was about this time that Miriam and Matthew learned that Mary had been safely delivered of a son. To Catherine the news was not the unalloyed joy it ought to have been. A degree of sadness tempered her happiness, making her feel afraid of the future, a future without him, desolate and empty as a winter sky.

꧁ ꧂

News of Annie was no better. Sunk into a morass of self-pity from which she had neither the will not the inclination to lift herself, she continued to blame Catherine for all her ills, both real and imaginary. Towards Miriam and Matthew she was openly brazen, their deepest concern only seeming to make her more vicious. Determined to dispense with any scrap of decency she owned and fling it on the sacrificial pyre that was Gerard, she sank lower and lower. She had taken up with a great bully of a man who only led her into further degradation; the house was a squalid mess, the two of them drinking themselves into oblivion or fighting like tom cats. She insisted on having her sons back at home with her, though Miriam and Matthew were loath to let them go. No sooner had they returned than the man they were made to call "uncle" forced them, on pain of a whipping, to do menial jobs in the town, all Gerard's plans for giving his sons a good education coming to naught. Drink and the means to obtain it were now Annie's major concerns.

꧁ ꧂

Summer 1347 and he had still not returned. She had noticed that there were longer intervals between each letter, eight months being the norm. The years were drifting by helplessly, and yet the memory of their parting never left her. In 1348 she received another letter. The same tenderness was conveyed in every line, but reading between them she detected a growing unrest. Calais had finally surrendered and was now, to all intents and purposes, a fief of England. He was weary of the campaign and longed to come home, which meant her alone, his sole delight and joy in life. The hostilities, such as they were, had also degenerated into time wasting skirmishes, mainly due to a dread pestilence that had swept across from Asia and was now beginning to ravage Europe. Ending on a cheerful note, he bade her take care and promised that very soon he would take her to Holy Island. To that hope she clung tenaciously.

The autumn of 1348 was wet and windy and the crops, unable to be harvested, suffered accordingly. Matthew, more dour than ever in his prognostications, foretold of want and deprivation and his neighbours were inclined to agree with him.

Burgoyne had returned from the rent day tired and visibly despondent. Since Elliston's absence he had resolved on collecting the dues in autumn, a much wiser proceeding from his point of view considering the availability of produce, but an unwanted inconvenience to the tenants whose busiest time it was. Not that it made much difference that year.

"I take it that the harvest has been all but ruined, Sir Edward?" Catherine enquired.

"Twould be telling an untruth to say otherwise Mistress Venners. It will set us back many a month yet."

"I knew as much from what my uncle was saying only a few days ago, and he is well versed in such matters. Have you aught to tell that bodes good?"

"There is something of cheer," he eventually said.

"Tell me," she asked with growing interest.

"One Geoffrey Frincham is from this day a free man."

"Really!" she laughed. "Then his patience has brought a just reward. Alice will be overjoyed."

"The whole family is overjoyed," he replied with a rare touch of drollery.

"I can well imagine. You have no idea how much it means to them."

"Oh I do Mistress Venners. Assuredly I do. Mistress Frincham does not exactly mask her feelings."

"Did she wear *the* dress?"

"She did," he replied, faintly smiling at her well directed wit.

"What other matter?" she enquired.

He looked at her uneasily, as if uncertain whether to proceed.

"Sir Edward?"

"Tis not of good import Mistress Venners. This pestilence that

Lord Elliston mentioned. It has reached the south of England."

A strange imbalance swam through her ears, her first thoughts being of Rob and Mary who had only journeyed south to escape the harshness of the northern climate. Would to God they had not exchanged one unfavourable circumstance for another.

"Where heard you this?"

"A clerk of mine was speaking with one who had fled north to escape the scourge. Already it had claimed many of his own kin. I believe it first infected Dorset and now has London in its grip. It spreads like flame, taking all in its wake. In the words of this man, Mistress Venners, London has become the city of the damned."

Wincing at the description, she drained her cup at a single gulp, her eyes expressing her unspoken fear.

"Think you it will reach here, Sir Edward?"

"I believe there is every possibility."

"Then we must be vigilant and take what precautions we can."

In her tense and nervous state she poured forth ideas for their deliverance, Burgoyne politely weighing the prudence of her schemes against an enemy literally invisible to attack.

"You speak with wisdom Mistress Venners."

"I would do anything to avert this cursed thing. Maybe a ban on trade at Bardwick."

He smiled. She was indeed innocent in many ways, a fact which Elliston in his quieter moments never tired of telling him. "She will not look to herself Burgoyne," he would say. "All this talk of others when I would sacrifice the entire world to save her alone."

"Sir Edward, are you listening?"

"Yes, of course, my dear," he affirmed, lapsing into a fatherly role, "but we can hardly prevent legitimate trade, and Bardwick, you must remember, is beyond our jurisdiction. If I may make a suggestion of my own?"

"Please do," she urged.

"We could be extra vigilant in our sanitary arrangements. They are nothing short of lax at times. Drains could be cleaned more regularly, open sewers emptied into proper channels. I can undertake to see that this is done in Runnarth, but I am afraid there is little I can do in Bardwick."

"You speak good sense, Sir Edward. We will put such schemes into practice at once. Cleanliness must also be our concern. The people must be told to wash more frequently, at least once a week, and the clothes that they wear must be reasonably clean. I will see to it that sweet smelling herbs are hung in each dwelling, and henceforth make herbal preparations and salves my sole task. There has to be something we can do stay this scourge."

He did not like to disillusion her, but he was convinced that it would take more than a simple infusion of herbs to ward off the sickness.

"God grant that our vigilance be rewarded," she said.

Never had Runnarth smelt so fragrantly fresh. Animals were tethered to prevent them from wandering at will, rushes renewed more frequently than ever before, decaying matter burnt or buried and strongly scented herbs strung in every dwelling. Those who ignored the injunctions laid down were obliged to pay a hefty fine or spend time in the stocks. Mother Jomfrey, deliberately defiant, had dangled her legs there already, but for the most part they were obedient, the mere mention of the plague being sufficient incentive to make them carry out all precautions to the letter. Father Craven's influence was also brought to bear, for where they might ignore others, they took notice of him.

In March 1349 she heard from him again. No letter could have been more welcome. His despondency was marked. With the spread of the plague the campaign was all but halted, his duties becoming sedentary ones allied to the governing of Calais. It would seem that the king had no intention of releasing him yet. The virulence and rapaciousness of the disease now seemed to totally obsess him. Apprehensive for her sake, he exhorted her to be vigilant and not hesitate to flee should it reach Runnarth, adding that since he knew she would never look to her own safety it behoved him to do so, for she was dearer to him that all his lands, nae the whole world. This time there was no mention of Holy Island or of his return. Laying the letter aside, she stood at the window and looked out on the blustery day; it was nature in transition, the time between the passing of winter and the advent of spring. Clouds were rushing overhead, fast forming and dissolving again, taking on the semblance of long necked birds, mighty towers, sun-tipped mountains and lastly the face of an all seeing God. She drew in her breath and exhaled. No, whatever came to pass, this was her country as much as his, and she would never willingly leave it.

The plague remained unchecked, Burgoyne having heard that large areas of Durham were already in its grip. They anticipated it with dread, for of a surety they felt it must come. Almost the whole of her time was now devoted to making up possible cures, pummelling and grinding until her wrist ached and her brow dripped with sweat. The granules were not more pummelled than her thoughts, for no sooner had she put her mind to solving one set of problems than another arose equally as pressing.

CHAPTER TWENTY FOUR

No one was ever to know how the plague came to Bardwick, but come it did, winding in and out of those fetid alleyways until hardly a soul was left living. What it did amongst the poor, it did amongst the rich in equal measure. The panic and fear were dreadful to behold. Those yet unaffected fled north, fled south, fled anywhere, in fact, where they might be assured of immunity, but most of them fled to Runnarth, and within a week of the plague taking Bardwick it struck at the village.

Father Craven remained unwavering. He had long expected the like as a mark of God's judgement. His church provided sanctuary for his flock who, through his intervention, called on God to palliate their distress and spare them an ill-timed mortality. Unable to equate their own paltry sins with the retribution visited upon them, they began to wonder what manner of God it was who could abandon them to suffer unheard. Demanding an answer of God, they made no such demands of their priest. If he believed in his mark of divinity, they believed in it more, his presence having so impressed itself upon their minds that they were in danger of rendering unto the man as opposed to the God. They gathered in the church, staying there for hours at a time, most of them standing, the old and the feeble sitting with their backs to the wall. The sickness was cutting a thin swathe as yet, but they knew that this was only the beginning and that worse was to follow. They looked to Craven for succour, but he had no words of comfort to give them. Though he went amongst them as Jesus went amongst the Gentiles, it was without any comparable feeling of Christ-like compassion. His was an empty and impoverished care, offering not so much solace and hope as strength and resignation to withstand the wrath that God had chosen to visit upon them.

"Oh God, you have judged your servants harshly," he intoned, "and rightly have we deserved your wrath, for we have transgressed Thy holy laws, blaspheming and profaning the commandments you taught us. We are base and corrupt in your eyes, for we have spat upon your word and forsaken the narrow path of the virtuous for the tempting way of the wicked. Smite us then oh Lord until we be fit to speak Thy name, but remove not the light of Thy countenance for we are truly penitent and have no other help but Thee."

Proof enough that adversity sat well upon Craven, safe in his belief that only through suffering on earth was there hope of redemption in heaven. A saintly precept necessitating the one virtue he did not possess. Humility.

The following weeks saw the swift progression of the sickness. Like a shadow that sweeps across the hills, it swept through their village with unremitting force. There was scarcely a family unaffected. Now and then Mass would be punctuated by a pitiful groan, those assembled watching helplessly as another of their number was taken away, the first signs of the sickness upon them, but Craven stood firm, resolved to carry the burden no matter the risk it entailed to himself. Not one of those stricken was allowed to die unconfessed could he prevent it, and so zealous was he in the undertaking thereof that many thought him divinely protected, for surely no ordinary man could act as he did and still remain free of the sickness. In him they detected the makings of a saint, and he did nothing to discourage the impression.

Disposing of the dead became of necessity a perfunctory ritual. Mass burial pits were dug to contain the stench of mortal corruption, a task that could only be done by men of strong stomach.

Dignity in death was dispensed with, some being literally thrown into their graves before the breath had scarce left their bodies. These were strange and disordered times. Men of previous good character were seen to flee from those they presumed to love once the plague was upon them, while those of more moderate repute found new strength in their trials like diminutive Davids facing an unconquerable Goliath. Terrified priests fled to the security of the great religious houses, trusting in their relative seclusion to afford them protection from the worst of the pestilence. The rich squandered fortunes overnight in last frantic hours of pleasure. Others hoped for deliverance through an excess of penitence, seeking to atone for the sins of the world by scourging their flesh and droning out moribund responses. Lesser mortals could only look on in amazement. Because of the shortage of priests and the fear of dying unshriven, a special dispensation was granted whereby men could confess to each other in the knowledge that such would be acceptable to God. But nothing was proof against the scourge. It thirsted and took.

ଓଃ ଃଓ

She defiantly faced the Burgoynes. Having come to a decision, they were not going to turn her from her purpose.

"Edward, make her see reason," said Margaret to her husband who pursed his lips without venturing to speak. "Catherine, what do you hope to achieve," she continued. "They are beyond your help, and if they have any concern for you at all they will thank God that you are here and safe for the time being."

"For the time being?" Catherine reiterated with a smile, "and what is a temporary safety to me Margaret when those I love may be dead or dying."

Burgoyne felt similarly helpless, except that he chose not to show it. Once Catherine had made up her mind, she could be as stubborn as Elliston himself.

"And think you that a few miserable herbs will miraculously heal the sick and restore the dying?" Margaret harangued, entirely forgetful of the usual restraint she imposed upon herself as the wife of Sir Edward. "You are a fool Catherine, a stupid irksome fool, totally without thought for those who only have your best interests at heart." So out of character was this outburst that Catherine broke into laughter.

"You may well laugh now Catherine, but believe me you will very soon weep. Treat me with contempt if you must. I do not care if it turns you from this madness."

Catherine's laughter was not in any way meant to be derisory. Rather was it the outward expression of her highly strung state.

"Hush woman!" Burgoyne reproved. "You are not improving matters. Have I not always told you to weigh your words before uttering them."

To be reprimanded in private was one thing; to be so corrected in public was distinctly another.

"You go too far husband!" she almost screeched. "I will not be reminded of what I should or should not say in such a manner." Her tiny body shook with unconcealed anger, hot piercing tears falling down her cheeks.

"Stop this, both of you," Catherine begged, putting her arm around Margaret.

"Tis you Catherine who are the cause of all our distress," Margaret sobbingly replied "and you alone who have sown the seed of discord between us."

Burgoyne bowed his head in resignation. Every day since the pestilence commenced he had been within the perimeter of the village to witness the extent of its hold, and with each succeeding visit he had returned noticeably lower in spirits than before. Wearied and dejected beyond measure, even he began to question the feasibility of a caring God. Like everyone else he floundered for answers, and it was only his responsibility to Runnarth and Elliston and his belief that things must improve that gave him the strength to continue.

Margaret had stopped crying. He knew her worries, her concern for himself, for their sons in Durham of whom they had heard no news, and for Catherine Venners who, like himself, had a similar tenaciousness.

"Mistress Venners," he began, "I will not attempt to dissuade you as my good wife has done – the addition of the "good" helped to mollify Margaret a little. All I would ask is that you think of your duty to us who have you in our care, or if you cannot think of that then the duty you have to Lord Elliston and the blame that would devolve upon us should anything happen to you."

"As assuredly it will," put in Margaret, markedly more conciliatory. "What is it you want, Catherine? An unnecessary martyrdom, for that is all you can hope to attain. Stay, Catherine, please. We have a great affection for you, much more than I think you realise."

She could hardly bear the look of pathetic entreaty in Margaret's tearful gaze, let alone the heavy eyed countenance of Burgoyne. She owed them so much, and yet she knew that she could not accede to their wishes, however well intentioned.

"I could detain you by force Mistress Venners," said Burgoyne.

"And would you?"

"I think you know me better than that, but you must understand that once you leave the precincts of the castle I cannot allow you to return should we, pray God, continue to remain free of this plague."

"I understand Sir Edward. No woman could have been more fortunate in her friendship than I have been in yours. You will both remain constantly in my thoughts. I cannot say more." Her voice was quivering in the excess of feeling she was trying so hard to suppress.

"I pray God protect you," said Margaret, fiercely embracing her.

"You are a singular woman Catherine Venners," Sir Edward remarked, warmly grasping her hand.

"No, I am nothing of the kind," she answered dismissively. "I am simply anxious for my family. Tis a perfectly natural concern."

Only when the drawbridge was raised behind her did the irreversibility of her decision begin to gain upon her. The weather was fair. Spring ploughing should have commenced, but the great open fields lay fallow unto the sky, neither man nor beast moving upon them, the few strips that had been planted becoming stunted from lack of attention. Weeds were steadily encroaching, the wild flowers being the loveliest she could ever recollect now that they had leave to grow where they willed. As the village drew nearer the scent of the flowers gave way to a strange sickly smell that made her want to vomit; it was a smell with which she would become very familiar. She turned to look back from where she had come. The castle was very distant now, the village inconsolably near. There was hardly a soul moving between the houses and those who did slunk past without a word, their eyes set to the ground, their hands clutching sprigs of sweet smelling herbs to ward off the sickness. It was oppressively silent, the silence of men who have no vision beyond their own immediate travail. The doors of the afflicted were daubed with red crosses. She saw one man flee from such a dwelling, wildly crying and throwing his hands in the air. "Tis with them, tis with them," he railed. "Oh God o' mercy save me! Save me!"

"It takes some of 'em that way," explained the man whose task it was to daub on the crosses. He kept licking his lips, whether through habit or because of his trade, it was difficult to tell. "Still someone's got to do it."

He was not known to her, but since there was no one else to speak to and he seemed in a mood to be amenable, she called him to her.

"Can you tell me if the home of Matthew Thompson is affected?"

"Holy Mother o' God," he replied, scanning her features with surprising indifference, another blight albeit of a different nature having little effect upon him.

"I dunna know anyone by name lass. I were one of the fools that fled 'ere fro' Bardwick. Thought to find safety we did," he laughed, his laughter having a frantic edge to it. "I do as I'm bidden. The priest give me yon chore. The money's good, so I think tae myself I may as well risk all and if the good Lord dunna smite me first, finish a richer man at the end o' it. Look to yesell lass. Keep breathing longer than the others, that's what I say."

She thanked him for his "selfless" advice, almost reluctant to reach her own home lest those within be similarly accursed. What if she were to flee like the man she had just witnessed. How could she be sure that she wouldn't. She was no more proof against the exigencies of the disease than anyone else. Life was precious and she loved Elliston too much to lightly cast it away. Had she been foolhardy in ignoring Margaret's advice now that she was confronted with the full horror of the situation? Of course she had, but absurd though it seemed and in spite of all Margaret's well meant importuning she knew that the choice she had made was the right one.

The sun, hitherto undetermined, now shone brightly, accentuating the dearth that lay upon the land. Overhead portentous rooks cawed mightily over their dying empire. The village was singularly empty except for the dauber of crosses, but then she saw a man coming towards her. She hardly recognised him at first, so marked was the change in him, but he recognised her. It was Geoffrey Frincham, an aberrant and strange looking Geoffrey.

"Kate," he quivered, "sweet Kate," his voice as fragile as the rest of him, a faint whistling sound accompanying each syllable as his teeth clacked in his gums. Gripping her hands, he stared at her wildly. The flesh had fallen away from him and his eyes looked hollow and haunted. The touch of his hands was like that of a skeletal impress.

"Geoffrey?" she said.

"Ay, and a free man too," he replied with the innocence of a child, a wide vacuous grin such as his son was wont to show suffusing his features.

"So I have heard," she humoured. "Tis well deserved Geoffrey."

"Ay, a free man I be."

"And Alice and the children? No doubt they share in your pride."

Looking momentarily puzzled, he paused uneasily before replying, the grin giving way to a grimace, the answer when it came all the more poignant for its glimmer of reason.

"Christ Jesu looks after 'em now," he wistfully informed her, pointing a finger up at the sky. "Heaven be a fine place, Kate, the Father be always tellin' us so."

"God protect you Geoffrey," she said, edging away from him, her mind ineffectually trying to cope with what he had told her. Alice no more, Alice who had evinced such a keenness for life, and every one of the children. To what purpose was Geoffrey's freedom now. And what of the exacting nature of God. If indeed God had chosen to visit such suffering upon them, as Father

Craven professed to believe, then it followed that He must be as flawed as the man he was said to have made in His image. Others might meekly accept. She, never! Rather did she rail at the injustice of it, at God, at the world in general, at whatever was to blame for having brought about such misery where none was deserved. "Tis surely not of God's doing," she said, biting her lip in defiance. Of a surety not the all forgiving Christ in whom she placed her trust. But if not Christ, who? The Devil? Evil personified? "Oh gentle Jesu, she began to pray, "deliver us. Let us live again. Love again." Not for others was the plea, but for herself and Elliston. It was for him she prayed, his life, his love. Was she selfish? Yes, for him, only for him.

Before she reached her own home, the Bardwick man had daubed three more crosses upon three more doors. With the onset of evening the all pervading quiet weighed on her senses. The shriek of someone in extremity caused her to start; then a blackbird burst into song as if its sole purpose was to blot out the cries of the dying, the two sounds mingling strangely together, equally imperative in their need to be heard. Dying men. Singing birds. Infernal. Eternal. It made her thankful to find no such mark on her own home. Matthew opened it warily.

"Kate!" he remarked in amazement. "Well I dunna believe it. Tis good to see ye, but surely the castle be not affected yet. Why Burgoyne were only 'ere a few days afore to see we dunna starve entirely."

"No Uncle, but I wished to be with you. I could not stand the uncertainty of not knowing how you were."

"Ye must be addle brained lass," he mildly rebuked.

"Ay," agreed Miriam, on hearing them. "Ye may be crazed, but I be glad on it," she said, her face puckering as she gathered Catherine to her and wept.

"And what good 'ull cryin' do," chided Matthew.

"As much as anythin' else I know," she sobbed, "but what would *he* say?"

Catherine smiled, the euphemistic 'he' never deserting her aunt even in a crisis.

"He knows me well enough by now," she replied.

Roused from her stupor Annie hiccupped. She was incapably drunk.

"As ye can see, we hae Annie with us," she sighed, hardly disguising her chagrin. "She brought the boys with 'er when the plague took Bardwick. Good boys they are. They be washin' afore supper. Tis bad for 'em to be cooped up as they are."

"Tis bad for all on us," Matthew added.

"Verily," Annie slurred, putting her hand to her mouth as she broke into high pitched hysterical laughter.

"Best not heed her Kate," Miriam whispered. "She be sadly altered and bad tempered withal. There's no reasonin' wi' 'er."

"Tis grief," put in Matthew. "We mun make allowances."

"Ye see, father understands," she slurred. "Playin' the good Samaritan again cousin Kate, are we?"

"Dunna answer," Miriam said. "Matt always makes excuses, but tis time she thought o' others besides 'ersell. Those boys need 'er more than ever they did afore."

Saying nothing, Catherine helped her aunt prepare the table. A frugal meal was soon laid, and despite the dismal circumstances she found herself clearing her plate with uncustomary relish, no doubt a nervous reaction to everything that had happened since her decision to leave the security of the castle. The boys were as hungry as she was. Looking at them, no one could doubt their Gallic inheritance; they had Gerard's looks and his same ease of manner. Indeed, so pronounced was the likeness that it hurt her to see it. Their mother's tipsiness did not appear to trouble them. Perhaps they had grown used to it. It troubled Catherine though. Annie's prettiness was tending to coarseness; she was putting on weight and painting her face like a harlot. And because it was largely self-inflicted it would have required the callousness of the truly hard to remark it unmoved and Catherine was anything but hard.

"What are ye starin' at Kate?" she pounced, aware that she was under scrutiny. "My good little cousin Kate, always wantin' to save someone. Ye didna save Gerard though."

"Annie, I think ye should rest," Miriam remonstrated, trying to drag her to her feet. Catherine noticed how her uncle bowed his head to his platter, feigning disinterest in the proceedings, though his eyes were heavy and his hands trembling.

"Take ye hands off me," Annie drawled. "I know ye dunna want me, not like ye want little Kate," and staring all her pent-up hatred at Catherine she staggered to her bed.

There was silence. The silence of children who did not understand, the silence of an unforgiving mother, above all the silence of a father's growing disappointment in the thing he most treasured.

"She'll be better in a while," Miriam at last spoke. "We try to keep the dratted stuff fro' her, but tis less trouble to let her have it. God knows we hae troubles enough."

"Ay, tis bad for all on us," said Matthew, anxious to direct the conversation away from his daughter. "We hardly go out now.

The land rots and we'll starve if matters dunna mend. I were out on it two days since, but we hae nae oxen to speak on, and pullin' a plough be beast's work, not man's. I may try again, but the heart goes out o' it when others give up."

"I saw Geoffrey," said Catherine, understanding her uncle's vexation. "I hardly recognised him at first."

"Ay," sighed Matthew. "When I look at that man I am hard put to understand the ways o' God. I try to help him as best I can and see that he dunna go hungry."

"He clems himsell," put in Miriam. "Forgets to eat, hae nae notion o' night or day. God be merciful," she said crossing herself. "Matt has been goodness itself to 'im, though he dunna take kindly to praise, like others I could mention," she continued, glaring at Catherine. "Matt tends his strips o' land when he can, but we mun pray that Geoffrey regains his wits."

"Ay, 'is freedom come dear," said Matthew.

"Uncle Matt, you are a good neighbour," Catherine said, pressing his hand.

"That's what I tell 'im," sighed Miriam, "but he dunna heed it. God knows what he'll do if I'm taken, not that I'm afeared o' dyin', well no more than most anyway. Ye'll hae to see to 'im then Kate. Without me, he'll forget to dry his shirt, stay out too long on his pieces of earth, and as for his shoon ..."

"Shoon?" Catherine questioned, smiling at her uncle's growing discomfort.

"Ay, shoon. He dunna dry 'em proper, just like 'is shirt, and when I'm gone ..."

"For God's sake, give over!" Matthew broke in, "whinin' about nonentities. We be livin' yet baint we? It dunna do to dwell on such things afore they've 'appened."

"Ye close ye eyes Matt. Tis a dreadful thing, this plague. Just because it strikes others, dunna think it 'ull conveniently pass us by. Remember what ye said about Alice? Nothin' ud fell 'er ye said. When I think of 'er Kate, I see 'er that vivid like, just as she were in that dress." At this point she began to weep.

"Stop ye drivellin' woman, I'll nae listen," he said, fondly ruffling the boys round the head. It made them laugh. Weighed against their grandmother's tale of impending woe, it came as a welcome respite. All this talk of death filled them with a feeling of mingled fear and curiosity. They could still recall that terrible moment when they had been told that their father had suddenly died of a fever. It was all very well to be told that he now dined with the angels in heaven, but heaven was a vague and faraway concept. Far better that the good Lord had left him to go on dining with them. Still, their father had been a good man and their grandmother had assured them that the good always supped with the angels.

"I'm only tryin' to prepare ye," Miriam persisted.

"And I say ye are mitherin' o'er trifles. Shoon, wet shirts, bah!"

The boys laughed again, and so did Catherine. It was the bickering that made her aunt and uncle so human, and looking at them she felt that she had never loved them more than she did at that moment. Gerard's sons liked their aunt Catherine. He had taught them to look beyond the mask to the woman behind it until they hardly noticed it at all. Their mother never had time for them in the way that their aunt did, and as for telling the most wonderful stories no one told them quite like Aunt Kate. They insisted that she tell them one now before Miriam sent them to bed.

"A really grisly one," said the youngest.

"As grisly as I can make it," Catherine promised.

"I want them to sleep, not be havin' bad dreams," said Miriam.

"And they will sleep, just as long as they remember to say their prayers," she affirmed, resorting to a ruse which her mother had often employed.

"Why childer will ne'er go to bed when they should is beyond me."

"Tis in the sequence of things, aunt. You must have been the same, and so was I."

Once the story was told, they went to their bed without a murmur, leaving the grown ups to speculate over the future.

"If only Rob were here," said Matthew.

"Ay," Miriam agreed. "He were ever considerate o' others unlike some."

He had grown used to these allusions to Annie and preferred to ignore them.

"To think we might hae a grandson we hae n'er even seen," said Miriam. Tis a long time since we heard fro' them Kate. Tis all a worry."

"You must be patient," Catherine enjoined. "Communications are not what they were. You will hear from them soon, never doubt."

"God willin', God willin'," droned Matthew. "I hae seen too much to be o'er confident," and forgetting his recent stricture to Miriam to desist from morbid speculation he recorded a list of those who had so far succumbed to the plague, investing it with the plea of a litany, names, ages and dates of demise of men, women and children, most of whom she knew, and some of whom had been known to her mother in the days when she had made up cures for the numerous complaints to which they were prone.

"Matt, dunna go on," begged Miriam. "Tis o' no use to them or us. The labourer Lord Ellis ...". She hesitated, blushed and started again. "That labourer of ours were one o' the first, along with Baillie Talbot."

"No great loss there," Matthew spat.

"For shame," she cautioned. "We are all God's creatures Matt."

"Well he were a creature right enough," mumbled Matthew, his voice trailing off incoherently into the cuff of his sleeve. Miriam frowned, but let him be.

Her aunt and uncle retired earlier than usual, leaving her alone to reflect on the topsy-turvy nature of life itself; Geoffrey's witlessness, Annie's churlishness, her aunt and uncle's resilience of spirit, but more than all of these she thought of *him,* the distance that separated them and whether he still cared for her as much as she still cared for him despite the intervening years. She felt for the ring on her finger, trusting in the sincerity of the commitment he had made to her in spite of what Craven or other men said.

The fire made her sleepy. She tried to visualise his features; it became harder the longer he was absent. She longed for his nearness, the touch of his hand on her cheek, the quizzical look in his eyes whenever she did or said anything that defied his comprehension.

She was very nearly asleep when Annie prodded her; Annie, dishevelled and partially sober, a petulant pout pursing her raddle stained lips, colouring she had obviously retouched like the deathly white powder she had dabbed on her face, blotched, grotesque and thinly streaked with the sweat of unnatural excitement. The same excitement shone in her eyes, their pupils dark and dilated. She was bold, defiant, like someone amorally inspired. Her hair spun round her head like some unkempt halo, debased gold, suffering and tarnished. Catherine almost felt afraid of her.

"I dunna see why ye should sleep Kate Venners when I canna." That she herself had slept for the past three hours without a care for anyone else was of no matter.

"I was not asleep Annie, merely resting my eyes."

"I hae a murderous headache," she whined, holding her hand to her agonised brow to give emphasis to the fact.

"I could prepare something for you, if you think it would help," Catherine said trying to appease her.

"Keep ye bloody cures. I want naught from ye!"

"Annie," she appealed, "are things not bad enough without this continual rancour between us. I did what I could to save Gerard, you must believe that. He died penitent and reconciled to God. I spoke with him before he was taken for trial. He did not regard himself as deserving of clemency. Rather did the nature of the crime weigh on his conscience. As for Lord Elliston, think what you will Annie, but he had no other recourse. Believe me, it caused us both pain."

"No recourse!" she howled in derision, her rocking motion reminiscent of the one she had adopted on their previous interview, but this time clipped of the softness that cried out for sympathy. "You did not care so long as ye kept *him* satisfied. Gerard was mine and ye let him die."

"I told you the last words that Gerard spoke. Why won't you believe me. I had them verbatim from those who were there at the end. He held no one to blame but himself."

"Lies to cushion ye conscience!"

"No Annie, the truth!" she maintained, raising her own voice.

"Damn ye!" she cursed. "Elliston's whore! Do you really think he cares that for ye," she continued, snapping her fingers. "Ye got him by foul means I reckon, but he'll soon be the wiser. Whoring his way across France, I wouldn't mind bettin', pressin' his mouth to many a face more fetchin' than yours."

"If he but retains a measure of the affection I still feel for him, then I would willingly forgive him all such inconstancy!" Annie effected to laugh, but her laughter was strained. The retort had taken her completely by surprise. "I did not invite your company Annie. I suggest we put an end to this conversation. It is doing neither of us any good."

"Why, because ye canna face facts?"

"More than you ever will Annie!" she flared, losing her temper. "You suck on your grief like a babe at the breast, but the babe knows when it is satiated. You, never! That has always been your failing. As for Gerard, he sacrificed everything for you, even his life. I scarcely think you worthy of the sacrifice!"

Silenced, Annie sank to the floor, drawing up her knees and holding them to her, a habit she had retained since her childhood whenever she became vexed, usually over something she wanted and was not allowed to have. It rarely failed to move Gerard. She now began to wail, sensing the truth and hating its sting. Drawing her hand across her face, the paint and the powder were wiped into smudges. She did indeed look like a child again, lost, bewildered and hopelessly inept at dealing with the complexities of the grown up world. Catherine wished she could have recalled those words, but they were out, cold and recriminatory, not even tempered with a little grain of compassion to soften their impact.

"Annie, I ..."

"I hate you!" she cried, getting to her feet and hitting out at Catherine, though still being in a sort of semi stupor she was incapable of inflicting any real hurt, and Catherine was able to push her away. "My worst is over Kate Venners. But yours is yet to come! And I'll make sure that it does."

CHAPTER TWENTY FIVE

It was a dreary dawn, made drearier still by the constant drizzle. Puddles formed in the paths as the Bardwick man with two of the villagers tramped through the mire to perform their terrible task of loading the cart with the bodies of those who had died in the night. They had wrapped rags round their faces to cope with the stench and ward off infection. So far they had collected twelve, but before the day was at an end the toll would have risen to twenty. If it continued to rise, a further pit would need to be dug on the common.

Thankfully Annie remained in bed, but her children were in good spirits, and ready for breakfast. Somehow they made life seem normal.

"Ye best take some gruel to Geoffrey," said Miriam, looking at Matthew. "Ay, best watch 'im eat it too, or he'll put it aside and forget. God knows he could do with some flesh on 'im."

Catherine cleared the dishes. After the altercation with Annie, she had past a miserable night. Now she was bound to incur further censure from her aunt and uncle by telling them that it was her wish to help Craven; this had not been a sudden decision, but was very much bound up in her decision to return to the village. When Miriam learned of it, she reacted much as Margaret had done.

"If anyone be doomed, then tis he. What has got into ye lass? Speak to her Matt. Holy Mother of God, speak to her!"

"Let be," replied Matt. "The lass must do as she thinks fit, and if ever a man were in need of help, then it be the Father. We are fortunate to hae 'im Miriam. Most of his like hae only looked to themselves."

"That's as maybe, but Kate hae no cause to put her own life at risk. Tis enough that she hae come to us when there were no need on it."

"I owe Father Craven a great deal," Catherine tried to explain, "and as Uncle Matt says he has need of assistance."

☙ ❧

The drizzle had ceased and the break in the cloud promised a brighter afternoon. Fewer people than previously sought refuge in the church, their numbers having been sadly depleted, and those who remained were noticeably subdued, God's house having afforded no more immunity than anywhere else. She thought of the last time she had been in this church, of how Craven had used the sanctity of his calling to persuade her to leave Elliston, and of Elliston's sudden intervention and his far more human appeal of love and desire. She had conceded that Craven was much the better man from a moral perspective, but to do good and live righteously as Craven had done, and yet to be lacking in the feelings common to most men was a fault in itself. Though Craven professed to love his Saviour, his love was imperfect, for only through the love of one's fellow human beings could one truly love God.

Nothing had outwardly changed, the paintings on the wall were more brilliant than ever and the Virgin looked beatific in a kind of expressionless way; had she been anything more she would have wept at the pitiful gathering who petitioned her with prayers and lit candles in her honour.

"Where is Father Craven?" she asked of Eve who was seeking escape from her crone of a mother in law rather than the plague itself. Before she had time to reply, he had emerged from beyond the chancel.

"Here Catherine," he said, holding out his hands in welcome.

"Father, will you let me help you?"

"Assuredly," he answered, making the sign of the cross. "You know, the ways of God are many and varied, Catherine, but I thank Him that He has led you to me in these times of great trial."

She smiled faintly. The phrase slightly discomforted her. She had no desire to be taken to task yet again.

"There is much to do," she remarked, conscious of his scrutiny and the shiver that ran down her spine.

"Much indeed Catherine," he averred, approving her sensibility without alluding to past events which were painful to them both. Nonetheless he still preached. "Do you not perceive the hand of God in all that has befallen us, His Judgement on the vanity of a world that closes its eyes to the commandments He has made for our guidance?"

Perceiving nothing of the kind, she could not lie to him now.

"I see only the Devil's," she replied.

There were one or two gasps of amazement. It was only what

many of them thought, but it took someone with more than ordinary courage to question Craven's belief in an all avenging God.

"I see you remain intractable Catherine," he said with a look of genuine pain. "Only in bending your will to that of God's will you see His truth more fully revealed. I shall pray for you Catherine."

"We have always seen things differently Father, but can we not agree to put aside such differences while these present troubles prevail."

"Differences, Catherine? I know of none," he equivocated, his features impassive, never impassioned.

Concerned that he might continue in the same vein, she was somewhat relieved when he began to speak of the more immediate needs of the village. Since the visitation of the sickness the land had lain untilled, its few crops aborted in the wake of neglect; rain had flattened the furrows and made streams in the ridges; weeds were freely rioting in both. The villagers were becoming too timid to venture outdoors for fear of contracting the plague, besides which there appeared to be little profit in tilling the soil if death was to claim them before they were able to reap the rewards of their labours. Even so, the ties of a man with his land went deep, Matthew often saying that it behoved him to keep faith with the little good he had inherited. Not to do so was to starve, and they only had to look at Geoffrey's pinched features to see what the outcome would be. Pilfering was taking place, perhaps to a lesser extent than might have been expected, but they were human and not immune to the temptations put in their way. Ironically, the diminishing population was helping to ease the situation, but survival depended on rigorous self-denial if the imminent threat of starvation was to be avoided.

"Your uncle, Catherine, I know, has been one of the few to persevere," said Craven. "He is a man well respected and I feel confident that were he to lead others might follow. If you could speak with him Catherine?"

"I will do my best Father," she promised.

"Catherine?"

"Father."

"God in his infinite goodness has sent you back to us. At least, in this you have obeyed His will. I pray it may be so in all other things too. Always be heedful of His call."

"I shall Father. I shall."

"Indeed you must, Catherine."

Catherine's return to the village only helped to strengthen his belief in the mark of God's special grace; he could now see that the error had been his for being impatient, but did not everything ultimately work out to the good of those who truly believed in Him. Elliston had been a test of his faith, but now at last all would be well.

Late silvery sun edged the clouds, hardly touching the earth beneath them. A quickening breeze heightened the sweet sickly smell of the invisible predator, and she suddenly felt cold and full of foreboding. Her fears were well founded. The man from Bardwick was daubing the tell-tale cross on their door; a dying beam of sunlight shone upon it as it dribbled down the wood like the oozing of blood. He slunk by to avoid her. She stood there, disbelieving. They had been so well when she had left them that morning, Miriam chiding her for seeking out Craven, Matthew preparing to take gruel to Geoffrey. But such was the nature of the plague that there was no telling where it might strike next; Miriam had said as much when she warned them not to be over complacent. Until such time as it did, it was possible to think of it in a detached kind of way, as something terrible that was striking down others but mercifully not striking them. Catherine had been guilty of precisely this sort of reasoning which was why the cross on her own door had such a chilling effect. Her eyes refusing to focus on anything else, it drew her and everything surrounding it into its smeared and blebbed colour; barely resembling a cross at all, it was as if God Himself was slaking the paint to deny His involvement. The knock she gave lacked definition. She was terrified.

"Kate, go lass," came Matthew's voice, holding fast the door against her possible entry.

"Uncle Matt, tell me who is sick. Is it you? I am your kin. I have a right to be told!"

There was no answer, but she had no intention of walking away, and it was not in her uncle's character to be deliberately evasive.

"Miriam and the childer," he gave out at last, each syllable stretched and strained, as if he found it difficult to believe what the words encompassed, "and I am only stayin' because I canna leave, she bein' a goodly woman and one who wouldna hae deserted me. Now go Kate. For pity's sake, go!"

"And Annie? What of Annie?" she asked, whereupon she could hear him drumming his fingers on the door in the manner of the fretful, the humiliated.

"Gone," he replied, as if he hated having to inform her of the fact. "When Miriam said she be hot and feverish, the childer likewise, she left. Unthinkin' Kate, that what she be, unthinkin'. I dunna understand 'er. I dunna understand anythin' nae more." The note of despair in his voice made her even more resolute. They were her people, just as Elliston was hers, to love and to cherish until the day of dissolution, be it now or some time in the future.

"Where is Annie?"

"As far as I know, with Mother Jomfrey."

She found herself smiling, not in humour but in knowingness of Annie. And in spite of her uncle's vexation, she was almost relieved to find she had gone.

"Let me in Uncle Matt. Tis not right that you should be alone."

"For sweet Jesu's sake, go Kate," he entreated. "There is naught ye can do. Miriam would not want it and neither do I."

"I am not leaving," she persisted, hammering on the door until her hand was streaked with the crimson. She was hoping that it would get to the heart of him, which it did, and instead of turning her away as he had fully intended he now let her in.

"Like ye mother afore ye," he mumbled.

She reeled from the stench, the stink of corruption seeming to taint everything it touched.

"Dunna go in there!" he cried, standing between her and the dividing piece of hempen. "I dunna understand ye lass. Are ye sae bent on dyin'?"

"No Uncle Matt. I want to live as much as anyone else, but if I can do anything in my power to ease their pains then I will."

She was beyond him, but then so was her mother. Strangers both, he reflected, leading her into the narrow space where Miriam and the boys writhed on their pallets. They manifested all the known symptoms. Buboes in the armpits and the groin, sickness, vomiting, fever.

"What hae they ever done to offend God?" he said, looking to her for some sort of explanation.

"Nothing Uncle Matt. Nothing."

"I hae shrived 'em Kate. Tis permissible. Though what she hae to confess I dunna know. As for them," he sighed, pointing to the boys, "mere innocents."

Some respite in her suffering, Miriam glanced up, listening with her eyes, which had in them a peculiar quality of intense observation, as if they saw beyond the surface of life as it waned, for in looking at Catherine she thought she saw Isobel, and in Matthew the youthful features of the man who had promised her the world for her portion. The setting sun bathed her face in glorious light. She weakly raised her hand to draw his attention. Despite the risk of infection, he clasped it tightly in his own.

"Matt," she whispered.

"Ay lass, I'm here."

"Hae ye milked Daisy. I would not hae her suffer on account o' me."

She never spoke again, her last coherent thought being for him and the beast he so treasured. Catherine turned away, her eyes clouded with tears. Gerard's sons died a few minutes later.

Evening fell. The cart came. Already laden high with the putrefying flesh of the dead, Miriam and the boys were unceremoniously thrown in with the rest. Matthew trudged some way behind, his face hunched up in his jacket to offer him what little protection it could. He was not brave. He simply felt a need to be with them on this, their last journey. Passing Mother Jomfrey's, Annie watched and wept.

Catherine stayed behind to sweep out the house, burn the bed linen, lay fresh rushes and prepare a special pottage of herbs to offset the lingering smell. Although she had pleaded with him, Matthew had forbidden her to wash their bodies. He was wise. No dignity could be accorded to the dead. To be quick and alive was all that mattered. Now that she had done all that there was to be done, the awful finality of it began to weigh upon her. She looked at the pot of broth bubbling over the fire. It was Miriam's broth, prepared only a few hours before and looking as appetising as when she first made it. The bread she had cut in readiness for her uncle's return was also of Miriam's making, as were the pots of herbs and spices. Catherine had pleased her by marking them up with the squiggles which she was never able to read for herself but which she had always regarded as little short of miraculous because others could. What a warm and generous person she had been, what a capable and hard working wife for a man as demanding as her uncle. Covering her face with her hands, she let the tears come, and then as suddenly stopped. Matthew must not see her thus. If only for his sake, she had to be strong.

He returned like the ghost of the man he once was. They did not speak. She urged him to eat, but at the sight of Miriam's broth his eyes began to fill. Breaking the bread into edible pieces, he spread them on the table as if they were the remnants of the host served at Mass.

"She were a fine woman, Kate," he said. "I had no complaints."

Left alone, she sat staring at their uneaten meal. Before very long she heard the sound of his sobbing.

They spoke little during the following days. What were words in the midst of their grief. And it was not just for Miriam that they grieved, but also for the children, and for Matthew the grief went deeper still because of Annie and his inability to excuse the inexcusable. She had not ventured near and he was too proud to seek her out. Catherine's time revolved around a routine she devised for herself, that of keeping house for Matthew and of assisting Craven in whatever way he deemed best. Craven had little to say of her own loss, hollowness of feeling preventing further expression, but then death was so commonplace that it was difficult to mourn in a healing kind of way.

For the first time in his life, Matthew had no heart for tending his land. Catherine did what she could to encourage him, but he would sit for hours in the same attitude, abstracted and vaguely staring into space, his eyes becoming heavy from want of activity. She reminded him that in spite of the four remaining oxen which had been deliberately fattened to cope with the burden of pulling the plough the earth was sprouting weeds rather than crops.

"I be thinkin' o' puttin' Daisy down," he said by way of an answer.

"No, Uncle Matt! How can you think of such a thing after all Aunt Miriam said."

"Ay, but the beast be clemmed. Tis cruel to keep her and the mite o' milk she gives is pitiful."

"Wait a while, I beg you. These terrible things must have their term and once they have, pray God, things will improve. As it happens, the weather is favourable to ploughing now did someone choose to undertake it."

"Maybe," he grimly agreed, the implied censure not having escaped him.

೧೫ ೱ

The following afternoon saw the arrival of a young rider dressed in the livery of the Ellistons. Drizzle soaked him through as he fretfully drew on the reins, the desolate scene showing gloomier still in the grey coloured weather. His agitation only increased on seeing the cross on Matthew's dwelling, but those free of them were few and far between. The letter he had brought her was dipped in vinegar in a pathetic attempt to prevent the contagion from spreading. He had pinned it to a stick which he dandled in front of her. The certainty that it must be from Elliston caused her fingers to fumble as she ripped off the seal. Her joy was short lived. The message came from Burgoyne. It was to inform her that plague had taken the castle with the loss of much life. Maud had been first to contract the disease and now lay buried with many more in a pit specially dug for the purpose. Poor Maud. What a dismal end to a dismal life. She ought to have done more for her, if only to rescue her from the indignities of the kitchen. There was certainly not much of cheer from Burgoyne. They had not heard from Elliston and Margaret was becoming pressing in her demands to find out how her sons fared in Durham. As ever, she feared the worst and because of the unsettled times he was reluctant to allow her to undertake the journey without him; he was therefore of a mind to leave the household under the control of his lieutenant, a capable man in whom he had every confidence, but only if Catherine agreed.

"I am to wait for an answer," the man agitated as she re-read the letter.

"Tell Sir Edward I am agreeable," she said, "and bid him and Lady Margaret God speed."

Matthew, finishing his gruel and listening to the proceedings from indoors, asked her what was amiss. She told him of her decision.

"A wise one Kate," he said, wiping his mouth. "Tis not right that a woman should mither after her childer."

With this, he rose from the table, but instead of moving to the fire as was his usual wont, he walked to the door and reached for his jacket. She watched him anxiously, not daring to speak lest she spoil the inclination. How old he now looked, but there was still an irrepressible store of strength in the man that refused to be buffeted by circumstance. Also he had lived long enough to learn that pain could only be minimised through effort.

"Well I'll be away," he remarked casually, almost afraid that she would make of it much more than it merited. He was not mistaken. Had she done what she wanted to do, she would have flung her arms round him, but realising how he would recoil from such demonstrations of affection she merely helped him into the jacket and smiled encouragingly.

"Thank you Uncle Matt."

He stared at her for a moment, pretending to pick the threads of the homespun, wanting to speak his gratitude, just as she wanted to speak hers, yet finding no words in which to properly express what her staying had meant to him.

"Well lass there's much to do, and Rob wouldn't want me to neglect his inheritance," he mumbled, despising himself for his apparent indifference though she was used to his ways by now.

"Do not overtire yourself Uncle Matt. Remember, I promised Aunt Miriam to keep a watchful eye on you."

"Ay," he sighed, suddenly catching hold of her hand and squeezing it roughly. "She were bonny, Kate, bonny."

Tears moistened his eyes, but she pretended not to notice.

A thin stream of men followed his example, and if the specks on the earth were fewer than before they were there and it was a goodly sight. They laboured until they were beyond toil, until the blue sky above them had deepened to night, ploughing their anguish into the land and turning it to account, tiring their bodies and strengthening their spirits, men of torpid emotion who had learned what it meant to silently endure. The day remained dry, intervals of sunshine breaking the dullness, nothing hindering their labours apart from the breeze that still blew upon them in little gusts of sickly sweetness.

He returned tired and weary, but decidedly the Matthew of old, and for a change uncommonly talkative, full of the kind of restiveness that denotes a fresh purpose in life and the strength and means to achieve it. She listened without interrupting, knowing that he had past the ultimate bound of his grief and could begin to think of the future.

"Let me take your jacket, Uncle Matthew," she eventually spoke, remembering Miriam's strictures on his welfare.

"Ay, and there's still much to be done," he continued, as if the prospect cheered him. "I canna remember seein' the fields as bad as they are now. Why my own strips are naught but weed patches, and as for Geoffrey's." He sighed deeply, handing her the jacket without demur and pulling the shoon from his feet in compliance with her wishes and those of his wife.

"How is Geoffrey?" she enquired, as he eased himself before the fire, the nights still proving chilly despite the overall warmth of the day.

"Nae sae bad as he was lass. He does as I tell 'im, and there are times when I think he understands better than we do."

"In what way?"

"I dunna rightly know Kate. There's summat death defyin' about 'im if ye take my meanin'."

"I think I do," she replied, feeling that perhaps Geoffrey too had learned to be gracious for the life still allowed him, his witlessness lending him a strange kind of strength and helping to heal him in the process.

The little niceties she had performed did not go unnoticed, and if the measure of his gratitude could only be evinced in a smile it was sufficient to make her content. Her sole concern was to keep home for him as Miriam would have done. Miriam's head had contained a store of receipts, both for famine and for feast, and whatever the circumstances it was to her lasting credit that she never failed to satisfy the appetites of those in her care. Catherine knew herself to be poor in comparison, but that did not prevent her from trying. Up until now her uncle had evinced little interest in food, but the labour had helped to sharpen his appetite. She had made him the flat cakes that were Miriam's speciality, but they did not have the appetising look of her aunt's.

"I made them with the little that was available," she said by way of apology. "I fear they are scarcely palatable."

"They be fair fillin' Kate," he commented wryly, fingering a particularly sticky bit from his teeth.

"You deserved better. I am sorry."

"Dunna fret lass. Tis unlikely Geoffrey will hae better."

Smiling, she set to repairing a tear in his jacket while it was still light enough to see, her thoughts straying to Elliston as she worked every stitch. Matthew, none the worse for his meal, was snoring peacefully.

"Uncle Matt," she whispered, gently nudging him.

"All right woman, stop ye naggin'," he muttered half asleep.

"Tis I uncle," she reminded him. "Best go to bed now."

"Ye mustna mind me lass," he said, rousing himself. "I get forgetful. Ah well."

As he had said so often of late, it was a strange world, and stranger still that they should be sitting together in that lonely house, their thoughts respectively turning to one man and one woman far beyond their reach.

The weather was squally the following day, and she urged him not to go out until it showed fairer. For breakfast they drank Daisy's thin milk and ate the remains of the cakes, even less appetising in their cold and stodgy state.

"I were wonderin' about gettin' news to Rob and Mary," he remarked. "The tranter who carries letters to and fro Craven should be here any day now. Do ye think he may hae a letter for us lass."

"I doubt it Uncle Matt. In any event I think Rob and Mary will have left London. Very likely, they are journeying back here, but remember they have a child to care for now."

"My grandson," he sighed. "God knows, I hae need o' one."

By mid-day the rain had ceased, patches of sun tinted cloud relieving the greyness. An occasional swallow reached into the blue, dipping its wings in the sunlight. Much of the sickly odour had been washed away and the air, though still tainted, held the promise of revivifying freshness. It somehow pointed to a change, not passing but permanent.

"I'll be away Kate," he said, anxious to take advantage of the change in the weather, almost boyish in his eagerness to start working again. "Must collect Geoffrey first."

Catherine looked at him and smiled. Collecting Geoffrey was now very much a part of their day. With Matthew left on his "collecting" errand, she concentrated on the household chores. She had also promised to see Craven. With all this in hand, she had little time for reflection, but keeping busy was better.

When she left the house the day was already well advanced, dull and damp with a gathering of cloud that had stolen the sun, though the air felt purer than it had in a long time. Her thoughts on Craven, she kept her eyes close to the ground where newly formed puddles mirrored the dark clouds above.

"Want to watch where ye are goin' Kate Venners."

She looked up to find herself confronted by Annie, the smell of sour ale on her breath.

"Annie," she replied, vaguely surprised.

"Ay, the very same," she spat out, her eyes bright in the shadows surrounding them, proof sufficient that conscience had deprived her of sleep. It was only on seeing the cart trundle away the bodies of her mother and sons that the full enormity of what she had done found her plagued by remorse, a nasty canker ridden guilt that laid her wrong-doing bare and made her squirm like a worm on a hook. The realisation that she had failed both as a mother and a daughter was hard enough to endure without the added indignity of knowing that Catherine had not been found similarly wanting.

It was this that really rankled and made her hate Catherine with a deep and unreasoning hatred. Wallowing in imaginary grievance until it took on the semblance of truth, it was much simpler to lay the burden of her guilt upon the shoulders of the woman whose care she despised. Even the taste of the ale could no longer console her. Nor was she Catherine's only detractor. She had another far more dangerous in the shape of Mother Jomfrey. The old woman had not forgotten how Isobel Venners had made her seem small in the eyes of her neighbours, nor how her plan for wreaking vengeance on the daughter had sadly miscarried, Catherine's time at the castle having resulted in anything but the humiliating lesson for which it was meant. She had bided her time with the ease of a snake slithering through grass, her tongue ready to fork and sting when the moment seemed ripe. Neither was she averse to making use of anyone to serve her own ends, and who better than poor feckless Annie.

"Naught to say on the neglectin' o' my duty," Annie goaded.

"Tis not for me to act the part of your conscience Annie," she replied, "but I wish you would speak with Uncle Matt. He has need of you. Now if you will let me pass, I am in a hurry."

"Hold her fast!" cried Mother Jomfrey emerging from her hovel and wielding her stick in the air. Annie did as she was told, gripping Catherine tightly by the wrist. The village Cassandra had changed very little, her face having darkened like leather, the neck of it puckered and pulled like the crop of a fowl's. She had also developed the habit of continually sucking on her two remaining teeth, though her eyes remained keen and prickingly pupilled.

"Well, Mistress Venners," she croaked, as Catherine tried to pull herself free, though the old woman grabbed her by the hair, "we hae not met for many a day."

"It has suited well enough," countered Catherine, recoiling from the stench of the hag's reeking breath.

"Such spirit," she laughed, winding a strand of Catherine's hair round the stick.

"She always had that," Annie mockingly joined in, her hand still tight on Catherine's wrist.

"Like her mother eh," Mother Jomfrey put in.

"Let me go!" Catherine spat out at the crone. The spittle trickled down the old woman's face. Wiping it away slowly with the back of her hand, she smiled faintly to herself, and then brought down the stick fiercely across Catherine's shoulders. Catherine cried out. It was that cry that unleashed all of Annie's fury.

"More!" she yelled. "More! More!"

At the same moment Mother Jomfrey lowered the stick and gazed at her disapprovingly. She had not expected much of Annie, but had reckoned on her showing a little more subtlety.

"Afraid are ye!" screeched Annie, attempting to wrest the stick from the woman's tightly clenched fingers.

"Ye hae nae sense Annie," she retorted. "Never did have. Now this one," she said, pointing a finger at Catherine, "she hae more o' it than is seemly."

Catherine, recovering from the ferocity of the blow, which had momentarily stunned her, decided to adopt silence as her defence no matter how much they were set on provoking her.

"Ye see Annie. Sense. I can see what she's at. Let us blather on, won't ye Kate Venners. Hope to play on our little differences, but ye'll not succeed, of that I can assure ye."

What Mother Jomfrey had guessed was partly true. Indeed, she trusted to profit by her silence in the hope that their divisiveness might simmer. Annie fell strangely quiet, hanging on every word the old woman uttered, somehow seeming impotent to act without her say-so.

A small crowd, attracted by the disturbance, began to gather. It mainly consisted of women, their menfolk not having returned from their labours. Others were from Bardwick, many of them having the menacing looks of her kitchen acquaintance.

"What be your game Jomfrey?" came a man's voice from the rear of the crowd.

"We be here to prove that Kate Venners is not what she would hae ye believe," Annie replied in response to a nod from her accomplice.

"She be your cousin," said another.

"Which is why I know her better than ye do," she winked in the direction of the man from Bardwick who had so liberally disposed of his crosses.

"There be nowt wrong wi' 'er," a tousle haired woman, arms akimbo, boldly called out. "She were good to me when I were taken badly, and what's more through 'er we hae all fared better."

"Ay," was the universal cry.

Annie winced uneasily. Not having anticipated this sort of opposition, she looked to the crone for support. She, on the other hand, was fully prepared for it. Just how susceptible they would prove was part of the challenge.

"Ye hae been made fools on," she commenced, weighing every word with parsimonious care. "Where did she come fro, this cousin of Annie's? Ye tell me that. Who were her mother?"

"Isobel Venners were fine by me," an old woman about her own age asserted, her extended span of years owing much to Isobel's timely intervention.

"Ay that's as may be, but who bedded her?" Mother Jomfrey continued, narrowing her eyes at the woman. They fell silent. And in that silence she knew she had them. "Let 'em see ye face Kate Venners. Come now, dunna be shy," she teasingly coaxed.

"Ay show ye face cousin Kate," Annie yelled, hardly helping matters as a look from the crone informed her. Catherine remained silent. She neither removed the mask nor stopped them doing so. It was this mild, almost total acceptance, that so disconcerted Annie who had expected her to show more spirit. For a moment their eyes met and Annie felt unaccountably chastened. At a sign from the old woman, however, she ripped the mask from Catherine's face like a fiend bent on spite. Instinctively Catherine bowed her head.

"Nae lass," said Mother Jomfrey, catching at her neck with the stick and thrusting up her head for everyone to see. "The good people want to look on ye prettiness."

Memory had dimmed in many of those who had previously remembered. Over the years they had accepted the mask as once they had accepted the disfigurement beneath it; most of them had forgotten what she actually looked like while others, too young to remember or having come from Bardwick, had no recollection of it anyway. As far as they were concerned the Venners girl was more remarkable for the efficacy of her cures than the strangeness of her looks. Moreover, her relationship with Elliston had done nothing to harm them; on the contrary it had brought them nothing but good. Mother Jomfrey was relying on the shock of revealing the full extent of Catherine's disfigurement to work in her favour and make them more receptive to her argument. She had calculated correctly as Catherine was only too aware. All those old sensations of being made to feel different and repellent came flooding back again as every face was fixed on her own. She felt degraded, humiliated, the principal character in a dumb show which had gone terribly wrong. Close to tears, she forced herself to hold them back.

"Now then, tell them who ye father were," heckled Mother Jomfrey, harmlessly prodding her with the stick, "and keep ye head high, such modesty is unbecomin'."

"She were always good at pretendin'," said an exuberant Annie, trampling the mask in the mud as if she was dancing.

Provoked beyond endurance, Catherine now spoke.

"You may detest me Annie," she charged, "but I never thought you would resort to using Mother Jomfrey."

"Nae one uses me," the old woman screeched. "No one. Do ye hear!"

"Only too well, and there is sense in your argument. I was mistaken. Tis you who use Annie."

She saw Annie flinch, the paint on her lips smudged like crushed raspberries, her face becoming white to the roots of her tow coloured hair. It was the truth and it hurt.

The crowd was growing, edging ever closer to the protagonists, eager to see the next scene enacted, admiring the modesty of the accused but deploring her obvious drawback.

"Who were 'er father then?" questioned the man of the crosses, "seein' as ye be sae clever."

Everyone began to laugh, even Annie who laughed louder than any of them in a desperate attempt to deafen her conscience. Then it grew quiet again, which was what Mother Jomfrey was counting on to allow her to seize the right moment.

"Whose testimony is written in fire?" she smoothly insinuated. "Who brands his disciples thus?"

Every eye was now on the crone and the girl, a murmur of expectation running through the crowd like a sibilant ripple through corn. Rain was falling. A crow squawked overhead like a bird of ill omen. Mother Jomfrey turned to Annie and smiled.

Out of sight of the crowd, Craven stood watching. Tightening the cord about his cassock, he viewed the spectacle with contempt. They were like chaff, readily expendable, save for a grain or two of worth such as Catherine Venners. As for the Jomfrey woman, she was the worst kind of abomination in using her cunning to prey on their credulity, but he too could speak to purpose when it mattered.

With the dismal break in the weather, the men had decided to finish their labours earlier than usual, only to find themselves drawn to the edge of the crowd with the impetus of a stone tossed in water.

"What be it," said Geoffrey, childishly clutching at Matthew's elbow.

"I'm sure I dunna know, but I mean to find out."

With Geoffrey still hanging on to him, he pushed his way through the crowd which was beginning to have all the makings of a mob set in motion.

"It be Kate," said Geoffrey, nervously pulling at Matthew's sleeve. "Your Annie too. What do it mean Matt? Mother Jomfrey hae a nasty face to her. I dunna like it Matt. I be feared."

"Dunna fret Geoffrey. Stay close now. I'll soon make sense o' it."

But he could not make sense of it at all. Here was the Jomfrey woman flinging her usual invective; that in itself was in no way surprising, but that Annie was standing there with her and blatantly condoning it was beyond his understanding. His first concern was for Catherine who looked amazingly calm considering her unenviable position, though he could see in her eyes her total involvement. The fact that the mask had been removed made her look even more vulnerable.

"The devil do leave his mark thus!" screamed out a woman beside him.

Gradually whipped up to a frenzy, they were a crowd no longer, but willing participants in the passions evoked by a vicious old woman and her ranting accomplice. Only a few remained timid or silent.

"I see most o' ye be clever at catchin' on," said Mother Jomfrey, reserving her stare for the less well enlightened.

"I bet there be a few warts on ye!" came the retort of one of them.

This was greeted with moderate approval by the less superstitiously inclined, but in the main they held back for fear of what the hag might do to them.

"Ye may mock," she hissed like a snake about to bite, "but I hae power to see through to evil, and ye mun believe me when I tell ye that Kane Venners were not sired by any ordinary man."

"Tis truth," added Annie, excitedly using her hands in a way reminiscent of Gerard. Unlike Mother Jomfrey who made an art of deceit, she could not quite bring herself to stare directly at the crowd, only over their heads to where the sky began to stir in notes of ominous thunder. Partners in a common aim, they did not share a common conviction, Annie needing to believe in her mission, Mother Jomfrey seeing it for the pretence that it was. "Why, ye only hae to look at the colour o' her hair," she continued to rail, twisting a strand of the said auburn round her fingers, so much so that it caused Catherine to flinch.

"Ay, the colour o' a wanton," said the woman next to Matthew, quick to catch at the inference.

Matthew now stood directly in front of them. Annie did not see him. Experiencing all the unreality of a real hurt, he drew his knuckles together, desperately trying to equate this abusive harridan with the pretty child who used to sit on his knee.

"She hae the devil's taint right enough," a timid looking girl announced in a sanctified whisper, as she made the sign of the cross.

"Tis just he got a mite carried away in 'er case," said her neighbour, a mean faced man, one of those who was making a mock of it all. There was laughter, most of it nervous. Annie continued to gaze heavenwards as if calling on God to give final judgement.

"She came amongst you wi' looks o' tender concern. Twas a ruse worthy o' her master, and do not think I refer to Elliston," Mother Jomfrey went on.

"Tis so," Annie maintained, her confidence increasing as their resistance proportionately withered. "Do ye honestly think any man would hae bedded her without bein' bewitched first." A groan of tacit assent was her reward. "And think carefully," Annie continued. "With her comin' our misery increased. More perished than before."

"Many more," Mother Jomfrey added emphatically, now leaning on her stick. Growing tired, she wished the matter to be brought to a satisfactory conclusion. Her bones creaked in their inadequate covering of skin and the hands that gripped at the stick were blue with cold and tortuously twisted. Catherine, having the advantage of her dithering proximity, could at last appreciate her for what she was, a warped old woman who sought notoriety in her penchant for making trouble. She even felt a little sorry for her, an emotion in no wise extended to Annie. In contrast to her cousin, she looked at the crowd. Indeed, once she had resigned herself to the loss of the mask, she had never removed her eyes from them. What she felt she could not explain. She was aware of the old woman's influence, but had never anticipated her using it to such telling effect; nor could she credit how easily they were led. Was she so defined by her disfigurement that they were unable to see beyond it? Were they turning against her for no other reason than that? Had they forgotten the actual Catherine Venners, the one who had devoted her time to their welfare? In her hurt pride, she could have despised them like Craven. Instead, she felt only pity. Geoffrey still clung pathetically to Matthew, though Matthew himself appeared to have completely forgotten his charge.

The air tangibly thickened, a mixture of sickly decay and newly washed earth, the cloud deepening round them to on-rushing blackness. Heavy rain was now falling and the crowd began to grow restive.

"Dunna keep us waitin'," came the sound of an isolated voice.

"Best put an end to it now," Mother Jomfrey inaudibly muttered.

"Work that should ne'er hae begun in the first place, but worthy of your foulness!"

The voice was that of a dark haired angular looking woman who had been too long in the old hag's company to be under any delusions. It was Eve, she who had nursed her son, suffered the rancour of her tongue and become necessarily inured, if not reconciled, to both the squalor of her surroundings and the sinful old woman. She had always liked Catherine, and to see her treated in such a way and through the agency of such a woman, hardly a murmur raised in her defence after all she had done for them, impelled her to speak where others kept silent.

"And ye are mad to believe 'er," she said turning on her neighbours. The ground was muddy and she slipped close to Geoffrey. Sensible enough to her needs, he prevented her from falling. She smiled her gratitude. There was warmth of expression in her features, and the touch of her hair felt soft against his skin.

"Dunna heed 'er!" screamed Annie, unleashing her final assault. "She took my mother! She took my children! She would hae taken me too had I not discovered her guile."

"Of a surety, she has robbed ye too," Mother Jomfrey added, her voice not so strong as it was. "The de'il's brood hae de'il's breath."

It was now Geoffrey who moved forward. The constriction in his head, which up until then had resembled an ever tightening band, perceptively relaxed, its dazed and cluttered state briefly intact. All the sensations of a man were briefly his again.

"They be lies Annie!" he cried, his thin wrist raised above them like a spectral threat. "Kate n'er hurt anyone. Why, I mind the time when she were naught but a tiny thing and came wi' her mother to tend my Alice. But for 'er I would hae been a widower much sooner. Lies, lies, I tell ye. Tis wickedness, all on it. The lass ne'er hurt anyone. Lies, lies ..." Feeling the band tighten again, he relapsed into mere repetitiveness.

"And will ye believe the wanderins of an addle pate," Annie mocked.

"You did well Geoffrey," said Eve, taking him by the hand.

"Lies," he muttered incoherently, looking to Matthew for some sort of guidance. By remaining silent, Matthew had been praying for the miracle that would turn Annie from her madness and make her once more the child he had adored. But miracles were illusory and not for the likes of him. He now called her by name. She could not avoid seeing him now nor the dreadful hurt in his eyes.

"Annie, gie me that," he said pointing to the mask beneath her foot. She mutely did as she was bidden, smiling vacuously as if puzzled by the crippling manner in which he looked at her. Taking the mask, he gave it to Catherine. "Tis fairly dirtied," was all he said. The crowd grew hushed, heedless of the rain that fell upon them. If there was one man they respected above all others, save their priest, it was Matthew Thompson. "I am ashamed of ye Annie," he said, "that ye my own daughter should speak so base before our neighbours. From henceforth I swear I hae nae child but Rob. May the Lord see fit to forgive ye, for I ne'er will."

The quiet conviction in his utterance took her by surprise. For an instant, she was totally shamefaced, but knowing that she had always been his favourite she had no reason to doubt she could still win him round.

"Father," she said, her voice softening to the coaxing tone with which she was wont to address him. "Tis all true o' Kate. Ye must believe it." But he would not take the hand she so touchingly held out to him. "Father, please," she pleaded, her eyes close to tears. He ignored her, though it cost him much to do so.

Mother Jomfrey sucked on her receding lip. She could see that it now remained with her to save the day even though her strength was giving out. "See how she turns a father against his child. The de'il looks after his own. Who else hae gone amongst ye, as she has, without takin' the sickness. Who I ask you!"

"I have," said Craven, coming amongst them. They immediately drew back from him like the Red Sea parting before Moses, wondering at the strength of spirit that leant his spareness of frame a dignity in which their own was sadly wanting. When Craven spoke everyone else became silent. Many knelt down to kiss the hem of his cassock, others taking hold of his hands which touched their brows with a blessing. "We are all sinful in the eyes of God, are we not?" he began, surveying them coldly. "You, Annie, Mother Jomfrey, Catherine and, of course, myself." He spoke simply for their benefit. "And who of us present would not claim to be under God's protection," he maintained, noting the look of dejection on the faces of several of his flock whose sins, real or imaginary, lay heavily upon them.

"The de'il protects his own," Mother Jomfrey cunningly appended.

"Speak of Elliston to Catherine Venners' detriment if you must," he replied, "but also remember that she forsook the former safety of the castle to be with her kin, to tend them in their ills, to assist me in giving succour to you."

"Tis true," said many in response, others as freely demurring.

"She has done much good for our village," he continued, pausing between each sentence to gauge their reaction. "That we owe both her and her mother before her a certain indebtedness I think you will allow."

Catherine had wiped the mud from the mask but chose not to wear it. She held her head high. It was as if she had at last found strength in the disfigurement and no longer felt the need to conceal it behind the obscuring piece of linen. She was comforted by the few who had spoken out in her defence, Eve, her uncle, Geoffrey, but she knew that only Craven would be capable of shielding her from the imputations levelled at her. The crowd were now listening attentively to every word that he said. But Mother Jomfrey was not finished yet.

"Then if she be what ye think, she will hae nothin' to fear. Put her to the test and prove what ye say to be right. I challenge ye to do sae here and now Father, afront o' witnesses!"

"You challenge me!" he retorted, staring at her scornfully, the light of his eyes ascetically blue in their clear sighted intellect. "I think you forget to whom you speak."

Only he could have silenced her thus. She gripped the stick, sucking in an oath, her anger confined to an involuntarily twist of her body.

"Come Catherine," said Craven, his voice firmly commanding. They let them pass through, his wayward flock huddled together like sheep bereft of their leader.

"Harlot!" screamed Annie in a last frantic attempt to retain their flagging attention. She might as well not have bothered. Her father's look was bitter and she fell silent, what feeling she owned smarting under the loss of his affection. No one heeded her. Why? She had only done what her conscience had prompted her to do, that compromising conscience of hers that compounded the truth to suit its own ends. The crowd were moving away. They no longer knew what to think, the arguments of the priest and the crone appearing to have equal validity, and whither either led they invariably followed, fearing to lose the blessing of their priest on the one hand and dreading to incur the wrath of the crone on the other. Matthew had gone with Craven and Catherine. Without the supporting crutch of his friend, Geoffrey started to cry. His head was swimming. He could neither think nor act for himself. A few of the lingerers, the most vicious, started to prod and poke him, twisting him this way and that and generally make sport of his idiocy. It took a woman to restrain them.

"I'll take care on ye Geoffrey," promised Eve, putting her hand on his. "Dunna fret yesell now."

"But Matt's my friend," he sobbed, his atrophied frame shaking violently.

"I know, but Father Craven 'ull know what to do."

"And Kate?" he blubbered. "She what ne'er harmed no man."

"Kate will be judged aright. Hae no fear o' that. The Father knows her worth well enough as do ye and I."

Geoffrey held on to her hand.

"That's it, move ye stinkin' carcass old fellow," someone yelled when they were well at a distance.

"What old fellow?" he queried, the rain rapidly drenching him.

"Dunna heed 'im," she soothed, "he were but jestin'."

"Dunna they know I'm a free man," he replied indignantly. "I ought to be given a measure o' respect."

CHAPTER TWENTY SIX

Protected from the rain a group of children huddled in the porch of Craven's house attempting to play toss stone.

"Remember to say your prayers," Craven cautioned. One word from him and they pocketed the stones and made for home. The rain seemed to buffet the world and night fell before its time. Was there haven for anyone?

Inside it was as cold and comfortless as ever. Even Craven shivered as he knelt to kindle the fire. In a further effort to dispel the gloom he generously lit two candles and bade them be seated.

"Well Catherine," he said, folding his hands, their smoothness of finger attesting to his love of the intellect. She did not answer. The ordeal had sapped her much more than she cared to admit and with the candlelight shining fully upon her she found it difficult to concentrate. Her eyes had a tendency to close against her will, reality spirited away in dreams more mercifully inclined to bring what it denied. Matthew gently nudged her awake.

"I appreciate how tired you must be," Craven resumed, taking measure of the situation and finding it blessedly to his advantage, "but it is incumbent upon us to consider your welfare. You cannot think for one moment that I would put you to Mother Jomfrey's so called test. Your innocence is affirmed in all things, save one, and to that I will not allude. As it is, your personal well being must take precedence over everything else."

"Ay," agreed Matthew, "once their spite is up ..."

"As it is," Craven interjected, "which is why I think it would be prudent if you were to leave Runnarth for a time."

"Leave!" she exclaimed, rousing herself from the lassitude that made thinking a burden.

"Just for a while," he continued, "at least until such time as it is safe for you to return without fear of persecution. I believe, praise God, that the plague has nearly done with us, but the people are credulous, easily influenced, and will seize on any excuse in the belief that it may charm away their ills. You know how Mother Jomfrey incites them. Indeed, better than myself."

Out of consideration for Matthew he did not refer to Annie.

"I think the Father be right," said Matthew, "best leave a while Kate, though God knows I'll miss ye."

"As will we all," Craven concurred, closely regarding her, while she watched the light flicker inconstantly round his head, one moment brightly glowing like an aureole, the next snuffed out like a candle.

"How can I leave now?" she questioned, "I have responsibilities here, and then there are the Burgoynes, they have a right to be informed. And I would not leave you Uncle Matt, alone and in that empty house so full of memories and precious little else."

"Ye must think o' yesell lass," he replied. "Dunna fret o'er me Kate. I hae enough to keep me occupied."

Although he had little to say unless it related to his strips of earth, they were both aware that Miriam's death had brought them closer together, and despite his insistence that she go she knew that he would be lonelier for her absence. She would also miss him, even those irritating yet endearing little habits that made life tolerable when all around was chaos. Their home was not as empty as Geoffrey's had become, cold, comfortless, devoid of human warmth to make it habitable.

"Be sensible lass," he insisted, mistaking her silence for the old obstinacy reminiscent of her mother. "Tis what Miriam would hae wanted. Rob and Mary too, would they were here."

"Maybe, but ..."

"You've little choice in the matter," Craven broke in. You may call it circumstance, though I would give it a different name. Though we have free will Catherine, the best is that ordained by God."

She liked not the veiled admonishment. It might have been applicable to anyone, but she knew that it was intended for her alone and that he had neither forgotten nor forgiven.

"And the way in which this is to be accomplished," she said, realising that further objection was pointless.

"I have a cousin in Yorkshire, head of a small religious order. You may have heard me speak of her."

"Ay, Father," replied Matthew in anticipation.

"She will afford you a safe refuge for as long as is needful."

"Needful?" she drowsily reiterated.

"Do as the Father says," Matthew entreated, marking her hesitance. "Tis sense he speaks."

She smiled at him. For Matthew there were never any shades. It was either right or wrong, black or white.

"Then it is settled," Craven said before she had time to reflect any further. She did not demur, any possible conflict between his wishes and her desires overridden by necessity and the dismal lack of choice. "I will write the requisite letter to my cousin now. I know my cousin, that is Ursula – here he paused as if he did not wholly approve of the name – will sanction my wishes."

Yorkshire. Ursula. Necessity. She could hardly keep her eyes open, his voice sounding hollow and distant like the cry of a bird on some remote plain. The plague, it would seem, had hardly touched his cousin or her order of women, another reason why he was not in any doubt that she would accede to his request. Ursula, she reflected, must be as rare as her cousin. Watching him through half closed eyes, she had the uncomfortable feeling that he was deriving a sense of pleasure in disposing of her fate, not exactly joyous but spiritually rewarding.

It was agreed that Matthew would escort her to Bardwick early next day where a man called Seldon, a tranter, was staying prior to commencing his journey. She was to give him the money that Craven was now counting out and to assure him that it was but part of the reward, the remainder of which would be paid on completion of the task. Moreover, she was to inform that he was to speak of the matter to no one and to ask of her no questions. She was also to impress upon him that Craven intended her to be treated with all due respect. The man being coarse, it was important that she stressed this at the outset. Did she accept and understand.

"I do Father," she replied, "but how will you explain my absence."

"Leave that to me Catherine. They will believe what I tell them."

Matthew nodded his assent. Craven moved the candle to assist him. They watched in silence as he wrote, the candle dripping tallow on to the table.

"I am in your debt Father," she said when he had finished.

"I do as God bids me," he replied, touching her hand. The touch was icy yet firm.

The route to Bardwick was familiar to them both from earlier and happier days. It was one of those beautiful, hallowed kind of dawns, and the rain having stopped the path was easy to negotiate.

The town was still in its slumbering state. Sun was spilling between the narrow alleyways and on to the streets. It looked more appealing in its deserted aspect than it had ever done before. They passed the house where Gerard and Annie had lived without remarking on it. The memories surrounding it were still far too painful. They soon found the street where Seldon was lodging, a grim looking place, half tavern, half brothel. In ordinary circumstances Matthew would never have left her in such an insalubrious quarter or to the care of such a dubious character as Seldon, but these were not ordinary times, and it was only on the assurances of his priest that he was doing so now. There was no sign of Seldon who was probably sleeping off the effects of the previous night. Matthew would have stayed to have a few salutary words with Seldon himself, but knowing that her uncle was not the most tactful of men she convinced him of the desirability of undertaking the interview alone, added to which she was reasonably confident that what Craven had told her to say would be sufficient to guarantee her safety.

"Are ye sure on it lass?" he said.

"Yes Uncle Matt, I am sure."

"Ay, well," he sighed, fidgeting awkwardly. "We mun part then I suppose."

"Yes uncle."

It was hard to find the proper words.

"Here, take my jacket Kate," he said. "The nights can be cold and ye hae a fair way to go."

"I will not refuse," she replied, "but if you have need of it I can send it back to you via Seldon."

"Nae," he refused. "Tis time I wore the new one. Anyway it will serve as a reminder o' me like, if ye want such."

"I need no such reminder," she said, her eyes filling now that the parting was near.

"I'm not a man o' fine words as ye know lass, and mayhap in the past I hae spoken harshly to ye and ye mother, but there were no malice in it."

"We knew that, Uncle Matt."

"That's as maybe, but I wanted ye to know that ye goodness to me and mine hae not gone unremarked, and as for the man who sired ye, why he hae no cause for complaint."

"Please uncle, no more," she begged tearfully.

"Come Kate," he comforted, drawing her to him and stroking her hair as once he'd stroked Annie's. "Ye hae been stronger than us all. Twill all come aright."

"Will it?" she sobbed. "Sometimes I cannot but wonder."

"As long as ye hae faith Kate, believe me. And, who knows, but one day he as ye cleave to 'ull come back to ye."

It was the first time he had ever referred to her relationship with Elliston, and the fact that he mentioned it now and in terms of condonement meant more to her than he could possibly know.

"Thank you Uncle Matt."

"God go wi' ye lass."

"And with you Uncle Matt."

She watched him go, his bent and stooping figure sharply outlined against the patch of blue sky.

CHAPTER TWENTY SEVEN

All the resilience she had exhibited for her uncle's benefit now deserted her. Moreover, Seldon was making her wait, not knowingly of course, but it seemed to be so. When he finally emerged, she recognised him at once. Strongly built, he must have been over six feet in height, his hair and beard black and of the tousled variety, but it was the errant look in his eyes that disturbed her. Wiping his mouth with the back of his hand, his feet splayed, his head raised to the sun, he looked the embodiment of worldly self possession. Having drank well, fed well and whored well, if loving life to an excess can be accounted a sin, then here was a man in need of repentance. To speak with him, let alone bring herself to consider the prospect of his company for an unconscionable number of days was dismal indeed. Only necessity stayed her nerves.

"Master Seldon?" she said, coming out of the shadows.

"Ay," he acknowledged, his look open and candid, the constant twinkle in his eyes roving over her person from every angle, from the mask on her face to the shoes on her feet.

"Father Craven wishes you to escort me to St. Mary's Abbey, in recompense of which he sends you this," she explained, dangling the purse in front of him. He went to grab it, but she withdrew it from his grasp.

"Wait. I have yet to finish. I am to inform you that this is but part of your reward, for if you do as Father Craven requests a further such amount will be yours on completion of the task. On no account are you to communicate to anyone the nature of the undertaking. Finally, Father Craven exhorts you to treat me with respect at all times. Payment of the other half of your reward will be conditional upon your promise." He threw back his head and laughed, swearing roundly as he did so. "Am I to understand that you are willing to do as Father Craven asks?" she said firmly when he had done.

He rubbed his fingers through his beard and looked at her boldly. He had no cause to doubt Craven's word. He had done business with him before, but this was new and intriguing. And she was nervous, he could tell, despite her attempts to disguise it.

"You are doubtful Master Seldon?"

"With a pretty lass like ye. Not a bit!" he grinned, advancing towards her. "Fretsome aren't we," he laughed as his fingers hovered about the mask. "I hae a mind to see what I'm despatchin' first. Likely fodder for St. Mary's by the looks on ye."

"You presume," she chided, attempting to push him away. "Remember what Father Craven said."

The mention of Craven had the desired effect. He moved his hands away and turned his attention to her hair instead.

"Not all bad, eh," he remarked, drawing his fingers through it.

"Do we have an understanding Master Seldon!"

She was becoming impatient, as well as apprehensive.

"Of course we do," he replied. He liked a woman with spirit, no matter her looks. Also, there was a lamb's lining beneath the apparent wolfishness, one which made him a favourite with the fairer sex. What is more, this woman had him puzzled and he welcomed the challenge.

"Yes, we have an understanding."

"Then I am truly obliged to you," she said, giving him her hand.

"Are you now?" he laughed, squeezing it warmly. "I take it ye hae a name. I canna be callin' ye mistress this and that every inch o' the way, or mayhap that be another of ye secrets."

"You may call me Kate."

"Pleasin' name Kate. Known many a Kate. Ye can call me Lazarus."

She looked at him dubiously, an involuntary smile playing about the corners of her lips.

"Tis truth," he affirmed. "My mother were a good Christian woman and believed in life everlastin'. Tis why I survive."

For everyone of his strides she had to make two, sometimes three, so that she found herself running rather than walking in an attempt to keep up with him. The cart stood at the rear of the inn. Now most of the revellers had left, it was reasonably quiet.

"Ye'll not be afeared to sit aside me Kate?" he quipped, helping her up. "I'll be glad o' Craven's money. My livelihood hae suffered. Everyone be takin' up more with dyin' than buyin'."

The goods on the cart were an odd assortment. A few rolls of linen, poor in quality and spotted with mildew, a number of pots and pans which made a fearful row considering how few they were in number, and two gargoyles destined to adorn a new church in York, their horrible grimaces and protruding tongues defying the pious to sin.

"On it is then," he said, jerking the horse into action, obviously enjoying the unexpected proximity as she attempted to lean away from him as far as safety dictated.

If Craven had thought to despatch her with haste, he would have scarcely approved of the leisurely manner with which the journey commenced. The sun was soon shining fully upon them and she had to shield her face from its glare. No hurry was evinced by the horse or its master, but with Bardwick receding behind them her mood grew less anxious. It was precisely the sort of change she was in need of to revive her waning spirits and restore her weakening strength. Occasionally he would turn to give her the benefit of his full candid gaze, but she kept her eyes fixed on the road. The pots and pans made ditties in the breeze which was more of comfort than annoyance.

Seldon fell into a mood of reflection, strange for a man who was not given to thought, but Kate was a riddle to him, as was the nature of Craven's errand. For the priest to interest himself on the girl's behalf proved that the business was no light one, but if this were the case why had he been given no inkling of it two days ago when the priest had entrusted him with the usual letter to take to his cousin. That Craven had little to say to him was true enough, but this new charge coming so rapidly on the heels of the first must have indicated some sudden change after their initial interview, a fact which would account for her lack of possessions.

"Not broodin' Kate?" he would ask from time to time in the hope of finding out more. But her replies, though polite, were always evasive.

"Got a comb if ye want it Kate. A little keepsake o' mine, but ye are welcome to have it," he said with a wink, "a gown o' sorts too if ye not be o'er choosy. Bit big for ye, but nae doubt ye could adjust it, ye bein' a learned sort o' lass if I'm not mistaken."

"You are kind Master Seldon," she replied, wondering how altering a yard of material or using a comb could possibly make her learned, and why he should assume that she was since she had not openly said so, he merely guessing and drawing conclusions therefrom. He now began to whistle.

"Tired Kate?" he muttered, wanting to hear the sound of her voice.

"Yes Master Seldon, I am very tired."

She rested her eyes and half slumbered, every village they came to bearing a similarity to Runnarth in the neglect of the land and the encroachment of weeds. Dreaming, she was with *him* again; they were going to Holy Island; she could actually hear his voice; he was keeping his promise.

"I can scarce believe it," she unwittingly spoke out aloud, the overwhelming desire for it suddenly making her wake.

"Gently Kate, gently," he said "twas, I take it, a pleasin' dream."

"Forgive me," she replied. "I have not slept in a while."

"Ye be too quiet by far I'm thinkin', mortal quiet I'd say. Canna stand silence mysell, it makes for broodin', and I'll tell ye here and now, tis nae good for anyone. Take Craven, for instance. Where 'as all is broodin' got 'im, eh, you tell me that?"

"It has made him the man he is," she said, alarmed at her own equivocation.

"Precisely. I couldna hae said it better mysell," he laughed, thinking to tease the truth from her by rousing her temper. Catherine seeing it, checked herself, but only just in time. Disappointed by his lack of success he started to sing, his voice unexpectedly pleasing, except that he was forever changing the words of the song to a level of profanity which ruined it completely.

"Passes the time," he remarked. "Pleasure, that's all there is to seek in this world. Get it whenever and wherever ye can."

"And what of the price of such pleasure?" she said, thinking it was about time she asked of him a question.

"I'll repent, dunna fear Kate. I'm all for repentin' when the time comes, but the Lord 'ull spare me a goodly while yet. Why I'd wreak havoc in heaven."

"And hell?"

"Wouldna hold me. Anyway I dunna intend to let it try," he replied, and with such a look of mock seriousness that she started to laugh, something she had not been wont to do of late.

"Ye be a fine one Kate. Goin' into a nunnery too in the hope of purchasin' salvation. Tis hardly respectful."

"I cannot help it."

"Ay, I can see that. Ye'd be pleasin' enough to any man I'm bound were it not for that cross ye hae to carry," he remarked, staring at the mask.

Strange that he too should refer to her disfigurement as a cross she had to carry, just as Craven had done all those years ago when she had not fully understood what he meant.

"Tis truth though, eh?" he winked.

Still wary of him and fearing that her untoward gaiety might have given him the wrong impression she again became grave.

Their progress was often halted by pathetic groups of

children, pinched faced, dirtied, and obviously orphaned, who begged alms of them and freely used the oaths their mothers had taught them when none were forthcoming. Only when Seldon raised the whip in their midst did they scatter.

"Gently," she would remonstrate.

"Desperate remedies for desperate times lass," he would reply.

More pitiful still were the solitary human scarecrows who haunted their way and attempted to climb on to the cart, their atrophied fingers clawing weakly at Seldon's sleeve in the hope that he would relent and take pity upon them. She would always remember their eyes, sunk and hollowed out to a resigned kind of suffering.

"Save a poor man sir. My land, my family all gone. For the love of the Holy Virgin, I pray ye hae pity."

They never asked of him where he was going. It was simply a longing to leave behind the scene of their own immediate travail that drove them hither. Nor did it take her long to realise that without Seldon she would have found the journey impossible to make alone. She once asked him how he had managed to retain his sound constitution and stay free of the pestilence, particularly since his trade was not one to lend him any immunity. His remedy was simple if crude.

"First and foremost, dunna fear. Them that fears most dies soonest. Second, dunna be choosy o'er victuals. Eat what's available and I dunna mean measly portions o' slop. I ate anythin', cats, dogs, fly bitten ox. I'd hae eaten dung fro' the streets had it helped to keep me alive."

The solution was a grim one and guaranteed to take the edge off her appetite. But she need not have worried, for whatever he claimed to have eaten in the past, he did not eat now, the simple slop he despised providing a poor if edible meal for them both.

"I'll see ye do better anon," he avowed, wiping his hand through his beard. "Now for Durham!"

The idea of Durham clearly pleased him, in consequence of which their progress gained pace, so much so that even the horse seemed bemused at the urgency suddenly forced upon it. Catherine held on tight, a queasy feeling in the pit of her stomach from having eaten so recently. The outskirts of the city were reached before sunset. It was a lovely time of the evening, the stone of the cathedral glowing warmly in the serenity of effortless sunshine. On seeing the city, Seldon looked jubilant, quickly making camp in a nearby field and setting about undertaking a toilet as elaborate as any woman's. Stripping completely, he waded into the river, inviting her to join him.

"I think not," she replied. His body glowed in the full vigour of health, and though she intended to avert her gaze something impelled her to watch. For all his faults he had a zest for life which was exhilarating. Having been the reluctant acquaintance of death for so long, the appeal was only natural. She too wanted to live, reach for the sun as this man was doing, gloat in its warmth with a similar abandon. He had a change of clothes in the cart and she willingly began washing those he had discarded.

"What think ye?" he bellowed when at last he was ready.

"Will admirable suffice?" she coolly remarked.

"Ye are grudgin' in ye praise Kate. Any woman ud be pleased to say better. Any ..."

"I am not any woman," she skilfully interjected.

"Ye wouldna be makin' merry at my expense little Kate?"

"A woman of my supposed calling Master Seldon. How could you think it?"

How could he indeed. She puzzled and perplexed him by turns, even promoted in him a kind of guarded respect which he would have laughed at where other women were concerned.

"I'll see ye anon," he said. "Dunna wait up. I may be late."

She reposed upon him a beautifully obtuse smile. She could guess what was tempting him into the city, and it was not for the purpose of pilgrimage. Taking advantage of his absence, she too washed in the river. As he had warned, it had an icy edge to it, but with the dust of days upon her it was good to get out of her clothes and into the water. She took off her mask and undid her hair. The sensation was blissful. The fact that he had gone to a woman did not perturb her. It merely gave force to her own wants and desires, bringing to her an awareness of what she hoped against hope was a temporary loss, her unassuaged longing laved in the water which she used like a salve on her pent up emotions. Again and again she cupped up the water and let it flood over her body. Was it wrong that she too should long for the touch of one man, the bliss of a passion once known to her and which she longed to know again. She vigorously rubbed herself dry, so afraid was she of losing control of her thoughts and dwelling on dreams that might never be realised. But to exist was to go on believing. The comb he had promised was lacking in teeth but sufficed. As for the woman's gown it was, as he had intimated, cut for a woman of more ample proportions, and she had to adjust it considerably to fit her own figure. Tidying the cart, she pillowed her head on the neatly stacked sacking and gazed out on the night, now filling with stars. She must have fallen asleep almost at once, for the next thing she knew the sun was full in her eyes and Lazarus was putting the horse into harness.

"Ye slept well I take it Kate?"

"Yes, I must have."

"So did I," he winked.

They set off at a leisurely amble, sometimes in sun, sometimes in shower. It was that time of year. And all along the way were the human remnants of the plague, the old, the needy, the young and the pitiful.

"Buy a flower, please!"

The plea came from a child grown old beyond her years, her frightened half-wilful stare the outer expression of one who has learned to endure. Although Catherine tried to explain her lack of money, the child persisted in giving her the gift, and eventually she took it out of pity, affecting a greater show of pleasure than was called for in an attempt to minimise the disparity of the bargain. The little girl looked utterly mournful until Catherine smiled, and then she too smiled as if this were more than sufficient recompense.

"God bless ye mistress," she cried, pressing the flowers into her fingers. "Tis no matter, the money I mean. Tis no matter."

She longed to speak a blessing in return, but the words would not come, and all she could do was to humbly hold on to the flowers, the figure of the child growing smaller, the distance immense.

"Hae ye no sense!" Seldon railed, quite untouched by the scene. "Throw 'em down. Did ye look at the eyes Kate. Did ye see 'er eyes."

"Yes, Master Seldon, I saw them," she quietly answered.

"Ay and no long for this world," he pronounced, willing the posy away and throwing it into the mud.

Deprecating the act, she turned her face from him. What a ludicrous distinction he made between the possible infestation of a bunch of wild flowers and the taint upon the city he had revelled in only the night before. Thus, they continued the journey in silence, the clip, clop of the horse and the rattling pots and pans sounding uneasily in the constrained hush of quiet. Before very long he resumed his ditties and she began to doze.

The surrounding country now took on a solemn grandeur, its mighty expanse of moorland and hill cut sheer against the sky, its music that of water, wind and wilderness, its refrain the song of old gods and obedient to none. Signs of human habitation were few, the land being given over to the pasturing of sheep, huge flocks of them which brought wealth to the abbeys who owned them. Betwixt the rain and the sun, the scene glowered and brightened, much as the seasons of life, intervals of light on a shadowy backdrop. There was no sunset as such, just an outline of silver that etched in the hills. Catherine felt as if she had drawn close to the edge of heaven, so awesome was the sight, and even Seldon grew quiet.

"Where are we Master Seldon?" she enquired.

"Yorkshire Kate, this be Yorkshire."

"Then Yorkshire I like," she enthused.

The following morning promised to be a warm one, the exposed chain of hills affording them little protection from the rays of the sun. It put colour into her cheeks and quickly restored Seldon's volubility. She found herself taking more delight than ever in the country; it spoke of fortitude and strength, of reflection in quiet places, and an assurance of God. But Seldon was not over given to reflection and was soon in his talkative vein.

"Only another three mile I reckon. Trust me Kate, eh?"

"Yes, Lazarus, I trust you," she said with a smile.

She took a deep breath and let the landscape absorb her.

"There's more gold to be made out o' them witless creatures than all ye ploughin' and diggin' put together," he said, marking her interest.

"Gold for whom?"

"I'd hae thought ye'd hae knowed. Why, all these men and women o' a prayin' persuasion, such as ye be hopin' to join. They 'old the wealth o' the country in their hands and little enough they do for it bar prayin'. Lesser beins do the bulk on it for 'em. Tis doubtful whether e'en the plague will hae weeded em down, cut off as they be fro' the world and all its troubles."

"Fie Master Seldon," she replied archly. She now recollected that it was Craven who had spoken of large areas of land only fitted for the rearing of sheep, and from the number of them that roamed hereabouts she concluded that this must have been the country he'd had in mind. That she had forgotten his lengthy discourse on the religious houses of Yorkshire and their contribution to the prosperity of her country was hardly to her credit and she could only blame the omission on recent events which had tended to outweigh all other factors, even making irrelevant the little store of knowledge of which she had once been so proud. How right Elliston was in his view that learning for the sake of it had no part to play in living itself. The horse had now steadied to a canter and she was able to fully enjoy the undulating spell of the land and the feel of the wind on her face. It was purer air too, so welcome after that of Runnarth, and for the first time in months she experienced just what it meant to breathe in the scents of an unravaged earth. Thus, when Seldon began to sing, she feared he would spoil it all. But he sang a song of creation and the beauty of God's gift to man when he gave him the world for a garden.

"Your song is fitting Lazarus," she said approvingly. "There is a special quality about this place. Though there are few trees to break the sameness, it is a sameness that does not pall."

"Well I suppose it is well enough if ye hae a likin' for wild and solitary places, but gie me a town any day."

Leaving the crest of the hills they descended into the valley. The sound of a stream was clearly audible and occasionally there were glimpses of it beneath them.

"Here ye be then. Canna go nae further, be too treacherous. Ye'll find the abbey up stream a bit. Tis fairly secluded, but ye'll come on it sudden like."

"I owe you much Lazarus," she said as he assisted her down from the cart.

"As does ye priest," he parried. "What about a brotherly kiss, eh?"

"You are incorrigible Master Seldon," she said, caressing his cheek with something less than a peck.

"I pity them sisters Kate. Ye try a man."

"But there I shall be among women!"

He laughed. Theirs was a gracious parting.

She walked slowly. A few silver birches straddled the bank of the stream, providing a barrier in times of foul weather or, as now, a shady retreat from the sun. No solitary could have asked for more. The birds soared above her, free and unfettered of the laws made of man, and as she watched them her thoughts turned to Elliston and Craven, so opposed and yet so intertwined that it was impossible to think of the one without the other. If Elliston was all to her, she owed her deliverance to her priest, though God alone knew she would rather have been indebted to anyone but him, and in spite of the warmth she felt herself shiver. All this thinking was doing no good. Seldon could have told her that. But was not an abbey conducive to thought. Again she felt herself shiver. She did not want a cloistered existence. What she did want ... No, she must banish *him* to the back of her mind as if she was ashamed of the feeling she owned for him. But how to do it when believing in him was as necessary as believing in God. God had brought them together, of that she was certain, and in her simplicity of faith she looked not for judgement but pity.

A thin covering of trees terminated the path, at the end of which she caught her first glimpse of the abbey. It looked to be only a small order, a point in its favour with Catherine who was already feeling humbled enough. In fact, the picture presented had none of the austerity one might have expected of an order recommended by Craven, its row of rectangular buildings and the church at its heart looking anything but severe in the mellowing sunlight. A generous covering of ivy helped to relieve the walls of their confining appearance. At a glance Catherine liked what she saw. Isolated from the clamour of worldly endeavour and bedded in quiet, it provided the requisite setting for the rule of an order dedicated to a life of obedience, work and prayer. In a corner of the wall a gate lay invitingly open. The scene within was revealing as she stood on the threshold and gazed. In contrast to Runnarth's near devastation and the misery and want attendant on her journey, she might have been forgiven for thinking that the abbey had not been visited by the plague at all. Those of holier inclination were doubtless immune to a pestilence that men of Craven's persuasion believed to be a visitation by God to punish the wicked. With this in mind, she crossed herself and entered a well tended garden leading on to a rougher patch of ground which was clearly in the process of cultivation.

The sisters had cast their hoes and spades aside to go to their devotions. She could hear them now, their other worldly hum resting gently on the ears like the hum of the bees in the garden. Only one of them remained, digging and delving away, as if God himself had been unable to deflect her from her purpose. Catherine tried coughing politely as a way of announcing her presence, but the nun paid no heed, other than to dig ever more furiously into the earth. Catherine had to duck to avoid one divit which barely missed her head. "If I might ..." she began, whereupon the nun finally looked up with anything but kindly forbearance.

"Well!" was all she said, clearly irritated at the intrusion.

Catherine had been expecting an older woman, made irritable by increase of years, but this woman was young, five and twenty at most. Her reticence showed in her eyes, dark and deep with a heavy under-lidded expression, distrustful and not a little soul wounded. More surprising still was the way in which she regarded Catherine who had become accustomed to provoking some kind of reaction, whether of pity or aversion, but she may as well have been blind for all the notice she took of her. It was not what Catherine expected, her obvious difference having developed in her a perverse kind of vanity which only her mother and Elliston fully understood. To be pitied and deplored was one thing. To be completely ignored was distinctly another. But as far as this girl was concerned, she was simply a nuisance who was getting in the way of her work.

"I have travelled some distance and wish to speak with Sister Ursula," she said assertively.

"You do," was all the reply it elicited. The girl was clearly resolved to be difficult, a hard flinty stare directed from under those heavy lidded eyes as she dug in the hoe. "There is an entrance for such as you."

"Such as me!" Catherine retorted, fast losing patience.

"Yes, you. Wayfarers, pilgrims, what you will," she panted, flinging up a shower of soil and tossing back her wimple as if she had a mind to rip it off altogether. "This is my garden and you trespass." The remark put her in mind of Craven and "his" church, so certain was she in her claim to sole ownership.

"Your garden?" teased Catherine, a jibe which the girl was not slow to grasp.

"I tell you, you trespass," she reiterated, raising the hoe at a threatening angle.

"And I presume I am to beg your pardon?" Catherine replied, growing hotter by the minute, though at the same time she had to admit to a certain admiration for this quaint little body who reminded her not only of her priest but of her uncle in the attachment she seemingly had to the earth.

"I expect no such thing," she firmly responded, casting aside the hoe to give Catherine the doubtful benefit of her censorious gaze.

"Just as well," Catherine said, wavering slightly under the strength of the penetrating stare. "My enquiry was in no way impolite."

"Tut, tut. You speak like the world in general. Worthless babblings, better not spoken at all."

Catherine coloured, her pride not exactly wounded but nonetheless pricked.

"It is clear that my presence is both annoying and irksome to the cultivation of an intellect as fine as your own, not to mention the cultivation of your little plot of earth. But worry not, I have no intention of interfering in your meditations, and as for your garden ..." Here she found herself effecting a flourish of fingers more reminiscent of Annie. "I assume it assists you in your singular musings, for singular I am sure they must be."

She finished on a sigh of frustration and hurt. Her introduction to St. Mary's had been less than encouraging when she had hoped for much better. Only pride prevented her from dissolving into tears. The effect of her outburst on the girl was quite unexpected. The dark eyes widened into a glint of amusement. It was a telling and spontaneous smile, like a sudden rush of sunlight after storm. She was just about to further the intimacy when the rest of the order, their offices dutifully performed, filed into the garden. The light airy day afforded them a welcome respite from the cold of the chapel, lifting their subdued whisperings to a veritable chatter. Catherine stood at the side of the path to watch them.

"You missed your devotions again Sister Agnes!"

The accusation came from an extremely tall woman with sharp features and a nose like a bird of prey. Catherine listened carefully. It would seem that her acquaintance had a reputation for being awkward.

"My devotions do not require the limits of a covering of stone to make themselves heard Sister Jocelyn," she was quick to reply.

Suitably chagrined, the said Jocelyn stuck her nose in the air. The rest of them tried to look as unaffected as possible, but Catherine had the distinct impression that their sympathies were somehow with Agnes. The truant sister resumed her labours without more ado. Clearly, Sister Agnes was no ordinary nun.

"Who are you?" Jocelyn exclaimed, turning her attention to Catherine. Immediately the others turned to stare at her too; where Agnes was incurious, their reaction was in keeping with that she was used to, but there was nothing of hostility in it, such as that she had often experienced. Obedient to their calling, they had learned to be charitable to the least that came amongst them.

"Fetch Sister Veronica. She will know what to do," ordered Jocelyn as if she alone were entitled to make demands of the others. Surprisingly, it was Agnes who went to do her bidding, Catherine was told to wait in the cloisters which, being late afternoon, were flooded with sunshine. Whoever Veronica was, she was evidently thought of highly, but Catherine was beyond the point of caring any more, her legs having taken on the heaviness of lead and her head the lightness of a feather. All she longed to do was lie down and sleep. The Veronica they all seemed to revere at least came quickly, her slim fingers clasped on her breviary. Immediately Catherine felt a sense of ease. If there was such a state of perfection on earth, then Veronica came very close to it. Even Agnes ceased to wield her hoe in deference to the claims of a superior nature. Veronica was very young and very beautiful, all the attributes of spiritual and temporal grace having fused into a Madonna like aspect of utter serenity. Her composure touched everyone with whom she came into contact. It touched Catherine now.

"You are tired," she said, putting her hand into Catherine's and bidding the women move away, "and no doubt troubled by our questioning. Come, I will take you to Reverend Mother. There is nothing to fear." She spoke as if she was acquainted with the whole of Catherine's history without actually knowing it at all. When she took hold of Catherine's hand, it was if she had indeed come to the end of her journey. Allied to spiritual awareness, she was also endowed with womanly intuition. Seeing that Catherine had no energy for idle conversation, she proved herself one of those rare persons whose companionship does not suffer through silence. For Catherine the touch of her hand was comfort enough.

The buildings of the abbey refused to take shape in her brain other than as a multitude of images blurred by her tiredness. When they came to the room where their head officially received visitors, Veronica softly pushed open the door, Catherine still holding on to her hand as if she was loath to let it go. A candle burned in a sconce as an increment to the light that squeezed in through a squint in the wall. It half illumined an elderly woman who sat at her desk gently snoring, above her a statue of the Virgin. The room was spacious, although there was little furniture within it, but unlike her cousin Craven's it was suggestive of warmth and serenity.

Ursula required no prompting to wake. Whether waking or sleeping, she was attuned to the needs of the moment. Of incalculable benefit to the order was her peculiar insight into the many faceted sides of the human condition. In features she resembled her cousin, but because she had learned how to use her emotions it was a modified resemblance. The skin was not stretched on her face. It relaxed into lines of self-knowledge. She knew her faults and her failings just as instinctively as she knew those of the women placed in her care, and her love was in no way impaired from this sense of self-knowledge. This woman knew how to laugh, knew when to cry, when to hold back and when to go forward. Her look was straight and candid. It said I am your friend. Speak and I will listen, but speak from the heart.

"I see we have a visitor Sister Veronica and I think I know who it is, my cousin having occasionally mentioned you."

She spoke with a lovely soft burr, quite informal and restful on the ear. Her smile was open and devoid of affectation. Catherine smiled shyly in return.

"If we might crave a little of your time, Reverend Mother?" Veronica enquired.

"My time is not my own to dispose of, but as God would direct. I see he requests of it now and I am ready. Pray, be seated." Veronica placing a chair at the opposite side of the desk, Catherine sat down in it in a tremulous yet half thankful state. "Thank you Sister Veronica. You may leave us. I trust the sisters are not over exerting themselves in this heaven sent weather. We will suspend further activity till the morrow."

"Yes, Reverend Mother."

"And all will welcome the generosity of my bidding, save one, which only goes to prove that God never intended us to be other than we are, dissimilar entities to make up the whole. Tell Sister Agnes she may do as she pleases."

"I will inform her, Reverend Mother," she replied, leaving them alone.

Catherine took note. Agnes was allowed licence to freely indulge her eccentricities. Whatever would Father Craven have thought.

"You have beautiful hair, my child," Ursula remarked, directing her gaze to the asset rather than the drawback as a means of putting Catherine at her ease. "Such a rare and lovely colour."

"I fear it is untidy," Catherine replied, appreciative of the tactful allusion.

"No, I beg to differ. Who would have the blessings of nature subscribing to a set and uniform pattern. Tis man who has impeded on nature and attempted to make her conform."

Catherine smiled her agreement. It was a poetic and appealing piece of logic and one with which Elliston would have wholly concurred. She bit her lip nervously. The idea of him was like an ever fixed star that expanded her thoughts into blissful horizons. Ursula, sensing her discomfort, abandoned the theme.

"My cousin speaks very well of you Catherine Venners," she said as she read Craven's letter, occasionally smiling at some form of expression and muttering to herself, "Very like, oh so very like." Catherine watched her with interest. Her eyes were blue, not of the striking blueness that brings hot summer days, but washed through with a sort of watery reflection, very different to the unyielding expression of her cousin's. The candlelight shone on her hands, pale and long fingered like Craven's, but work-like in their rough skinned appearance. Having finished reading, she laid the letter aside and looked closely at Catherine, her hands cupped in thought to her chin.

"You must be rare indeed," she said after some consideration. "My cousin positively sings forth your praises, and from all that he tells me you are in no wise undeserving of such praise. Nonetheless you have suffered. The world has not treated you as it should have. Tis a contradictory world at best, and I for one never cease to question its injustices."

Catherine's eyes widened in growing disbelief, that she, a cousin of Craven's should question the fairness of things.

"I can see that I am not as you suspected I would be?"

"I ... " she stumbled.

"You expected a pale copy of Francis, no doubt, or may be an even more exacting one as if that were possible?"

Catherine, not sure of what she expected, could think of nothing to say and sat stiff and formal.

"You are discreet Catherine. I take it I am a little less severe?"

"Yes, Reverend Mother," she admitted, whereupon Ursula clapped her hands, obviously delighted. "Your prevarication is to your credit. Francis would approve. Poor Francis. The day may come when he will discover that he is very little different from those he professes to instruct." She now looked grave, even sad. "I look on that day with dread Catherine."

"Father Craven has not failed us, Reverend Mother. Indeed, we have looked to him for guidance throughout our recent trials," she replied, quick to defend him, though in her heart of hearts she knew she would always recoil from his perception of things.

"I do not doubt it. But you must know why I speak as I do. My cousin is, dare I say it, immoderately zealous, but he demands too much of himself as I suspect he does of those in his care. He forgets that he is mere clay like the rest of us and keeps his own demons at bay by denying their existence. Self knowledge, even unconscious self knowledge, is the first requisite of love and compassion; it is ruth on ourselves extended to others that brings us to a state of inner contentment. Francis is crippled by an image of what he would be and not what he is. Tis a cross he has made for himself and I pity him. I appreciate your respect for my cousin. He is a good man and I love him very dearly."

In her telling description of Francis Craven, she had put into words Catherine's own troubled thoughts on a man whose intellect seemed greater than his soul.

"I can see you understand, but let us speak of yourself. Francis leads me to believe that you have a natural vocation, which is pleasing, for we are but a small order and always in need of new and suitable novitiates."

Craven then had told her nothing of substance and less still of fact. His cousin was kind and she would not have her remain in ignorance, but it was difficult to speak of a relationship which was ripe for narrow minded censure, especially now she found herself with the delicate task of having to justify her so called sin to a woman whose province it was to roundly condemn it.

"I fear Father Craven has only sung my praises Reverend Mother, but I would have you know the truth, which has already cost me much of Father Craven's good opinion and will doubtless influence yours."

"Proceed. I would hear it nonetheless."

Such a confession was difficult, but her conscience was clear. It was those who condemned her who were cruel in their ignorance. It was strange that she never thought of Craven as being one of their number. Fully expecting Ursula to concur in her cousin's opinion, she watched anxiously for a change in her expression, but it never came, even when her feelings for Elliston were keenly exposed. Instead, she listened with that quiet understanding that lends itself to ease of confession. Neither did she interrupt, nor adopt the moralising looks of her cousin.

"So you see, Reverend Mother, not only am I base born, but the mistress of a wedded man," she concluded.

"Catherine, I appreciate your candour. No wonder, my cousin has chosen to keep me in ignorance of such facts. Naturally they would be at variance with his liking for you, and what he considers to be in your best interests. It was a courageous confession Catherine, wisely made in spite of his mistaken belief that it were better left unspoken. What you have told me will not go any further."

"Father Craven is bitterly opposed to Lord Elliston," Catherine explained, her eyes threatening tears.

"But you genuinely love him.

"I do."

"And there is no truth in the vocation my cousin claims on your behalf?"

"None, Reverend Mother."

"And Lord Elliston? You look on his return in the certain knowledge of his regard for you?"

"I do."

Ursula rose from the table, walking to and fro for a while in a mood of deep reflection. Already it was turning to evening and they were solely dependent on the candle for light.

"We will say no more of this, my child," Ursula spoke at last. "Tis not for me to condone or condemn. Neither is it fitting that Francis should do so. Such belongs to God and to God alone. St. Mary's is at your disposal for as long as you wish."

Catherine felt the weight lift from her shoulders. Her confession had decided her sentence and she was glad she had told it. Kissing Ursula's hand, the one that bore her marriage ring to Christ, she knelt in submission at her feet.

"Thank you, Reverend Mother, thank you."

"Come now," Ursula said, bidding her rise. "Francis informs me that you are well versed in the usage of herbs. Tis a talent St. Mary's could ably employ. We do what we can within the infirmary, but healing is a special gift in which we are not wholly versed. Your superior knowledge will benefit us greatly."

She then chuckled gaily to herself. It was not the kind of behaviour Catherine associated with the austerity of her calling, and far removed from that of her cousin.

"Why, you look surprised Catherine. We are but human after all. Laughter is a gift of God, is it not? When He walked amongst men, was He always so solemn? Recollect how the children gathered to him. I doubt if his charm for them sprang from a mournful expression."

Catherine smiled. She had never thought of her Saviour in quite that way, or rather her priest had drawn a distinctly opposite picture.

Ursula then called on Sister Veronica to conduct her to her room. Veronica held the candle high to guide her, Catherine watching their shadows thrown up on the walls like so many phantoms. She only carried the candle for Catherine's benefit, knowing the way perfectly well without it, as did the women going to prayer who emerged from the gloom, their faces showing tired but radiant in the sudden pool of light. Voices hushed and remote ascended from the chapel below with a distant and dreamlike appeal. Arriving at a guest room which adjoined the main dormitory where the majority of the sisters slept, Veronica kissed her gently on the cheek and bade her goodnight. The room was in accordance with the order's rule of simplicity, plain whitened walls, a thin mattress laid on the floor and a tiny cupboard on top of which stood a bowl and a ewer. The black wooden cross over the bed was the only form of decoration, and even that was austere. Catherine lay down on the bed and slept. After days of fear and uncertainty, she was thankful for any sort of haven, no matter how meanly furnished.

Throughout the night she was half conscious of the bell's periodic summons to prayer, but other than that her sleep was unbroken. The following day she adopted the dress of a lay sister, and joined the order for a simple breakfast of bread and porridge which was taken after early morning prayers. It was eaten in silence as was the rule of the order. Ursula sat at its head beaming contentedly at her bevy of children as she liked to think of them. Agnes chose to sit next to Catherine and passed her the bread with that narrow under-eyed look with which she appeared to view the world at large. At the conclusion of the meal Ursula formally introduced her to the women who softly bade her welcome. They then went to their respective duties, leaving Ursula and Catherine alone.

"I have arranged for you to work in the infirmary Catherine. There it would seem that your talents would be best employed."

"Thank you, Reverend Mother."

"Adjacent to your room is that of Sister Agnes who refuses to sleep in the dormitory itself much to the annoyance of some few of my children who think she ought to be flung back into the world from whence she arrived. She says little and will not pry."

"I met her in the garden when first I arrived."

"Ah, that would follow," she sighed. "Hardly the welcome you would have hoped for, I take it?"

"She did not like her labours being interrupted, it is true," said Catherine charitably.

"No, she would not. She remains a lay sister and is yet to take her vows. Her nature is a singular one, whether by inclination or through some other cause it is difficult to know. I took her under my wing when she arrived here as a girl of thirteen asking for sanctuary. She gives us little trouble and works well for her keep. All her love she devotes to the garden which she clings to with an obdurate passion. She prays with us and eats with us, but we do not really know her. Tis a pity, and I fear the blame lies with us. But I digress. I will get Sister Veronica to take you to the infirmary."

Without divulging anything of Catherine's past history to the sisters, Ursula made her entry into the order a relatively smooth one and for once her disfigurement worked in her favour, most of the women seeing it as a good enough reason for her wishing to enter their order. Like Craven, they saw it as a natural desire given her dubious prospects in the world outside.

Contrary to what Seldon had led her to believe, these women were far from idle, their rule revolving around a strict routine of work and prayer that varied little from day to day. It was not incumbent upon her to attend prayers during the hours of darkness, but she went nevertheless, feeling that she wanted to be as one with the women while she was amongst them.

Bridget was in charge of the infirmary, a small and genial type of body, fresh complexioned and having very blue eyes with a kind of twinkle in them. Of Irish descent, she had inherited its lilting way of talk from her parents, its legends and ballads being trilled off her tongue to entertain the sisters in their few idle moments. She immediately made Catherine welcome. Possessing not a jealous bone in her body as Ursula well knew, she was only too happy to place the running of the infirmary in more capable hands if it would redound to the benefit of the order as a whole. They worked well and amiably together. Two elderly nuns were permanently in their care and in need of constant attention, other beds being reserved for guests, some of whom were sick beyond cure, and had nowhere else to go. The only disadvantage to this near perfect arrangement was Bridget herself, who now began neglecting her tales of Ireland in preference for a daily account of the wonderful things she and Catherine were doing in the infirmary. Small wonder, the sisters began to yawn and even show signs of irritability, much preferring the soft Irish brogue when it related a tale less prosaic.

The weeks past, neither slowly nor quickly. They simply past. She had now been at the abbey for nearly six weeks and summer was approaching which meant that Agnes could devote more time to the garden. The bell had rung for supper and they were gathering on the lawn to go inside. Only Agnes spoiled the symmetry of the Noah's ark file, sauntering alone at its tail, her head defiantly raised to the sun. White winged butterflies flitted about them, pale and luminous like the faces of the women themselves, whose whispered confidences were no more than the play of the breeze on her face, the tiniest sound promoting rather than impairing the bird cradled silence. Finding herself similarly alone, Catherine slipped in beside her. Agnes ignored her, although Catherine was aware of an oblique kind of scrutiny. Suddenly she touched Catherine and pointed at her sleeve.

"Look, a ladybird," she said tersely.

"Hush," was the retort of the sister immediately in front of her. It was Jocelyn, once again asserting her right as grand dame of the order. Agnes was quick to respond. Putting her fingers to her ears, she wagged them furiously at the unsuspecting victim and then kicked her fiercely in a place that would hurt. Jocelyn squealed like a pig. A little muted giggling went down the line, Ursula who was at its head, turning to glance along it with a look that required no addition of words.

"It bears more red than black," Agnes resumed quietly.

"The ladybird?" Catherine whispered.

"What else, silly. The red is the blood of atonement, the black the sins of transgression. Do you not see!"

"Yes I see, but what do you mean by it?"

"That virtue far outweighs sin."

"In the insect?" Catherine innocently enquired.

"No, you simpleton!"

"In the world then? Is that what you would have me interpret?" Catherine continued, her voice distinctly less guarded now that her wits had been called into question.

"The world!" Agnes tut tutted, throwing out her hands in frustration and unintentionally ruffling Jocelyn's wimple, but this time Jocelyn made no protest. Rather was she straining her ears to seek for signs of heresy. Again Ursula stopped and looked down the line.

"In you, in you!" Agnes confided in a loud kind of whisper. "Tis an omen!"

It was the impassioned way in which this usually silent and uncommonly reserved girl spoke that left Catherine feeling utterly perplexed. Why she should attach such significance to a simple garden insect was beyond her understanding, and yet for some obscure reason it somehow seemed pertinent to her present position.

Agnes said no more as they filed in for supper but she sat beside Catherine and occasionally regarded her with that singular under-eyed look. Grace preceded the sharing of the broth and the breaking of the bread. Occasional slurps cut through the silence until they were counteracted by the near-perfect voice of Veronica whose turn it was to read to them. If it had depended on Catherine, she would have had Veronica read to them every day, but each sister had to take her turn, and not all of them were pleasing on the ear, such as Jocelyn who stretched out her words in a highly sanctimonious manner.

It was not all work and prayer. There were periods of leisure when the younger women would indulge in high spirited ball games on the garth of grass enclosed by the cloisters, Agnes hitching up her habit with the rest of them, as if to prove that her prowess with the ball was equal to that with the spade. The older women watched or dozed in the sun telling over their beads. Their eyes were passive and calm. What was to come they faced with prayerful acceptance.

Catherine's preferred pastime was to sit alone in the chapel and wait for the sun to pierce through the staining of glass and spill out its colour around her like the touching hand of God. Owing to the dowries the nuns brought with them, it contained far more in the way of decoration than her own simple church. The statues were many and beautifully carved, there was gilding on the altar and a jewel encrusted cross; as to the paintings on the wall, they were just as vivid in colouring as those on the walls of her own church, but done by a more proficient hand. A reliquary casket contained their most precious treasure, reputedly a splinter of wood from the cross on which the Saviour was crucified.

For Catherine the repetitive round of daily work and prayer provided a welcome respite from a world that had not dealt with her any too kindly. She felt at peace with herself and less afraid. Even her prayers were invested with a growing equanimity, but it was the future that she still looked to, a future with *him* and all that he meant.

CHAPTER TWENTY EIGHT

Matthew was up before daylight. Without Miriam by his side, he did not sleep so soundly as he once did. It was true that Catherine had helped to relieve him of some of that terrible aching void, but now that she was gone he felt it all the more keenly. The darkness played havoc with his thoughts as it had never done when Miriam was alive. He could even hear her voice, chivvying him for his failings, his lack of sensitivity, but what would he not have given, even his precious strips of earth, to have her badger him now. Miriam could have told him that he was needlessly punishing himself, but then to grieve properly is to be filled with feelings of guilt and remorse, and Matthew was only suffering as others have suffered.

And now Annie had left, the rift between them never having been mended. It had happened in spring when a group of travelling players had arrived in the village, trundling their props on a wagon. They were brazen and bold and she had no morals. Tired of Mother Jomfrey and tired of herself, she squeezed on her red flannel gown, painted her face and went along with them. Her departure was hardly remarked upon, so unconcerned were the villagers as to her fate. Matthew cried, not so much for the loss of his daughter as for the pain she had caused him. Neither was there news of Rob and Mary and he naturally feared the worst.

Craven had explained Catherine's absence satisfactorily enough to the remainder of his flock, impressing upon them that since it was clear that some amongst their number were still disposed to deal with her harshly he had seen fit to send her away to a place of safety until such time as they had a change of heart. Having thus made them feel guilty for having driven him to this course of action, his authority went unquestioned.

Glad of the daylight, Matthew pulled on his shoon, smiling sadly to himself as he did so. Sweet Jesu, it was damnably lonely without her. Geoffrey and Eve did what they could, but sometimes his loneliness seemed beyond cure. Under Eve's care Geoffrey was not only growing stronger but his wits were beginning to mend, so that now he was fit enough to tend his own strips of earth without assistance from Matthew. It was Matthew that they worried over now. He was working harder than ever, but for no other purpose than blotting out the past and filling up the long, lonely hours. Then there were times when a fierce stabbing pain would come into his chest, making him stop and fight for breath, but when Geoffrey and Eve asked him what was amiss he insisted that it was nothing and would pass as quickly as it came. He did not tell them that such attacks were becoming more frequent. But the land remained his refuge, the only one he knew.

Eve was a good cook and Geoffrey had regained his appetite, but Matthew ate as if it were a duty rather than a pleasure. They were eating now on this hot July day. As ever, Matthew had little to say.

"Blue sky Matt," Geoffrey remarked trying to be cheerful. His wits were still far from keen, and when Matthew did not respond he bawled out the same phrase again.

"I hae ears," Matthew retorted tetchily, "and I dunna need ye to tell me what I can see for mysell," whereupon Geoffrey's eyes grew watery with imminent tears.

"I'm sorry Geoffrey, I dunna feel mysell today. Twill pass."

"Ye be thinkin' o' them no longer wi' us," said Geoffrey with unknowing perspicacity. "Naught be the same Matt, eh."

"Naught," sighed Matthew, pressing his hand, "nor ever will be."

It was really too hot for work, lethargy getting the better of them in the face of an unrelenting sun, more burning than warming. Towards evening it became very still and dark..

"Best finish now Matt," said Geoffrey, "afore the storm comes. Why not come and take supper wi' us. Ye look wan Matt."

"I be right enough. Ye be gettin' like an old woman."

And then the pain came, but this time like the stabbing of a knife. He gripped at his chest and squatted down on the earth, the sweat oozing out on his forehead, his face contorted by agony.

"Matt what be it!" cried Geoffrey, kneeling down beside him. "What be it? Speak man, speak."

Matthew could not speak. His agony was too intense. Poor Geoffrey, blubbing and shaking at the knees, was at a loss what to do. "I best go for help, fetch Eve."

"Nay," Matthew managed to say. He knew it was over with him and wanted no fuss. "Tis o'er Geoffrey. Ye understand."

Geoffrey stopped blubbing, his mind suddenly being blessed

with extraordinary clarity. His friend was dying, the finest friend a man ever had. There must be something he could do.

"I'll get Father Craven, eh Matt?"

Matthew stretched his body on the ground. It was just bearable to do so. The earth made a warm bed to lie on and the sky showed a dull patch of blue. The rain was yet to spill. Even if Geoffrey went for Craven now, it was doubtful if he would arrive in time. No, Geoffrey must shrive him. He held out his hand to him.

"Ye shrive me. Tis permissible."

"I canna Matt. I dunna know how," replied Geoffrey, his eyes growing wide in alarm.

"Ye can Geoffrey. Ye must."

"Nay, I canna do it."

Matthew gave out a gasp of agony as the pain rent him further.

"Ye'd let me die unshriven?" he groaned.

Geoffrey caught at his hand; he could not bear to see him so vexed.

"I'll do it Matt, but ye mun be patient, me havin' a poor sort o' noddle."

"We'll help each other, eh," whispered Matt.

And so it began, this strange confession of one friend to another, Matthew making it as simple as possible for the sake of the other's poor head. Geoffrey had to kneel closer to listen, Matthew's confession being punctuated by sharp pangs of pain, but Geoffrey was no silent witness, there being an almost comic aspect in the way he fiercely took to task what he saw as some of Matthew's wilder admissions.

"Unthinkin' Matt? Ye were never that!"

"Often," Matthew insisted. "Get on wi' it man."

"Swearin'?" Geoffrey mouthed, scratching his forehead. "Ay, I'll grant ye that, but we all on us do it. Tis hardly worth the mention."

Thus, the shriving progressed, Matthew confessing all of the sins with which he felt he was burdened; Geoffrey in his simplicity of heart doing all that he could to refute them. And when it was over, Geoffrey continued close by his side with dog-like devotion.

"I'll tend ye land Matt. Dunna fret. What ye did for me I'll do for ye. Twill be just as ye would hae it for when Rob returns."

Despite his extremity, Matthew smiled approvingly. Speech being beyond him, Geoffrey cradled his head. The rain had yet to come and the earth crumbled warm in his fingers. Once the storm had past, he was sure that the morrow would be good.

"Twill be a fine day the morrow I'm thinkin'," said Geoffrey, innocently echoing his thoughts, but Matthew saw no more, though his eyes were set and staring as if they believed in the good day he promised.

"He were a good man withal," sobbed Geoffrey. "A good man."

Closing the eyes of his friend, he went to tell Craven; a more dejected man it would be hard to imagine. On hearing the news, Craven spoke a few consolatory words devoid of any real feeling. In Matthew Thompson's death, he only recognised the hand of God made manifestly perfect. Everything came of God, the plague, the suffering, and now the vindication of any doubts he may have harboured in his duty as a priest. Twas Christ gave authority. Twas for him, Father Craven, to use it as he willed. Little did Geoffrey guess of this inner exultation as they carried the hurdle to where Matthew lay. There would be no storm; it had passed before it had begun but the air remained oppressive. The burden of the man was heavy on the hurdle. Divested of the soul, mortality is like a clod, a limp and expendable prison once its inmate has flown.

"I wondered if we might gie him a special space o' ground Father, he bein' a good man withal and well liked by his fellows. Twould be fittin'."

"I agree Geoffrey," Craven smiled to himself. Yes, of a surety, Matthew Thompson was deserving of some special favour.

"A place where he can look on the sky and watch the crops a comin' up through the earth. He'd like that, I'm sure," Geoffrey continued.

"In truth he would, and I shall see that it is done. The ways of God are strange, are they not, Geoffrey?"

Once a month at a pre-determined time, Craven met Seldon a mile or so from Bardwick, the tranter having been given to understand that his presence in Runnarth might lead to problems. It was a dreary meeting place, a desolate and open stretch of ground where the wind was never quiet and the few trees that managed to grow were grey leafed and stunted. He felt an aversion for Craven and the feeling was mutual. Self-interest was the one thing that bound them, and where money was concerned the tranter owned to no scruples. Few words passed between them once the bargain was struck, Seldon dividing the coins into pockets of pleasure, Craven consumed with his nearness to God like some second Messiah intent on avenging the first, that Saviour of compassion and love he presumed to believe in. The wind added its dull rushing sound like so many whisperers gathered together. When Seldon was gone he listened for God in the silence. The work had to be carried through quickly, before the return of the Burgoynes or, worse still, Elliston himself.

"Oh God, make me resolute. State thou the time and the hour in which to accomplish Thy will."

Catherine soon received his letter. Heavy on fact and cold in sentiment, it told of her Uncle's death and briefly alluded to Annie's disappearance with doubtful companions. Since Miriam's death they had grown closer, and she was counting on Matthew to wait for her homecoming. Now there was no home to go to. She was inconsolable, and it was only through the aid of prayer and the kindliness of the sisters that she gradually came to look on the death of her uncle with something approaching acceptance. Separated from Miriam he had grieved, but now they were together again, in virtue of which she should give thanks to God as the sisters made her believe. Matthew had earned his just reward; it was now for Rob to return to give meaning to the struggle. In replying to Craven's letter the tears that she wept were not for her uncle, but for a future that seemed more uncertain than ever.

In reading it Craven saw that the time was very near, in pursuance of which he imposed upon himself a stern test of resolve, prostrating himself nightly before the altar of his church and calling on God to give him strength to carry out His purpose, and as he lay there listening in the silence the still, small voice began to beckon, gradually gaining in resonance until it flooded his being completely. So great was the clamour that he grovelled on the floor, his hands on his head to stifle the roar. "So be it. So be it," he cried. "Thy will be done. Thy will. Thy will". Had any of his flock been witness to it, they would have thought him possessed. Only through an enormous effort of will was he able to still the voice in his head, for it came of himself and not of God as his pent-up desire made believe. Utterly spent in mind and body, his face took on a strange deathly pallor, though his eyes were ablaze. Having cast God in his own sorry image, what else could he do but consign the true one to some dark and arid recess of his own troubled mind.

In the presence of his flock, he was the Craven they knew, assured and self-possessed, and when he told them that

Catherine Venners was dead they had no reason to disbelieve him, for he was their mouthpiece to God and what he told them they accepted as they accepted the change in the seasons. It was a plain and unassailable fact. Beyond it, he had little to say, other than that she had contracted the plague whilst ministering to a sick woman in Bardwick. It was a fitting explanation considering her former care of them. It also introduced an element of guilt on their part. They were shaken and filled with remorse, beset by his unspoken inference that in many ways they were to blame for the outcome, that it might never have happened without their connivance. Such feelings owed as much to her uncle as Catherine herself, he having given them the encouragement to continue when most it was needed. They went back to their homes downcast and humbled. Geoffrey and Eve wept for them all.

CHAPTER TWENTY NINE

It was a good time of the year to be at St. Mary's, for the earth was coming to fullness and the hours lingered warm into evening. The hills were purpled in heather and the sky showed blue and intense. Birds hovered their song high above and the air was soft and sweet scented. No promised paradise looked sweeter than this one to Agnes. Leaning on her spade, she longed to escape from the chatter of women and seek out a language more distinctly her own, for with Agnes the profundity of all things lay in nature, not in man. When compared with the grace of one bird in flight, her own kind was barren of spirit. If God was really so infinite in wisdom, he would have finished creation with the creatures of earth, sea and air, instead of spoiling it all by making a man in his image. Thus, she mused as she watched the others fuss over Catherine in her grief. She offered no words of sympathy herself, regarding them as ineffectual. Early in life she had learned to survive with a mask-like forbearance. Despite her reserve and contempt for humanity, however, it was noticeable that she was permitting Catherine a greater degree of intimacy than was normally her wont. The sisters had remarked on it amongst themselves, though never to Agnes. That would not have done at all. It was not that she spoke more gently to Catherine or as one usually does to another who would seem to have things in common. No, her behaviour was curt and suspicious, simply because she was afraid of the feelings that friendship engendered. It went against her rule of detachment and becoming involved, but in Catherine's marked strength of character she saw a little of herself, though it was allied to an over sensitive nature and hence a capacity to suffer. Of course, the sisters were only being kind in their expressions of sympathy, but to Agnes's way of thinking a surfeit of kindness can be worse than a lack. What Catherine needed was taking out of herself.

Opportunity offered on a bright windy morning later that week, a storm on the preceding evening having helped to clear the air and temper the heat of the sun. Catherine came into the garden as she was tending her vegetable patch. Oblivious of Agnes, she wandered up and down the gravelled paths, her eyes downcast and heavy in thought. They were completely alone and the time was perfect. Too perfect for Agnes, who now began to waver. The order did not allow for close friendships, which was one of the reasons why it appealed to her. She much preferred her own company to that of anyone else's. To her friendship meant compromise and a willingness to forgo one's own inclinations in order to please those of one's friend. Invariably it ended by one friend becoming selfish and making too many demands of the other. She had seen such attachments before, deeply felt at first and little by little eroding into sufferance, a little like love when it grows stale and they who have loved cannot let go. Such thoughts were troublesome, so why this sudden impulse to meddle in what was none of her business. The whole thing was tiresome. Nonetheless, she suddenly threw down the hoe.

"I propose to go for a walk," she said. "You can come if you wish, that is if you have no prior claims on your time."

"Agnes!" said Catherine, completely caught off guard.

"Well?"

"If you really desire it," she replied, seeing the familiar under-eyed look, not to mention the grudging way in which the invitation was made. "I think you would really prefer to walk alone, and you must not be kind to accommodate me."

"Accommodate you!" Agnes reiterated sharply. "You flatter yourself. As you will. I shall not ask again."

"Wait," Catherine said, becoming hesitant. Dare she be awkward. A smile played about her lips. "Yes, I will come Agnes. I should like to."

Agnes made no attempt to look pleased. By refusing her proposal one moment, only to accept it the next, she was left with the infuriating impression that Catherine was being deliberately contrary to try her. If her suspicions proved right, then it meant that Catherine was feeling better already without any effort on her part and that she had needlessly wasted her time, that precious time which she had wished to spend as she pleased. Still, there was no getting away from it, and she had to console herself with the thought that Catherine was a more tolerable companion than most.

"You better show the way," Catherine said, smiling demurely. "I will follow."

She reposed on Catherine a long withering stare and then strode ahead as if she would love to leave her behind. Confound her silly promptings of kindness. Damn what her conscience professed. In future, she would trust to her instincts alone. So the Venners girl wanted to walk. Then walk they would. Seething with annoyance, she deliberately set a heart thumping pace, but Catherine matched her step for step.

As they climbed higher, so the wind blew full in their faces, occasionally bringing tears to their eyes. Their habits flapped behind them like so many wings. Sheep shied away at their approach, bleating timidly at the untoward sight. Nothing was still, least of all the women themselves, who seemed as emotionally charged as the elements they moved in. Birds broke cover in the bracken, alarmed at the sudden disturbance, just as they were alarmed in their turn. Eventually Catherine had to stop to catch her breath. The full sweep of the heather covered moor lay before and around her, the abbey looking tiny in the crook of the valley from which they had come. The grandeur of it clutched at her soul. She felt as if she had reached the edge of some unattainable heaven and the sensation was one of pure exultation. There was nothing passive in this land. It said "I am," and what it meant was forever.

Agnes continued to climb, Catherine now easing her pace as the path grew steeper. When she finally caught up with her, Agnes looked utterly different. She had taken off her coif and her hair flowed wildly about her face, short and dark except where it was burnished to copper by the sun. The sheer joy of being alive was expressed in her every feature. She was one with the landscape, her whole being projected within it, her face shining and radiant from some inner knowledge that transformed her from mere mortal clay to burning bright spirit. Catherine felt as if she had no right to be there, as if she was witness to some profoundly personal experience that belonged to Agnes alone.

"I should not have come Agnes. Please forgive me."

"Why? I asked you, did I not." She smiled reflectively, the wind restoring the colour to her cheeks. "Tis over. Please stay. Such feelings only come when I am here, never at St. Mary's."

Agnes was calm and composed, though the experience had drained her of colour. Such ecstasy of feeling is necessarily of a transient nature and afforded to very few; a glimpse beyond this life to something glorious beyond it.

"Come. I will take you to the outcrop. Tis not far."

A wilderness of heath, boggy and treeless, led to an outcrop of stones which was said to have been sacred in the days of the old gods. To Catherine it seemed one of the loneliest places on earth.

"This is where I think," explained Agnes, positioning herself on a flat slab of stone. Catherine did likewise. "Do you believe in God?" she suddenly asked in a matter of fact kind of way.

"That is a strange question coming from one who professes ..."

"Why so? It is not as if I have taken any vows. I asked of you a question and you commence to turn it into a homily on my faith or lack of it instead. It is the kind of answer I would expect of the others but not from you."

It was a challenge that Catherine was not to let go.

"Believe in an all caring God. Yes, I do Agnes in spite of such trials as have tested my faith. But you Agnes, what are the beliefs that bind you?"

"I believe in this," she replied, spreading out her hand. "In the earth I see before me and everything on it but for my own vicious kind. Tis man the despoiler. This is my God, none other. This is the extent of my belief. I am of it, and it of me. We are one."

Catherine did not know what to say. What Agnes was confessing was tantamount to heresy. Men and women had suffered less in their divergence from the teachings of Holy Mother Church.

"You must be circumspect Agnes. It would never do to speak of such things within the hearing of the others."

"Jocelyn, for example," she retorted, shaking with laughter. "So that is your counsel. I should take heed for my welfare in the knowledge of what the church professes to teach and what I profess to believe. You see how I quake, how I tremble."

Allowing for everything she had suffered, Catherine remained strong in her faith, Agnes's laughter sounding cruel in her ears, but like so many Christians before her she had not the wit to defend it. Her defence became muddled and devoid of any logic, but then Jesus himself did illogical things. Agnes listened, tapping her fingers on the rock.

"You have a care for others. You like your own kind. That is the difference between us. I have seen evil beyond your imagining."

"And I have seen goodness in equal measure," she contested, though her defence by its very nature seemed weak.

"Small in relation I warrant. There is tittle tattle enough within St. Mary's, the sneaking, the mean paltry acts, not to mention the petty little jealousies."

"Tis a part of human nature to gossip. Neither is it always malicious. Anyway think of Sister Veronica and tell me of her faults."

"You choose a very rare example. Why should I see the good in my kind when my mother was a whore."

So taken aback was Catherine that she knew not what to say in response, though it helped to explain Agnes's distrust of her own kind. "Now that is a bit of history of which St. Mary's is ignorant, and I thank you not to make it known either. Tis a measure of my trust in you that I speak of it now. God alone knows who my father was. As for the woman who bore me, I learned to despise her."

"Then we have more in common than you think, for I too am baseborn, but my mother was a good and kind woman, and nearly everything I hold dear I owe to her teaching. She gave me the strength and courage to face the world as I am and I miss her even yet."

"She is dead?"

"Yes."

"So is mine. I was with her when she died. I felt nothing for her. She stank of disease and I feared the proximity would fester in me. Your mother gave you good counsel. I had to tutor myself in the ways of the world."

"Mayhap she did the best she could."

"Fie now! I might have known that you would attempt to find ways of mitigating her shame. You will see no tears rise to my eyes. I am immune. I was a mere child when she died, and I could have become as she had, there being men enough, even at that tender age, to show me the way. But I was no fool. I came to St. Mary's and here I shall stay. All humanity is foul Catherine, but men are the foulest."

"You must not think thus. There are good men in the world, just as there are good women," she maintained, her indignation emotionally tied to the man she adored.

"You speak as if you knew?" Agnes coolly remarked, adopting the inquisitive trait she presumed to deplore.

"I have no vocation Agnes. I have told Reverend Mother as much. I long to return to the world."

"Then there is a man in your longing?"

"A good man Agnes. One that genuinely loves me as I am. Doubtless, you find that surprising?"

"No, I do not. I am not at all surprised that a man should find you pleasing. Pray God, he is worthy of you." It was Catherine's trusting nature that had made Agnes willing to confide in her. Usually she reserved such outpourings to the free air around her, relying on nature as a more than safe repository for secrets untold. That Catherine had seen fit to confide in her was owing to her absolute honesty. It was the kind of trust and honesty that was guaranteed to bind them together.

CHAPTER THIRTY

It was late March and Catherine had been at St. Mary's for nearly a year. It had been a long and exceptionally cold winter. Traces of snow yet remained on the hills and frosts were a daily occurrence. With the wind raging outside the sisters gathered for warmth round the fire. So cold was the weather that Ursula had even seen fit to relax the rules on fasting. But Agnes was itching to get out of doors.

"I still think tis hardly gardening weather," Catherine remarked as Agnes rolled on her stockings with that dogged look of determination she reserved for anyone who threatened to thwart her resolve.

"Tis time enough," she replied. "The garden has need of me, and, more importantly, I have need of it."

Catherine tried hard not to smile. Agnes treated her garden like a substitute child, miscreant and loveable by turns, but hers was a nature to which Catherine warmed, while on her side Agnes was beginning to learn what it was to be liked and to like.

Catherine joined Bridget in the infirmary where they spent the morning renewing their small stock of physic which the rigours of winter had sadly depleted. Two of the older nuns had died during the winter and two others remained in their care. The sun filtered through the window along with the song of birds eager to begin nesting, Bridget adding the lilt of her voice to augment their chatter. By noon, when it was somewhat warmer, they were summoned to the guest house to attend to a man wearied and foot sore.

"And what can we be doin' for ye, praise God," Bridget brightly enquired, Catherine standing a little aside as was her custom with strangers.

"Canna take another step for the blisters."

"Let me see."

Wanting to assist, Catherine came forward, even though it necessitated exposing herself to the gaze of the man, whose reaction was that of the pitying kind. Mentally taking note of the women, he found the plumper of the two decidedly good natured, the latter being one of those poor unfortunates for which a nunnery was the only fit place. If he was inclined to recoil from Catherine, she was much more inclined to recoil from his feet which were a mess of blisters and pus.

"Beggin' ye pardon," he said by way of apology. "It be the walkin' but what is a man to do. I hae to find work now I hae nae family to think on, God rest em."

For a space his mood became thoughtful, but he was too caught up in his own immediate cares to be maudlin for long. "At least the plague hae provided a mort o' work for the few that be left, or so I thought till I came to this God accursed country, beggin' ye pardon sister." The apology was directed solely at Bridget, since he could not quite make up his mind whether the strange looking one was a simpleton or not.

"We'll need more bandages," said Bridget, leaving Catherine to bathe his feet, whereupon the man was soon to discover that Catherine was far from being simple. Such discovery in one so unfortunately marred made him doubly circumspect, such is human nature.

"Sister Catherine has more than the ordinary skill in matters of this kind," Bridget remarked, unwinding the bandages. He winced audibly as Catherine applied the ointment to his feet, Bridget trying her utmost not to bind them too tightly.

"Ouch!" he cried, once again begging their indulgence.

"Have you been on the road long?" Bridget asked as a means of diverting his mind.

"Ay, ye could say that. York to Newcastle and further still. A man should get good pickings with the scarcity o' labour as it is."

"And yet you found nothing to profit you?"

"Nae sister and me a free man and all."

The phrase caught Catherine unawares, bringing Geoffrey Frincham right to the forefront of her mind. She had heard little of him since leaving Runnarth, and in answer to her queries Craven was often vague and evasive.

"Mind ye, there was a time when I thought I'd fallen on my feet so to speak."

At this Bridget dissolved into loud peals of laughter.

"Ay, I take ye meanin'," he laughed warily, as if he were mindful of his surroundings, and when Catherine smiled too his face straightened out altogether. Unfortunately, he came under the category of those who would never accept her. "Anyways," he resumed, "when I reaches a place called Runnarth, I thinks to mysell, this might be the very place I be lookin' for."

Catherine dropped the ointment. Her face turned white. Her eyes were wide and enquiring.

"Why, whatever is it?" Bridget exclaimed. "You look about to swoon. Come, sit down now."

The man eyed them dubiously. He did not like the look of Catherine one bit, fearful that she might have the remains of the plague lingering in her.

"She hae a sickly look to er, I'm thinkin'."

"Sister Catherine is too diligent for her own good," Bridget made haste to explain. "Should you not rest Catherine."

"No I am perfectly well. I cannot think what came over me. I feel better already, but our guest was telling us of his visit to ..."

"Runnarth, sister," he continued, looking at her warily.

"Yes, Runnarth," she whispered.

"Ay well, this Runnarth be fair blighted, but tis the same all o'er. Things hae changed since the sickness. We mun hae a decent wage for a decent day's work, but when they tells me what they be willin' to pay it seems clear to me that they be stickin' to the time afore the plague and no man worth 'is due 'ull now stand for that. It be 'is lordship's doin' so I am told, so here I am back on the road."

"Lord Elliston is at Runnarth?" Catherine said, her voice close to breaking under the strain of speaking his name.

"I presume tis so."

"Do you know of this Runnarth? asked Bridget, much intrigued at Catherine's obvious interest.

"Yes, it is close to my home," she replied. She might have added her heart as well.

"I see. Then naturally you are interested."

The man could tell them no more and was soon on his way. Catherine watched him go with a blank expression, though inwardly she was bubbling like a cauldron about to spill over. Elliston at Runnarth. Could it be true. If so, why had Craven kept her in ignorance of the fact. Even allowing for his aversion to Elliston and their own past differences, she had never had cause to question his integrity.

The man limped cautiously into the sunshine, reserving his farewell for Bridget alone.

"Bless ye, sister, bless ye," he said, pressing a coin into the palm of her hand. "That for ye troubles sister. I hope yon poor creature be better anon. Tis a mercy ye have her in ye keepin'."

The poor creature was left in a daze.

From thereon her day resembled an airy procession of hours,

more dreamlike than real. She did not know what to believe. If only the man could have been more definite, she would have left there and then without any forethought. As it was, she went to ask for Ursula's guidance, Ursula being Craven's cousin and the only person within St. Mary's who was fully acquainted with her history. Ursula responded in her usual feeling way. As head of the order, she was also a woman, and realising what the news would mean to Catherine if it proved to be true, she promised to write to her cousin, counselling Catherine to be patient in the interim. Word of mouth, as she wisely pointed out, was not always the most reliable means of obtaining the facts.

Craven read the letter with obvious alarm. A foolish nobody was threatening to ruin his plans. Immediately he promised Seldon an immoderate sum of money if he would take him to St. Mary's at once. Two days later Ursula went to the infirmary to inform Catherine of his arrival.

"Now, pray God, you will have everything verified to your liking," she whispered, leading Catherine into the house reserved for guests. "Francis, she is here. I trust you will find our care of her to your satisfaction." As he did not answer, she took it that her presence was no longer wanted and left them alone.

To cater for the needs of its visitors, the guest house was more amply furnished than the rest of the nunnery, and he had chosen to sit with his back to the sun in the large recess formed by the window. His hands were folded and the light made a frame for his profile. She was struck by the change in him, particularly the downward pucker of the lips that had not been there before and spoilt his look of immunity to worldly concerns. He looked altogether older. He smiled in welcome, but as usual it was a forced kind of smile, which left her with the uncomfortable feeling that her long awaited happiness was in some way impaired.

"You look well Catherine. Pray, be seated."

"As I trust you are Father," she replied, seating herself at an equable distance, "but you must not overtax yourself as is your wont."

"I trust in my faith to sustain me Catherine. All else is irrelevant."

The gulf was widening between them. In obedience to the inner voice of God as he chose to interpret it, he had rid himself of all feeling. She, by contrast, was all feeling and entirely at his mercy. The directness of his gaze made her tremble, if not on the surface, then wholly inside.

"My cousin tells me that you have heard of Elliston's return," he began, going straight to the source of her disquiet with matchless composure. "It was only of recent date I assure you. I was fully intending to inform you by letter. However, on reflection I thought my presence would serve better to avail you of the circumstance."

Circumstance! Another word she put on a par with necessity, wide of interpretation. He was trying her sorely with his neat apposite phrases. She felt her chest tighten, hardly being able to breathe for the effort of repressing what she felt. Would that he spoke soon or she would rebel against the calculated strain he imposed upon her, and then he would see her as she really was, not a dedicated novitiate, but a dedicated woman, motivated by all the needs and desires of her sex. The palms of her hands were held tightly together, tiny beads of sweat dampening her forehead.

"You have spoken with him though?" she broke in abruptly.

"I have not spoken with him myself. Burgoyne has acted as intermediary between us."

"Then Sir Edward also has returned?"

"He has, along with Lady Burgoyne. They returned a little ahead of Elliston, having lost their eldest son to the plague. I thought you would wish to be made privy to such news."

"Indeed. Poor Margaret. I am aggrieved to hear of it and shall write to both her and Sir Edward as soon as I am able, but in the meantime let them know of my sorrow."

She was genuinely sorry, but because she was human she was selfish for her own concerns too.

"And Lord Elliston?" she reiterated, determined to stick to the issue in hand.

"As I said, Catherine, I have not actually spoken with him, Burgoyne consenting to act as mediator between us. I thought it the wiser course considering our past and continued dissension."

She bit her lip in frustration. He saw the thin smudge of blood appear upon it. The more she gave vent to her feelings, the more imperative it became to have her news quickly, the more inclined he was to prevaricate. Resolute in his belief that he was obeying his God, he was proof against all such appeals. Aware that he disapproved her lack of restraint, she realised that she must temper her feeling or suffer in consequence.

"My lord is ..." she stumbled. "My" implied possession, and such in his eyes might appear unseemly. She corrected herself, though not a word or reaction escaped him.

"Lord Elliston is well?" she resumed, casually putting the question as if she was discussing the weather.

"From what Sir Edward tells me, I believe it to be so."

"And Sir Edward and Margaret?" she added, naively trusting in this change of approach to promote her appeal.

"Well also, apart from grief at the loss of their son."

"Of course," she replied with a rote-like awareness. "Tis only to be expected."

Oh when would he speak! When!

The silence then hung heavy. Craven's studied evasion was serving him well, well enough to increase her anxiety and place her in a position of weakness. She attempted to wait on him to speak first, as her uncle was wont to do, trusting in the privilege afforded him to draw on his sympathy, but he was seemingly oblivious, looking beyond her into the shadows like some self-confessed mystic intent on worlds outside her vision. A wasp searching for egress frantically circled the silence.

"You find such quiet oppressive?" he asked at last.

Proof sufficient that he was perfectly aware of her presence. She ought to have known him better than to doubt it.

"It depends on the quality of the silence Father," she replied. "There are degrees, as in everything."

"Am I to infer that you hold discretion a virtue?"

The implication in the question increased her discomfort.

"I do Father, but even this has a qualifying limit."

"And you would have me speak to a degree exceeding that limit?"

"If it affected my happiness, yes," she said. There was a note of vanity in her answer and she regretted that she had not spoken in more general terms.

"And of what does this future happiness you speak of comprise, Catherine?"

She could take no more. The time for pretence was over.

"You know without my being discreet," she entreated. "Father, I beg of you, I would have news of my lord, his welfare and mine being inextricably bound by ties of love and affection."

He looked at her dispassionately. How freely she used the word "love" and how much it rankled within his hearing.

"Have you forgotten your uncle so soon?" he accused, introducing an element of indecency into the haste of her appeal.

"How could I ever forget him!" she retorted, incensed rather than chastened. "Surely you know me better than to even suggest it, but the dead are beyond our recall and I would have news of the living. If you think my manner unseemly, then I have nothing to say in defence other than what I have already spoken. Affection alone disavows the discretion you speak of. Surely it is not a sin to be ruled by such impulse?"

She appealed to him in all innocence, quite unaware that the love she spoke of had all the weight of a feather borne on the wind when compared with his crushing resentment.

"You are your mother's child Catherine," he said. Again the inference was plain.

"And proud to be called so!" she countered. "My mother was a good and virtuous woman."

She felt she had a right to be indignant, for what he implied was a flaw in that virtue, a flaw passed on from mother to daughter through the sin of an illicit union. How dare he suggest it.

"Virtuous to a fault!" he coolly replied.

"You will not say so!" she cried, tears of anger welling up in her eyes. "I cannot endure it."

Seeing her thus, he knew he had gone too far. It had been foolish to allude to her mother when he knew with what fervour she would spring to her defence. God forgive him his error, he inwardly prayed, crossing himself as he did so.

"Indeed, she was as you say Catherine," he said, effecting a softness of tone. "You mistake my meaning." He now spoke as if her sentiments were entirely in accord with his own, but it was merely a means of deflecting her anger. He succeeded. She believed he was sincere.

"Forgive me Father. It is delay that makes me intemperate."

His eyes too evinced softness. He even owned to a feeling of sorrow, but the ways of God were not his to question. Neither did they entail ruth upon others. He would speak as God had prompted him.

"Lord Elliston is well," he commenced, adopting a conciliatory manner. "I have it from Sir Edward that he speaks of you with affection." That affection sounded poor requital on his lips. She had looked for so much more, but consoled herself with the fact that Craven may have measured the terms in which her lord had spoken to a degree more befitting propriety. Doubtless, he had a letter to give her written in words more expansive.

"You have a letter for me?" She spoke excitedly, like a child in anticipation of a treat.

"No, Catherine, I have no letter," he replied. His voice might be gentle, but to her it echoed on the stillness like lead.

"I do not understand Father. There is a vagueness in all you have told me that seems to make hollow the joy I had hoped for. If there is something further, I beseech you to tell it." Oh that he would, his equivocation filling her with fear. "Father Craven," she pleaded, "I beg of you."

"Catherine, I would spare you such news as I have if I could, but tell it I must. There is a rule of inconstancy in most men. Do you know to what I allude."

"I think so," she shakily returned, her body becoming rigid.

"There are men of a certain temperament, such as Elliston, who will adapt to any change in their circumstance."

"I have not changed!" came her agonised cry, her eyes empty of the tears she refused to let spill in his presence.

It was a cruel and tortuously clever way of drawing her into the net, but with God on his side he only saw triumph. Little by little the good work was being brought to its rightful conclusion.

"Lord Elliston, according to Sir Edward, is shortly to be married to a lady of no little standing and much accomplishment. Indeed, I have it on good authority that she is considered to be most suitable in all the attainments befitting such a wife."

It fell from his lips as simply as that. Where Catherine was involved, he knew that it behoved him to speak in the particular as opposed to the general, and in part he spoke truth, except that the women Elliston was now to be seen with were devoid of attraction, either particular or general.

"A wife," she mouthed, half closing her eyes. "How can that be? There is a Lady Elliston already."

"No longer, Catherine. The marriage is annulled."

Again, this was a deliberate distortion of the facts, the divorce having been expressly obtained by Elliston during his absence as a means of regularising their union on his return, a circumstance which he knew would both pacify and please her, and one which he had deliberately kept secret for the purpose of springing its welcome surprise after their lengthy separation.

"And what of the Lady Blanche?" she enquired, surprised at the control she maintained in her voice.

"Wed to Lord Baring as is right and proper. Tis all as was meant, Catherine, or rather as God Himself intended."

"Meant! Meant!" she exclaimed, covering her face.

"Catherine," he coaxed, almost bringing his hand to touch hers. "You will be strong and outgrow this affection in time. Pray for it daily, I urge you."

The struggle was over and he had not been found wanting in the test. It was no simple matter to witness her anguish, and he was surprised to find himself stricken by a twinge of remorse, but by attributing it to the weaker side of his nature and not to the tiny grain of compassion which ever cried out for mastery inside him, the feeling was quickly disposed of.

"You are happy here, are you not, Catherine?" he asked, gently persuasive.

Still not having wept, she uncovered her face and stared at him, a blighted smile bringing the wound clearly to the surface. What manner of man was he, she thought, who could still enquire of her happiness having all but destroyed it.

"Catherine, all this will pass in God's good time."

Time. How could he possibly understand that his so called time would be to her an eternity. The desecration of a smile refused to leave her lips, studied, scraped over the welter of emotion that must follow the moment he left.

"What I purposed to say ..." he began.

"I know what you purposed, Father," she said. "The sisters are kind, your cousin especially." The underlying calmness of her reply astounded herself.

"Then this will be a comfort to you, Catherine, in overcoming your ...." Unable to think of the appropriate word, a trace of agitation showed in his features. This putting to right of a wrong was even more exacting than he had reckoned.

"Disappointment?" she said, a sting in the utterance.

"Yes, Catherine, yes. Bide here a while with the sisters. Think over what I have said. Returning to Runnarth might cause you pain, and although the plague has left us, tis too soon to test the temper of the people. The times remain unsettled and Mother Jomfrey continues to exert an unhealthy influence. You must not worry for your uncle's lands. Geoffrey Frincham, his reason all but restored, faithfully tends them."

At the mention of Geoffrey's name, her look mellowed. To hear of him in the midst of her anguish was to be given a little taste of some sweet in the sour, though it was taking a singular effort of will not to weep openly in Craven's presence.

"Make known my indebtedness to Geoffrey," she said, holding on to the little dignity left her. "If he could read, I would write of my gratitude. As it is, I shall rely on you, Father, to make known the sincerity of my feelings. I would have him know ..."

"Catherine!" he exclaimed, as her voice trailed away, half broken on a sob.

"It is of no moment," she assured him. "I cannot think quite aright. What am I to do? What is required of me?"

"You should know Catherine, without any prompting on my

part. God has brought you thus far. Tis for you to heed Him now."

He slowly rose to his feet. It was done. Everything about her convinced him of the fact and he saw that it was good, notwithstanding the hurt it occasioned. In a few carefully chosen words, those words that he believed were divinely inspired, he had pointed the way. And she, being vulnerable, received the impression, alien though it was to every thought that she owned.

He now took her hand, an involuntary gesture that dismayed him as much as it disquieted her. Its touch was very cold.

"I know that God will guide you in all things, Catherine. Trust in Him. My prayers will be with you."

Releasing her hand, he walked away. The sun left with him. Even the wasp ceased to hum. She was conscious of nothing, neither the length of time she sat on in the dark, nor indeed of the darkness itself. The flicker of her eyelids was all but suspended. She was lost in her petrified moment of time.

Ursula began to worry. Her cousin had left without a word of farewell and Catherine had not been at supper. The sisters were now at their midnight devotions, but she was not of their number. With an unaccountably sick feeling at heart, Ursula went to the guest house, holding her candle aloft to search through the gloom.

"Why, whatever is it, Catherine?" she cried out, seeing Catherine flinch from the light. She took hold of her hands and rubbed them vigorously, trusting to animate the body as well as the mind. "Oh Catherine, I can see that my cousin's news has not been of the kind to reassure you." Catherine had no reply to give her. "Come with me. There is nothing so lacking in hope that it will not look better for the blessing of sleep." Catherine allowed herself to be led. "I know Brother Anthony is our Father Confessor, but there are some matters beyond the comprehension of the stronger of the sex. I am not here to pry. I only wish to help in what way I can. Tomorrow will be time enough. Meantime, remember Catherine that no sorrow on earth goes unmarked by God or his Blessed Holy Mother. Ask and you shall receive. God have you in His keeping this night and always."

Catherine looked at her vaguely. When Ursula held up the candle to guide her, the ledge where it had rested revealed a thin layer of dust and in it the wasp.

"Tis terrible to die confined," Catherine murmured on seeing it.

Ursula took her by the arm. She did not understand.

"You are tired, my child, so very tired."

Ursula had given her a sleeping draught and the morning was well advanced before she opened her eyes. The nightmare was in waking, not in sleeping. She found herself gazing up at the ceiling in the same way she had done as a child when day after day she had learned to cope with the agony of physical torment, but that was as nothing compared to the agony of mind she was now undergoing. Then she had been able to bring her will to bear in blotting out the worst of the suffering, but for this there was no remedy, no cure for an affliction that fed on the very heart of her and turned all its accepted beliefs into chaos. The bell was intoning its summons to prayer and the sun made a shadow of the grille on the floor. She was imprisoned and her faith began to crumble. Despite its illicit nature, she had believed that what she felt for Elliston was inherently good and therefore impelled the blessing of God, and now she was being punished for her arrogance. She watched the sisters filing out of the chapel, Agnes dawdling a little behind them, as was her wont. Rain had fallen during the night and the sudden shock of sunshine was giving the day the baptismal quality of a fresh and new beginning. She squeezed her hair beneath the coif and made ready to join them. Her absence from supper the night before had been noted, but only remarked upon by Jocelyn who chose to speak of it now.

"Good morrow sister. I trust nothing ails you."

"No, nothing," she mechanically replied.

She was with them and yet she was not, a part of her having flown she knew not where. It was as if she had lost her very identity.

The sun poured upon them at breakfast, though Catherine continued to stare at her dish long after the others had finished. Out of obedience to their rule they affected not to notice, but as women they were curious. Ursula had cause to be anxious and Agnes, with her uncluttered mind, could feel her anxiety.

Catherine scarcely raised her head. Base born, base bedded, what right had she to sit with these women, share in their discourse, partake of their food, profess to a calling which must offend the very God she presumed to believe in. She understood herself now, even the facial flaw which was nothing more than a poor reflection of the inner defilement. Her very vision seemed impaired, the room narrowing to the confines of a tunnel without any visible end, the sisters retreating down its labyrinth to escape from the taint of her presence. In their looks of concern she saw nothing but scorn. Indeed, so disturbed was her reasoning that she fancied she saw in those shining faces of theirs an emanation of the pure light of God which would pierce through to the core of her being where the maggot of sin squirmed for authority over her soul. The day seemed without end. She spent most of it in the cloisters until their shadow half covered the grass. Birds came and went pecking at the crumbs put out for their benefit and for a moment she drifted blissfully into sleep. She deliberately isolated herself, and they wisely let her be.

At the close of the day, she went back to her cell and resolved to commence the atonement, make proper reparation in the hope of remission from a sin which she had formerly accounted a blessing. She never doubted what Craven had told her, for he was her priest and a man renowned for the honesty of his beliefs, even though they did not always accord with her own. The hours between her devotion and work she spent in private prayer, such hours as she would call on Mary, gentle Mother of Jesus, to intercede on her behalf and make Christ aware of the measure of her repentance, but even so the past found a way of intruding. It came in cold, haunting lapses of thought, too often beset with earthly desire and want of true penitence, moments when her visioning was not of Christ but of Elliston who enacted the role of his own intercedent. Promptings of the devil, she persuaded herself.

"Holy Mother, Gentle Mary, have pity on me. Protect me from the corruptness of my thoughts. Let me be cleansed. Let me be freed from the oppression of my sins. I believe in God the Father, Maker of Heaven and Earth. I believe ..." and so she would continue until she drowned all remembrance of Elliston and what he had meant to her by a tortuous process bordering on madness. Indulging in every form of self-abasement said to ease the soul of its burden of guilt, she fasted, worked and prayed to the extent of imperilling her health. The sisters could only marvel and pray. They liked her. They had learned to accept her disfigurement. Though as yet a novitiate, she belonged to their order and when one of them suffered, all of them suffered.

In the meantime, Ursula was patient, though she looked to the time when Catherine saw fit to unburden herself. She had tentatively enquired of Father Anthony, who shared her concern, but assured her that Catherine's confession contained nothing that might assist them in mending the matter. She knew he spoke truth. Their priest for many years, he was a kindly man, white of hair and gentle of speech, and Catherine had evinced a liking for him because he reminded her of Peter. It was now all in God's hands, though Ursula trusted that He would not be too dilatory over such a pressing concern. She wrote to Francis, convinced that his visit had been instrumental in effecting the change in Catherine, but his reply was what she expected, evasive and full of theological musings which were merely annoying.

And so matters continued. It was now autumn and they often awoke to the mists of the season. Catherine was noticeably weaker. Not proof against her own thoughts, despite the long round of tasks she imposed upon herself, she was now reduced to a trance-like condition driven by mere strength of will. For one thing she could not help but conjecture on the woman who had taken her place. "Not like me!" she reflected, stressing the "Me" with utter self loathing and pity. No mirrors were allowed at St. Mary's, which was just as well considering her thin and wasted appearance; as for the one thing she prized, her hair, it was now so neglected that it resembled a skein of colourless tangle.

With the passing of Christmas came the first heavy snows, so much a part of those testing months of the year when to keep warm is the main occupation of every living thing. Once again the sisters were allowed the luxury of retiring to the kitchen where they took it in turns to huddle over the fire. Catherine's atonement was nearing its end. She was now so weak that she could hardly walk without effort. Ulcers inflamed her mouth and made the taking of nourishment a misery, and what little food she did eat could be likened to the wafer served up at the Host. In keeping with her vow of self-mortification, she had not changed or washed her clothing, blisters and sores adding to her bodily discomfort where the habit began to adhere.

Mercifully, it was a short, sharp winter, the unbending of the worst of the weather happening well before March. It suited Agnes perfectly. She went to look at her garden, but the sun was elusive and certainly not conducive to digging and delving.

"Devil take it!" she gave out and she meant it. Nor did she cross herself as a mark of contrition. Catherine came out to watch. She walked very slowly and the early morning chill made her cough.

"Maybe in a week or two Agnes," she said. "You will have to be patient."

"As you are?" Agnes retorted.

"Yes, as I am." Her throat hurt terribly and she could barely see Agnes at all.

"For what, Catherine!" came the bitter rejoinder. It was the first time Agnes had called her by name and the address was hardly tender. "Though I have scant understanding of friendship, you have taught me the little I know, and for you I do have a care."

"I thank you for your concern Agnes, also the fact that you regard me as your friend." A sudden ray of sunlight flooded the garden. "I was wrong Agnes. I do believe that it will be a fine day after all." Shielding her eyes from the glare, an involuntary fit of coughing stayed her speech and a tiny trickle of blood oozed from her mouth where an ulcer had burst.

"Catherine," Agnes sighed. "You tell me you believe in God, but is this what a saving Christ demands of you? Were it so I would spew all such faith from my lips and openly confess the doubt I confided in you."

She put her arms around Catherine's shoulder, a surprising gesture from Agnes, and helped her to the infirmary where Bridget was sorting old linen for the making of bandages.

"Holy Mother of God," she exclaimed on seeing Catherine.

"What do you expect" said Agnes indignantly, "from one who is so intent on leaving us. She seeks an early reward in return for her pains. Then let her have it! Tis her right!"

Agnes intended the sting as a kindness, as a short and sharp lesson in bringing Catherine to her senses before it was too late, but Bridget was furious. For a long time she had regarded Catherine as specially favoured of God, her rigorous self-denial part of some divine plan, the revelation of which was very near at hand.

"What do you know of it?" she railed, pointing a finger at Agnes, her accent more pronounced than ever. "She who is chosen of God can teach us His ways."

Catherine stood by impassively, leaning to support herself against the table. Both women were possessed of a temper. And Agnes did not improve matters by laughing out loud. She was cruel in her ridicule.

"Stop it at once! Stop it!" cried Bridget, raising her hand.

"Please Agnes," Catherine appealed.

"You see, Catherine, the cause of your infirmity is discovered!" she mocked.

"You blaspheme!" Bridget accused.

"And those who cannot have miracles will ever invent them," Agnes derided. "Oh, Catherine, I beg you be careful. Sister Bridget seeks a martyrdom for you. If you must have a saint, sister, go look at Veronica, for she is nearer to your dreams of perfection."

Thus their contention was sealed once and for all. Bridget busied herself over her bandages, muttering at intervals to herself. Agnes gazed out at her garden. The weather had dulled into drizzle.

Catherine now seated herself at the table. She felt in pain, not only from the physical discomfort she had brought on herself, but from an irrepressible agony that continually scratched at her thoughts. She saw the man and not his Creator. And the shame of it was that she longed to hold on to *his* image, to absorb the lost part of her being and feel whole again. A tinkling sound echoed in the silence. The cord holding his ring round her neck had broken and the ring had slipped and rolled across the floor in circles of unrelieved brilliance. There was nothing of tarnish upon it. Shining as brightly as sun after rain, it was the symbol of everything she had always believed in. Whether God condemned her or not, she would hold fast by the error, glorying in a past happiness which better men called sin. She slowly rose to her feet, intending to retrieve it, but the room swayed back and forth. Agnes and Bridget ran to assist her. The ring, the ring, she must retrieve the ring. The light of it was fading. She must reach it. She must, must ...

Ursula wasted no time. She had been fully expecting such a crisis. Catherine, no longer being in a position to rebuff their concern, Agnes and Bridget made up a bed for her in the infirmary.

"She is weightless," sighed Ursula, as they lifted her on to it. It was so. A bird like fragility was all that remained.

"Tis worse than I thought," said Ursula, as they set about removing the habit from her body.

"We will have to cut it from her," said Agnes matter of factly.

"I fear you are right," Ursula agreed, knowing full well that beneath Agnes's icy exterior lay a very real concern.

Veronica was sent for to assist in the task. Ursula warned her that it would be a painful undertaking, but Veronica only smiled. She had faith in her God. Such faith was lost on Agnes. Her belief was neither submissive nor humble. She only knew that Catherine was suffering as all women suffer. Bridget went to tell the others, her natural way with words assuring her of an appreciative hearing. The mention of the ring gave rise to speculation, but it was generally assumed that it had been worn as a keepsake of her mother. Only Agnes and Ursula knew differently.

While the sisters prayed for her recovery, the three women

worked hard to effect that recovery. It was disagreeable and tiring, but they did not flinch or recoil, a common compassion binding them to the unpleasantness of the task. Their only wish was to see her well again. Once divested of her habit, which had to be cut away in pieces, they washed her body and applied ointment to the sores. Only on removing the coif was the state of her hair fully revealed. They gave out a gasp. Ursula held up her hands despairingly. Veronica was very close to tears. Agnes did the practical thing by getting the shears and hacking away at the knots. Within the space of an hour Catherine was shorn like a sheep.

"We should cleanse her face too," Ursula remarked, swallowing hard. They had never seen her without the mask and though Christianity stressed the precedence of the soul over the body they were human and fearful.

"I will do it," said Agnes.

"Pray, proceed, sister," said Ursula.

By now Catherine's eyes were starting to flicker. It was as if she guessed what they were about and was desperate to prevent it from happening. Her arms struggled ineffectually, such was the power of the mind though it slept. Once it was actually removed she gave up the struggle and sank back into torpor. Not a word was exchanged between the women as they gazed unopposed on the ruin before them. Their reaction was in keeping with Elliston's, initial shock and revulsion overcome by love and concern for the person they knew.

"Tis a face, much as any other," said Agnes at last.

"And dear in its difference," Veronica appended.

"You speak as God directs you," said Ursula approvingly. "She is Catherine and fast in our love."

The crisis lasted for days, her bodily weakness not helped by her morbid condition of mind. Incoherent and feverish, sometimes half awake, mostly asleep, she fought for the right to forget. In her mind she wanted to die and it was only their tender resolve that prevented her from doing so. She had failed in her penitence. Now God would never forgive her transgression. In her rare moments of awareness she appealed to Him again and again not to send her to the hell she deserved. Then she would hear one or other of them whispering words of assurance, Veronica so tender, so gentle, Bridget with her soft Irish lilt, Ursula serene in her care, and lastly, Agnes, unflinching, defiant. Their prayers flowed over her like waves on a beach. And then she would dream, sweetly of Sulburgh.

ᘓ ᘐ

The day was bright with spring sunshine. Warming her face, it folded the scent of flowers into her dreams, and when she awoke a pleasing lethargy made her stretch out her limbs.

"So you have decided to come back to us, Catherine," said Ursula, smiling warmly.

"Reverend Mother, I ..."

"You have been very ill, Catherine, but God has been good and seen fit to return you to us."

God could be so trying at times, she reflected, giving with one hand, only to take away with the other, invariably introducing an element of compromise between the human desire and His will, but He alone knew the right of it, He alone was goodness and He alone was wisdom, and here was an instance where He had seen fit to compassionate their cause and generously accede to their prayers. Ursula was as human as the rest of them, and her faith would have been sorely tried had all their efforts proved in vain.

Catherine reached for her hand, Ursula gave it willingly. She looked around her. There were flowers at the side of the bed; the scent of them was sweet.

"Bluebells, Catherine, the first of the spring, and picked by Sister Agnes to please you."

"How good you have been, Reverend Mother."

"Not at all child."

Gradually she became more and more aware. Touching her face, she accepted the exposure of it much more readily than she would have done had she been well; it was the loss of her hair that she found more upsetting.

"We had to cut it, "Ursula explained, a note of regret in her voice. "And you look, if I may say so, rather engaging, certainly much better than you suppose, but so thin. Why, twould scarce take a hand's span to encircle your waist, but we are all determined to fatten you up. No fasting for you, sister."

Such kindness made Catherine turn away. Once again she was assailed by feelings of guilt, of having no right to the care and concern they had lavished upon her. For nothing of God belonged to her now, neither the gifts of His earth nor the promise of His heaven. She had made of herself a deliberate outcast. She had tried so hard to atone. She had tried so hard to be saved. But she could not deny her feeling for Elliston, for if his was an outworn emotion hers only grew stronger. It was the burden of this that made her fling her arms round Ursula's neck and cry out her soul in a passion of weeping.

"Help me, Mother, I who have been such a burden, I who have no right to call on your care. Death should have claimed me. Tis only oblivion after all. Tell me it is, for heaven is no longer vouchsafed to me and an everlasting torment fills me with dread."

"Catherine, Catherine," Ursula soothed, hugging her close.

"Do you not see," she sobbingly continued, "there is no heaven. It is but a comforting notion to make more bearable the nothingness of death. This abbey is mere stone, cold and icy, built to the glory of a God that does not exist. Tis vanity. There is naught but disillusion in belief." Then she looked up, her eyes bright with conviction. "I sought for my paradise here on earth and I found it. Neither God nor man can tear me away from the dream I so nearly attained."

"Child, child," Ursula coaxed, but she would not be quieted.

"I know it was but a dream, but maybe our lives are composed of our dreams. If dying is but a semblance of sleep, then my fears are assuaged, but if it is not, and there is a God after all, meting out punishment to those who persist in their sin and express no contrition, then I am accursed. You, Reverend Mother, you who would seem to know the secrets of eternity, tell me the meaning of faith."

Thus, she continued in a kind of rambling coherence until Ursula began to grasp at its meaning. "I tried to atone, but I failed. The prayers that came from my lips were not from my heart. What I renounced I still worshipped, and though I longed for forgiveness I held fast by my sin. I have chosen and I cannot retract." She turned aside, her face a blotch of tearful resignation. Ursula stroked the sweat from her brow.

"Catherine, I think it is time that we talked. If you cannot talk to Father Anthony, then maybe you can talk to me, since I am a woman with a woman's understanding."

There was encouragement in her smile and considering the trouble she had caused them Catherine felt she was more than entitled to be given an account of its cause. The bell would chime twice before she had finished. Ursula listened intently, sighing occasionally whenever her cousin's name was mentioned. She also found herself smiling. The sin was not the enormity Catherine had imagined, Francis's exacting code of morality no doubt having worked upon a mind already overwrought by what it had borne.

"How is it that you can be so forbearing?" Catherine said in amazement.

"Because my child. Because ..." She still held Catherine's

hand and patted it reassuringly.

"Reverend Mother!," Catherine appealed.

"Because it is my turn to speak. You say that you have failed in your commitment to God?" Catherine nodded. "Well, is it surprising? Consider the matter as it is. You offered Him hate instead of love. You endeavoured to despise what you formerly loved. Do you think God looks on such penitence with favour? What is He to do with such a confession? Why, it is grosser than the sin for which it purports to atone. Whatever his faults, you loved this man. I suspect you always will. God also loves this man. He will not despise him for your sake. Our God is a compassionate God."

Catherine was confused. She was expecting to be chastised and given a long string of penances.

"I did not presume to hate," she explained, "but as soon as I learned from Father Craven that Lord Elliston had replaced me in his affections with another, I realised that I was mistaken in thinking our love innocent, for now I knew it to be tainted as Father Craven had always insisted. You cannot condone what is tainted. No innocence attaches to it."

"Of course, it cannot be condoned in the letter, Catherine, but what of the heart? Surely it was innocent at heart, that is in your heart at least."

Catherine recoiled. Why was she speaking like this, reading her every thought as if her soul was a visible page whereon everything was written.

"I thought that it was, but I was mistaken," she replied, scarcely daring to glance at her inquisitor.

"Are you sure of that?"

"Yes! Yes!" she rigorously maintained.

"Which compounded your feelings of guilt and remorse, but this was not enough. You wished to undergo a keener contrition, the kind my cousin would no doubt approve. Through self-mortification, you thought to expiate not only your own sin, but that of Lord Elliston's, but in your heart you could neither despise him nor disown the feeling between you. Am I not right?"

"If only I could have been blessed with the looks of the plainest of women," Catherine mournfully reflected, her thoughts suddenly turning askew.

"Catherine, Catherine," Ursula sighed in exasperation. "Such self-pity ill becomes you. No man takes a woman for her pleasing face alone, and if he does, he is a fool, and from what I have gathered Lord Elliston is no fool."

"But a pleasing face is an asset," Catherine insisted.

"Naturally, but there are other assets to be prized far above it, assets which in you are not deficient, and if nature takes away with one hand, she always bestows with the other, and since God is in all things it is for us to determine how we use those assets to reflect a little of Him. God gave us free will Catherine; what we do with it depends on how much we genuinely love Him.

Catherine became silent. Ursula was as persuasive as her cousin, but in an entirely different way. Unlike Craven, she was not lacking in humility to make allowances for the failings of others, and for the first time in months Catherine felt herself relieved of the terrible burden she had made herself carry.

"You were very close to your mother, so Francis tells me," Ursula continued.

"Yes."

"And if I recollect, she too was deserted by your father."

Catherine nodded. "And did you ever hear her speak of your father in anger."

"No, Reverend Mother. I believe her love was unwavering."

"As is yours Catherine. God wants your honesty Catherine. He wants your happiness too. There are many kinds of love. All have their time and their place. Only God's love is forever enduring. Acknowledging this is to be humble before Him. My cousin would do well to learn this one essential truth. I know you love God, Catherine, but this does not prevent you from loving Lord Elliston. Come now, no tears."

She clasped Catherine to her.

"May I stay at St. Mary's, take my vows?"

"We turn no one away, Catherine, but ask yourself, is this really what you want? Better still, ask of God."

"I am content with what I now have," she maintained.

"Devote yourself to getting well first, and then we will think of the future. And Catherine?"

"Yes, Reverend Mother?"

"Do try to look a little more worldly."

CHAPTER THIRTY ONE

Geoffrey regarded his own strips of land and those of his friend with justifiable concern. It was a dismal sight, days of heavy rain having reduced the three great fields to three muddy lakes, the water from which was only now beginning to recede. Two oxen were all that remained of the livestock, and the men were losing heart. Eve took his hand and squeezed it reassuringly. Under her care he had regained the appearance of a man and his reason was all but restored. Defying the conventions of their neighbours, they now lived openly together, uncaring of what anyone said, save Father Craven who reminded them daily of the sanctity of wedlock. But Geoffrey had every reason to be circumspect. Having lost so much through the first union, he was reluctant to hazard a second. Eve was not pressing. At first she had loved him as a child, but with the clearing of his wits as a man. In their separate ways, they had suffered too much to be confident of the future. To live one day at a time brought problems enough. The land was their main concern, most of it still lying untended, and along with their neighbours, that is the few that were left, they were struggling to survive. With Elliston's return, they had hoped for some betterment, but they might as well have looked for cuckoos in winter. From the time he learned of Catherine's death, he became a man without purpose, full of self-pity and immune to the needs of his land or the tenants who tried to maintain it. Flitting from one empty pleasure to another, none brought him solace and once again it was left to Burgoyne to shoulder the burden at a time when he could have done with the strength and support of a younger man to assist him. Too much was expected of him and he was tired of being taken for granted. The plague years had robbed him of energy; they had also taken his son.

This day in particular had gone badly. One of the free men had left to go elsewhere in pursuit of higher wages. Since the plague it was now common practice. The insufficiency of labour was enabling men to bargain for their services in a way that they had never been able to before. Others doubled their precious strips of earth by acquiring those of their deceased neighbours, nothing more being required of them than a willingness to continue working their lord's land. There was little in the way of commutation for labour any more, so desperate were the lords of large domains to hold on to their peasants. Geoffrey Frincham had been one of the last obliged to purchase his freedom on Elliston's domain and those, like Elliston, who resisted the new ways only fostered resentment.

"What am I to do?" Burgoyne said, wearily tapping the table with his fingers.

Margaret looked at him anxiously. Ever conscious of her inadequacy, following the death of her son she felt herself even less capable of lending him any practical help, much as she longed to be of some comfort.

"If you were to speak to Lord Elliston," she suggested softly. With her woman's intuition, she had realised what the loss of a woman like Catherine would mean to a man of his uncertain humour. She herself had been deeply distressed. In every book she read there were echoes of Catherine Venners, remarks she had made in regard to some passage, illuminated pictures for which she had expressed a special liking, even the book marks she had so carefully inserted when called to her duties. If these things recalled her so vividly to mind, what must the sum of memories recall to him who had cherished her as a wife.

"Clearly, you know not what you ask Margaret. Trying to reason with Elliston is like trying to reason with the devil."

"If only Catherine ..." she began, tearfully abandoning the sentence.

"If! If!" he threw back at her. "There are too many ifs in this world."

"I test your patience I know," she replied, still on the verge of tears, "but what will become of the land? Who will be left to continue the Elliston line?"

"Not him, I'd venture. He is only fit for whores now!"

"But we must try, husband. We must."

"I am tired, Margaret. Tired, tired, tired."

But he did as she asked. A few torches cast their meagre light in the corridor. Most of the servants had died or been disposed of, apart from two slatterns who trundled inedible platters of food from the dirt of the kitchen. A state of neglect was being encouraged. It was a blessing that old Lady Elliston was not alive to see it. Burgoyne was not a man who easily lost his temper, but on finding Elliston fondling one of his women he gave way to it now.

"Get rid of her!" he said, without even addressing Elliston formally.

Elliston merely laughed, sending her forth with a slap.

"Why so censorious Sir Edward. A man must have his pleasures."

"I thank God above that your pleasures and mine are distinctly dissimilar."

"That is where we differ Sir Edward. My gratitude to God is non-existent."

Without wasting any further time, Burgoyne thrust some documents into his hand relating to the parlous state of his domain.

"So?" he weakly replied, returning the papers without even glancing at them.

"Is that all you have to say, my lord, but then why should I feign any degree of surprise. A pig that wallows in its swill is hardly susceptible to reason."

"Sir Edward, I should forbear if I were you. On this occasion, I shall forgive your insolence because I see you are tetchy and overwrought. Anyway, what have I done to merit such chagrin?"

Pouring out wine, he handed a cup to Burgoyne. Burgoyne took it, but his mood remained distant and disaffected.

"We have all suffered, my lord, but none more so than the people in our care, nay, your care." Elliston attempted to speak, but Burgoyne refused to be silenced. "But we try not to wallow, my lord. We do not sink. We rise above the flood of experience. We act like men and let God do the rest."

"I never thought you inclined to the poetical Sir Edward," he cryptically replied. "Pray continue. Your flood of experience, your God, they intrigue me. Teach me to know their significance, Sir Edward. I am listening."

"Here is your meaning, my lord," he said, taking up one of the discarded documents and thrusting it under his nose.

"The name Frincham occurs with some frequency, I grant you. I seem to remember this is the man who finally bought his freedom?"

"Yes, my lord, tis so, for all the good it has done him. Frincham is distantly related to ..." Burgoyne, suddenly pausing, looked awkward.

"Say it, Sir Edward. Does it pain you so much to speak it as it does me to hear it?"

"I ought not to have ..."

"Sir Edward," he said, rising to his feet. "A moment past I was damned in your eyes. Now you speak softly and petition me sweetly."

Suddenly their eyes met in the old way. Burgoyne was again sympathetic.

"Frincham is related to Catherine Venners. Since her uncle's death, he has striven to tend Thompson's land as well as his own. He is a good man, my lord, and deserving of all the succour we can lend him. There are others too who are greatly deserving of our support. My lord, your domain is wasting away for lack of labour, and I am helpless to remedy it without your approval. I fully share your belief in the old ways, but times are different now. The price of labour is high, but we have to afford it. I believe it is what Mistress Venners would have wanted, my lord, she who helped them most in their affliction. They were her people, my lord. They are yours too. Succour them now for the love of Sweet Jesu. I am an old man, my lord, but I would rather leave your service than live to see Runnarth of no account. I can no longer cope alone. I need a man's strength to aid me. I have want of you, my lord."

Elliston held out his hand. He was close to tears.

"You make a fine appellant, Sir Edward."

"I have had occasion to practice, my lord."

"Do not leave me, old friend. As ever, you utter good sense. Do anything you think meet. For her alone we will put Runnarth aright. This man Frincham?"

"My lord?"

"Place him at the head of our priorities. Tomorrow I will view the extent of the need for myself."

"Thank you, my lord," he said, taking his hand. Margaret had been right to ask him to try one more time. He must not forget to tell her of the fact.

Elliston kept his word. Indeed, he adopted the cause with the same reserves of energy he had formerly applied to empty pursuits. Nothing was spared to bring Runnarth back to how it was before the plague. He laboured alongside his tenants, even ploughing his own team of oxen. They marvelled at the change.

And everything he did was shaped by her, the sky above, the earth beneath, the very air he breathed. She was in his waking and in his sleeping and in the very dreams he dreamed and the haunting was sweet.

With June came the roses and a scent of remembrance that hurt. Much against Ursula's advice, Catherine had resumed her duties in full. She was tired of being a burden and was anxious to repay the kindness of the women in any way she could. The daily routine of the order would help to occupy her mind and strengthen her body, or so she believed, and she had resolved to spend the rest of her days there. No task was too menial, all her work being undertaken with a zeal over and above what was needful. Most of them thought her recovery complete, but there were those who knew better like Ursula and Agnes. To them, it was plain that she chose to be cheerful and that the effort was wasting her strength. Though her appetite had improved, the habit still hung on her body. Of her own state of mind, she took no account. She thought she was happy. But sometimes on mild summer evenings when she found herself alone in the garden the old dream would threaten to haunt her again, but now she felt free to indulge it, together with all the sense of regret it occasioned. Then would come the strange sob in her throat which she accounted a weakness. With her future secured at St. Mary's she felt it ill became her to waste tears on the past.

It was on one such evening that Ursula came to a decision. Approaching Catherine in the garden, there was no disguising the anguish she saw in her face. It stared out at Ursula like a rebuke.

"Do not stay too long Catherine. The nights soon become chilly," she said, resuming her walk as if nothing untoward had occurred.

The following day Ursula announced that she was going on a pilgrimage which would necessitate her being away for several days. She had little further to say, other than it was a decision taken on impulse and one she could not delay. They were not to worry on her account, but to look to the well being of the order during her absence. The women were naturally puzzled. Never having left them before, they were concerned for her safety, but she only smiled at them indulgently, which meant that her mind was made up and that there was nothing they could say or do to deter her.

The early mist of morning lay soft on the hills as she started out on her journey. She gave the sisters her blessing. Some of them were weeping. Others suggested she carry a stick. What did they think her, a beldame, she said! As for a crutch, her two feet would suffice.

"Pray God, I am not on a fool's errand," she sighed, once they were well out of sight.

Reaching the highway, the day barely brightened, and she

listened carefully for the rumble of wheels. As she had surmised, it was the proper day and the proper time. Coming out of the mist, Seldon sat atop the cart, cracking the whip in time to the song he bellowed forth. Ursula put out her hand to stop him.

"What is this then, Mother?" he asked. "Another letter for ye cousin?"

"No, tis not a letter," she replied, assuming her most gracious demeanour. "I would ask of you a favour, Master Seldon. I wish you to take me to Runnarth. It is a matter of some moment concerning my cousin." He looked at her closely, but Ursula was not the kind of woman to be intimidated. "Well, Master Seldon?"

"Does your cousin expect you?" he enquired, fearing to incur the priest's rancour, especially since they had made the bargain together.

"No, he does not, but as I said it does greatly concern him. Master Seldon, to speak plainly, it is not a matter that can be conveyed in a letter."

"I see," he replied, stroking his beard. On reflection it appeared a reasonable enough request and he was not one to forgo the opportunity of a little company that might relieve the tedium of the journey, even if it was a woman of years and a Reverend Mother at that. "Climb up, Mother, I will take ye."

The horses lunged and the cart rattled forward. He struck up another song and she said a prayer. Eventually the weather brightened and the moors emerged from the mist bathed in sunlight.

"Twould seem the weather be smilin' on ye mother?"

"Verily," she replied.

Allowing for the customary stay overnight in Durham, they reached Runnarth on the following evening. The weather was now deteriorating into drizzle and a dense veil of mist was obscuring the hills.

"I wish to be put down here Master Seldon, if you please," she said as they drew near to the castle.

He reined in the horse and looked at her keenly.

"I thought you wished to see your cousin. By my reckonin', it be a mile or two yet."

"I do, but I have other business to attend to first. Now if you will kindly assist me."

"As you will. It be more to my likin' anyway. I can turn me back to Bardwick. There'll be summat o' cheer there I'm thinkin', eh Mother!"

The drizzle was matting his beard, a thin lipped grin widening his mouth at the pleasure in prospect. She took up her bundle, and with his assistance climbed down. The creak in her knees was audible.

"I thank you Master Seldon, but before we part I would have you know that I am neither your mother, God pity her for her pains, nor your good woman, though I pray you'll find such a one ere long."

"I'll think on it Mo ..."

"Do!"

CHAPTER THIRTY TWO

"The woman is insistent my lord," said Burgoyne, wearing his habitual look of long suffering like a tried and trusted garment.

Elliston looked ahead of him sullenly. Cold and fatigued, he was not in a humour for idle conversation, this being the fourth such occasion on which Sir Edward had interrupted him with some tale of an abbess who would not take no for an answer.

"Damn the woman!" he muttered between gritted teeth. Dressed in the garb of a labourer, his nails were ingrained with the dirt of such toil; the light from the fire blazed in his eyes which had the burnt in look of a man consumed by one thought. All that he said he would do, he had done. Runnarth was beginning to prosper again. The fields were looking neat and productive and the villagers were moderately content. He had employed three or four labourers to help in the task, despite the high wages they asked. His conscience was eased, but the peace of mind he had hoped to find in the doing of it was as far removed as ever. Where was his prize, where his reward for doing God's will? Where God come to that? Fear of evenings alone no longer oppressed him. The dark was his solace, filling his mind with the light of a happier time.

"My lord, what am I to tell her?" Burgoyne continued.

"Tell her to go to hell!"

"My lord," he appealed. "She is a woman of God."

"So?"

"I did suggest that she leave the gist of the matter with me, but she still persists that her news is of such a nature that it is pertinent only to yourself."

"Impertinent!" he flung out, venting his ire on Burgoyne for want of anyone else.

Burgoyne drew his hand across his forehead in an attitude of extreme vexation. He could hardly see for tiredness and his legs began to totter.

"Forgive me," Elliston said, grabbing him by the arm and easing him into a chair. Burgoyne took it willingly.

"Let me get you some wine."

"Thank you, my lord," he replied. "Tis vexing, this onset of years."

"To your health, Sir Edward," he said raising his own cup.

"And to yours, my lord," he replied, doing likewise.

"Doleful toasts both, eh?"

"I am getting old, my lord, that is my excuse."

"False modesty, and you know it. Where would I have been without your consistent good counsel, more likely than not floundering in that pig swill of a mire you spoke of so eloquently."

Burgoyne's face relaxed into a smile. The wine warmed his spirits. It was a night for the telling of friendship and Elliston took hold of his hand, gripping it tightly?

"You know tis not for them that I've striven!"

"Perhaps not, my lord, but in doing it for her you do it for them. Tis one and the same."

The words appeared to have a soothing effect, though Burgoyne could tell that he was still continuing to wrestle with the imponderabilities of existence.

"What is it all for, Sir Edward, eh?"

"All, my lord?"

"Aye. Life, for want of a better description."

"You need a philosopher, my lord, not a simple plodder like myself."

"Then God grant us plodders," Elliston asseverated, raising high his cup.

"And the lady abbess, my lord?" he reminded.

"You say she refuses to leave?"

"She is adamant, my lord."

"Then I suppose I must needs speak with her. My evening companioned by a nun! These are strange times, Burgoyne," he said, slapping him upon the shoulder. "Go fetch me this virago in a habit."

So Ursula had her way, and quite an impression she made, notwithstanding her years and the length of her journey. He was set on being sullen, but the pleasantness evinced in her smile overcame his detachment, she employing it to such good effect that it almost made him feel timid. In a word, she nonplussed him. Were all nuns like this, he reflected? Did God indeed bring such joy to his spouses?

"Pray be seated. I hear you have travelled far and have something of import to tell me," he heard himself saying. Already it seemed as if she had reduced him to playing the host, making him forgetful of the intrusion and the graceless hour at which she had sought to inveigle her way into his presence. He even gave her his customary place by the fire, the flames lighting up his face for her benefit. She, sitting in shadow, could scrutinise him the better. In an instant she could see the nature of the attraction between Catherine Venners and this man, that lovely alliance of opposites that helps keep the savour in wedlock. She noticed how her calling caused him unease. He rarely looked at her, twiddling his fingers and folding his body into awkward positions.

"It is true that I have something of importance to relate concerning yourself. I think you should know that Francis Craven is my cousin." She heard his involuntary groan of dissent, but was in no way perturbed. It was, after all, what she had expected. "Lord Elliston I have travelled a great distance for a woman of my years." She had found that age can be a positive boon in pleading one's case, indeed the only one that readily sprung to mind. "My news is bound to distress you. But I know it will hearten you too. I pray you be calm. It is of Catherine Venners that I wish to speak." The effect on him was immediate. There was no mistaking the feeling he had for her. It blazed up in his eyes like a flame in a fire. "She who loves you dearly, my lord."

His breath seemed to be impeded. What news did she bring him. What news could she possibly bring him. In that look, she saw what she feared; that her cousin had lied.

"Loves," he repeated dully, his accent on the present tense. Then he was irked and distressed all at one and the same time. Who was this woman anyway, that she should come to torment him with talk of the dead. That she was related to Craven should have been sufficient to dispose him against her, but there was something more to it than that.

"Should it not be loved, Reverend Mother," he replied with the underlying bitterness of a man dispossessed. No doubt, it is Francis Craven who has prompted your visit, though I find it hard to believe that his charity would extend to me in any guise, so what profundity of knowledge do you propose to expound?" His speech became forcibly sneering, but she did not trouble to interrupt it. "A life everlasting? Some blessed abode where she and I will be reunited and never know sorrow? Is that what you would have me believe in? Well, let me tell you now, I have long lost such faith. I would have her here with me now, not in some airy fairy hereafter I know not the meaning of. Come, Reverend Mother, enlighten me as to what you would have me believe."

When she failed to reply immediately, he sprang to his feet, seething and ashen.

"I would have you calmer, Lord Elliston," she eventually replied, whereupon he sat down again, aghast at her presumption. "What I have to say is not easy and even less so for you who have to hear it. You speak of wanting Catherine now. Well, you shall have her. Contrary to what you have been led to believe, Catherine is not dead, but is alive and residing within my order of women at St. Mary's Abbey. You have been the victim of a cruel and needless deception.

"You jest! You trifle!" he cried, gripping the arms of the chair, but still remaining seated, for in spite of his quick accusations there was nothing in her bearing to suggest that she was not speaking the truth. And why would she lie to him anyway, not that he allowed himself to be taken in by the fact that because she was a bride of Christ she was bound to tell the truth. In his experience, it was the simplest thing in Christendom to put on the robes of religion and dissemble as much as the next man. Indeed, many of the clergy were more hypocritical than those they professed to direct. But the news was so startling that he permitted her to continue in silence.

"She is alive Lord Elliston. Francis Craven is my cousin, God pity him, and it is he who has sought to deceive you, and indeed Catherine, but, worse still, he has deceived himself, thereby relinquishing the trust of those who rely on his guidance."

"Craven!" he cried, as if the word and the man were as one. He was about to spring to his feet, but sat back with his hand over his mouth, too shocked to speak further.

"Shall I continue, my lord," she asked "or would you prefer that I left you a while."

"Proceed," he said, almost inaudibly.

"Catherine is a novitiate at our nunnery, where she has been a valued and much loved member of our order for nearly two years. No doubt, you will have heard of the circumstances surrounding Catherine's return to the village, of her selfless devotion to the needs of her family when the plague was at its height, of how she and my cousin tried to succour the villagers in their time of most need. Other things may have been kept from you."

Moving his hand away from his lips, he glanced up at her.

"I believe there is a woman in the village who goes by the name of Mother Jomfrey, an evil minded woman by all accounts."

He nodded.

"Annie deserted her family when they were dying to live with this woman. For reasons of which you are already aware, Annie bore a grudge against Catherine, and together, she and this Jomfrey woman, conspired to make a scapegoat of Catherine by accusing her of having a hand in the plague. Many of the people believed it."

Now he did leap to his feet, his vanity wounded.

"Those weak minded fools I have succoured for her sake. Oh what a jest God has made of my pains!"

"Consider their plight, my lord. Such times discover the best in men, but also the worst. And some will grasp at anything to make sense of the misery they endure. Those who differ in any way from the rest, such as Catherine, are easily suspect. Francis did what he could to hush their wild clamour and because he was their priest, they were inclined to ..."

"Craven is a fiend!" he interrupted, dashing everything from the table with a sweep of his hand. "A fiend, God damn him!"

Ursula stayed seated, her heart thumping, as a plate rolled towards her feet. The clatter seemed to calm him. She was surprised that he had managed to stay calm for so long. He turned to look at her.

"Go on. Go on."

"If you are ..."

"Go on!"

"Being their priest they were inclined to place their trust in him, but the Jomfrey woman had played on their superstitions and Francis thought it wise for Catherine to leave, as did her uncle, until such time as it was deemed safe for her to return. Thus, it was that she came to us at St. Mary's. Francis had led me to believe that she had a natural vocation, which of course we know is not so. She was honest and told me as much. Worse was to come following the death of her uncle as it left my cousin free to do as he willed, or knowing my cousin as I do, he would see it as doing what God willed. Francis is sick, Lord Elliston, grievously sick." Here she paused, finding herself in the unenviable position of having to mediate on behalf of her cousin. Elliston sat rigid. "Now you must bear with the hardest part of my story and, pray God, you will find it in your heart to reserve a measure of pity for a man sick in spirit. My cousin, as you know, had always wanted Catherine for Christ, and had it not been for you I believe she would have eventually seen the benefits of such a life. But you spoiled it for him, my lord, you who seemed to represent everything of which he was most envious in his sex, the ability to love and be loved. With her uncle dead and Catherine safely with us, he was tempted to tell an untruth, persuading himself that it was not so much a temptation as a directive from his Saviour. It was only by chance that she learned of your return. Puzzled as we both were, I wrote to my cousin, who sensing his plan under threat, arrived at St. Mary's within a day or two of receiving my letter. Only recently has Catherine told me what passed during their interview. May I have some water, Lord Elliston." He gave her wine instead, thinking that if ever woman was deserving of it, she was.

"I fear that the worst is yet to be told?" he remarked as she took sips of the reviving liquid.

"Your fear is well founded. Catherine trusted my cousin, Lord Elliston. It was only natural that she should, for had he not helped her in the past, been anxious for her welfare at a time when she found herself virtually friendless. She had no reason to doubt what he told her."

"Which was?"

"That your affections had changed, in a word that it was your intention to marry."

"Blessed Jesu!" he sighed, putting his hands to his eyes. Ursula gently laid her hand on his arm, but for all her concern she realised that there was no way in which she could cushion the facts. She only wished that there was.

"If only she had told me sooner, I might have prevented her from suffering as she did, but she kept it from us. Confronted by your supposed desertion and the feeling of guilt engendered by my cousin, her spirit began to break. In matters of conscience, Francis can be very persuasive and Catherine was quite at his mercy. How was she to think dispassionately, my lord, when everything she had believed in was suddenly sundered. He showed her the way, the only way, and she took it, believing it to be her only hope of salvation." Elliston slumped at the table and sobbed. "She fasted to excess in atonement for her sin, the sin of affection for you, but it brought her no peace. Torn between her commitment to you and her commitment to God, her mind and spirit were unequal to the burden of guilt placed upon them." Again she paused out of feeling for the man. There was no stopping the well of emotion her story occasioned. "She sickened, and for a time we feared for her life, but thankfully God heard our prayers and she was restored to us."

"Tell me she is no longer in danger," he wept, his hands drawn away from his face so that she could now see the full extent of his suffering.

"No, my lord, she is not. So far as her debility of body is

concerned, we are greatly encouraged, but her spiritual well being is still of concern to us, and it is this and her continuing want of real contentment, combined with my growing suspicion of Francis, that has brought me to Runnarth. I can only thank God for his prompting."

"Damn Craven! Damn him!" he cried in his agony.

"Come now," she urged, kneeling beside him as Catherine herself was wont to do. "We have spoken much of you, and I do now believe that she has learned to reconcile her commitment to you with that of her commitment to God, although she knows nothing of my visit and still believes you estranged which is sufficient proof of her constancy. Of necessity I had to conceal my purpose under the guise of a pilgrimage, just in case my instincts proved faulty. Be assured, her lethargy of spirit will now soon be mended."

"And I believed her dead in some pit. The villagers believed it. Everyone believed it. Your precious cousin had given them to understand that she had been taken ill while tending to a sick woman near Bardwick. No-one exactly knew where. He did not even allow me a grave over which I could grieve. Oh, God, what sort of man can he be!"

"A suffering one, my lord. And although I plead no defence on his behalf where you are concerned, none being merited, I would ask you to bear in mind the good he has shown to the people in his care. For this alone, I pray you will find it in your heart to show him a little compassion." He could see she was in earnest, but wished to hear no more of Craven, either in this world or the next, and she knew better than to press him. He took her left hand, kissing the ring on her finger.

"I have rarely given way to tears in the presence of a woman," he said, "but I am totally unmanned and ask your indulgence."

"You have it, Lord Elliston. From infinite suffering comes infinite joy, for God will never suffer a wrong to go unrighted."

He was all for starting out at once, but she bade him be patient. "It has been a testing time for both of us, and my bones are in need of repose. Remember too that Catherine knows nothing of this, and I would prepare her first before you see her. The good lord has brought us this far. He will not disappoint you now."

He did as she wished, though naturally everything within him railed against it.

The morning broke softly, the promise of sunshine discerned through the haze. Having hardly slept, he still felt more refreshed than he had in many a month. Dressing hurriedly, he called for Burgoyne.

"Is it not a supremely fine day?" he enthused, pointing to the misty prospect, his manner buoyant and over excited.

"It augurs fair, my lord," Burgoyne replied, scratching his brow, for the unremarkable change in the weather could hardly account for the remarkable change in the man.

"And so it should. Why so solemn, my friend. This is a day above the ordinary. Tis a blessed day. A day to rival days."

"If you say so, my lord."

"Oh Sir Edward, life is too short, and your serious aspect sits ill with my pleasure. Go see to our guest at once. No, wait."

Burgoyne turned, a look of bemusement on his face.

"I have to tell you now, Sir Edward. Tis a miracle, a miracle."

Ursula had slept soundly, content in the knowledge that her pilgrimage had been a success. Indeed, she thanked God for it, but her joy was not without sorrow, and when she prayed it was principally for her cousin. Seated at the window of the unfamiliar room, her recollections were of him. She thought back to the time when they were children. Even then, he had been a withdrawn and solitary child, reserved and remote, always holding back from the rough and tumble of the games the others enjoyed. An only child, he had spent many summers with her family. Her two brothers disliked him, looking on his presence as a necessary encumbrance that had to be borne, but mercifully not forever. To them he appeared a sour tempered child who refused to dirty his girlish white hands and it was left to her to keep him amused, that is assuming it was possible to amuse a child like Francis. For his part he resented these visits as much as they did, but it was his mother who insisted upon them, she being widowed from an early age and finding him singularly difficult to deal with. It was not that he was in any way a naughty or disobedient child, but a very self-absorbed one who found it hard to inspire or show affection. He did not make friends or appear to want them, devoting all of his time to his books. His father had been an educated man and his mother likewise, but they were warm hearted people who knew the value of kindness over learning, whereas their child appeared to see nothing beyond it, except for a devotion to the church which was more intellectual than loving. He had not been a child to be hugged or made a fuss of. Ursula remembered one instance in particular when after falling and bruising himself, his mother had gathered him up in her arms and ruffled his hair, only to be met with his fist in her face and the demand that she put him down at once. From this rebuff she never quite recovered. By contrast, Ursula had been an extremely loving child, and his seeming isolation made her feel sorry for him. She tried to take him under her wing, sisterly like, and because she had an interest in books he was willing to tolerate her, albeit in a condescending sort of way. Poor Francis, reserving his love for God alone, having little or none for those He had made in His image, until the lack of it totally ate him up. Now it seemed that she alone was left to salvage the good in him.

She found Elliston eager to start.

"My lord, if I might speak"

"Speak away."

"If we might delay the start of the journey."

"Why so!" he exclaimed, turning a baleful eye upon her.

"I realise your eagerness to commence, but I would beg your restraint for a little while longer."

"Restraint," he replied, looking at her guardedly.

Fearing that his happiness might get in the way of her purpose, she began immediately in the hope that at least he would give her the hearing she craved.

"It is a matter of the deepest concern to myself."

"Proceed," he said curtly, as if he already guessed the nature of that concern and resented it fiercely.

"I wish to speak with my cousin." His look became bitter and hard, but then he relented.

"Reverend Mother, you have restored the meaning to my life, and although I grudge the matter in hand it would ill become me not to grant it. I am, after all, in your debt."

She smiled graciously, a trifle conciliatory too. Yes, this was the only man worthy of a woman like Catherine.

"I thank you, my lord. It means much to me. I know that there is little I can say in my cousin's defence as regards yourself. He has caused you to suffer and knowingly so. But I believe that I can still plead for him as a man who has kept faith with his people in a time of uncertainty and suffering."

"So, you would have me feign tears, cry over his so called virtues as well as his grave misdemeanours. Well I cannot. Forgiveness does not come that easily to my nature. I cannot speak for Catherine, only myself. Where the heart is concerned, she is made of more malleable stuff than I am."

Ursula hesitated to say anything further. His restive mood was becoming more marked, the line of his mouth more rigid and set.

"There is something else?" he enquired.

"I would ask of you a favour, my lord."

"Go on. What rancour I exhibit is not towards you, merely for your kin."

"As you will. It is simply this. Let not my cousin's wrong doing become common knowledge. Think of the harm it would do him in the eyes of those people who honour and respect him, let alone the harm it would do to himself. Permit him a little dignity in the knowledge of the past good he has done. In these troubled times things often happen awry and it would mean much to me if it can be so arranged that my cousin was misinformed as regards Catherine's death."

The corners of his mouth began to tremble as he glowered at her darkly.

"I cannot credit what I hear! Practice deceit in return for deceit, perjure the truth for the sake of an honour sufficiently tarnished already. A strange sort of request to issue from the lips of an avowed bride of Christ!"

"Strange maybe, but an untruth I believe that God would approve."

"I see. Sophistry in religion, the recourse of a doubtful belief."

Ursula grew hot, her own temper rising.

"And lack of it, the resort of the cynic," she countered.

He had not expected such a rebuke. It provoked him to laughter when he had meant to be stern and as a result saw the ire in her own face relax.

"I would say we are quits, my lord," she said, returning his glee with a wry look of humour.

The silence that followed was long and earnest. It was a time to weigh matters and reflect on the outcome. She could see the inward struggle he underwent, his predilection for vengeance on the one hand as opposed to the promptings of conscience on the other.

"Is it what she would want?" he asked at last.

"I believe that it is."

"Then so be it. Now go speak to Craven, the sooner, the better."

CHAPTER THIRTY THREE

Provided with a small escort. she soon arrived in the village. Her arrival was noted, but not remarked upon with any degree of interest. But when one of them asked in passing who she was and she told them, their attitude changed, as if the notion of her kinship to Craven called for a conscious show of deference on their part. Obviously, the mere mention of her cousin's name provoked in them a rather chilling note of respect. Becoming a little irritated in the face of their ever increasing solicitude, she was tempted to tell them that she was Ursula on a nag and not Christ on a donkey.

It was noon and time was languishing in the soft summer haze. Bees sucked at the flowers in Craven's garden and within the vicinity of the church it was peaceful and calm. She knocked at the door and quietly entered. He sat at the desk, his long fingered hands lying prone upon a book which as yet remained unopened. Even in the short time since his interview with Catherine, he had visibly aged. What had it cost him, if anything at all? She wondered. He looked what he was, solitary and alone, detached from the reality of his own life or the lives of those over whom he exerted such influence, the inward looking child having grown into the self-absorbed man. In contrasting what he was with what he might have been, she could only feel regret. But for his vanity of spirit and his inability to make himself humble before God and men, he might have attained what he wished, the measure of sanctity that makes men into saints. It was a dreadful waste.

"Francis."

She spoke his name softly. It was not her intention to stand in judgement, just to guide him to a realisation of the truth. Glancing up, he knew that it was all over with him.

"Why Ursula, what a ..."

"Surprise?" she assisted.

She noticed how his eyes seemed to retreat into the dark of their hollows, empty, resigned, lost to the light.

"Yes, you are discovered Francis, and tis bitter for us both."

Rising from the desk, he went to close the door, thus shutting out the light. The room was shaded like dusk, but somehow it seemed more fitting to talk in the gloom. Like Catherine, she experienced a keen sense of chill, much more akin to autumn than the summery weather outside. Resuming his own seat at the desk, he bade her be seated, she facing him across it as Catherine and her uncle had done on that memorable evening so many months ago.

"You do not see things as I do Ursula, but you will. What I did for Catherine Venners, I did for her good and to the glory of God. I did what He instructed me to do, and who am I to disobey the dictates of my Saviour."

"What Saviour Francis? To whom do you pray?"

His eyes looked away and his fingers began to tap on the book. It was his consciousness that she probably knew him better than anyone else that moved him to feeling.

"I obeyed the will of God. I had to protect her," he equivocated."

"From what did you have to protect her Francis? From Elliston?"

"No!" he cried out in denial.

"Or was it from any man who threatened to take her away from you?"

He did not answer. He felt she was being unnecessarily cruel. Tears brimmed up in his eyes. She saw their latent shine and detected the throb in his voice. With lightning perspicacity she had laid bare the truth, seen into his heart as no one else could, forced him to acknowledge what before he had refused to admit and watched his face pucker.

"Close confined in a nunnery and shut away from what she held most dear. Tis a poor deliverance, Francis."

She did not want to speak thus. She did not want to hurt him. But if she was to help him at all, then she had to make him receptive to the truth. In his agitation, his hand swept the table, just as Elliston's had done. The book fell to the floor with a thud. Had she been one of his flock, he would have crushed her with a glance, but she was his woman cousin, the only person on earth with intellect sufficient to reach out and touch him.

"Catherine was pure and innocent," he spluttered, "but he had to sully her. She was not fitted for any man, only to ..."

A choking sensation came into his throat. The spittle frothed out on his lips.

"You Francis! You!" she accused.

He felt faint. If it was a dream and she the apparition, then

God grant he would quickly awaken.

"Jesu, Jesu," he mumbled incoherently, clawing his face.

What words of comfort could she give him? Few, if any. She had done what she had to. In time, this alone might bring its own form of healing. For how many years must the feeling have lain dormant within him? For how many years had he tried to suppress it?

"Francis," she said softly, thinking it better had he openly wept. "What strange manner of love did you feel? Not the usual kind of love betwixt a man and a woman I warrant. Neither the love of a father for his child. What then, I pray?"

Not knowing himself, he could not provide her with a satisfactory answer, but at least she was glad that she had brought him to an awareness of the fact, for in it lay his help. When he uncovered his face his features were blank of emotion, but having made him see she was satisfied that the repression of years could no longer be buried.

"Francis, I pray you reprehend the deed, but not the feeling that gave rise to it. God will assist you in this. Elliston has given me his word that what you have done will not be disclosed because he believes, as I do, that it is what Catherine would want. He cannot forgive you. Of necessity, Catherine must be told, but her heart is a loving one as you very well know, and I believe that in time she will learn to forgive you." She was careful to spare him the knowledge of Catherine's illness, feeling that for the present he had enough with which to occupy his mind. "You are no different from other men Francis. God knows our capacity for good, as equally as he knows our capacity for evil. He loves each and every one of us. Our individuality is special to him. He wants only our good. Tis not for us to confuse God's will with that of our own. He only prompts what is right. Other promptings are those of our own selfish nature. Listen for Him Francis. He understands us as no one else can, and He will always be there to forgive us. Pray with me now."

He stayed silent, dismissing her call to prayer with a crook of his finger. Then in a loud voice he cried, "I believe! I believe!"

It was his witness to faith, but in it she detected his witness to failure as well. Picking up the book, she placed it before him. His hands flipped through its pages in an abstracted fashion. She chose this as her moment to leave.

"I shall go from Runnarth," he said. "For some time now, I have been thinking of entering a monastery where I can devote myself more fully to God."

"As you will, Francis. The villagers will miss you, but I doubt that you will miss them. Will you write to me? We are both growing older and our ties of kindred should bind us."

"I know little of kindred," he replied, "but, yes, I will write."

She thanked him, beseeching him to remember her in his prayers, as she would remember him in hers.

"I shall pray as I have always done," he said.

"Then for your sake, Francis, I pray you let Him take the burden."

Closing the door on the shade, she entered the sunlight. He did not write nor did she see him again.

CHAPTER THIRTY FOUR

Elliston would brook no further delay. Be the weather fair or foul the journey had to commence on the following morning. Restless and impatient, it was almost as if he doubted the veracity of what Ursula had told him and must have his miracle confirmed before he could actually believe in it. His behaviour was irrational if impassioned. Alternating between extremes of elation and rage, it leant all he said and did a curious fervour, from the string of oaths and commands thrown out at Burgoyne to the sullen periods of silence that followed. Although there was nothing consistent in his speech it made its own sort of logic, or at least it was a logic with which Burgoyne was familiar. In giving precedence to their efforts on the land the household had tended to take second place and it was up to Sir Edward to bring it into a state of repair fit to greet her.

"It is a difficult task you set me, my lord," he ventured to say with a slightly worried air.

"But you can do it Sir Edward. You can do it," Elliston maintained. "It has to be done!"

Such conviction was touching and Burgoyne had not the heart to contradict him. Moreover, he was well practiced in the art of the impossible. Margaret gazed up at him wistfully as they watched the small party leave the castle, streams of hazy sunshine washing its path in the first light of dawn.

"I feel as if I too want to live again," she whispered, resting her head on his shoulder.

There were tears in her eyes and suddenly her mouth was on his in a rush of emotion she could not contain. Burgoyne accepted it graciously.

"Margaret. Margaret. My own dear wife."

Though Elliston was all for going on without pause, Ursula's age demanded such pause, and out of consideration for her years they rested overnight. Elliston managed to curb his impatience with a show of commendable restraint, but once they came within sight of the goal it took a good deal of tact on Ursula's part to prevent him from seeking her out there and then. Catherine was now her main concern and she was naturally anxious that the news be broken to her gently and of necessity in private, in pursuance of which she begged Elliston to wait. He made a brief groan of protest, but such was the wisdom of her proposal that it gained his grudging assent. After all, it was she who had brought him a joy beyond measure.

No sound came with a sweeter appeal than the charmless chime of her beloved abbey bell as she neared the end of her pilgrimage. Returning to the world was all very well for a space, but the world of the cloister drew her to it like a love beyond equal. The sisters were waiting to greet her, their welcome being proof of the special regard in which she was held. They did not question her, for it was not in their calling to do so. Just to have her with them again was a blessing in itself. Pleading fatigue, she retired to her room as a refuge for thought, but not before entering the chapel to fall on her knees and thank God for enabling her to put a great wrong to rights. She thought of those who would benefit most, of Catherine and Elliston and of the resumption of their happy life together, and of the one who would not, for what of the future for Francis, so alone, so eaten up with his own invented truth because of a reality too bitter to bear. And it was not over yet. There remained the difficulty of how to tell Catherine in such a way that it would call forth the element of pity to which she felt her cousin was entitled, not that there was any question of doubting her compassionate nature. St. Mary's had sufficient evidence of that, but would she be able to forgive in the knowledge that he had not only betrayed her but betrayed Elliston, anything that touched him, be it sorrow or joy, of a certainty touching her. There was only one thing of which Ursula was certain. Given the nature of Craven's strange possessive feeling for the girl, she realised that for Catherine's own peace of mind it was better if she remained in ignorance of the part it had played in her fate. Only God could reconcile Craven with his own troubled conscience. But Elliston was waiting and she had so little time at her disposal in which to prepare Catherine for the full impact of the news she was about to relate. "Holy Mother, please guide me through your blessed son Jesu," she appealed in a softness of tone belying her qualms.

"Be seated Catherine," she began, studying to look at ease.

Catherine felt a pulling sensation at her heart. All that came into her mind was Elliston's face.

"Can it be that you have already guessed the nature of my pilgrimage Catherine?"

Catherine felt herself redden. Was her longing so obvious. It should not have been so had her vocation been firm.

"Does it appertain to my ..." she hesitated. Not mine, her conscience retorted.

"It does. You see how he is always in the heart of you."

"Forgive me, Reverend Mother. It is a frailty which I cannot amend," she replied, clenching her hands.

Ursula smiled. Perhaps her task was not going to be so difficult as she imagined.

"Amend it not. It speaks for itself."

Catherine remained silent, but her heart began to thump against her breast and droplets of sweat showed the strain on her face.

"Gently Catherine, gently," Ursula enjoined, holding out her hand in a gesture of compassion. "I wish I could delay this interview until you are better able to cope with its import, but alas it is not possible. It is good news though, of that be assured. Nothing can now mar your happiness, Catherine. Nothing."

Catherine grew calmer. These words spoke of hope, but it was Ursula herself who wrapped them round in the promise.

"Pray continue, Reverend Mother. I am composed."

Ursula had her doubts. This sudden transition from passion to calm filled her with anxiety. Also, there was a chilling detachment in her features, rather as if she was making an empty vessel of her mind in readiness for a flood of new images. The high spirits of sisterly chatter drifted in from outside where the women were enjoying an hour of leisure, all the more marked for the silence within. Omitting nothing that might add to Catherine's understanding or plead for mitigation on her cousin's behalf, Ursula proceeded, relating the whole of her meeting with Elliston. He had chosen well in choosing her for the purpose. Sensitive and kind, she allowed the story to slowly unravel, again and again emphasising Elliston's continued regard and the fact that his affection was changeless and constant.

Having finished, she waited on Catherine's reaction. Her face was bereft of expression, almost a blank. It was as if the revelation had failed in its impact, and yet she knew that this was not so. Suspended feeling was visible behind the empty expression with which Catherine regarded her. All it wanted was courage to evoke from it the proper response. Ursula prayed to

God it would come. If only she had given way to the violent but simpler emotions of Elliston. As it was, she was trapped in her own extremity of feeling.

"I think I should like to go into the garden," she said, her voice as distant as her look.

"Catherine, I was afraid that this news would greatly disturb you."

"No, no. Tis not so. The air will do me good and the afternoon is pleasant."

Reluctantly, Ursula let her go, but not before summoning all of the sisters, including Agnes, to tell them the news, reflecting that in this way Catherine would be able to gather her thoughts.

Shielding her eyes from the sun, she walked over the garth of grass into the garden. The scent of the honeysuckle was sweet, the hum of her near-waking thought as busy as that of the bees in the flowers. Her love was intact. Craven had lied. At the thought of him, little quivers of cold crept up and down her spine, just as they had always been wont to do in the past. Comfort came from the steady clang of the bell and the distant voices of the nuns singing out their devotions. She would never be part of their life. She realised that now. How could she ever have considered becoming a bride of Christ when it was impossible for her to break free of the ties that bound her to Elliston. What a mockery it would have been, and indeed He would have seen it as such. It was true what Ursula had told her. She belonged to God, but she belonged to Elliston too. There was a white rose in the garden, not a particularly fine one, but a white rose nonetheless, and in gazing at it she recollected how he had likened her to just such a flower. She remembered him picking it and describing it as the bloom of his choice, though the meaning behind it was plain. She was that choice. It was she that he loved.

"Catherine" her name echoed faintly.

It was Ursula concerned for her welfare.

"It feels so strange," she began. "Nothing moves me to pleasure or pain, yet I know that it should."

But how was she to know, Ursula thought. Such a sudden and unexpected joy can be as hard to absorb as that of a sorrow. Ursula sat beside her, companionable but silent. In her need to understand Catherine had unwittingly taken off her wimple and set her hair free. It brought her relief. "Among his many praises, Catherine, he often spoke of this," Ursula said softly, brushing the loose wisps from her brow. "You know, Catherine, he loves you very dearly. You say you cannot feel, but you will. What I have had perforce to acquaint you with is too weighty to be absorbed in a moment. It needs time to be felt. I asked Lord Elliston for a little more of it, but so anxious was he to see you that he refused to wait any longer. Catherine effected to smile. This indeed was like him.

"Can it be as you say? I so want to believe it."

"You must Catherine. You must."

She sat perfectly still, trying to assimilate the miracle as Ursula had told it until little by little it seeped into every pore of her being. The breeze brushed the ends of her hair into wisps of soft colour and before very long she was crying.

"This is good, Catherine," she said as Catherine sobbed in her arms. You will feel better ere long, and when you do you will be ready to leave us."

Within the hour, it was just as Ursula had promised. It had been a strange and solemn thing to divest herself of her nun's habit and revert to the old Catherine Venners. Feeling a need to thank her God, she went into the chapel and prayed. Around her the floor was stained with lozenges of colour as the sun slanted in through the great east window with its depiction of Christ in Glory. And so it would continue for another two hundred years until the Abbey was dissolved and all of its beauty quite swept away.

"Do the sisters know of my leaving?" she asked of Ursula when she was ready.

"Yes, but not to the extent they would like. To speak truth, their curiosity is aroused rather than cured, a healthy state of things for women who deserve a little vicarious pleasure. They are saddened too at this sudden turn of events. We have grown very fond of you, Catherine. Your gain will be our loss. But what is our loss compared to your gain. You go to a new life. Tis a day for rejoicing."

"How can I possibly thank you?" she replied.

"By being merciful to my cousin, Catherine."

"You ask the impossible, Reverend Mother. If I could find it in my heart to forgive his wrongs towards me, those towards my lord I can never forgive."

"You have a duty towards another Lord, Catherine, one who has sustained you and upheld you. Is He not entitled to be listened to also?"

Catherine pursed her lips in thought.

"Let nothing come between you, Catherine, and the perfecting of a God-given joy. Think on it, I beg you."

Catherine knelt at her feet and kissed her hand.

"I will try for your sake."

"Do it for God's Catherine. Do it for God's," she replied, bidding her rise.

Out on the grass the sisters were gathered in the sunshine. Catherine had tied back her hair, but the sun brought out its fiery red tints and the sisters were glancing at it with unconcealed admiration. All were there except Agnes.

"We now come to that most difficult of moments, saying farewell," admitted Ursula, "but it is meet and fitting that we do so properly, for Catherine you have been much loved and valued during your time here amongst us. Not only have you taught us to remedy our inefficiencies in the infirmary, but you have taught us what it means to bear the disadvantages of an unmerited affliction with dignity and courage."

"God save ye," Bridget involuntarily added, her cheeks a lovely shade of scarlet.

"You have all been so kind," Catherine effected to say, her voice trembling.

"We thank you for the gift of yourself," Ursula resumed. Only Jocelyn irritably tapped her foot, no doubt wondering how long she had to endure this laudation, quite undeserved according to her. "We trust that what you have willingly given to us, we have in some wise returned."

"The giving has all been on your part," Catherine replied, whereupon Jocelyn looked appeased.

"And to express their gratitude," Ursula continued, "I believe the sisters have a few small gifts with which to bid you God speed. Is that not so, Sister Veronica?"

"It is Reverend Mother," she answered, her whole bearing as beautiful as ever.

One by one the sisters stepped forward with their gifts, each of them kissing Catherine on the cheek and giving her their blessing. It was not so much the gifts themselves, but the simple love displayed in the giving thereof; allowing for what few faults they owned, these women were genuinely good and it was this that made their gifts precious. From Bridget there was a brooch roughly cut in the shape of a shamrock, guaranteed, or so Bridget said, to bring long life and happiness, particularly since she had asked for the Holy Virgin's blessing upon it. A beautifully illuminated page of the Paternoster was Veronica's gift, whose kiss was a blessing in itself. Lastly, Ursula presented her with a scroll containing a brief history of St. Mary's.

"You must come and see us, Catherine," she said.

"I shall, of course, I shall."

"And if you can pray for my cousin, Catherine?"

"I will try Reverend Mother."

The sisters slowly withdrew, some of them weeping, others turning to take one last backward glance, as if they were set on retaining her features.

"But tis to the future you must look, Catherine. It will bring you great happiness, of that I am certain, for all is now as it should be. God bless you, my child."

"And you Reverend Mother," she replied, as they warmly embraced, "but there is yet someone missing. I cannot leave without bidding Agnes farewell. Where is she?"

"I think that you of all people should know the answer to that particular question."

"In the garden."

"Naturally!"

Agnes was not at work. She sat alone on a bench, her eyes closed and raised to the sun like its own special votary.

"Agnes?" Catherine whispered. "I have come to say goodbye."

"You need not have bothered," she rejoined, opening her eyes, "but if you insist, farewell, and there is an end. I see they have plied you with gifts." She glanced dispassionately at the various packages tied to Catherine's baggage.

"Yes. Everyone has been most kind."

"Then on your way Catherine. I have nothing more to say. The eking out of farewells is not a fancy of mine."

"And what of our friendship Agnes?" retorted Catherine. "You wish to part thus, without one kind word, without any touch of feeling."

Agnes turned aside her face. She resented her going.

"Why not. You have other concerns now, other claims upon your affection." Her tone was fiercely independent, almost dismissive. "You will forget me soon enough. That is the way of things. We both know that."

"Then your reckoning is faulty," Catherine threw back, her voice high and indignant. "I do not forget those I love. I came to say farewell because I have a care for you, but it seems I am wasting my breath. You were ever an awkward and uncompromising creature."

At this Agnes laughed, but not derisively.

"If anyone else were to utter such unwavering tokens of affection," she replied, "I would dismiss them as like as not, but with you Catherine I may be inclined to believe them. You are novel in this world."

"Novel or not, what I say is the truth. And as for being

different, I am only so in my obvious difference. All of us are a mixture of contrary emotions, some good, some bad. Just thank God that for the most part the good within us prevails."

"Always man's proud defendant!" Agnes exclaimed with a smile on her face. "It will ever be thus with you I warrant, and the pity of it is that I see no hope of any change."

"I do not propose to change!"

They laughed easily.

"If it was left only to me, I would not have you leave Catherine Venners," she remarked with that under-eyed look of hers that always helped to mask her feelings, "and that is more than I ever thought to say to a fellow human being, but there I have said it."

"Tis an admission I welcome Agnes."

"Tis the best you will get."

"I shall come and visit. I have given my promise to Ursula."

"And I take it we are to rely on such promises?"

"Indeed you are."

Agnes then rose from her seat and walked to the edge of the path where she knelt to pick something up.

"Here, take this, if you will," she said. "Twill maybe remind you of me. Maybe not."

What she gave to her was a sprig of heather, well hewn from its soil. It bore no flower.

"Nurture it well and it should bloom next year, when its flower will be white. It grows in a special place only known to me. You should be flattered. Tis rarely I plunder the earth."

"Thank you Agnes. I shall treasure it always."

"Sentimental twaddle! More likely than not it will perish in those wilds where you come from. Now go, and be happy. And if there is a God, I bid him go with you."

"Such a God as I believe in will always be with you, Agnes."

They hugged one another like sisters in flesh. Catherine then ran from the garden, tears streaming down her face. Agnes picked up the hoe.

"Interruptions," she grumbled. "Damn this prickly eye. Tis the wind makes it smart so."

CHAPTER THIRTY FIVE

Elliston had been reluctant to go to St. Mary's itself, relying on Ursula to smooth the way for him, added to which he had no stomach for finding himself in close proximity to a religious house for women. Men and women of such persuasion would always be a mystery to him. He was too much a man of this world to think of the next with any great longing. That aside, he owed much to Ursula, her intervention having strengthened his belief in his Saviour, in virtue of which he was endowing the abbey with a considerable sum of money. Having arranged for his small retinue to continue to Durham, he was now alone. Not until he saw her with his own eyes, held her in his own arms and kissed her with his own lips, would be believe in the miracle vouchsafed to him. Would she even recognise him. During the five years they had been apart, he was aware that he had aged, and not greatly to his advantage. He was stouter and his hair had turned grey. His face was more heavily lined, not only with the scars won in battle but with those acquired in living itself. It was true that they had never cared for one another on the strength of mere appearance, but nonetheless he felt obliged to take such matters into consideration. That the longed for reunion might end in disillusion and disappointment made him unusually fretful and anxious.

Imagine her feelings then, she who had nothing in the way of good looks to work in her favour. The afternoon having kept her busy, it was only now, entirely alone and surrounded by silence that she could fully give vent to her thoughts. Like him, she feared that the lapse of years might have worked to estrange them, that the love they had known was of that time, not this, and could never be rekindled. She thought of his being obliged to confront her poor blighted face once again, for what if in the intervening years he had forgotten the full extent of it, and were now to recoil. The possibility filled her with dread. In her mitherings she was setting aside the ties that bound them, depriving the future of hope. Filled with self-pity and self-doubt, the twin banes of her nature, she was beginning to regress to the past and the fear of rejection. Other than herself, she had nothing to offer.

Ursula had reassured her that he would be waiting where the river path turned into the valley, but so uncertain had she become that she found herself sinking down on the grass, Agnes's sprig of heather held tight between her fingers. She could not go on. All anticipation of any joy to come was gradually fading. She was only conscious of her foolishness in thinking he would still want her as she was.

Meanwhile he was growing more fretful. Why was she late if all was in order. Finding inaction intolerable, he saddled the horse and went in pursuit. As always, activity helped to overcome his impatience. Hearing the horse, she knew it was him. The pounding of the hoofs on the ground was no greater than the pounding of her heart. The sun was directly in her eyes as she got to her feet. He rode straight through it and at last she could see him. Dismounting, he walked towards her. They were now just a footstep apart. Eye read eye. Feeling met feeling. The years were receding, hurtling back to the day when he had left her. She only saw him. Him only her. There was no time, no place, no nothing. Only the man. Only the woman.

"Kate? Kate?"

And then she was held. She was safe. The intervening years they were both so afraid of were rendered of little account in the immediacy of the moment. His kiss was like balm and she wished to be healed. They could see they were older, but that did not matter. In heart they were young. In soul they belonged. They laughed. They cried. What they had lost, they had found. Happiness was not illusory after all. No words passed between them. For a while there was no necessity of speech. Content was in being together. When it was needful they found the words, surprised and relieved to discover that their special kind of banter was in no way diminished.

"And what is all of this?" he asked, pointing to the bundle and the sprig of heather that she still held in her fingers.

"My belongings, plus tokens of affection from the sisters. The heather is from Agnes, my special friend." She did not inform him of Agnes's aversion to men.

"And I presume they all loved you?"

"I trust so, my lord, for I loved them. Tis a great debt we owe to those women, Ursula in particular."

"In truth. In truth," he replied, growing solemn, though his eyes never left her.

"Come here," he ordered, holding her close again. She was readily obedient. Setting free her hair from its clasps, he then removed the mask from her face.

"I love you Kate Venners," he said, running his fingers through her hair and kissing the scars on her face.

"And I you, my lord," she whispered, beginning to weep.

"Roger," he corrected.

"Roger," she whispered

"Why did you not tell me of our child Kate?"

She struggled free, looking up at him contritely.

"Margaret informed me," he explained.

"I swore her to silence."

"You did wrong."

"Forgive me." Happiness consumed her, but sadness was part of it too.

"We will have children Kate, lots of them. I want daughters like you, red haired and wilful."

"My lord," she smiled, "you shall have them, but what of a son? The Elliston line must continue. For my part, I shall pray for a son like his father."

"You are kind Kate, ever kind, ever loving." She touched the chain round his neck, wishing to make sure that he still wore the cross that had once belonged to Peter. "It was my lucky talisman Kate. I shall always wear it. And the ring I gave to you Kate. I see it not on your finger."

She drew the cord from her bodice to show him.

"Tis now too large to wear on my finger," she explained.

"And I am unthinking as usual. Ursula tells me how ill you have been."

"I am better now, Roger, and shall be henceforth."

"I swear I will never let you out of my sight again, never. The past is behind us Kate. You are my present. You are my future. You are all to me that matters."

☙ ❧

Staying overnight in Durham, they continued to Runnarth next morning. It had been sunny at first, but by the time they reached the outskirts of Runnarth drizzle of the thick and vaporous kind hid everything from view. Hence, she saw none of the improvements he had made in her absence.

"Well, Catherine Venners, here you are at last, where you belong," he said, helping her to dismount. "What matters the rain, eh!"

"Nothing," she opined as he gathered her to him.

Margaret was waving from across the courtyard, fluttering

and dithering in the rain like a fledgling flung out of its nest.

"You best go and pacify her," said Elliston, stepping aside.

It did not require him to point out her duty. Within a moment the two women were warmly embracing, laughing and crying and generally being of comfort, one to the other. When at last they drew breath, it was Margaret who spoke first.

"Catherine! Oh Catherine, tis so good to see you! Tis a miracle, a miracle indeed, and to think twas all because of some error." From this remark, it was obvious to Catherine that Margaret had not been permitted to share in the secret of Craven's deceit, which considering her nature was probably just as well. "Indeed it is," she went on, cupping her hands in sheer pleasure, "and I have said as much to Sir Edward on numerous occasions, so many in fact that the repetition of it is beginning to irk him."

"Not a bit of it!" inserted Burgoyne, coming to lend his own welcome. Catherine only had to look at him to realise that it was he who had borne the brunt of their troubles.

"Sir Edward," she said, extending her hand, "what a welcome this is."

"None more deserved," he replied. "We have need of you Mistress Venners."

"Catherine, please," she insisted.

"Oh, Catherine," Margaret enthused. "I am so immeasurably delighted that I cannot think what to say or do next. I am afraid I shall blather. I know that I will."

"Well blather on woman," said Sir Edward indulgently, "but if you must, do it indoors and out of this rain."

Elliston was about to follow, but Burgoyne drew him aside, allowing the women to continue without them.

"I see the wisdom of what you say," he laughed.

"No, my lord, tis not that. During your absence things have proceeded apace, so much so that I needs must speak with you at once."

"Come, tell me, but make it brief," he said, leading the way.

While Elliston was away, Burgoyne, in obedience to his commands, had made considerable efforts to bring the castle into something approaching good order, a fact that did not go unnoticed by his master.

"This is good. Good," he remarked approvingly. You are to be congratulated on your endeavours, Sir Edward, considering time was against you."

"Tis not remarkable at all, my lord," replied Burgoyne, impeccably dismissive, "but I will convey your gratitude to my lady wife and the household in general."

"Do. Do."

Closeted together in a room rarely used, but which was guaranteed to give them privacy, Elliston made generous with the wine to offset the unseasonable chill. In the more frequently used apartments, fires had already been lit.

"Well, Sir Edward. What news is it that is so pressing?"

"Craven has gone, my lord. I discovered as much when I went to speak with him regarding our previously agreed plan to conceal his duplicity and explain Mistress Venners' return. He had left a document with Geoffrey Frincham to give to myself. He had also given Frincham to understand that after much searching of soul he was of a mind to enter a religious order and thenceforth to devote the remainder of his days to a life of fasting and prayer."

"Apt!"

"Further, he said that he had only delayed his decision on account of appointing a priest in his stead, and that now such a one had been found by the name of Father Barnabas, a young man who will be arriving within the next day or two."

"Young," remarked Elliston, fingering his mouth, "and less meddlesome I trust."

"My lord," acknowledged Burgoyne tactfully. "Craven wishing to leave quietly, he begged Frincham to keep his intentions close, though Frincham did say, and I quote, that his look betokened a man tired of this world and anxious for to seek the next." Elliston shuffled uneasily in his chair. "The document," he continued "was couched in clear precise language so as to be readily intelligible to his flock, to whom he bade me read it. I have it here if you wish to read it for yourself, my lord."

"Later."

"It explains very succinctly the confusion that had arisen over Mistress Venners' supposed death, and his genuine mistake in the matter ..."

"Genuine! Damn him!"

"Shall I go on, my lord." Elliston nodded.

"A distortion of the facts certainly, my lord, but even so most beautifully worded."

"Expedient I grant you," Elliston concurred, biting his lip.

"I then arranged for Frincham to have every man, woman and child assembled to hear the parting testament of their priest, just as he willed it. It affected them deeply and I have to say that the news of his going tended to take precedence over that of Mistress Venners' return which, I hasten to add, was greeted most favourably, that is with the exception of Mother Jomfrey."

Here Elliston smiled, as he knew that Catherine would have done. There was no getting rid of the besom, even the plague would not have her. "Without a doubt, Father Craven must have decided to leave the moment he heard that Mistress Venners would be returning."

"Fitting indeed."

"Despite our opinion of him, my lord, it was rather wondrous to witness the reverence in which he was held."

"Enough Sir Edward, enough," he replied, though in soft resigned tones. "You have other news?"

"Yes, my lord, which will please you far more. The day after Craven's departure, the Thompsons returned."

"Thompsons?"

"Mistress Venners' cousin and his wife, my lord, not forgetting their child."

"Ah, of course. Rob was his name, was it not?"

"Yes, my lord. As soon as the plague arrived in London they began to make the long journey home, and by God's good grace stayed free of the sickness. It seems to me that this Thompson is a far seeing man who looks to his own and uses his head. His wife is of a gentle nature and most caring of her child, a small boy, who, incidentally bears a remarkable likeness to his grandfather. Their grief on hearing the news of their parents' demise has been tempered somewhat on learning of Catherine's survival. If I may venture to say so, my lord, I think that this Robert Thompson is a man whose services would be of value to us."

Elliston thought for a moment. Sir Edward's remarks had put him in mind of a plan.

"Have you told your wife of their return?"

"No, my lord. I thought it better to wait until you and Mistress Venners are ..."

"Married?"

"Well, yes, my lord. She looks so frail and I did not wish to anticipate matters on account of her health."

"Excellent, Sir Edward. Tonight we will marry. Tomorrow she and her cousin will be reunited. In the meantime, I exhort you to silence. Keep mum, Sir Edward, keep mum."

The two women were now deep in talk, the missing years having provided them with a wealth of news to exchange, much of it sorrow, some of it joy. When two women of affinity have things to confide the time is of little significance and it was only when the candles were lit that Margaret remembered her duty, or rather that imposed upon her by her husband.

"Goodness, how a drear day takes away the light. But now, my dear, I have things to attend to."

"What things, Margaret?" she asked, quite bemused by this sudden bustle of activity.

"You must not chivvy me. I gave my word to Sir Edward, and I will not break it."

She stood surveying Catherine from tip to toe, the kind of hard critical state that is not meant to give offence, but so often does, particularly with someone as ill at ease about her appearance as Catherine.

"Margaret, what are you about?"

"Naught," she replied, the denial clipped and nervous.

"Well for naught, you seem greatly agitated."

"Tis just that you are mortal thin child, and I doubt that the gown we had in mind will now fit. Did they not feed you at the Abbey? I have heard of those places. All prayer and small comfort. Tis no wonder you were ill. Still, we must do what we can."

"Margaret, I beseech you to tell me what you are at. Secrecy ill becomes you, and since this particular secret puts you so out of countenance I beg you reveal it this minute."

Without answering she disappeared into the small ante-chamber adjoining her room, leaving Catherine more bemused than ever. Before very long she returned with a gown of green silk draped over her arm.

"There, tis for you Catherine," she said, ordering her to stand up so that she could match it against her figure.

"For me! But tis far too fine for me."

"Now go wash and comb your hair."

"Margaret sit down." Margaret sat, a harried look on her face. "Now, tell me."

"I cannot. I gave my word to Sir Edward."

"Then I shall sit here until you do."

At this Margaret was clearly alarmed, her fingers stroking the silk as if she was stroking a cat.

"You must not be trying, Catherine."

"Trying!" she countered. "It is not I who am trying."

"If I tell, will you promise to do as I ask?"

"I promise."

It took her an hour to wash, brush her hair and put on the gown. Margaret gazed at her admiringly.

"You look beautiful Catherine, truly beautiful," she said,

clapping her hands in excitement.

And just for a moment Catherine believed it.

☙ ❧

He waited within the apartment that they had formerly shared together and which Burgoyne and Margaret had been so at pains to have prepared in readiness for her return.

"I have brought her Lord Elliston, as you requested," she announced. "Sir Edward and I will wait in the chapel."

"You are prompt Lady Burgoyne. Just a few moments longer and we will join you."

"Well, Kate," he remarked gazing approvingly at the transformation.

"Well, my lord, as I trust you are."

"You little tease," he laughed, gathering her to him. "You like the gown?"

"You know I do," she answered.

"Good, because the colour was of my choosing. On such an occasion a woman should look her best."

"Occasion?" she mused, though her bottom lip trembled.

"You know!"

"If it is what I think, my lord, then I deem it an honour," she replied, shyly touching his hand.

"Kate. Kate. You address me as if we were strangers and I was conferring upon you some special favour. Honour be damned. Tis your due."

And with that he held her closer. Their kiss was sustained and passionate.

"I have the priest waiting," he said, as she rested her head on his shoulder. "Not the thin and cadaverous kind, but one that is obliging and rotund."

At this a tiny frown appeared on her brow and he wished he had resisted the allusion.

"I should not have said it."

"Hush, my lord, we are happy."

"Roger," he corrected.

"Roger."

"Have you the ring? I would not have you wear other than that."

"Yes," she replied, detaching it from the cord round her neck.

"Then let us proceed. I think we have delayed long enough."

Burgoyne and Margaret acted as witnesses, there being no other guests present. Elliston had arranged it as such, his desire for privacy being wholly in accord with Catherine's who had always expressed her preference for a quiet wedding should the occasion ever come to pass.

The wedding supper was brief. He had no wish to prolong it, and since the Burgoynes were the only guests present he knew he could rely on their discretion to leave without the bother of having to labour the point.

 ❧

As he lay on the bed watching her disrobe by the light of the candles, her slim outline casting its large shadow on the wall, her hair tumbling down her back like a skein of red silk, he knew she was all he had ever desired. Bewitching but good, the woman of his idle dreams made reality.

"Roger," she avowed, lying beside him.

"Kate, my dear, sweet Kate."

The sun was there to greet them on the morrow. He awoke first, watching it warm the contours of her face. She lay on her right side, so that only the unravaged side of her face was exposed, soft and beautiful in the early morning light. He lay there simply gazing, knowing that she was at last truly his and nothing, save death, would divide them, and then, pray God, not for long. Slowly rousing herself, she reached out to touch him.

"Good morrow Lady Elliston," he said, pulling her to him. "Did I weary you Kate."

She nestled up to him, tracing his face with her fingers.

"It was an exquisite weariness, Roger."

"You are happy then?"

"Why ask when you know."

They breakfasted but ate very little, feeding on each other for sustenance.

"You are rare Kate," he murmured, "rarer than air. Rare. Rare."

"I am very ordinary, my lord. Simply your Kate and nothing more."

"Oh, much, much more."

After the dismal weather of the previous day, this was a glorious one, and they took full advantage of it. To her delight, she discovered that she still enjoyed riding. He took her to a vantage point high in the hills where the whole of Runnarth was spread out before them, the castle, the river, the village, the church and the neatly tended strips of earth. Without wanting to boast of the part he himself had played in restoring his domain and assisting his few remaining tenants, he was anxious to gauge her response.

"My lord, tis so changed, so different from what I remember when I went away."

"A change for the better, I trust?"

"In truth. In truth. Tis you, my lord, tis you? I know it!"

"Of course, tis me. Here I am standing beside you."

"No. Do not jest with me Roger. You know what I mean. Tis you have done this for our tenants."

"Our!"

"Why, yes," she replied. "I feel for their welfare as well, probably more so now I am your wife."

"Wife!" he laughed, tapping the rump of her lightly with his whip. "Then wife dismount."

She did as he asked, but his bantering mood did not deceive her. He might make light of his achievements, but she knew differently.

"Roger, you are a good and kind man," she affirmed, her eyes washed with tears.

"Kate. Kate. It was naught. Tis Burgoyne you should thank. Twas he who chivvied me into taking such steps as were needful instead of wallowing in self-pity. And what I did I did for you. Only you, Kate."

"And I still say you are a good man," she persisted, drawing him to her and kissing him full on the mouth.

"I am relieved to discover that I am not overly cruel to my tenants."

"Never cruel. Never."

☙ ❧

She eluded him for a time after supper, and it was only on enquiring of Burgoyne that he discovered her whereabouts in the garden.

"What are you doing!" he asked, referring to her kneeling position on the ground.

"In our happiness, my lord, I had overlooked Agnes's gift to me," she explained, firming the sprig of heather in an open space of earth which was suitably wild and windswept. "She said it would not grow in these wilds of ours, but I maintain that our wilds are no different to hers, which is why I wish to prove her wrong."

"Come, let me help."

"No, tis done. Besides Agnes would have resented any help from your sex."

"Would she now. Doubtless, she is a sweet faced nun committed to good works and prayer."

At this, she laughed out aloud.

"My lord, you know not Agnes."

"But I know you," he replied, gripping her firmly round the

waist, "which is why I find it annoying that you seek to avoid me already. Come inside Lady Elliston. We have yet much to discuss."

"Who is this Lady Elliston?" she countered. With that he hurried her indoors.

There were, as he said, many things still to discuss. Mindful of the manner in which Craven's transgression was going to be kept secret, she was yet to be told of his leaving. When he informed her of it, she was surprised at her confused state of mind; in her present state of happiness it had been easier to dismiss him from her thoughts, though he was never entirely erased, and when he did come to mind it was more as some ghostly presence that needed putting to rest. The likelihood of her never seeing him again was somehow inconceivable. Indeed, she was anticipating just such a meeting in the hope that it might provide her with some insight into why he had acted as he had; whether he would show any contrition or whether, as she feared, he would lay the blame on her for not obeying God's will. If only she could have understood even a little, then she might have forgiven. By depriving her of such opportunity, she felt as if he had deceived her a second time.

"Do you think he was shamefaced into leaving?" she enquired.

"I know not Kate. We must put him behind us, as we would Satan."

"But you feel something for him."

"I feel nothing Kate."

"But you have agreed to protect him from censure."

"Only out of consideration for his cousin. I cannot forgive him if that is what you mean."

"Ursula asked me to forgive him."

"You must do as you think fit. I do not wish to speak of him now or ever. Please, Kate, let us think of more pleasant matters."

"As you wish."

"Do you not recollect the promise I made to you."

"My lord?"

"You disappoint me Kate. As I recollect, you had a yearning to see Holy Island?"

"Why yes, of course I remember, but tis so long ago."

"No matter how long, I intend to keep my word. Tis meet we go away from here for a while. I thought Sulburgh first ..."

Before he could continue, she was begging for news of Joan, her face rapidly changing from anxiety to relief when he was able to confirm that Sulburgh had escaped the worst of the plague and that from what he had gathered Joan and Watkins were fairly content and had another two brats to add to the first.

"Oh Roger, this is good news indeed. I am so, so ..."

"I know Kate," he said, catching her to him. "What say you, we set out tomorrow."

"So soon?"

He guessed her concern, indeed had deliberately provoked it, for it brought him to the matter of the ploy he and Burgoyne had devised specially for her.

"You do not want to go?"

"Yes, you know I do, but I was thinking of ..."

"The village and 'our' tenants?"

"You think me foolish."

"No. I think I know you. As it happens, I can arrange for an escort to take you."

"I need no escort, my lord. I pray you let me go on foot as I always did."

"You are Lady Elliston now."

"But your wife first. Titles hang loosely on your Kate, my lord."

"As you wish," he sighed.

She kissed him in gratitude, this time a sweet, lingering kiss.

"Before you go?"

"My lord?"

"I was speaking to Sir Edward yesterday. I have had to let your uncle's dwelling and land to new tenants."

"I see," she replied, slightly taken aback.

"You are sorry?"

"A little. Tis only natural, I suppose. I spent so much of my life there that I was still hoping that Rob might return. I realise it was but a faint hope."

"Well, the new tenant is a good man, or so Burgoyne would have me believe," he went on, ignoring her reference to Rob. "Apparently his knowledge of land and tenure is such that Sir Edward is of the opinion that he would make a good bailiff or something of the sort."

"We are in need of such men, it is true."

"Exactly, which is why I wish you to speak with him. I relied on your judgement as Kate Venners. As Lady Elliston, I shall rely on it more. You will do this?"

"I am honoured that you should rely on my judgement."

"Oh, this honour business Kate! One minute you are speaking in terms of 'our' tenants, and the next you are positively servile."

"Then I shall try to do better in future," she replied, feigning resentment.

"Are you jesting Lady Elliston?"
"As if I would."
"A kiss will convince."
"There, you shall have it," she said, readily concurring.
"I love you, Lady Elliston."
"And I you, my lord."

CHAPTER THIRTY SIX

How strange it was to be walking the old familiar path. It was two years since she had last walked it with Matthew on their furtive journey to Bardwick. Then all was desolation and waste. Now the corn grew tall and green again, the wind rippling through it like waves upon water. Then it had been wanting in human activity. Now it was filled with it. She walked slowly, contrasting the then with the now, revelling in the changes she saw, knowing that they came from man's own resilience and the continuing trust he placed in God. She did not resent the flow back of time. It brought her consolation and a kind of acceptance. Her one regret was that Matthew was not there to see it too, but maybe he did, for as she had discovered nothing was impossible through the goodness of God. Was it not He who had effected her reunion with Elliston. Was it not He who had prompted her lord in the care of his people.

Many of the faces she previously remembered were absent, taken by the plague, but there were new ones in their stead, their candid looks of curiosity in keeping with what she expected of strangers. As she drew nearer to the old home her heart began to beat faster. It was the familiarity of it that hurt, those ties between her and her childhood that could never be weakened.

Most of the villagers were out on the fields, but a woman with whom she was slightly acquainted, one who had escaped from Bardwick in the early days of the plague, stiffly gave her good day, conscience having something to do with the manner of constraint in her greeting. She did not stop to talk.

She gazed wistfully across to this place of her birth, her eyes becoming blurred with remembrance of golden hued days that were good. A woman was busy outside, a slight and gentle looking woman that might have been Mary. "Might," she whispered sadly. Doubtless, she must be related to the man Sir Edward had in mind to be bailiff. As Elliston's wife, she felt it incumbent to bid her welcome. Just as she was about to do so, the woman half turned as if she was expecting her. The sun blazed between them, but not sufficiently to hide the woman's face from view.

"Mary!" she exclaimed, fearing she was under some sort of self-inflicted delusion.

"Catherine."

The utterance of her name finally convinced her. She was hugged and embraced amidst a tearful if wordless reunion.

"Oh Catherine," Mary sighed, her face radiant with joy.

"I have been looking for you all morning. You see how your coming has affected us, despite Sir Edward's forewarning. Have I not looked for her time and again Rob?"

"Rob? My own Rob? Where is he?"

"Here," announced Rob, coming from inside the house.

It was hard to hug Rob, but he let her, his bottom lip even trembling in the emotion of the moment.

"You expected me?" Catherine asked in amazement.

"Yes, we knew," admitted Mary. "Lord Elliston wished to surprise you."

"And of a surety he has," she replied. "I shall have to take him to task. Too many surprises of this kind must not become a habit, for I fear I cannot withstand them."

Though the remark was intended to be flippant, the tears continued to stream down her face. Rob left them to it, ostensibly to attend to Daisy, in reality to stem a blubber in the cuff of his sleeve.

It was gratifying to find that little had changed in her home, that it was much as she had left it, uncluttered and clean and with the scent of newly laid rushes. There were even wild flowers in a jug to brighten the scene.

Mary had laid the table in preparation, Miriam's best pewter having been brought out in honour of the occasion. In looking at it, Catherine could not help but think of that last Christmas when they had all been together and so little knowing of what was in store.

"Here, drink this. It will settle you," said Mary, pressing upon her a cup of milk mixed with honey and spices, a receipt much employed by Miriam to steady the nerves.

"I shall be quite myself in a while," she assured. "But such a surprise is bound to ..."

"Shake you," put in Mary, sympathetically cupping her hands round Catherine's to prevent the vessel from shaking. "We wondered at the wisdom of it, particularly upon hearing of all that had happened during our absence, but from what Sir Edward said it would seem that Elliston was set on having his way."

Catherine smiled. He invariably did was her thought.

"Such unexpected joy," Mary continued, as Rob rejoined them.

"Ay, so tis," he agreed, "for ours hae been a sad enough home-coming."

"Oh Rob," said Catherine, pressing his hand, and trying to console him. "They were so full of courage. You would have been proud of them, and as for Uncle Matthew, he was the very rock on which everyone leaned."

"Ay, so tis said," Rob concurred, his eyes filling with the knowledge of it.

"Geoffrey so loved him," said Mary, intuitively resting her hand on Rob's shoulder.

"He was goodness itself to Geoffrey, but when it was time Geoffrey repaid it."

"Ay, he's a true friend," Rob agreed. "Yet who would hae thought it fro' what they do tell us o' the man he became because of his troubles. Quite lacking in wits so I hear and naught but a mass o' skin and bone."

"I can vouch for that," replied Catherine, "and but for Uncle Matthew I fear he would not have survived."

"Now he has Eve," put in Mary.

"Ay, and that's a strange sort o' business," said Rob.

"Tis not strange at all," Mary denied.

"Eve?" questioned Catherine. "Luke Jomfrey's widow?"

"Ay the same," Rob said in taciturn tones.

"It seems that Eve took it upon herself to have a care for Geoffrey," Mary explained, "and was in no little way responsible for clearing his wits of their muddle. Now they live as man and wife, but without the blessing of Holy Mother Church."

This unexpected liaison between Geoffrey and Eve was certainly cause for reflection, but it gave Catherine pleasure. As for them living outside of wedlock, why she herself had done the very same.

"I should like to see Geoffrey," she said.

"And so you will," replied Mary. It is a blessing that he has Eve. He lost so much in losing Alice and the children. When I think of them it breaks my heart. Alice was so good and honest and ever cheerful. Tis hard to think of her gone."

"Tis hard indeed," agreed Catherine.

And suddenly the gap in the years was closing again, and the blessing of it was that they could think of those happier times without the plague destroying the memory completely. Naturally, they were obliged to speak of it now and again, but they did not dwell on it to the exclusion of everything else. Rob and Mary said little of their time in London or of their return to Runnarth, just as Catherine said little of her time at St. Mary's. It was the future that now seemed important. Thoughts of the plague and what it had done to them were reflected on in silence, and when that silence became too oppressive one or other of them would break it quite effortlessly.

"She's nae very bonny, Eve, but she's loyal," Rob suddenly remarked for no apparent reason. "Look at what she had to endure fro' that old hag o' a mother, or rather Luke's mother. Geoffrey could do a lot worse than make an honest woman of 'er I'm thinkin'."

Catherine, thinking this time as good as any, to tell them of her own news, held out her left hand to show them her ring. She had cleverly intertwined it with a thin strip of linen to stop it slipping from her finger.

"You are wed Catherine!" Mary exclaimed.

"Yes, Mary, I am indeed. We thought it best to do the deed with the minimum of fuss."

"Come, let us kiss," said Mary. "I am so very, very happy for you."

"Not afore time," Rob commented dryly, pecking her cheek.

"No, not before time," Catherine agreed, "and in my role as Lady Elliston I shall do what I can to impress upon Geoffrey the merits of wedlock."

"Twould be a good beginnin' for our new priest."

"The new priest has arrived?"

"Tomorrow," said Mary.

"Mind you, fro' what I heard, Father Craven will be hard to replace. The stories we've heard of 'im, not to mention the way he took your part Catherine," Rob observed. "Why Geoffrey said he were a man amongst men, and I hae nae reason to doubt him, but tis said it cost him dear and his health is near broken, but then tis not surprisin' considerin' what's he's been through."

"I owe him a great debt," agreed Catherine, "and so do the people."

Maybe she was imagining things, but to Mary Catherine's avowal sounded distant and icy, an element of restraint contained in its utterance. As ever, her intuition was keen. She also noticed that at the mention of the priest's name Catherine became withdrawn and pensive, for the truth of it was that Craven would go on exerting an untoward hold upon her for many years to come. Often she would try to envisage him in his house of austerity and wonder whether this was the ultimate denial he had sought all his life and whether within it he would find rest for his soul.

"You helped him though," said Mary. "We heard of that too."

"I did what I could."

"And more I warrant."

"Leastways, ye are back wi' us now, Kate. Had ye been dead as the good Father thought twould hae been a double blow to us," put in Rob.

"Well I am not, and tis good that you are back too."

"Tis just a pity that Father Craven ..."

"You look tired Catherine," Mary thankfully intervened, "and we have talked too much and too soon. Rob go and fetch Matthew while I prepare supper. Tis time Kate and he were introduced."

"I am greatly looking forward to it," said Catherine.

Mary refusing all offers of help, Catherine was allowed the privilege of sitting in the chair once favoured by her uncle, but now reserved for visitors owing to Rob's reluctance to sit in it himself, the very idea of him doing so implying a usurpation of long held authority. Besides the impress of his father's figure still lay upon it, not to mention the wooden arms of it whereon he had drummed out innumerable problems. As it was summer the fire burned low and she felt peculiarly rested. She was asleep when Rob returned from his chores, a tousle haired child, the image of Matthew, holding his hand.

"Hush now," whispered Mary, putting her finger to her lips.

Rob took his place at the table and the child climbed on to his knee where he could see the stranger more clearly. He looked at her warily. So this was the woman he was to call aunt. Her history he knew, Rob having told him of the accident which accounted for the piece of linen which covered one side of her face. But his father and mother had said she was kind and that it was incumbent upon him to try and make allowances for a difference that might make him timid at first. Above all, he was to be polite, he was to be friendly. Cupping a hand round each eye he regarded her closely. He thought she looked forbidding, but then Catherine showed to little advantage in her slumbering state and the idea of her waking somewhat dismayed him. When she did wake she started violently, thinking for a moment that she was back at St. Mary's and the bell was summoning her to prayer.

"You were tired, Catherine," Mary spoke softly.

"You should have wakened me. Tis unseemly of me to sleep,

and on such a day too."

"Tis the excitement. You were in want of a little respite."

It was then that she noticed the child, who conscious of his father's scrutiny, gazed at her shyly, his immediate thought being that she looked marginally better awake than asleep, though he remained very circumspect. Notwithstanding, he was mindful of his manners. Rob had seen to that. Looking at him, Catherine guessed as much and smiled shyly in return, for it was no less a testing time for her than it was for the child.

"Go and bid your aunt welcome Matthew," Mary whispered in his ear.

Descending from the security of his father's knee, he went over to her.

"Welcome Aunt Catherine," he dutifully said, Catherine tactfully turning the better side of her face to receive his peck on her cheek, both of them conscious of Rob's rigorous surveillance.

"Thank you, young Matt. You know, you are so like your grandfather," she said, gently holding him from her and smiling to draw forth his confidence now that she had come through that first crucial test.

"Father says tis so," he replied a little more confidently.

"Your grandfather was a fine man, Matthew. Tis a pity you will never see him. He would have been so very proud of you. As for me, I am, as you see, a little different from what you are used to, but in time I trust that my difference will become so commonplace that you will no longer heed it. We shall see, shall we not."

For reply he kissed her on the other side of her face, the side that was hidden, and he did it without any prompting and because he liked the way in which she spoke to put his childish fears at rest. Rob and Mary smiled at one another approvingly. The little scene just witnessed seemed to augur well for the future, but then Catherine had a gift for putting people at their ease.

"Do you like stories Matthew?"

"Not now Catherine!" said Rob a trite sharply.

Matthew looked at him soberly under his eyes. There was just the hint of rebellion in his gaze. Had he inherited the Thompson stubborn streak? She genuinely hoped so.

"Later then," Catherine promised on seeing his look of disappointment. "Shall we make it a bedtime story?"

"Yes," he replied with alacrity.

"Yes, what?" reminded Rob.

"Yes, if you please, Aunt Catherine," said Matthew, resenting this one apparent slip in the face of his seeming success.

Catherine winked at him in a way that the others could not see, but Matthew was sharp and screwed up his right eye in response. He liked this touch of conspiracy. Catherine breathed deeply. Thank goodness the transitional stage between acquaintance and friendship was over, she thought.

Mary now had an errand for young Matthew to perform, that of going to collect Geoffrey, which quite put Catherine in mind of old times.

"Right now?" he questioned, suspecting, and rightly so, that the grown ups had things to say which were not for his hearing.

"Yes Matt, if you will," Mary replied, chucking him under the chin as he went. "We love him so much Catherine, but there are times when I think that Rob is a little too strict."

"One spoiled child in the family was lesson enough," he returned, a clear allusion to Annie.

"Try not to be too hard on Annie, Rob. Her sufferings made her unmindful of others. Remember, even before the plague, she had lost Gerard."

"Her sufferings!" he spat. "Show me the man, woman or child who has not suffered; she suffered no more than anyone else, but why should you be so lenient towards her, after all she was hardly kind to you. And what woman would leave her own childer to die?"

"She is your sister Rob."

"Was. I have none now!"

"Fie Rob!" Mary remonstrated. "Blood is blood and you cannot disown it. In a way I feel for her weakness."

"You and Catherine both then," he sighed. "Well I cannot forgive her."

"Let us not speak of it further," said Catherine. "I have a boon to ask of you, Rob, on my lord's behalf. We wish you to be our new bailiff, both my lord and Sir Edward seeing you as supremely fitted to the role."

"I agree wholeheartedly," said Mary.

"Well I dunna. Raised up because of my cousin's position. You think I'll not be proof against such favour."

Mary's face dropped to a look of dejection.

"Just as I anticipated," said Catherine. "If you think tis favour from my lord, then you know not my lord. He has worked hard for the care of this village and its people."

"So I hear," Rob grudgingly agreed.

"Which is why," she continued, "in order to maintain a goodly estate he is in need of a man capable of seeing to its day to day running. You are just such a man. There is no other now that Uncle Matthew is dead. Your neighbours loved and respected your father, and they will love and respect you. To refuse would be churlish."

"Catherine is right Rob," Mary softly appended.

"I'll think on it," he replied.

"Then I shall tell my lord of your acceptance," said Catherine.

Nothing more being said, they then spoke of other matters, one such being the survival of Mother Jomfrey.

"That sort always survives," Rob said emphatically.

"Still, I am pleased," announced Catherine. "Runnarth would not be Runnarth without her."

Just then Geoffrey arrived, his head poking round the door in a broad faced grin, though mercifully absent of its former inanity. Young Matthew was clutching his hand chivvying him to step inside. When he did so, it was the Geoffrey of old that she saw, true a Geoffrey chastened by circumstance, but a Geoffrey grown strong through his troubles. His figure had filled out again and his hair was restored to its fly-away appearance. The sunken hollows were gone from round his eyes and his expression was alert and alive.

"Geoffrey," Catherine cried, as he grappled her to him like a big friendly bear.

The tears were coursing down his face simply because he was happy, and was unashamed to give way to his feelings in front of the others, unlike Rob who still thought it unmanly.

"You look so much better," said Catherine at last.

"Ay, lass, thanks to ye uncle."

"And Eve," put in Mary.

"Ay, and Eve," he agreed, somewhat sheepishly.

"Your kindness to us will never be forgotten," said Catherine.

"Nay lass, twas long times past. Matt were my friend and the best that I had. I merely set about doin' for him what he done for me. Like for like as they say, but tis good to see ye lass. Matt were that fond o' ye, and ye with them sisters o' mercy all this time."

"Yes, Geoffrey, all this time."

"And she has news for us. Come, Catherine, show him your hand."

Doubtless this was Mary's way of bringing Geoffrey to a rightful course of action where wedlock was concerned. Smiling at Mary, she showed him the ring.

"I am now Lady Elliston, Geoffrey, but you shall still call me Kate."

The smile went from his face and he tidied his hair as if he had suddenly found himself in the presence of his betters.

"Geoffrey, what is it?" she teased.

"You, our little Kate, wed to yon great lord," he replied, scratching his brow.

"But still little Kate," she insisted, kissing his cheek.

"Well he be a lucky man, that's what I say, a lucky man."

"Indeed he is," said Mary "and there be others who might be lucky too were they similarly disposed."

Geoffrey blushed, right through to the roots of his hair, but remained silent. Supper was one of the happiest Catherine could remember since Miriam was alive, and everyone ate heartily and well.

"To Lady Elliston," said Geoffrey, pledging his cup.

"To Lady Elliston," they responded.

When the supper things were cleared away Catherine kept her promise by reading Matthew his story, at the conclusion of which he put his arms round her neck and kissed her. It made her confident of the future with her own children. God was indeed good.

Geoffrey promised to walk with her part of the way as he wanted to show her where Matthew was buried. It was now nearing dusk and she knew that Elliston would be waiting as he had promised. Geoffrey walked slowly but purposefully. He was a different man altogether now that Eve was caring for him. The fields looked softly at rest in the twilight. It was wonderfully still and peaceful.

"Did you hear somethin' Kate," he suddenly said.

"No, did you?"

"There again, like a scratching of mice."

And then it drew nearer and with it the shape of an old twisted woman.

"Tis Mother Jomfrey," he said between gritted teeth. "We can pass on the other side."

"Why Geoffrey? Is she not my tenant, so to speak?"

"A bad one. You could now wreak havoc on 'er if ye were so minded. Twould only be what she deserves."

"Fie Geoffrey!" she jested. "Expend my energies in wreaking vengeance on a defenceless old woman. Why the mere thought of it is shameful."

Geoffrey assumed the look of a man clearly rebuked, but

Catherine only smiled. She had no intention of being anything other than Kate Venners where her neighbours were concerned, and Mother Jomfrey was a neighbour of long if dubious acquaintance.

"So ye be back at last, Mistress Venners," she croaked, tottering to a halt, her eyes gimlets of life in the sere waste of flesh. Now regarded by most of her neighbours as a pathetic old woman devoid of any special powers, she still refused to be shamed in the knowledge of what she had done.

"As you see Mother Jomfrey."

Geoffrey gazed at the ground, scudding his feet with a look of disdain.

"Ye always had more brain than Annie," she rasped, the night air causing her to break into a sudden fit of coughing.

"You should be indoors Mother Jomfrey. You are not well."

"Well enough for a woman o' my years, with neither son nor daughter to tend 'er."

Geoffrey now looked at her, but there was not a vestige of pity in his usually good humoured countenance.

"You deserve nae succour," he gave out in a tone that left her under no illusion that he meant what he said.

"Ye be welcome to my son's bitch," she countered. "She were never o' comfort to me."

"Eve be worth a thousand o' ye," he retorted, raising his hand.

"Enough Geoffrey," said Catherine. "I will see what can be done to alleviate your ills Mother Jomfrey. You shall not want if I can help it."

The old woman cackled derisively, setting Geoffrey's teeth on edge and inclining him to make her aware of a few important facts guaranteed to wipe the smile from her face.

"Hae a care woman," he began. "Ye not be speakin' to Kate Venners now. Ye be addressin' Lady Elliston!"

Saying it, he raised himself on his toes and looked slightly pompous, considering the kind of man that he actually was. It made Catherine smile.

"Yes Mother Jomfrey, I am wed to Lord Elliston. Thus, I am in a position to assist you."

The old woman paused, narrowing her eyes, and obviously thinking deeply.

"My doin'!!" she shrieked out at last. "My doin'!"

"She be gettin' enfeebled," said Geoffrey, trying to drag Catherine away.

"No Geoffrey. Permit her to speak. How your doing, pray?"

"Twas I that got ye sent to the castle," she laughed, tears of glee starting to stream down the lines in her face. "Ye mind the day when Baillie Talbot came lookin' for a wench to serve in the kitchens? Well, twas I told 'im where he could get one. Ye take my meanin' Lady Elliston?" And with this she attempted to bow.

"Indeed I do," replied Catherine, looking amused. "Then you are indeed deserving of all the aid I can render. Is she not, Geoffrey?"

Geoffrey scowled. He wanted no part of it. For all he cared, she could go to the devil.

"Rest assured, Mother Jomfrey, I shall not forget you."

The old woman shook her head knowingly. Her smile was as crooked as her body, but there was an attraction in the evil that somehow redeemed her.

"Like mother, like daughter," she tittered, continuing on her way, mildly triumphant.

Matthew's grave lay close to the church, a simple mound of green that commanded a view of the fields which had governed his life, and indeed his death. Flowers sprang upon it, wild, fragile flowers that grew in the meadows or on the baulks dividing those fields. It was lovingly tended by a people who would not forget. She stood by it quietly, tears clouding her eyes, but she was more proud than sad.

"He were a good man withal," reaffirmed Geoffrey wiping his eyes. "Ay, a good man."

"Yes, Geoffrey, he was."

"Just as Father Craven were, only different like." She felt herself tremble as she always did at the sound of Craven's name. "I'm sorry that he chose to leave us Kate. He were a strange man in some ways, but always fair and honest, and ye hae cause to thank 'im more than most."

"Yes, Geoffrey, I have." And for the first time she was able to say it from the heart and not from the head.

"He were like a man spent Kate. I could see it in 'is eyes, so sad and so wearied. He spoke of ye, said that ye'd understand that what he did was all for ye good, and, of course, so it were."

"I know that Geoffrey."

The irony of the words did not escape her, but the wrong of it all was beginning to heal.

"Geoffrey," she said, after pause for reflection.

"Ay."

"Marry Eve."

"Ah, I mun, I mun. She's a good woman."

"A very good woman Geoffrey and deserving of her own portion of happiness, as we all are."

"Ay, ye speak sense."

After parting from Geoffrey, she went as far as the hermitage. Looking across the water, she fancied she could see the vision of a man, his hair white like a prophet's, his smile the smile of a friend.

"I knew you would come here, Lady Elliston."

She turned to find Elliston beside her.

"Kate, my lord, please. Call me Kate."

"Or should it be Catherine."

"Whatever pleases you best."

"This pleases me best," he said, kissing her softly.

It was a still and warm night. The stars were out and a new moon was shining. It shone over Runnarth church and on to the door of the priest's dwelling which was open to let it flood in, such was the custom of the village when one priest departed and a new one was to come on the morrow. By "departed" they usually meant dead, but for men such as Craven is there not a death in life which is equally valid?

A smell of lavender hung on the room where he was wont to sit chained fast to his vision, but happily the feeling of cold was no more. The breeze occasionally turned the leaves of the tome left behind him. It was quiet. It was calm.